CW00674831

Also by Miles Nelson

Riftmasters

The Forge & The Flood

RENEGADE

Miles Nelson

Elsewhen Press

Contents

For those that need them, trigger warnings for this book can be found at http://milesnelsonofficial.com

To my husband, Chris.

I'd cross the universe just to be with you.

Prologue

Rain pattered softly against the broad, red leaves of the bright rainforest. Strange creatures cried and bird-like scavengers cackled. The woods were alive with light, excited creatures leaping from branch to branch. A pair of stormy grey eyes watched them go, but did not make a move to follow.

Beneath the tree canopy, a human was settled by a campfire, dainty hands wrapped in black leather. With long, slow rasps of stone against metal, they sharpened a silver knife, spraying the ground with a shower of sparks.

Most back on Earth would see a girl, perhaps, her shoulders broad and strong. Or maybe a boy, his hair long and body stocky and short. But whatever they were didn't matter out here. They themself hadn't thought about it in almost eight hundred years.

These were the first, and only human eyes ever to see this place. It was a forest full of life and edible fruits, and the creatures which lived here were quite harmless.

The fire crackled alluringly before the Rifter, yellowish in colour and casting a pleasant warmth along sleek leather armour and hand-stitched hide coat. This was a roughly done set; made long ago by inexperienced fingers. The prickings and cuts earned from the effort had, luckily, long healed. The threads holding the outfit together were made from woven grass strands of a brown-red colouring, whilst the leather itself was black as congealed blood. Mottled red fur stuck out between the seams and around the collar to warm the neck, just a shade darker than the wavy red hair that fell in a shock about their shoulders.

A bug-eyed amphibian was roasting on a yellow-green spear above the fire. The human's stomach growled. Very rarely did anything ever smell delicious, out here in the Rift. But this was enough to set their stomach pining, reminding them of the many weeks of scant living before reaching this planet.

The scent, however, brought a measure of risk. Something would smell this, and something would want it. They'd have to eat fast and move on quickly. Luckily, that was one of their specialties.

The Rifter's head jerked upright as a flurry of shrieks erupted from the underbrush. Creatures which had been hiding in the treetops sprang from trunk to trunk, croaking and barking warnings. The human froze momentarily, skin prickling. Finally, chest heaving, they stood, silver knife glinting wickedly in the firelight.

They listened for a while to the sounds of the night and the fire's crackle, cocking the freshly-sharpened blade.

A quiet rustle set them on edge, and the Rifter tensed. A moment later there was another, louder. The survivor's blood ran cold. *I'm being hunted.*

They rose, stalked around the campfire and pushed through a curtain of leaves. No hunter in its right mind would attack fearless prey. When they reached the place the noise had come from, nothing remained but shallow footprints in the moss. They crouched, running a hand across the tracks, taking note of the pattern and depth. *Strange...* the Rifter mused. *I don't remember any bipeds living on this world...*

The Rifter straightened up. *Well... at least it doesn't seem very big.*

They looked out across the clearing as another quiet rustle reached their ears, and they felt their heart beating hard beneath their breast. They pressed deeper into the foliage. Another sudden noise told them that their quarry was trying to escape. Lips tightening, they held the knife at arm's length, and quickly advanced.

They placed their feet carefully, and hesitated before emerging into an open clearing, sweeping leaves aside, poised to drive the weapon into the unfortunate creature.

…But never did.

The Rifter's eyes widened, knuckles white where they gripped the knife. A human man stared back at them, blue eyes wide in fear. Back on Earth, he might have been considered handsome, with long, grey-streaked blonde locks and an angular face. But now, he was emaciated, with torn, unkempt clothes and a wild beard that clung in scraggles to his chin.

They met his gaze, eyes narrowing, uncertain of what to say. It took them a moment to recall the words, rearranging the tongue in their mouth; it had been many, many years since they'd last used their native voice.

"Were you trying to rob me?"

The voice that spoke was sharp and rough from years of misuse. The man stared back at them, wordless, terrified – and after a moment, the Rifter realised that the tongue they had snapped in was not English at all, but was trade-speak used only by a race of small, round earth-dwellers they had met centuries ago. A tongue that was rough, snarling and brittle, with an accent that rumbled and cracked like breaking rocks.

With a low grumble in the back of their throat, they tried again.

"You're here to steal." It didn't sound like a question as they'd intended, but it was close enough.

This time, the stranger's eyes lit with understanding and profound relief. "God, no!" the man said, voice high with indignation. "I would never, ever rob a…" He trailed off, looking them briskly up and down. "…A lady!"

Understanding came more readily than the Rifter had expected it to. "Ah… I see." They said at length, then grinned at his visible discomfort. *How fitting that the first human I've met in 900 years would be a complete pillock.* A smart person would already be miles away, having swiped their dinner the second they left the clearing. "…You should have tried, at least."

"You'd want me to steal from you?"

The Rifter shrugged with a lopsided grin. "No. But you don't need permission to try."

The man's face reddened, and he shifted uncomfortably in the silence. "I ah… simply wanted to ask for some."

"And… If I said no?"

The stranger had no answer.

"You'll never survive," the Rifter said, shaking their head lightly. But then they smiled, rarely seen dimples marking those freckled cheeks. "Not out here."

"Out… here?" the stranger asked. Although he tried to sound sure, his voice wavered. "Where is… here?"

Slowly, but surely, the Rifter was rediscovering a long-forgotten tongue. They glanced up to look for a direct answer, though the tree canopy obscured any hint of stars. "Not far away from your home. We are only a few light-years from…" They paused, hesitating on a name that they hadn't spoken aloud for centuries. When they spoke, it was only a little above a whisper. "…Earth."

The Rifter moved on, shaking their head. "But knowing the Rift, we could be anywhere."

"Th… the Rift?"

"Your last moments on Earth. There was a bright white light… and pain. And when your eyes opened, you were here?"

"…Pretty much."

"That's the Rift. The pathway between worlds – you belong to it now." The Rifter smiled again. It was a plain, simple smile, but it felt cruel. It didn't spread to their eyes.

"There's… no way back?" the stranger asked in disbelief.

"In nine hundred years, I think I would have found a way." The Rifter spread their hands. "Congratulations –

and condolences. Welcome to your new life."

The stranger looked as though he wanted to say something more, but was interrupted as his stomach let out a pitiable growl.

"Come, then," the Rifter said. "It's burning."

Several minutes later, the pair had settled by the fire, and the Rifter was dividing their portions carefully. Their mind was still reeling from the unexpected encounter. In their head, they found themselves rehearsing words in a tongue they thought they'd never hear aloud again – and feeling appalled at how little they remembered. They watched the stranger's changing expressions with a mixture of curiosity and suspicion.

Finally, they divided a lump of meat the size of a fist for themself, and about half that for the newfound acquaintance.

He fingered the meat briefly, before asking "Is that all?"

The Rifter sputtered out an involuntary laugh.

"This is your first meal out here, yes? I don't want you to lose it."

"How did you know?"

"Aside from your clothes, you strike me as the kind of person who couldn't catch a marsh-hopper if it hopped right into your open gob."

The stranger flushed red and avoided their gaze, glaring down at the food in his lap. He thought for a second. "Don't congratulate yourself," he muttered after a while. "This is barely edible."

The Rifter unwittingly smirked. "Alright, then. Our next meal is on you."

The stranger looked up in panic. "Excuse me?"

"I'm saying I can teach you. The attitude will need to change, but it's been far too long since I've had company."

"Attitude!? I don't have an attitude, and fat chance I'll let a… someone like *you* teach me!"

Ah, there it was. They waited for his rage to cool before speaking, expression unchanging.

"Alright," they smiled wryly, holding out an empty palm. "You can give that back. A kill like this could keep me going for a week, but instead I wasted it on you."

"You can't be serious." The stranger blanched, looking at them in disbelief, so the Rifter flexed their fingertips and raised a brow.

"If you won't give it, then I'll take it back myself. Starvation isn't exactly peak physical condition for a…" – they looked him up and down as he had them, and sniffed – "…*man* such as yourself. It won't be hard. Unless, of course, you'd like to show a little more grace."

Finally, the stranger hung his head and avoided their gaze. He stuffed the meat into his mouth a little quicker but said nothing.

The Rifter, though, smiled, finally lowering their hand. "So… Do you have a name, stranger?"

The stranger's eyes narrowed. He remained silent, begrudgingly swallowing another mouthful. "It's Oliver. You?"

The Rifter's eyes glittered. "Back on Earth, they called me Aria. But you can call me Riftmaster."

Chapter 1
In Loving Memory

Riftmaster Ari's hand clenched, grip tightening on the necklace in their palm. The surface of the jewel shimmered with droplets. The rain fell around them in icy sheets, tangled knots of red hair falling around their face. For the first time in months, they were alone. Blissfully, yet chokingly alone.

The Riftmaster looked up only once to see the retreating back of the boy... no... the man they'd known as family for so long. Bailey's cloak swayed gently with the motions of his movements, hood pulled up to shield himself from the rain that Ari had willingly embraced. Before he could look back and offer one last glimpse of his face, Ari hastily turned to the memorial at their feet, worried that the sight of him would change their mind. Sodden, cold, and beginning to shiver, they knelt, gently placing the blue-stone pendant upon the lichen-covered rock. The pendant was bound to both of them now; it would be no use to either of them anymore. Their gaze trailed up the headstone to linger on old, long-worn lettering.

```
ARIA JAMESON
1936-1960
BELOVED DAUGHTER
OF JOSEPHINE AND
ROBERT JAMESON.
```

Finally, Ari hauled themself to their feet and stepped back. The distant sound of an engine throbbing over the pattering rain told them that Bailey was gone, leaving to see the family he had left behind. His *true* family.

Although Ari knew that they'd done the right thing, the thought burned itself into their brain, and they felt their vision grow blurry, and soon warm tears mingled with the cold of the rain. They slowly lowered their gaze, and settled, sitting cross-legged before the graves of their kin. And there they waited; Ari wasn't sure whether for minutes or hours, but they waited.

It was over.

All they could do now was wait for the Rift to come back for them.

Luckily, they didn't need to wait long. Soon the cold was pierced by a sudden pain of burning fire, running from their head to the tips of their toes. Fingers curling into the wet stems of grasses as though it would help them stay, they doubled over and let out a silent cry.

Through the pain of Rifting, the Riftmaster stole one last look at the familiar church beyond, committing the sight into their brain. They glanced around, taking in the sight of the flowers resting on the graves, fresh and wilting; roses and pansies and even the occasional rogue dandelion. Ari savoured as best they could this one final glimpse of familiar soil. Of Earth.

The last thing they saw was their own tearful face gazing back at them from the shining pendant resting on the foot of their grave.

And then, like a kitten being wrenched limply into the air by its mother, Ari felt their feet leave the ground, and vision faded into whiteness.

They tumbled to a grinding halt against hard, red soil. The Riftmaster lay where they had fallen for a time, drenched with fists clenched, hot breaths curling into a wisp of steam from flared nostrils.

The air was cold here. Cold, but new.

The time had come to let go, once again. And yet... this time, they somehow found that they couldn't. The thought of leaving Earth behind *again*, and what little surviving family they had there, wrenched their heart clean in two. Tears squeezed out from beneath tightly closed eyelids. They let out a choked sob.

Within these months of my life, I've lost everything. Any hope that my children lived a long and happy life out there in the Rift... any hope that they might be out there still. I've lost Oliver... Again.

Ari searched for the anger. The sheer abhorrence for everything their old flame had stood for, and what he had brought back into their life after so many years. So many times he had forced them to relive everything they thought they had left behind on Earth. But all that remained was a crushing sense of loss.

Oliver hurt me. We argued, we fought, we never saw eye to eye. He refused to call me by my name because it represented something that he thought I shouldn't be, and everything I did had to be in defiance of his ideals.

Ari let out a choked sob.

But God, for so many years he was all I had. And I never, ever would have thought it'd come to this.

What Oliver had done didn't change the fact that he was now gone.

If the only way to soothe their pain was forcing themself to relive their hatred for a dead man, perhaps they deserved this. Any anger that remained seemed fruitless.

Ari's eyes were closed, the ground cold and hard against the back of their head. They didn't try to get up and simply lay there on the cold extra-terrestrial earth.

Even their parents, for whom they had thought any lingering feeling was gone, were dead. They had lived out their days under the shadow of grief, never knowing what had happened to the daughter they must have always thought they drove away.

Their mother had died forty years ago. Their father had spent the rest of his long, lonely years waiting for the return of a girl who no longer existed.

And now, all these years later, Ari knew how they had felt.

What's the matter with me? The Riftmaster asked themself, forcing their eyes open. Through the tears, the world was blurry with lights. *I've done this before, hundreds… no… thousands of times… I've got to get up. I've got to survive. Something out here will find and eat us if I don't.*

They stopped themself.

No, not us… Just me.

Their only surviving kin was gone. Bailey had returned home, to his true family. He was happy. Happier than he'd ever be with Ari, because of them. Their duty to him was done.

All Ari could do now was pray that he never found their bones.

Somehow the thought made getting up even harder.

Do I want that? They asked themself. *After all this time, do I really just… give up?*

They squeezed their eyes shut, but failed to block out the agony, and felt the tears forcing themselves out to roll down their cheeks. For once they didn't care about wasting the moisture.

What a waste of five thousand years…

Slowly, surely, the Riftmaster drew their hands into fists, rolled onto their side, and brought their knees up to their chest. *I have to go on,* they told themself. *I killed Oliver for this chance.* Their tears cooled rapidly against their cheeks. *This can't be how it ends.*

They thought back to the faces they'd known, to the

years they'd shed like snakeskin. They searched in vain for something to force them to go on, anything. Ari found instead the agony of grief that they'd endured, again and again and again.

First with their parents. They had pushed through.

With each and every world they had grown to love.

Then with their children… a family they thought would never end.

Ari squeezed their eyes shut, but they couldn't shake the memory of dusty plains and weathered bones. Instead they tried to remember voices. The fresh, smiling faces and rosy cheeks.

The memories wavered, oddly misty.

After years of fighting for survival, it was the ordinary days that Ari remembered most. The days where nothing happened – when their bellies were full and the children played.

An image rose to the forefront of their mind; a memory of a small blonde boy stumbling towards them with a scraped knee, an older child holding his hand to lead him, a shock of red hair about her head. The Riftmaster's soothing laughter echoed in memories as they washed Toby's scrape clean. When anyone in their family had ever felt afraid or hurt, lost or alone, it was always Ari they turned to for comfort. For some reason, the others always thought that they would know how to help.

Adeline glanced back as her brother scampered off to play once more with his twin. Ari saw a fire mirrored in Adeline's eyes that had once lived in their own.

Adeline, Toby, Peggy… if there was something I could do to spend one more day with you…

Their memory meandered among silken stems and fragrant leaves as the four of them played, reliving the excitement they had for the growth of their tiny family.

From three, to four, then to five, and then six. It was a hard life, but Ari wouldn't have given it up for the world. And then finally, there were thirteen.

In those days, before the first loss, their children seemed to look to Ari as eternal, infallible.

There was never any doubt that the Riftmaster would make it through.

And yet, here they lay. No one left to comfort them. No one to clean their wounds.

What I wouldn't give for someone to look at me like that again.

The image lingered. They clung to the sight of their sons and daughters while it lasted behind their closed lids, trying to relive that feeling of joy.

Finally, though, they opened their eyes.

None of them would want me to lie down and die. Not after everything I've sacrificed to be here. Pip, Martin, Katrina, Lily… All of you… I'm not going to be joining you just yet. Maybe one day, but not yet.

Bit by bit, they uncurled, forcing themself upright, and onto their knees.

I just have to make it through today. While there's one person left in the universe who I still care about, I'll always find a way.

Bailey… this is for you.

Their eyes felt hollow, sore with tears and dust, and vision slightly blurred. They blinked it back as best they could, and then staggered to their feet. For a moment, Ari pitched forward, extending a hand to steady themself against the rough surface of a large boulder. They hadn't eaten in days. Grief had made it difficult to stomach anything in their brief time on Earth, and before that… well… raw terror had not been kind.

Finally, though, after a few moments of steadying themself, Ari looked up. They were standing on a wide, flat plain with a scattering of boulders like the one they leaned against, in varying shapes and sizes. The soil, hard and packed under their feet, was cracked as though it had once been the bed of a river or lake. It was a muddy red-brown, with greenish swirls of copper and rust.

This world failed to fill them with the wonder that so often kept them going. Perhaps the most intriguing part of the sprawling nothingness was the rapidly brightening stratosphere, where the moon hung as a great, purplish orb around ninety degrees beneath the apex of the lilac sky.

The sun was rising quickly over the distant horizon, bluish in tone, and the Riftmaster could already feel its heat falling across their face. Even still, Ari shivered, drawing their sodden cloak about them. Perhaps as the morning drew on, it would grow warm. Maybe even *too* warm.

But from the look of it, the days were short here, and Ari did not trust the night to be over just as fast. If they wanted to survive the day, they would need to move quickly.

As far as the eye could see, there seemed to be no life, not even the hardiest scrub. Ari turned, but each and every direction looked the same. *Better to follow the moon*, Ari finally decided. *It'll be easy enough to orient myself, that way.*

They finally cast their gaze skyward, looking out towards the stars that were fading in the pale morning light. They searched the constellations they knew, trying to pinpoint their place in the universe. A few were intact, and Ari could almost pretend they were stargazing from a distant, uninhabited corner of Earth. Some, though, were scattered, constellations fragmented and displaced.

I must be a few hundred light-years away, they thought. *Not too far. So then, that means...*

Ari turned their gaze sharply upwards, and their eyes narrowed as they fixed on the dark areas of a familiar constellation, the void filled by a distant glimmering point. Ari's jaw quivered as they beheld Earth's star.

One day, Ari vowed quietly. *One day we'll meet again.*

They waited until the sun had risen, and the stars had finally faded away before forcing themself to move. Step by step, they set off towards the distant horizon.

And as long as that promise remained unfulfilled, Ari knew that they would somehow find the strength to go on.

***

The sky seemed empty, save for a few clouds that rolled lazily past the sun and moon. A fine mist of drizzle disturbed the warmth once or twice, before quickly clearing. Ari tried their best to filter the rain from the air to drink with a sheet of leather, but it was far too fine. They salvaged what they could of the rain that had soaked their clothes, but it yielded no more than a few mouthfuls.

They silently cursed not having the foresight to fill their waterskin with the fresh, clean water of Earth.

Whenever the sun shone through the clouds, coils of steam rose from their cape. Ari found that it rapidly grew far too hot to continue. So, they staggered into the shelter of an enormous boulder, resting their back against the cool stone as they waited for it to pass them by. Heatstroke was a very real threat out here, and one that they couldn't afford to take lightly.

Resting their head back, Ari was still, half-listening to the surrounding world but mostly conserving energy. The Riftmaster doubted there was much that could hurt them out here, but if there was, they needed to be able to escape it. Gradually, they became aware of a low humming sound, trembling in through the back of their skull. They listened, trying to pinpoint the direction, and ran their hands across the earth to feel for vibrations.

Ari's eyes narrowed. They pressed their head slightly harder against the boulder. *Could it be water...?* They wondered, feeling the vibrations growing stronger. *There must be something under there. There's a rhythm to it. Perhaps organic. Perhaps a subterranean stream.*

Ari turned, hugging the shadow of the boulder, as they ran their fingers across its rough surface. Again, they felt nothing more than cool rock. Caution coloured their movements as they inched away, peering at the dry, cracked sediment around its base. After a moment of scouting the small area of shade, Ari knelt, and drew the silver knife from a belt on their upper thigh.

The knife felt cold, icy cold in their palm, and for the first time, they hesitated to use it. The last time lingered, heavy on their mind. Even now, they felt the weight of a life draining away into their hands. The leather hilt of the weapon felt sticky with blood. It slipped under their grasp, and Ari tried not to look in case some remained, oozing out from between their fingers.

I can't believe I'm still using the knife that ended his life.

A chill washed over them. Their chest grew tight.

*The knife **I** used to end his life.*

Ari transferred the knife to their left hand, running their fingers across their palm. After a moment, they forced themself to look. Their skin was coated with a thin layer of sweat, and nothing else. Their breaths shook, and they sat back down, relieved, but only slightly. Their heart pounded, hands beginning to tremble.

I can't keep going back to this. He gave me this chance. He knew there was no other way. When I find another Riftworld, I can get a new knife. I can trade this one away.

For a moment they hesitated, nausea rising in their stomach. Their heart beat faster. Ari tightened their grip on the knife with a shudder, pushing their thoughts away from those awful moments.

Finally, they held it tight in both hands, and let out a sigh.

I'm wasting time.

Fumbling carefully, Ari felt at the base of the rock and eased up a plate of hardened sediment with the tip of the blade. The soil beneath was damp and soft, and their heart swelled quickly. Ari hastily sheathed the knife. Cautiously, they dug a little bit deeper with their hands. Water welled in the bottom of the hollow, and their excitement mounted.

Steady, steady. Where water exists, there will always be something living in it, they reminded themself. Cautiously, they removed a small clay bowl from their satchel, and continued digging until the water formed a shallow pool. The sun had climbed until it was very nearly overhead, and Ari shifted until they were in the shade as best they could. Then, the digging continued.

Finally the pool was deep enough to wash out their

bowl and gather a few drops. As they did so, though, the surface of the boulder trembled. The plates of dry sediment around its base shivered and Ari jumped back, heedless of the sun on their neck. A moment later, a cluster of tendrils emerged from beneath the soil, and the boulder tilted wildly. The entire formation emerged from its hollow on four stumpy legs, dripping wet and covered in tendrils of pondweed.

Ari jerked away, hiding in the shade of another rock, heart hammering. Was this one alive too? Ari shrank behind it even so, watching as the rock-creature's dripping tendrils tasted the air. It broke into a lumbering trot, rumbling low in its throat, and bumped sides with another, which lifted itself from its pool as well. Ari watched in fascination as tendrils locked and growls echoed throughout the dry riverbed.

Whilst the creatures were distracted, Ari hurried over to the hollow the rock-beast had left behind. They peered down into a tiny pond, eyes widening in amazement. As well as a faint covering of algae and strings of yellow pondweed, Ari had found a veritable treasure trove of tiny aquatic creatures.

Yes! If I'm lucky, these will keep me fed for a while…

From their satchel Ari withdrew a small pinch of dried herbs, and crumbled them into the bowl. The herbs, black at first, swelled and fizzed as they made contact with the water. The foam that formed across the top had a faint yellowish tint.

Ari squinted, letting the reaction take its course before emptying the bowl onto the sand. Finally, they filled it one more time, raising it to their lips to drink. The water tasted faintly coppery, with the barest hint of salt. Knowing this, Ari didn't drink too much. Instead, they filled their waterskin and resolved to filter it later over a fire.

In any case, they still needed sustenance.

Ari looked up as an enormous crash erupted from the two clashing beasts, sending chunks of stone clattering to the ground around them and splashing in the two empty ponds.

The first rock-beast finally appeared victorious. With deep growls, the second one was forced out of its hollow, and lumbered away across the dry riverbed, seemingly oblivious to Ari's invasion of its neighbour's pond. As it walked, inky tendrils slithered over the ground before it, and it soon turned in a wide circle and began to return.

Quickly, Ari removed a linen pouch from their satchel, and stuffed it until it bulged with creatures, wriggling grubs and pondweed. Reaching into the lukewarm water up to their elbow, they retrieved a palm-sized sphere, coated in a thin layer of slime. There were many of them, hidden in the muck at the bottom of the pond. *Eggs?* Ari hoped, bursting with excitement. *It doesn't matter what world I go to, eggs rarely disappoint.*

They couldn't stay for much longer; the rock creature was mere metres away now, walking at barely a crawl as it fumbled its way ahead with searching tendrils.

Finally Ari tied the pouch shut, feeling it wriggle and squirm, and hearing the pondweed slosh within. It was suddenly heavy, and Ari quickly darted into the shade of an undisturbed rock. The creature's searching tendrils finally found the pond. It scouted the moist banks and snuffled at the tracks Ari had left behind.

Finally, with a hearty grunt, it settled down into the water, and became little more than an unassuming rock once more.

Ari let out a sigh of relief, and stood upright, backing away from any and all boulders in the nearby vicinity. The sun was beginning to sink. Their freckled cheeks felt hot, and the back of their neck was probably already sunburned. But it wouldn't be long before dusk brought back the cold. Ari needed to build a fire before then, so that they could filter their water and cook themself a meal. After they knew it was edible, of course.

With a spring in their step and a slightly renewed sense of vigour, Ari set off towards the distant horizon, hoping that even though the riverbed was dry, they'd find an ocean at its end.

***

Soon after night fell, the faint drizzling of rain became a sprinkling of snow. They walked for many hours, and still found nothing that could possibly serve as firewood. The night was chilly, and they pulled their cloak tightly about their shoulders. Breaths steamed in the air before them.

I can dry out some of the pondweed in the sun tomorrow... perhaps that will burn for a time. Until then... I just have to keep moving. Stay warm.

So, Ari stumbled on, trembling all over, as they held their belongings close and their cloak tight about them. With face bare and legs covered by a thin layer of purple scales, though, they still felt the chill.

Luckily, the dark was not unnavigable, lit by the pale light of the ever-present moon shining overhead.

Although the days passed quickly, the night seemed to last forever. The stars above glittered and winked. Ari glimpsed the tiniest speck of Earth's sun once more, and felt a familiar ache as they walked, fingers clenched tight to their palms, and hands withdrawn into the heat of their chest.

Preserve heat, they repeated mechanically, bringing everything they could as close as they could, and making themself as small as possible. *Don't shed, transfer. Little lost, little wasted.*

Their legs grew numb, and eyelids heavy, breath steaming around their face. Their ears and nose turned red, and they stumbled over any slightly tilted plate. They forced themself to watch out, scanning the world ahead. But it all looked the same. Flat, too dark to see the treacherous cracks.

Once they fell fully down, landing on their knees and grazing their palms, losing precious lifeblood to the earth. They licked the wounds until the bleeding stopped, then rubbed their hands dry against their cloak and brought their closed fists back towards their chest.

Keep moving. Movement is heat.

Ari trudged on.

Eventually midnight passed and the world grew lighter. The days cycled quickly, but Ari knew that they shouldn't relax, not until the sun was high.

The weariest travellers always perish when hope rears its ugly head.

When dawn finally arrived, and warmth shone down on their face, Ari settled in the early morning light and fished in their pouch for some pondweed. Despite the added freshness, it had perhaps been unwise to bring the pond creatures alive. Slimy things rippled and wriggled under their touch, squelching disgustingly among the weeds. Something trembled as the Riftmaster's hand closed about it. A moment later, it bit. Ari snatched their hand back, blood oozing from a tiny cut.

Ari cleaned the wound with drops from their waterskin, swearing under their breath as the sensation stung.

"Alright, that settles it, you're getting eaten first," they muttered, feeling their stomach let out a low and pitiful moan. "For your sake, I hope you're edible."

Finally, Ari withdrew the pondweed, as much as they could without being accosted again. They laid it out to dry in the sun.

Whilst it warmed, the Riftmaster prepared their bowls with pinches of powdered herbs. They had very little left, and they feared this world would be unsuitable for growing more. If the whole planet was like this, it would be difficult to ration remaining supplies, and when they reached the next world… poisoning would be a very real risk.

For now, though, they had other things to worry about. It would take time to test the creatures they'd foraged, and even longer to cook them.

With a small metallic hiss that sent chills down their spine, Ari drew their knife.

They opened up the leather pouch, and looked inside. They reached first for a palm-length, worm-like creature with large, knife-like mandibles. "Sorry, little chap," Ari muttered, hastily dropping it onto the ground. It squirmed, mandibles clicking, and hide crinkling grotesquely. Its green-flecked skin may have hinted at toxins on earth, but on this world, rippled with veins of copper, Ari was certain those colours just meant camouflage. Even still… they raised their knife, not wanting to prolong its suffering as it squirmed frantically on the dirt.

Their stomach growled, knife flashing wickedly in the sunshine.

Still they hesitated, a brief jolt running through them.

A moment later, Ari blinked. *Come on, Riftmaster. It's a worm, of all things. And it's suffering because of me. It'd be crueller to let it keep squirming for escape.*

Ari faltered again, their chest aching with held breaths. They watched as the worm's thrashing brought it towards them, across the plate of long-dried sediment.

Why is this so hard? I've done this a thousand times before. To hell with it!

Shame rapidly boiled over into a flare of frustration. The Riftmaster tightened their grip, clamped their eyes shut, and plunged the knife down into the cold, hard earth. There came a high-pitched whistle of escaping air, and a small pop. Ari opened their eyes.

The worm writhed, skewered. Thick, blue blood dribbled onto the ground in a way that was all too familiar.

Ari shuddered, wrenching the knife back from the dying worm and holding it away from them. In their mind's eye, the blood looked crimson as it stained the blade, creeping down towards their hand with awful intent.

Ari shivered, their stomach twisting with hunger, and yet their appetite somehow lost. They threw the dagger to the ground by the still-twitching worm, and then sank down onto their knees with an enormous sigh.

With shaking hands, Ari picked up the creature and twisted its head from its body, ending its suffering for good. Then they sat back, catching their breath and pinching some herbs into the bowl. With a trembling hand they added in a dash of water. *See?* They chided themself, like an unruly child. *That wasn't so bad, was it?*

As the sun grew too hot, Ari retreated into the shadow of a boulder. They rested their ear to its surface to see if it was alive. Then, satisfied that it was at least dormant, they kept on mixing, letting the colours work themselves out and the liquid settle. Finally, Ari dumped the half-full bowl onto the sand. They stalked back to the remains of the worm, picked up the ravaged chunks in one hand, and hurled it towards the distant horizon.

A distant splatter faded into silence once again.

***

When the night grew dark, Ari stared into a fire which burned in a sickly shade of green and munched solemnly on a pale sphere.

Unlike the worm, these weren't toxic. That said, it tasted like sour meat, its texture like slime as it slid down their throat, leaving a burning sensation as it went. The Riftmaster tolerated it with all the grace of a polite aristocrat.

Soon after that, Ari rested their back against a rock, gaze never moving from the fire and the bright coals in its depths. Their knife lay where it had fallen. Desperate to sleep, Ari's eyes kept cracking open and finding its silver gleam in the dark beyond the flame, as though it was watching them.

If I'm attacked here... they thought. *I won't have anything to defend myself.*

They let out a breath.

...And what if it's stolen?

Exhaustion lingered in every muscle. Their side slowly rose and fell, as if already asleep. Finally, they eased themself into a sitting position, and stood. They moved around the fire, plucking the blade from the earth. They felt the sticky, cioying feeling of bug-blood as soon as they touched it, and their expression soured in the dark. In a fluid motion, they flicked off a spray of liquid and sheathed it against their thigh.

Then they put their back to the rock, basking in firelight, and drew their cloak tightly about themself.

With their eyes closed, there was nothing to keep them from memories of aged bones and empty sockets. Their eyes kept flicking open again. It took some time, but finally exhaustion got the better of them. Their breaths grew longer and evened out.

The fire swam in their vision, before swelling in hues of orange. On the other side of the fire, they saw a ring of familiar faces waiting to welcome them.

When their eyes opened again, the sun had risen and was already setting.

Ari was alone, their cheeks were encrusted with salt crystals, and eyes wet with fresh tears.

Their fire had burned itself out hours ago.

Trembling slightly, Ari dug in their satchel, and withdrew Oliver's knife. They hadn't looked at it since they had taken it from him. It was a beautiful weapon, though undoubtedly fragile. The blade was crafted painstakingly from ivory, the handle wrapped in leather that was probably taken from an unfortunate sentient being. They stroked their finger along its blade as though in a trance. It could be useful to them, yes... But it held too many memories. Ari dropped it to the ground and bent it beneath their heel.

Piece by piece, the knife cracked into tiny shards.

When Ari finally stepped away, it was barely recognisable.

Ari sniffed, and finally looked up. There was no way of knowing how long they had slept, but exhaustion tugged at their limbs.

They had to keep going.

Ari turned away from the shards, gathering their supplies together as they prepared to move on. But before they did, they risked one glance back at the shattered knife. They hesitated.

Do I really want to leave it here? This is all I have left of him.

After another few moments of consideration, Ari

removed the leather wrap from the broken pommel, and knelt down beside the shards of ivory. With careful and deft motions, Ari used the length of leather to tie the fragments into a new necklace. *They might even be more useful to me like this.*

Looping the leather around their neck and letting the fragments fall against their bare skin, Ari turned their back once more, and this time when they moved away, they didn't look back.

Chapter 2
The Nomadic Ocean

Days became weeks as Ari walked across the bleak surface of the wide, dry plain, following the path of the moon.

They ate frugally and drank as little as they could. Still, the endless trekking combined with the daytime heat was not ideal for preserving moisture.

When the need arose, they'd provoke the pond-guarding creatures by digging under them, though only sometimes did they rise to the goading. Most of the time, Ari was able to simply hollow out a small opening, fill their waterskin, and then quickly retreat. Only some of the pond-guardians possessed the fist-sized white spheres that Ari subsisted on, and those that guarded them seemed far more easily provoked.

Although it was easy to imagine why, Ari tried not to think about it.

They walked and walked, cutting a long yet direct path across the long-barren floodplain. *Perhaps the waters will come again,* Ari thought. *The ponds have to come from somewhere. Perhaps the rock-creatures are simply waiting.*

The lack of incline worried them. If an ocean did lie at the end of this barren riverbed, what if they were going the wrong way?

Whenever awake, they followed the position of the moon, hoping that the answer lay somewhere beyond.

They walked for miles, the sun rising and setting over them. They ate, and slept, and ate again. *Just one more day,* they told themself each morning as they awoke. *Just get through this one more day.*

Eventually, the agony of leaving Earth faded to a dull ache that was pushed to the very back of their mind. Survival took centre stage.

I've dealt with worse, they reasoned. *I've lost far, far more, and in far worse ways. At least I know that Bailey is still out there. And... that he's finally home.*

Finally, one day, they awoke to find sunlight shimmering on the horizon; they tried to blink the mirage from their eyes before realising that it was real.

The end of their journey was in sight.

The sound of the winds whistling through the stones soon changed as well. The sound became deeper, richer, rising and falling in a low hiss. They stepped onto dry foliage that crunched beneath their feet, but even that was soon replaced by healthier plants, purplish in tone. Ari picked up the pace; hours later, they came upon a beautiful sight.

Waves crashed at their feet, waters soaking the parched earth. Gnarled, purplish trees spread bare branches above the water's surface, their roots resting in the shallow waters. Thousands of tiny creatures flitted between trees or found rest among the branches. Massive stones moved in the shallows as herds of rock-beasts grazed, their tendrils sifting through the shallow waters.

While the forest clung to the shallows, the water stretched as far as Ari could see, the light of the moon glittering lilac across its surface.

Ari sank to their knees at the water's edge and drank. The cold water tasted clean and mineral-rich, so unlike the stagnating pools beneath the rock-beasts. As they straightened up, looking out to sea, they forced the faintest smile to their cracked lips. *This is why I'm here,* they thought. *Through it all, this is why I keep living.*

The sun set soon after, and Ari took off their boots to hunt in the shallows. There were creatures moving under the water, serpentine and fish-like, along with amphibious little herbivores with wide, buggish eyes. Whilst Ari still had trouble hunting, vegetation was plentiful, and occasionally even delicious.

Over the next few days, the tide went out. Each time Ari awoke, the water had receded by a foot or more, following the moon. The trees moved too on broad, vast tentacles pulling them on their slow way. Ancient rock-beasts, heavy on their feet and too exhausted to keep following the sea, dug themselves nests and were left behind.

The little ones, though, roamed in vast herds. They were splashing and playing in the shallows, breeding and hunting among the tree roots. And as they all made their slow way in the world, Ari too found their place. They took the nomadic lifestyle in their stride, following the forest, living in its shade. They hunted in knee-deep waters and plucked blossoming flowers from the surface.

The days of living on scraps had long gone; among the trees they had everything they could ever need.

So why did they not feel whole?

***

For the better part of a year, Ari shadowed the roaming forest. In that time, they suspected they had not covered even a fraction of the planet's surface, and still the tide moved on in an endless cycle.

The cycles of their body ticked off the days, the months, a year. They counted just as they had when they'd first entered the Rift at the tender age of twenty-four.

If I'd never left Earth, I'd be in my eighties… I might have had grandkids, or great grandkids. Now would be the twilight of my life.

But they never changed, never aging, never growing. The more light-years they were from Earth, the more their grip loosened on the progression of time. They found themself wondering once or twice just how long it had been for Bailey since they'd left. Two days? A month? A year? Ten years? There was no way to know until they made it home. All they knew was that back on Earth, time seemed to slow.

When they'd first encountered Oliver after 900 years in the Rift, it had been 1971 – only 11 years after they'd left. Four-thousand years on, and it was 2019 back there.

Trying to pinpoint exactly how time worked in the Rift was like trying to find an egg yolk in a bucket of paint, and just as messy.

So they kept on going, through months and years and decades, then centuries.

Nothing had changed, and everything.

Even now, not a single grey hair marked their auburn mane.

The usual aches and pains never came.

In their time following the ocean, their hair grew, tumbling in a mess of red curls about their shoulders. The Riftmaster spent many hours examining their reflection, wondering if they should draw their knife and crop it short. Eventually they decided to simply let it grow, reasoning that change felt good. To keep it out of their eyes, they tied it back with a length of fabric into an explosive ponytail that cascaded down their back like lava.

Eventually, the Rift came for them, sweeping them away and dropping them on a planet even further away from Earth. Now one hundred lightyears stood between them and the actualisation of their silent vow.

And it was time to start again, renewing the cycle and finding their place anew.

This planet placed forest canopies and clouds between themself and the stars. As soon as they reached it, they ached to leave. The next, they touched down into a narrow canyon, and could see only a narrow sliver of sky. For months, the Riftmaster lurched headlong from world to world, always looking ahead, and never able to stop. Reality spun around them as though they were caught in a hurricane. Each time they blinked, another year had passed.

Until finally, as the fresh waves of pain faded from their skin and the light of the rift died from their eyes, they opened their eyes to a river of stars. They were perched on the crest of a clifftop overlooking a scarlet sea. Above them, millions of tiny lights winked in an abyss of deep maroon. It took them all of a few moments to recognise the sight of the milky way stretched out before them. All of the constellations visible from earth, glimmering billions of light years away, and fragmented in disarray.

And in that moment, time seemed to slow. They felt all their years come crashing in.

The Riftmaster's stomach sank. For a brief moment they were overwhelmed with emotion, and their heart felt suddenly leaden as they gazed up at the universe that they loved.

All those planets, hundreds of thousands of worlds… and only one of them is where I want to be. What's the chance that I'll ever make it back?

Ari closed their eyes once again, hardly daring to look at their new surroundings. They steadied their breaths as they sank cross-legged to the ground. The moss was soft and dewy beneath their fingertips, and they drew in warm and humid breaths.

This pain brought them back by thousands of years, forcing them to remember the first steps they had ever taken in the Rift. When they'd spent each day on the run, and each night in tears. Missing their parents, their home, and the hot food on the table.

And then again, when they had found themself separated from their love and their children for the first time.

Every time they opened their heart, the Riftmaster knew they could only have it broken again. As long as they lived, that was the only way it could ever be. To break a heart or be broken themself; until their immortal existence ended, that was all they could do.

I've been away from Bailey now longer than I knew him, and I'm still fighting to get back to him. That boy is the only thing in the universe I have left.

Love was addictive, and the one thing they couldn't seem to control.

They just kept on falling into the same trap, over and over again.

But…

This isn't like the first time… the Riftmaster reminded themself. *I made it back once. Thanks to Bailey, I know now that the Rift can be controlled, our paths reversed. If I can just find my way to another Riftworld, then…*

Finally, the Riftmaster sat upright, their jaw tight and teeth clenched.

What am I sitting around and moping for?

Ari rubbed a tear from their cheek with the back of their wrist, then licked it from their skin.

He may be gone, but he's exactly where he should be, because of me. Back on Earth, it's probably only been a day. I have a thousand lifetimes to make it back to him. He's the first of my own ever to truly leave the nest. And I'm happy for him.

It was a sentiment that was easier thought than felt. They cast one last, wistful glance up at the stars.

I've lived like this before. I've found joy out here in the silence, and peace in being alone. I can do it again.

The Riftmaster stood sharply.

I should be celebrating. Enjoying my time out here knowing I'll never be able to lose him again.

***

Years passed.

Worlds flashed by in a blitz of colours and motion. Ari kept themself going in a state of perpetual motion, never stopping for fear that the loneliness would crush the life out of their lungs.

Through rain and storm, sea and plain they leaped between worlds as a dolphin leaps the waves, carefree.

It was only a matter of time before they were forced to slow. The Rift dropped them unceremoniously into a pit of foul-smelling mud. They struggled, panicking briefly, before finally finding solid ground somewhere below. As luck would have it, it was shallow enough to stand. The mud came up to their waist, tepid against their skin as it seeped its way into their clothes. With no way of knowing what lay beneath, Ari frantically looked for a way out.

The swamp was crisscrossed with foliage that formed a dramatic ceiling of immense plates. Twisted, pillar-like stems split into an elaborate knot of roots, rising like cages from the mud. Seeing no way out onto dry land, Ari forced themself to trudge on.

Steam rose in coils around their body and leaked out into the sky through cracks in the canopy. The air reeked of organic decay.

The swamp-forest was loud with deep, throaty grunts and chesty calls, but Ari could see only the smaller denizens of the swamp. Balloon-like creatures floated on coils of steam, without a means of powered flight or a care in the world. Ari passed bubbling patches of escaping methane gases and gigantic, naturally-formed cauldrons of gelatinous algae each containing a world and life of its own.

They hurried towards a hillock of dirt and moss, only for the mound to croak frightfully, and begin to haul itself away, leaving Ari to hastily reverse.

It was like wading through syrup; their limbs ached, breath heaved and trying to move faster only made them more exhausted.

Frequently, they felt something beneath the mud nipping at their skin or sliding against the outside of their clothes, leaving them to hurriedly scramble up onto a root. After long minutes of stillness they would reluctantly lower themself back into the mud and keep going, keeping their hand firmly on the sheathed knife at their thigh.

After what felt like hours of trekking, the mud became

shallower. And finally, a slope materialised out of the mist.

Renewed life seeped into Ari's tortured limbs as they finally hauled themselves out onto the semi-solid shore. Just a few paces more, and the mud gave way to a bank of moss. There, Ari fell to their knees, gasping for air beside a gurgling river of mud. Frantically, they dug muddied hands into their satchel and removed everything they had. Their bowls were covered in an ugly layer of slime, their herb pouches very nearly ruined; the valuable powders and seeds sodden and unusable.

Ari felt a spark of panic.

I need to get these planted if I've any chance of surviving another world.

They knelt, hastily driving the contents of each pouch into small furrows in the ground, regardless of whether they had a chance of lasting. As soon as the remaining plants were buried, Ari returned to their satchel.

Three old photos, given by their surviving earth family had been stashed at the bottom of their satchel, wrapped in leather. They were blotchy, barely recognisable. Ari sniffed faintly, smoothed them out as best they could, and laid them out on the bank to dry.

The few teabags they'd been saving were muddied, reeking of methane.

Ari had no choice but to toss them to the marsh creatures.

Finally, they poured the remaining mud from their satchel into the river.

Only then did Ari finally look down at themself, and cringe unhappily. Layers of clothing carefully made over years of interstellar travel were ruined; tunic coated in a layer of mud, boots filled to overflowing. Their furred garments were dripping and brown, terribly heavy.

Ari forced themself to strip down to the iridescent – and fortunately, waterproof – underlayer and leather belts. Those would wash just fine.

But they needed water to do that. Wiping the mud from their palms onto their pile of ruined clothes, Ari stood, and looked around. Their gaze was drawn to the river of mud. *There has to be a source somewhere. And perhaps that source will be clean. If not, I'll have to find a way to make a fire, and filtration systems.*

Ari glanced back at the marsh, at the steam crawling slowly across the surface.

But then… the gases here will make that risky.

And as for food… Ari shuddered.

It could be a week or more before their tester herbs sprouted. Even longer before they were remotely usable. Just this once, Ari would have to risk poisoning, and go without.

Heaving out a small sigh, Ari began to move. They followed the river of mud to its source but found no clean water. They widened their search, and found their safe haven to be no more than a tiny island. They found more rivers that joined together to make a slow-moving mudbank, rendering a large section of the land impassable.

This isn't working. I'll need to find firewood and make camp.

They pulled themself up to the peak of the island with straggles of vegetation. A small stand of trees slowly materialised out of the mist. Searching among them, Ari came upon something strange. A tree stump, gnawed and disfigured with fresh wounds. The fallen log lay on its side, a former giant that was once hundreds of feet tall. Hard, plate-like leaves of a dull brown were scattered across the local area. Pleased to have found something useful, Ari began to gather them.

When they began to explore, they came upon the unmoving body of a creature, hind limbs trapped beneath the fallen tree.

Ari held their fingertips just above its huge jaws and let out a small sigh of relief.

It's dead.

Certain now that they were safe, Ari allowed themself a closer look. Thick, ivory skin hugged tight to sinewy limbs and leathery muscle, and a rubbery carapace hardened into sharp, blue-tinged spikes above its shoulders and back. Six stocky limbs hung limply, tipped with wicked claws. Its throat hung loose like a leathery balloon.

Its jaws were massive, built for crushing, yet narrowed to a sharp and almost beaklike point. Leathery plates shielded the holes which might have been its ears, once.

The impact of the tree had crushed two of its six limbs, wounds leaking silvery blood onto the hillside. *Not minor wounds,* Ari thought, perturbed. *But they shouldn't have killed it.*

Four eyes, small and narrow and grey, had not rotted. The creature was freshly-dead. Not even the scavengers had reached it yet.

Ari stepped back, blinking, and they felt their head spinning with the possibilities. *Its skin is thick. The hide will be valuable for new armour,* they thought, rubbing their cheek. *And there's a good chance it might be edible.*

Ari realised for perhaps the first time that they were incredibly hungry. They felt their spirits rise. *I'll make camp here. I can't test it, but this is the best chance I'll get at making it past this world.*

Shortly after, the Riftmaster lit a fire, which burst into existence and burned furiously no matter what they fed it, and their gaze combed the sky until they were certain it was safe. They filtered enough marsh water for a few clean mouthfuls.

They built up a wall of mud, rocks and branches until their prize was hidden from hopeful scavengers.

Then Ari knelt at the creature's side, and drew their knife. It had been almost a year since it had last left its sheath.

The creature's carapace was thick. Far too thick to cut through easily. Clamping their eyes shut, they steadied their breaths and sawed strips of meat from its open wounds.

After cooking it, they took a few tentative nibbles, then stuffed themself until they could hardly walk.

When they dropped off into slumber, they dreamt that

they were choking. On what, they could not say, but they jerked awake with the acrid taste of metal on their lips. After that, they felt a strange spell of sluggishness and lethargy which quickly deepened into nausea. For a day, they did not return to the carcase. Hunger eventually drew them back.

They ate, slept, and ate again, cautiously monitoring their body's systems for any sign of abnormality.

The sickness deepened each morning and the torpor bit deep, but as time passed they would experience nothing more severe. Nothing, that is, except for a near-constant feeling of being watched. They felt it when they woke. They felt it as their consciousness drifted before sleeping, and a tiny part of them stayed wide awake.

Unsettled, the Riftmaster searched, yet found nothing. Even the drifters seemed to avoid this place, and they were well and truly alone. Still the feeling remained.

There was little they could do but hope it passed.

After spending a day or more trying various methods of cutting through the carcase's hide, they skinned and tanned it by firelight, putting the scraps aside for a new set of armour.

When scavengers caught the scent of meat, Ari defended it. They took position, lingering and even sleeping next to the carcase until it was long past its best. The creatures were small enough to not be much of a threat; mostly Ari's duties involved flicking bugs back to the marsh or stomping to scare off small winged scavengers.

All things considered, things were looking up.

Having eaten all they could, Ari took the carcase apart and used a leg bone, a fang, and strips of hide to create a spear. Although their hunting knife was sharp and always reliable, Ari still felt strangely reluctant to draw it.

The spear, on the other hand, felt strange and different. They rarely used spears, and this one felt new, better, and it didn't fill them with the same sense of dread.

Plus, when it came to fending off predators, distance was more useful than sharpness.

They cooked and preserved whatever they could, and used any spare drops of water to clean their clothes. Their satchel no longer held a cloying scent, and their fingertips came up clean when they touched it.

Finally, all that remained were a scattered array of bones, and Ari, with their satchel full of leaves, headed back to where they'd first come ashore. Their garden was beginning to flourish, pushing out buds in various hues.

As Ari harvested their herbs and placed them back into freshly cleaned pouches, they grinned in silent celebration, knowing that they had once more been victorious over the Rift.

And, as sunlight began to filter in through the canopy for the first time, Ari finally left that treacherous world behind in a sear of white light and pain. As the glare of the Rift faded, they opened their eyes to a familiar sight and the rarely-seen grin faded from their cheeks.

The Riftmaster squinted their eyes against the bright glare of a sky threaded with the ribbonlike pathways of the Rift.

Chapter 3
New Blood

It was no secret that Ari despised baths, ordinarily. But for the first time, they revelled in the opportunity to cleanse themself of layers of filth. The warm springs that formed equidistant to one another across the planet's surface were faintly warm, mineral-rich waters soothing as it cleansed the filth, sweat and grime from their skin and clothes.

Once they had finally scrubbed themself clean of clinging mud, they gazed out in a moment of rare stillness across the curved surface of a world they had seen in so many different parts of the universe. The grass shimmered lilac tinged with golden dewdrops.

As their stomach dropped, they realised in that moment that a small part of them had hoped never to set foot on another Riftworld. But they shook it off. *This is perfect,* they scolded themself. *Now I can start looking for crystals.*

Even so, Ari walked the planet's surface as if it would crack beneath their feet, placing each step carefully and monitoring the planet for any sign of unrest or change, resolving to find a way offworld just in case things turned south. But the quakes here soon proved infrequent and comparatively gentle.

The lingering nervousness from their last Riftworld gradually began to fade. It had been a long time since they'd seen a world in its infancy, but this one *seemed* new. It was sparsely populated, and had yet to acquire its own settlers or naturalised lifeforms from those originally brought by Rifters. The jungles were thick with the invaders of a thousand worlds, roots coiled and entwined, steadily choking the life out of one another in silent stasis.

It would be a long, long time before the victors of that struggle were decided.

As on any other Riftworld, fallen meteorites had been repurposed into quaint little houses and support beams for larger wooden structures, as fellow Rifters settled into temporary homes before their inevitable disappearance.

But something lingered from the last world; lethargy still clung to their movements. Ari tried to rest it away, and frequently awoke feeling woozy. They became hungrier more quickly, and even when they were satisfied, never felt energised.

Days passed, and it did not end.

In time, they pushed it to the back of their mind, returned to their routines, and tried to convince themself that they felt better.

It didn't work.

Stubbornly resisting sleep, Ari spent time searching around the fallen meteorites for the smallest shard of rift crystal from beneath the soil. And, in the woods, choked by vines, half-hidden beneath a chunk of moss-covered metal, they found one.

It was around the size of their thumb, a dark cluster of crystals that felt wickedly sharp in their beauty. It didn't look like much. But Ari knew these crystals held great, and largely unknown power. Power that Rifters the universe over would die for if they knew such a thing existed.

The power to keep the Rift at bay.

The Riftmaster's euphoria was tempered only by the realisation that the crystal was, right now, completely useless.

Perhaps I'll end up on a world with electricity, one day, Ari thought, sighing, as they tied the crystal onto one of their necklaces.

This world was scarcely populated, but there was a distinct sense of community among the denizens who seemed completely unaware that they were residing on a ticking time bomb. The town was small and new, bustling with the constant activity of peoples from throughout the universe.

There were no days or nights, here; Ari snatched an hour of sleep when and where they could having taken up residence in a hidden thicket of long-dead plants.

With no one to watch their back, the Riftmaster preferred to sleep alone, with plenty of distance between themself and anyone with sticky fingers.

They still sometimes woke with the curious sense that they were being watched. Feeling particularly vulnerable in their weakened state, they erred on the side of caution. After searching their thicket again, Ari was left not only baffled, but alone. As the day wore on, both feelings would fade.

As a result, they kept mostly to themself, becoming increasingly nervous that someone would notice their uncharacteristic illness.

That wasn't to say they were completely unpleasant to the other Rifters, though; in fact, they were quite friendly to those on the outskirts, and made sure to help out anyone who needed it, as long as they were within arm's reach.

It was always good to have allies.

One or two even spoke broken versions of languages Ari was familiar with, and Ari welcomed the conversation, revelling in the distraction.

Once, as they returned home after foraging, they found that the entrance to their thicket had been intruded, broken branches and snapped stems forging a path into the thorns.

Blood running cold, stomach turning, Ari tightened their grip on their spear and pressed inside to see if any of their belongings remained. They came face to face with a Rifter huddled by their sleeping hide. Crouched beside their belongings, a tall, almost-humanoid creature regarded them with fright in the orbs of their huge, green eyes. Faintly spotted skin was torn by thorns, and even crouched as low as they could, branches ticked softly against the spines upon their forehead. The stranger's skin was a pale desert brown, dappled with darker spots, and their impressive mane of quills was brown. Long, pointed ears were folded into its mane.

The stranger spoke in a slurred, hissing tongue. It took Ari a moment to realise that it was a tongue they recognised and, not only that, spoke fluently.

"Peace," the Rifter said, in heavily accented Renohaiin.

Ari glanced around the thicket. Though their bowls were scattered and the hides they used as a bed were strewn, everything seemed to be still here.

The Riftmaster's gaze snapped upwards at the first sign of movement.

The stranger raised trembling, pawed hands to its chest, and quickly gestured and bowed. After a moment's bewilderment, Ari did the same.

"Why are you here?" Ari demanded.

The stranger's relief at hearing a familiar tongue was matched only by fear at the ferocity in the Riftmaster's tone.

Ari knew, instinctively, that they had the advantage here, and so any lingering fear deserted them. They held themself tall and channelled that fearlessness into an authoritative stance. The strange Rifter, although large, could not hope to outmanoeuvre them in such a place.

"Hiding," the Rifter said, lowering their head.

"From?"

The Rifter's ears flared out. They cast a long glance out to the bright, grassy plain beyond the thicket. Through the broken brambles, the Riftmaster saw the shape of a sleek, black ship drifting over the surface of the plain. Ari's curiosity piqued for a moment. *A Renohaiin ship?* they thought, with a thrill of nervous excitement. *I haven't seen one of those since I served the empire myself.*

It wheeled past them, above the plain, before quickly vanishing across the horizon.

Finally, Ari turned their attention back to the matter at hand.

"So you weren't trying to steal from me?"

"I… I have everything I need."

Ari let out a small huff of acknowledgement.

Letting the tension drain from their stance, Ari took a moment to smooth their hair and slowly settled down beside the crushed foliage of the entranceway. After a successful day of foraging and a lush world beyond, there would certainly be enough for two.

Wordlessly, Ari began to stack firewood and kindling within a purpose-built circle of stones, keeping a careful eye on their uninvited guest. Ari knew, though, that they were being watched just as cautiously. Slowly, they laid out the fruits they had gathered and shuffled back.

"Can you eat any of these?" Ari asked.

Slitted nostrils flared uneasily. The creature's snakelike eyes darted from fruit to fruit. Finally, they reached out a shaking hand, and patted a large, bulbous melon. Ari nodded. Slowly, they stood, edging to the side of their clearing, and picked up three sticks sharpened to spear-like points. It still took quite an effort to pierce the melon's hide, but eventually it was skewered precariously over the fire.

For their own, they selected a small, round specimen resembling a folded avocado, and simply tossed it into the burning coals. By the time the fire died down, it could easily be teased out into the open, and would be deliciously caramelised inside.

Ari glanced up then. "Do you have a name, Rifter?"

"Reina. Yours?"

"Riftmaster." Ari said.

Reina tipped her head slightly. "Quite a name."

"Thank you," Ari shrugged, although they hid a smile. "Easier to translate."

Reina's ears flicked in acknowledgement. "Clever, clever," she murmured.

As their food cooked over the fire, Ari turned their attention to the creature's wounds. Her skin was torn and clothes ripped by the entrance into their domain. Orangeish blood leaked onto a grubby white jumpsuit from a particularly nasty gash on their shoulder. With a small, slow movement, Ari pulled their satchel closer, and fished into their bag for a length of spare linen.

They offered it, gesturing to the wound.

Although she flinched when they first held out their hand, Reina cautiously but gratefully accepted. She pressed the fabric to her shoulder, and briefly winced.

Then she glanced up. "Why?"

Ari smiled slightly. "You seem new out here," they said. "And I have something of a way with newcomers."

Reina nodded, seeming to understand.

They were largely silent after that, watching one another closely in companionable silence.

Not much conversation was shared past then, but when she left, Ari had the distinct feeling that this wouldn't be the last of her they saw. After that day, though, Ari started hiding their belongings, nervous that nearby denizens would take advantage of the widened entranceway to the thicket.

It was, they thought, a little over a week later by the time they saw her again, waiting outside of their humble abode.

"Reina? What are you doing here?" they asked curiously.

Reina's tail flicked from side to side. She looked a lot more comfortable out in the open, where she could stand up to her full, rather impressive height.

"I was waiting for you," she said, seeming, if they could guess, pleased to see them.

"How come?"

Reina smiled and for the first time, Ari found themself invited out into town for a pleasant drink.

Ari took a moment to consider, a brief thrill of suspicion sweeping over their skin, though they tried not to show it.

Examining Reina's body language didn't reveal any ulterior motives, and the thought of knowingly ingesting something mildly toxic was almost too good to resist. Besides, Riftworlds were some of the only places which could offer semi-palatable drinks. Humans weren't the only creatures in the wide, wide universe that knew how to party.

After a long pause, Ari offered a hesitant nod. Shortly after, they followed Reina into town, but not before slinking into their thicket to make sure everything was safely hidden away, and sweeping a length of hide across their shoulders. As they walked, the Riftmaster took the chance to glance over at their companion, who had dropped to walk on all fours with a long, slinking gait. Even then, her head was level with their shoulders. With an impressive mane of sharp quills down her back and an outfit that was adeptly sewn, Reina looked like a hardy creature despite her inexperience. A long, whiplike tail, tipped with a spray of spines, trailed out behind it.

"Do you shed your quills?" Ari asked as they walked.

"Heh?" Reina asked, tilting large ears curiously.

"Your spikes?" Ari asked. "Do you shed them?"

Reina blinked, then widened green eyes. "Oh. Yes. Often."

"Can I have one?" Ari asked, curiously. "I have things to trade, if you like."

The Rifter paused for a moment, as though processing the question, and then let out a low rumble that Ari soon understood to be a laugh.

"No trade," the Rifter said. "Just give."

Ari was warmed. "Oh, thank you. Are you sure?"

"Yes. Too many on the floor of my home. What do you need them for?"

Ari gestured to their scaled garment, ragged and tattered. "New clothes," they said.

"Clever, clever," the Rifter said. "I use quill for such, as well." They tapped the makeshift fastening at the top of their jumpsuit.

"Fascinating."

"Useful. On homeworld, we use them for medicines. No need for needles."

"Huh," the Riftmaster said. "You should consider trading them. I'm sure many Rifters here would be eager to find some good medicine supplies."

"I've tried. Difficult without tongues, though."

"Ah. I see."

As they walked, Ari let Reina take the lead, showing them the way to a tavern she seemed to frequent. They kept the pale hide pulled tightly around them, hiding their arms, knife and satchel, and using a hand to ensure it remained closed.

As they walked, Ari took the chance to look around at the peoples who milled about the streets, murmuring to one another, moving on their way or entering various buildings. Perhaps most strikingly, above the homes there lifted an enormous, mammalian head. Even from here, Ari could feel the deep bass grumbles of its speech as it growled around the stripped log held in muscular jaws. Ari watched, eyes blinking slightly wider.

I wonder what you'd pay a creature like that for building work?

They glanced down to see that Reina had stopped to look as well.

The great head dipped slightly under the weight, disappearing from view. Shortly after, Ari heard a great crash erupt from somewhere deeper in the town.

Ari glanced around as startled Rifters began to rush towards the source of the noise. Soon the pair were alone.

Bailey would have wanted to go. He'd have needed to make sure everyone was okay.

Ari, however, needed a stiff drink.

Ari blinked and met their guide's questioning eyes. They flushed slightly. "Just reminded me of someone," they said. "Still want a drink, Rifthopper?"

Reina nodded, turning into a back alley, where shining runes were polished into the side of a meteorite.

Most were unreadable to Ari, but they probably all said the same thing.

The tavern as they entered was small, dark and dingy, smelling strongly of earth and soured berries, along with the musk of decayed foliage. As they entered, they drew the eye of several colourful quadrupeds, who looked up from where they were gambling iridescent crystals on a table by the door. As they passed, Ari noticed one slide a few into its belly pouch. His opponent noticed as well, and let out such an uproar that the thief snarled back in protest. With deep, throaty growls an argument ensued, each creature huffing and coughing its part, digging great talons into the wood. They were so distracted that Ari couldn't resist sneaking a few into their palm as they brushed past the table. By the time the creatures noticed their disappearance, Ari was settled placidly by the bar as if they'd been there for hours, the gemstones safely hidden under their cloak.

By meagre shafts of light and the faint blue glow of a fire burning in the hearth, they picked out words embroidered into lengths of fabric hanging from the wall.

Unlike on earth, these signs depicted the languages each bartender spoke. The menu, Ari concluded, must be given verbally.

"What do you want?" Ari asked their companion. "First drink is on me."

"Give me a lumpfruit ale," Reina said, startled. "The only thing that doesn't taste of dung."

"That's a good sign," Ari chuckled. They made their way over to the bar and took stock of the scrawls of embroidery on the walls.

If Reina comes here often, there's got to be at least one Renohaiin speaker.

That said, while spoken languages tended to be well known and passed on throughout the Rift, written languages were rather less so. Ari's brow furrowed in concentration, but then relaxed noticeably when they finally found the name of a bartender written in Renohaiin script.

Ari stood and cleared their throat.

"Aldair!" they barked.

There was a clatter, then a splash. A tall, insectoid creature pushed his way through a tangle of vines from a side room that might have been a kitchen or a brewery. Four compound eyes locked with theirs and Ari smiled slightly. A Renohaiin, masculine-presenting. Polishing two valuable-looking metal tankards at once with four arms, Aldair slowly made his way over to them. A segmented tail slowly thrashed, adjusting a lopsided leather apron that was covered in burn marks.

The tines upon his head formed a crown of tiny thorns.

"Yes, Rifter?"

"What have you got? Been too long since I picked my poison."

"What atomic preference?"

"Carbon based, ideally."

Aldair paused to process this. "Well, in that case, we have fresh-brewed lumpfruit wine, essence of lard, Feverdrop tipple, and ice-cold hornet stew."

Ari thought for a moment, before digging in their satchel and withdrawing a small array of bowls. "I'll take a micro-measure of each for now. Excuse the manners, but do you mind if I…?"

"So long as you have something good to trade, go ahead."

Ari nodded, satisfied, then settled onto a tall half-log and unwound a length of leather from their neck. As the drinks were poured, they offered the bartender a gleaming pendant.

After a moment of examination, Aldair seemed pleased, and placed their offering aside. Shortly after, Ari began the long process of testing each drink in turn for various toxins and compounds. As they worked, they drew the gazes of a few curious creatures dotted around the tavern. A roaming bard looked up from where they plucked a dozen strings with six elegant limbs, its tail coiled elegantly around a wide and platformed fretboard.

Huge, green eyes blinked curiously, a small and reptilian smile tilting its fins before it quickly glanced away.

As the Riftmaster turned back to the bar, they heard the bard return to its tuning and ignored the other patrons.

Two of the three drinks were toxic. Fortunately, though, it was exactly the kind they were looking for.

"Would you wash these for me?" Ari asked Aldair, offering the small clay bowls, and gesturing to a fountain that was fed through a bubbling spring.

As their bowls were taken, they added "I'll also take a double of Feverdrop tipple, and a lumpfruit wine."

Holding out their palm, Ari offered the gemstones that had been swiped from the gamblers.

Aldair's mandibles twitched with mirth, but with a subtle glance up across the tavern, he gracefully accepted the payment.

Finally, Ari made their way over to where their companion awaited them, carrying a pair of heavy ivory pitchers.

"I'm sorry, they only had lumpfruit wine," Ari said, as they sat down.

The strange creature shrugged with a small smile. "Wine, ale, it's all the same to this one."

"Ah," Ari said, raising their pitcher to drink. The Feverdrop tipple tasted so cold that it left their mouth numb, and a bitter taste erupted in its wake. They must have had a startled expression on their face, because their companion rumbled with laughter. Shaking their head to clear the fog from their brain, Ari grinned and changed the subject. "Have you seen any other worlds?"

"No. This is my first, apart from Homeworld. Hopefully my only. I like it here."

"What was your homeworld like?"

"It was nice. Very hot, and very peaceful. A few cities scattered across a great, wide desert. We travelled to each one in turn, following the winter. We didn't have a name for it. Thought it was unique. At least until the Empire came. But the Renohaiin-kind called it the ninth colony of system forty-four; overnight we went from thinking there was no life out there, to realising that we were one planet of millions. Have you been?"

Ari listened in fascination. "No, I haven't been. It sounds incredible."

"Oh… Shame. What about yours?"

Ari blinked in surprise.

"I came from a planet called Earth. It was independent, not a colony."

Reina blinked in surprise. "How did you learn this tongue?"

"I've stumbled into more than a few colonies in my day. They prize Rifters highly among their ranks, especially if you're experienced. I served as a navigator for a few star cycles before the Rift moved me along," Ari answered curiously, looking their companion up and down. Now that they thought about it, their companion's outfit, although aged and torn, was vaguely familiar in design. The materials, threaded with shimmering lines, could only be made from Homeworld Silk, a light and easy-to-produce material spun by Renohaiin infants that was good for just about any climate. "And you… your homeworld was just a recent colony?"

Reina looked hesitant, then nodded. "At least by the time I left."

"Then… why were you fleeing from that ship? Don't you want to go home?"

"I…" Reina hesitated. "I like it better here. And I will always, as long as my home is a part of the Empire."

Ari hesitated. "I'm sorry. It must have been…" they hesitated, taking a drink, and then coughing softly. "…Difficult."

Reina said nothing. "Harder for the ones that rebelled," she finally said, flicking her whiplike tail. Ari heard the spines scraping softly against the floor. "The rest of us were… Fine enough. They treat us well, but it's not the same."

There was a long silence between the two. Finally, the Riftmaster spoke, subtly changing the subject. "How long have you been Rifting, then? You seem to have been here a while."

Reina shook her head. "No way to tell. But it must be at least an orbit."

A year, then. But there was no telling how long years lasted on Reina's homeworld. "So, not long. How have you found surviving so far?"

"Easy enough. When the Renohaiin sent me away, they had no idea where I'd end up. But I was very, very lucky."

"…Sent you away?" Ari blinked. "How?"

Reina jiggled her head, as though she had no answer. "They have a number of ways to trigger the Rift."

"That's a terrifying thought," murmured Ari.

"It is," Reina agreed.

"Why?" Ari asked softly. "Why did they do this to you?"

Reina shrugged. "I thought at first it was a punishment. I'd been in contact with some rebels before it happened. But I wasn't the only one, and some of the others were loyalists, so I'm not sure."

Ari sipped their drink and considered this, the hairs tingling along their back. Whether it was the drink, or the news of the Renohaiin expansion, they weren't sure. Placing down their empty pitcher, they glanced up as the bard began to play a bouncing tune.

The Riftmaster glanced across the tables, feeling their spirits lift at the sound of music. Reina's tail whipped as she stood fully upright, almost cracking her head on the ceiling of the tavern. Fully standing, she was easily over eight feet tall to Ari's five-two, and looked down at them with green eyes aglow.

"Another?"

Ari hesitated. *I shouldn't…* but the thrill within them was joined by a comforting warmth in their belly, an unexpected and uncharacteristic feeling of daring suddenly sweeping them.

Do it, a small inner voice told them. *You're happy and safe.*

It wasn't often that Ari got to experience company like this. They might as well make the most of it.

Although an odd twinge in their belly made them wonder if it was the best idea, they glanced up with eagerness shining in their eyes.

"Another Feverdrop, if that's okay."

As Reina picked her way across to the bar, Ari found themself watching the musician, tapping their foot lightly. The tips of their fingers had begun to tingle, and their chest swelled with excitement as the creature played. Using six long limbs to pluck at the strings, the bard produced a tune that bounced and wavered, sounding as though it was played by a band of five. The coils of its tail twitched and writhed as it adjusted the fret, sweeping the sound into a whole new level of organised chaos. The music was bright and playful, with never a moment of quiet or pause. It made the tavern feel crowded and alive, and the other patrons seemed to feel the same as they laughed and talked among themselves in dozens of tongues. Ari watched in pure amazement as the bard worked his magic, so entranced that they hardly noticed when Reina returned.

"I don't understand how you drink this," Reina said, as she placed their drink on the table.

Ari beamed and stuck out their tongue before taking a long swig. "Different tastes."

"You do know Feverdrop is brewed from worm venom?"

"Wouldn't have it any other way."

"Want to try mine?"

Ari narrowed their eyes slightly, casting their mind back to the process of testing. While it certainly wasn't toxic, they remembered the Lumpfruit wine smelling atrocious. Finally, they began to smirk. "Sure. Hit me with it."

As Reina passed them the pitcher, they closed their nostrils and took a sip. It was warm. And it tasted like freshly-laid manure.

Ari forced themself to swallow and hastily handed it back. "Not bad," they managed to choke out, as they took a long draft of their own.

Reina could only let out a rumbling laugh.

As the hours wore on, Ari's vision grew hazy, their tongue difficult to control, and they laughed more than they had in years. Before they knew it, they had got up to dance, and Rifters turned to watch in amazement as the clumsy-looking human tottered and spun on two gangly legs, cape billowing around them, yet somehow never fell. Reina banged her head on the ceiling as she got up to join them, even though she had had the same amount, and had twice the body to keep it in.

The atmosphere was truly intoxicating.

When Ari finally sat down, they were panting, the lines around their eyes etched with laughter. They fizzed internally as they sipped at spring water to ease their dry throat. They glanced up, and saw that Reina's chest was heaving, her ears half-folded with exhaustion.

"So… this is the only world you've ever seen," Ari said, as their heart rate slowed and their breaths steadied. "And the Renohaiin sent you, so you're not going to leave any time soon."

"Yes," Reina said.

"But that means you've never seen the universe. Only the fragments that the Rifters bring."

"That's right."

Ari looked up, eyes suddenly flashing bright with an idea. Somewhere in the back of their head, they warned themself not to say it out loud. But somehow they found themself asking anyway, the words tumbling from their lips in thoughtless eagerness.

"Would you like to come with me?" Ari asked suddenly, looking up into Reina's startled expression.

"Into the Rift?"

Ari nodded vigorously. "Yes. We can be companions. I can teach you, mentor you. I'll show you all the amazing and terrifying and wonderful things that the universe has to share with us."

Reina stared at them for a second as though stunned.

"Riftmaster… this is my home," she finally said, hesitating with every word. "It's safe here; I've rebuilt my life. I can't imagine always being on the run, and never being able to find a home. That's just not the life for me." Reina's ears drooped. "I'm... I'm sorry."

Ari felt as though they'd just taken a punch to the gut. The joyful music seemed to fade, the world blurred. All they could see was the sadness in her eyes, and the way she seemed to fold into herself.

"I... when I say terrifying, I– I didn't mean–..."

Suddenly the memories came crashing in. Piercingly, Ari felt again the terror of their flight from the last Riftworld. A sudden nausea tugged faintly at their belly, but they forced it down and shook their head.

"But this... this world," they stammered out. They saw the way that the world cracked open, the panic of the crowds that tried desperately to force their way towards a hope of survival. They saw the planet's surface shattering into space, flinging shards to every corner of the universe, sparking with lights as the Rift came for the lucky few who survived. Finally they remembered exactly how they'd managed to get away.

Ari found their voice. "These worlds... You can't stay here, Reina."

The world tilted under their feet.

"Why not?"

"This... This is not a planet. One day, the surface will break open, and everyone on it will die."

They tried, and failed, to read her expression as she met their eyes. "Why?"

Ari took a short, sharp breath. She was listening. "This planet is an egg. There is a creature the size of the world nestled beneath us, just waiting for the chance to break out. I've seen it. I've survived it."

"When?" Reina asked. She still looked at them uncertainly, but they didn't recognise any doubt or disbelief.

Relieved that she was listening, Ari sucked in a deep breath through their teeth. "I... I don't know." They shook their head and tried to think through the fog that was settling in over their brain. "You'll know when it begins. Rifters stop leaving, and then the earthquakes get bigger, more frequent. It could be a hundred orbits, or a thousand, or a hundred-thousand. This Riftworld... seems new, but it could happen at any time."

"Then..." Reina's tailtip curled slightly. "I think I'll chance it. I'm staying here."

"Wh-what!?" Ari's vision blurred. "Didn't you hear me?"

"I did. But there's time yet to stop it. I'll be long dead by the time anything happens, and that's a whole lifetime to prepare. It's better to live a long, full life that ends slightly before its time than to die young, and on the run. Besides..." She paused, ears flicking as though to give her next words some thought. "...You survived, didn't you?"

Ari stared at her, speechless, mouth slightly open. "I... yes, but..." The words failed them.

Reina slowly looked away, leaving Ari to gaze dejectedly into their half-finished drink.

There was a long silence between them before Reina finally spoke. "I'm finished. I'll bring you my quills in the morning." Slowly, Reina stood, nodded her thanks, and said, "It's been nice."

Ari nodded numbly. "It has," they agreed.

Then she dropped to all fours and exited the tavern without a word, leaving Ari alone once again.

The esteemed Riftmaster didn't remember much of what happened after that, but they awoke with a throbbing headache and a desperate thirst the next morning. They were cold, lying on the bare earth beside their bed of hides, covered in small cuts. As they tended the wounds and groggily made their morning checks, they found a linen package stashed just beside the entrance of their abode. Ari opened it up to reveal an array of fine, sharp brown quills of varying sizes. Although they knew the spines would come in useful in the days to come, they couldn't help but feel a little hollow.

Using one quill as an awl and another as a sewing

needle, Ari was finally able to stitch their new armour from the hide and tough carapace that had been taken from the swamp carcase.

They spent many hours kneeling surrounded by thorns, serenely joining the pieces together one by one, with ragged stitching and messy knots.

And finally, looking down at themself in the glassy surface of a pond, they felt their ego swell again. Their new armour was quite adequate, with blue-tinged pauldrons joined by a fashionable yet pointless cape across their shoulders, and an off-white breechcloth draped across their hip. The creature's carapace had allowed them to create a new breastplate, and iridescent scales beneath caught the bluish tinge with style.

A spare length of hide had been repurposed into a long, hooded cloak, made for warmth and practicality, as well as to obscure the figure and trick potential predators into misfires like the wings of a butterfly. Folded neatly around their belongings, they slipped it into their satchel.

Despite gazing into the pristine waters often to admire their new look, Ari couldn't help feeling like all that work was hollow with no one around to see it.

Their time on the Riftworld would end soon after, and the Riftmaster didn't even have the chance to say goodbye.

Chapter 4
The light in the depths

Ari was on their feet before the white-hot pain had faded from their skin.

And as soon as the light of the Rift fizzled out, their vision plunged into blackness. The Riftmaster slowly stood and glanced around, squinting against the dark. They felt their heart beginning to hammer as their vision adjusted.

By starlight they began to see.

A blue planet swirled with clouds hung framed by distant hills across a great, flat moor. Beyond grasses and twisting heathers they saw the distant winking of lights scattered across the plain, like tiny earthbound stars. Some moved with jerking motions, echoing comets in the night. The world was silent except from the whispering of a faint, warm breeze. Ari supposed that they were lucky the wildlife of this world had evolved to bear lights of their own.

Without their own, though, Ari felt sufficiently camouflaged.

Glowing flecks of dust and spores swirled about them, and the air tasted dry and rich, with the smell of fresh-fallen rain mixed with the faintly heady scent of minerals. Ari dumped their cloak and satchel onto the ground, digging around for some linen bandages to cover their mouth and nose. When they picked up their satchel again, it left a luminous imprint in the moss beneath.

Blinking, Ari swept it over their shoulder, and then stepped back from the light. Their feet left glowing marks.

Ari looked up and gazed around. Now that they had adjusted, their eyes could easily pick apart the landscape, drenched in starlight. Ari stepped forward, glancing around cautiously, leaving a trail of glowing footprints in their wake.

So much for camouflage…

They brushed past a cluster of foliage, to find that the tips of the leaves began to faintly glow with the contact. Ari flinched, then crouched to take a closer look. The glow lingered for all of a minute, before fading once more into darkness. Glancing back to their path revealed the mossy ground to be slowly fading as well.

No matter how lightly they placed their feet or how much they spread their weight, the Riftmaster could not find a way to stifle the glow.

This isn't good. I can be tracked easily here, they panicked. *I need to keep moving.*

And so Ari fled, the bright glow springing up behind them. They made their way quickly across the bright moorland under the stars, glancing back and forth rapidly. Where they could, the Riftmaster hopped up onto rocks and stones to avoid leaving a telltale print, and crouched there until it faded away. Despite the brightness of the stars, the shadows were all-consuming. Even once their eyes had fully adjusted, it was often hard to see what lay in their path. Once, the ground before them fell away into nothingness, and Ari froze on the brink of a vast chasm. Foliage clung to cracks and ledges just below the overhanging lip of the cliff, but they could not see what lay at the bottom.

After a moment of thought, Ari knelt and pulled a clump of glowing moss from their footprint, and tossed it over the edge. The glow faded before they could see the bottom, and its landing was so soft that they couldn't hear it.

For all Ari knew, the chasm might as well have been a bottomless abyss. They decided after a moment's consideration that they'd rather risk the open sky.

Clusters of pale berries grew from wiry branches beneath the lip of the sheer drop. They had to lie down and stretch alarmingly out over the edge, but were just able to drag the fruit into their grasp. The scent of rot drifted up to meet them, and somewhere in the depths, they could hear the lonely trickle of water.

With a strained grunt, Ari managed to drag a branch from its perch, and shove an armful of fruit into their satchel.

Along the edge of the vast crevasse, Ari slunk, looking for a way across or a way down. The ravine forked, and Ari hurdled a web of smaller cracks with relative ease. Finally they found themselves standing before a precarious bridge of worn rock.

Ari guessed that the crevasses, ravines, and naturally-formed bridges had once been an entire network of underground rivers that had long since collapsed.

When Ari looked back, they watched their snaking track across the land gradually fading into darkness. A little orb of light came bounding along it.

Something was following them.

Ari's stomach dropped.

Ari turned back to their chosen path and broke into a brisk trot. They glanced back occasionally, to see the lights bobbing distantly like will-o-the-wisps. They blinked to one another, made drastic leaps, or simply hung twinkling in the distance.

Ari watched them in fascination.

Then something changed. Before their very eyes, Ari watched them wink and flash, waves of light passing across the plain. Ari stood perfectly still as though hypnotised.

Then, just as quickly as the display had begun, all the lights began to wink out, starting from the far distance and ending at the light closest to Ari. The Riftmaster's breaths quickened. Why had they stopped? Was Ari being hunted? If there was one thing that was worse than being followed, it was not knowing where you were being followed from. Ari was rarely scared, but not knowing just what lay out there was unnerving to them.

And then they heard a faint whistling sound; some of the stars above winked out into darkness as something cast a vast shadow across the plain. Something circled them. Ari suddenly, belatedly, realised their mistake.

The lights weren't a show. They were a warning.

Closer, closer, it loomed. Ari caught the light dancing across luminescent wings, and gleaming in enormous, highly reflective eyes. Something was coming. And it was coming fast.

The way the feathers shimmered, iridescent, made it hard to keep track of, and even harder to find again.

What were the chances that it was friendly? Slim, at best. Ari had met very few large creatures outside of Riftworlds which thought of them as anything more than a light snack. Ari didn't blame the predator, of course, but being eaten wasn't their preferred cause of death.

Ari turned back to their path and bounded across the land bridge.

They followed the chasm once again, hearing the water churning deep below, and looking over the edge to see if luck offered them a ledge to hide on. When their efforts were unsuccessful, Ari pulled down their makeshift mask to heave great breaths of thick, muggy air and kept on running, hurtling across the moor and leaping deep rifts in the earth.

When they finally looked back, lungs aching, and chest heaving, Ari felt their heart drop. The creature was toying, like a great airborne cat. It circled, its movements long and slow, high above the plain. It did not seem like it was in a hurry to reach them.

Perhaps it was contemplating the wisdom of ingesting alien meat.

They probably had only a minute or two before it made up its mind. Ari turned and kept running. Five-thousand years had granted them time and means to hone their strength, and their lean body was packed with endurance that a lifetime of training on Earth could never hope to match. But even so, no human could run forever.

Lungs aching, they began to slow.

A shining orb blinked into existence ahead of them and waved enticingly. Despite their better judgement, Ari plunged after it. Soon they skidded to a halt, panting, at the edge of a precipice.

The earth below them fell away into darkness.

Ari looked back, hardly daring to hope that they were alone.

The great thudding of wingbeats answered their question as the great flying beast beat its wings once, and then folded them into a plunging dive.

It's coming.

Ari paced back and forth, searching across the abyss for somewhere to go. What was that? Starlight shimmering? Movement? Something flashed in the dark, and Ari caught sight of a ledge, slick and glistening with much-needed water. Ari tensed up, preparing to jump, then hesitating. Ari could almost feel breaths on the back of their neck, and sense great claws extending to snatch them up. It was so hard to see, and so dark. If they didn't make it, they'd plummet to their death. They glanced back. The sight of the creature's outstretched claws was all they needed to abandon their reluctance.

The Riftmaster had no other choice. They didn't let themself think and hurtled into empty space. An immense thud echoed after them, and fragments of stone and moss rained down into the ravine. It was as if they were falling forever.

Ari thought for a single, awful moment that they'd missed. Then they clattered to a halt, winded, pain shooting through their shoulder as they landed awkwardly.

Ari let out a breath, scrabbling across the rocky ledge and pressing their back to the cliff face.

They looked up.

Starlight reflected sharply white in a pair of enormous

eyes and slick black wings reflected the sky in the colours of an oil spill. Glowing particles of vegetation shrouded its shadowy form as it brushed against the luminous heathers. Ari met its eyes, and for a long moment they thought it was about to pounce. But its wingspan was impossibly broad; it would never have fitted into the ravine.

Ari pressed themself down into their newfound shelter. Suddenly, with a deep boom, and a rush of air across their face, it lifted off again, and disappeared into the sky.

Ari watched it go, catching their breath, until even the echoes had faded into the dark.

As the adrenaline faded, Ari's head began to spin, and they felt bile rising in their throat. The air felt thick as the nausea pressed in on them from all sides.

Closing their eyes, Ari forced themself to wait it out. Minutes passed before their head stopped spinning, and their world stabilised.

The Riftmaster finally opened their eyes.

Then, and only then, did they realise that they weren't alone. There was the sound of small claws scrabbling in the dark, and then something hopped up from behind them onto unseen ledges, and out into the starlight. A small silhouette appeared on the edge where they'd leapt, and glanced back for a moment, revealing enormous eyes. An orb of light appeared just beyond. And then, another and another, until the Riftmaster shielded their eyes from the brightness.

Ari sat up and watched in fascination.

The orbs hung in the air, bobbing and swaying. A few dark shadows appeared to join the first, more eyes shining curiously in the dark.

The shapes lingered for a long, long moment, and then disappeared over the brink. Ari let out a long breath, remaining where they were, and closing their eyes tightly. For a long while, all they heard was the pounding of the blood in their ears, and the hammering of their heart. They felt the slick, cold surface of damp stone against their fingertips, and a dull ache in their shoulder where they had landed heavily.

But they had survived.

As the pounding of their heart faded. Ari became aware of the gentle trickling of water, running beside them from a divot in the rocks.

Their throat clung to itself as they swallowed and, shivering, they eased themself over to the spring, letting the water run cold and clear into their palms. It had been a long time since they had drunk without making sure it was safe. Raising their hands to their lips, they hesitated, and felt their throat crying out. Their hands trembled, and head ached. Their lips were dry and cracked, their lungs still stinging.

They needed water, and they needed it desperately.

But they hadn't survived potential predation just to poison themself moments later.

In something of a daze, Ari put down their satchel and mixed their herbs, exhaustion making their fumbling fingers feel leaden. In the starlight, they couldn't pick out the colours of the concoctions, but it remained dark, and fizzed lightly as they added in the red-toned leaves. It was enough for them. Ari put their lips to the surface of the stone and drank. Then they rested their head against cold stone and slept exactly where they were.

***

When Ari awoke, their fingers felt cold, and limbs stiff. The planet hung vast overhead, and they could see a jagged fragmcnt of it through the ravine. The sun still had not risen, and somehow, with the planet blocking out most of the starlight, it was even darker. The chasm beneath them fell off into an inky void, glowing powders swirling up from the depths.

They shivered.

I can't light a fire. The spores might catch.

They had two choices; to climb back up to the moor and brace themself to be hunted again, or to head down into the unknown, with the strange glowing spores and the scent of decay. Neither was an attractive proposition; but they had no better options.

Ari paced on their ledge, very nearly slipping, and tried to work out a way off. Up or down, either would suffice.

Looking up, they struggled to pick out the ledges that the light-creature had used to escape. But they were narrow, and slick with grime and mould.

In the end, they let themself down, inching slowly and cautiously along the cliff face. They pulled up the fabric over their mouth and nose once more, and descended into the deep chasm.

It got brighter the deeper that Ari went, the spores and creeping tendrils glowing with an eerie green light. Soon they landed with a squelch into a shallow marsh and looked around. Their gaze tilted up towards the distant crack of sky.

Soft trills of small creatures and insects rang out around them. An enormous worm with glowing segments slithered off into the muck. Muddy water swirled around their boots. Glowing tendrils lit the murk, some of them bearing bulbous fruit, which Ari plucked. Wind whistled faintly from above, but down here the air was still.

Vertically growing foliage and enormous caps crowded the sides of the crevasse, and Ari wondered, hopefully, if they might be able to use them to find a way back up.

Before they moved any further, Ari cut a piece of foliage free, and painted a glowing mark onto the cliff face, marking their path back to the ledge.

Maybe I'll find another water source. But for now, this will be a good place to come back to.

And then Ari squelched off into the dark and dank depths of the moor.

They searched for a time, gathering samples of plants, fungi, and vines. It was almost like a maze in these murky depths, with spores swirling and cracks disappearing off into every direction. It was like another world entirely separate from the moorland above.

Ari tried to climb one of the walls using the caps as footholds, but the spongy object came away beneath their hands. The glow soon faded, but Ari kept it anyway.

Soon after, they tripped on something hidden beneath

the mud, and stooped to find a massive, pointed skull, the size of their torso. For a moment they had a fleeting sense of familiarity. That enormous head, four eyes, and great, crushing beak… With sweeps of their foot, Ari unearthed more muddied bones, wrapped tightly by coils of hungry sediment-dwellers which disappeared as quickly as Ari unearthed them. Disgusted, Ari let them be. They dropped the skull, and it sank slowly back into the murk.

Other than the worms, Ari saw very little living in these inky depths, although the skeleton, along with chunks taken out of the local flora, suggested that they were far from alone. Closer inspection of the plants' strange wounds revealed them to be long-healed, glowing white with scar tissue.

Soon Ari began to fear that they might never find a way back up to the surface, but they also began to wonder if they really wanted to. Nevertheless, they kept track of the way back to their home ledge and kept going straight on, ignoring branching pathways in favour of having an easy route home.

The crevasse seemed to go on forever; although usually it was several metres wide, at times it was so narrow that they had to squeeze just to keep on going.

Finally, it opened out into a vast corridor, many metres wide and filled with marshy terrain. The cliffs rearing up around them seemed to have collapsed many times, with many different levels and ledges, and boulders scattered around the nearby area. It was open to the sky and covered in a blanket of foliage, with great, wide plates of leaf-matter forming a welcoming carpet between Ari and the mud. A small troupe of waist-height herbivores startled and fled as they came too close, mossy hides making them almost indistinguishable from the walls of the crevasse. Ari felt their spirits lift.

Finally, something other than worms.

They gratefully scrambled out of the mud and rested under a rocky ledge as they looked around, listening to the distant call of something circling the plain.

This would do.

Down here, among the leaves and glowing flowers, the Riftmaster felt at home. They tested the local flora and found a couple of kinds which, whilst chewy and tasteless, would fill their belly for a while. When that was done, they moved onto the nearby fauna.

They managed to trap a herbivore without too much difficulty. There were only a few of them, but they seemed unused to predation, their movements slow and purposeful. They were stout and moss-backed, with long-fingered feet that allowed them to traverse the mud with ease. Looking into eyes that were dark and watery, it took a lot for Ari to convince themself to make the kill. Eventually, though, they decided that it would be a merciful end.

After allowing themself a moment to steady their breathing, Ari dragged the body over the rocks until far enough from the marsh that they felt confident the worms wouldn't reach it. Then they climbed the levelled cliffside, hopping nimbly onto a ledge that felt secure.

Above the heady mist of spores, they lit a fire, and their gaze combed the sky until they were certain it was safe. By its light they tested the meat and filtered enough marsh water for a comfortably clean drink. The meat was not toxic; and after cooking they ate with gusto.

After eating, Ari glanced up to see greenish orbs of light hovering just above the lip of the chasm, watching them.

Although Ari did not know what those creatures were, they knew enough to be able to guess why they were here.

They lingered closest when Ari cooked meat over an open fire.

It seemed, for now, that the light-creatures were unable to, or perhaps unwilling to find a way down, and Ari's worries faded into the back of their mind. They were content to battle with scavengers until their food source was far past its best.

When the meat was no longer edible, they subsisted on leaves and stems. While these had very little nutritional value, they contained a lot of water.

Even still, Ari felt fatigue creeping in, and was forced to hunt once more.

In time, the herbivores started to grow scarce. After much deliberation Ari speared a slimy creature from the mud and dragged it out into the open. It looked disgusting, but it tasted delicate, and almost perfumed.

As long as their belly was full and their weapon sharp, Ari was more than content to stay in the chasm forever.

It wouldn't last, though. Awoken from slumber by light piercing their eyelids, Ari regained consciousness, to find themselves bathed in light.

Rolling over, they looked directly into a pair of great wide eyes. They sat up, and scrambled back. The creature watched them go with head tipped, greenish eyes gleaming above a tiny nose. Its body was tall, slim, and almost catlike, with tiny forelimbs and velvety skin with faint patterns that resembled the heather of the moor. A long, prehensile tail bobbed and twitched, pulsating with a large, fleshy orb of green light. Membranes slid across both eyes as the creature blinked.

Ari could hardly dare to tear their gaze away, but the moment they did, they regretted it. In the chasm beyond, a crowd of dancing and bobbing lights that surrounded the remains of their last kill. The throng of creatures had buried their heads in the flesh, tearing and chewing, fighting with shrill squeals over the food.

"H...hey," they muttered gently.

Their spear rested against the rock face somewhere behind them, out of reach. Ari's hand slid down towards the knife sheathed against their thigh. Their fingers grazed the pommel, and they froze as they felt it beneath their fingertips. Catching their movements, the creature's tail lit up, and the group in the crevasse froze, a dozen pairs of eyes turning towards them. Suddenly the horde surged up the cliff face towards them, hopping from stone to stone and boulder to boulder. Faces, large and small, appeared around the Riftmaster's tiny camp, and Ari could do nothing but shrink back against the rock wall.

Another light-hopping creature joined the first one and

stood upright on enormous hind limbs. Ears went back. This one was far larger, and its body was muscular, almost plump. Its tail-light blinked, on and off. In reply, its companion's tail-orb dimmed slightly, before pulsing brighter than ever. A shimmer of light rolled across the leader's hide. The pair winked and gleamed back and forth for a time, occasionally glancing back towards Ari.

Ari's hopes suddenly rose.

They're communicating… More than that, they're sentient!

Ari leaned forward, then knelt, lowering themself beneath the creatures' height, and pressing their face to the ground. *The key to making friends,* Ari silently recited, *is to make it clear you're not a threat.*

The creatures flinched, looking confused, and then hopped closer, curiosity written on their faces.

With a shaking hand, Ari opened up their satchel, removed the last of the fruits they had gathered, and placed it in front of them.

All around them, the strange creatures exchanged glances. Ari held their breath. Finally, the largest gave an immense sweep of its tail and shoved the berries off the ledge and into the marsh. The hairs along the back of Ari's neck bristled.

Oh no…

But a moment later, the strange creatures lost interest, hopping back down onto the ground to continue ravaging the Riftmaster's meal. Ari could only watch in stupefied amazement until they were finished, and one by one, skipped along a jagged path, bounding up and onto ledges Ari could not see from below. Their curiosity satiated, they quickly disappeared up and onto the plain, except for one, who cast a single glance back towards Ari, pulsed its tail, and then vanished.

Ari thought about it for a few seconds, and then hastily followed the creatures out of the chasm and back into the starlight.

***

For the next few weeks, Ari began to track the creatures along their strange, starry home. Although the group seemed wary at first, they soon learned to ignore the Riftmaster's presence. And Ari's occasional offerings of fruit they'd found seemed to help. Even though they weren't usually eaten, it showed their willingness to share resources.

The light-hoppers' paws were so small and their leaps so long that they left minimal prints in the mosses, and Ari had to fight hard not to lose them. Luckily, though, the creatures were curious; and whenever Ari had to stop to gather berries, or test potential food sources, the group would gather round to watch.

When Ari emptied their small testing bowls, the creatures would sniff at the herbal substances left behind, eyes wide. They'd examine, sniff, and lick at anything Ari left unattended, growing close… at times far too close for Ari's comfort. But they allowed the creatures in, never once shooing them away or making themself scarce. Patience was key; the fact that the little creatures were drawing near at all was a blessing Ari reminded themself of every day.

That being said, there were… certain elements of human nature they'd never wanted to show off. As much as they tried to hide away, the light-hoppers always seemed to sniff them out. Ari tried to make it clear that they wanted to be alone, at first… until they had the realisation that the more they tried to escape embarrassment, the more curious the group became.

When they weren't investigating Ari, the creatures seemed never to slow or stop, whether to sleep, eat, or anything else. After several days struggling to keep up, Ari was finally forced to slow, build a fire, eat, and rest. They awoke hours later to find themself alone, their stomach turning, and their head spinning.

A sigh left Ari's lips as they stood and packed their belongings to go.

But a movement caught the edge of their vision; and Ari glanced up to see a light dancing in the distance.

They picked up the pace, gripping their spear, and hurried after it. They reached the little nomad to find that it was alone. It waited until they were almost in touching distance before springing away.

It did this a few more times before Ari finally realised that it was leading them. Their heart warmed. A few hours later, Ari and their companion finally saw the glimmer of the group across the plains.

After that, Ari was no longer reluctant to stop to rest. Whenever the group took off ahead, Ari would always find one little creature waiting for them.

It took them a while after that to realise that it was always the same one. His hide was a plain, dull grey and ears slightly torn. His sides were always slim and slightly sunken, but his tail was always bright. Although the names of these creatures could not be verbally spoken or written down, Ari knew this one by the slow, patient flashes. This light-hopper's communication was distinct; consisting largely of slow fades and long movements. In this manner, he seemed to be trying to teach them.

When Ari lost their way, he would guide them with a single pulse. So that was how they came to know him.

Ari was not certain why Pulse was helping them, but they tried to make up for that kindness by helping the group whenever they could. If a young hopper could not reach the branches of a fruit tree, they could lift it up towards the lower branches. If a creature was hurt or wounded, they could bind, wrap, and clean the wounds with scraps of fabric, and droplets from their waterskin.

In return, Pulse, and sometimes another grey-blue adult, would always bring Ari strips of meat from scavenged carcases and dead things. Though the group ate first, Ari slipped in to take what was left. They'd cut out the bones, and store away strips of meat and leather for later use.

Whenever they did anything like this, the entire group of Light-hoppers would gather around and watch in fascination.

Ari soon began to recognise that Pulse was a bit of an outcast. He would signal the group frantically, but never received anything more than a nip on the ear for his troubles. He rarely seemed to linger anywhere other than the very outskirts of the group. Ari, on the other hand, seemed to fascinate him. Frequently, they'd sit together as Ari's food cooked on the fire, and he allowed Ari to gently stroke his back. Ari was entranced by the velvety texture of his skin and the way that the lights seemed to swell and blossom from within his bulbous tail.

His biggest antagonist, on the other hand, appeared to be the leader of the group. With his dramatic, sweeping motions and startlingly sudden lights, Ari came to know him as Blinker.

In time, Ari tried to replicate their language themself. They watched the creatures with their bright tail movements and pulsing lights and tried to replicate them with movements of a hand. They echoed the light-hopper's pulses by spreading their fingers. Replicated the fade-out by clenching their hand into a fist. The first time, they were rewarded with a sharp nip of their fingertips, and Ari had to assume that they had been rather rude. They tried their best to apologise and resolved to be extra helpful in the coming days.

One day, they used the hide of a prey creature to create a sling, which Ari then used to aid with hunts. After a while practising on fruits, they used it to knock a flying creature out of the sky, ending a hunt far earlier than what the Light-hoppers were used to. They crowded around the fallen prey, hesitant to eat it, and hung back from Ari in a wide circle. As soon as Ari put their sling down, the light-hoppers destroyed it.

It wouldn't be the last time.

Blinker seemed to be the instigator of this. He was always the last to leave the scene of the crime, making sure that Ari saw.

At one point, the nomadic group found themselves climbing a rise at the very edge of the plain.

Blinker signalled wildly from the highest peak and from that height Ari could see the pulses of other groups right across the plain. Over time, they learned to read those pulses; and found that the groups of light-hoppers would signal one another from great distances. Each group was always aware of a predator's movements, no matter where they were.

Although Ari had begun to communicate with gestures and open palms, there was no way that their words would ever carry so far.

When possible, Ari tried to help the group on their way. They laid makeshift bridges of knotted foliage across the crevasses or dug ramps down into secluded ponds so that the creatures within could finally be hunted.

Strangely, these ponds seemed far more alive than the larger crevasses. All manner of small creatures swam in even the shallowest pools.

When Pulse climbed down to hunt, though, the others snapped, nipped, and flashed until he was forced to retreat. Ari slowly climbed out of the pit and waited with him until their turn. Ari tried to signal with their palm, but Pulse's tail-light remained dark.

At least Ari was well fed for their troubles.

Once, they were even trusted to be a nanny as the adults left to scout.

This is the life, they thought, sitting cross-legged in the moss as youngsters tumbled around them. *Before, I had everything I could ever need. Now I have everything I could ever want. Company… Warmth… Friends… I couldn't ask for anything more. This is why I keep living.*

Why, then, did they feel so hollow whenever two noses touched? Whenever they watched two tails entwine and lights ripple with joy?

I just wish that I could stay.

One night, as they settled by the campfire, Ari heard a quiet rustle in the heather. A moment later, Pulse appeared, limping badly, and his hide torn open to reveal luminous lifeblood pouring down his side. Ari bound, cleaned, and tended the wounded creature until he was able to go on his way.

After that, though, Pulse lagged even further behind the rest of the group. The wound didn't seem to have slowed him down too much, but Ari suspected that there was a deeper reason for his hesitation.

The odd duo walked and hopped side by side.

As time passed, the group seemed to leave them further and further behind.

Until one day, when the blue-grey Hopper appeared at the edge of their campfire. Ari was surprised as Pulse moved forward to greet it. The two creatures pulsed softly to one another, and a new face appeared.

A tiny creature, all eyes and legs, emerged from the undergrowth, blinking and glowing softly.

Ari's heart warmed. *A baby! How sweet. Is it his?*

They looked at Pulse expectantly, and watched their companion nuzzling the youngster's forehead, while the stranger – presumably the other parent – glowed with pride.

A moment later, the parents moved to press their hides together, nuzzling one another softly. The little one licked its parents' faces with a tiny green tongue.

Ari couldn't help but lower their gaze, feeling their eyes well up. They remembered the feeling of parenthood as though it was yesterday, and it was hard to believe that that feeling was all but gone.

No… Not gone. Bailey is still out there. And he will be until the last star in the universe draws its last breath. That's why I have to get back to him.

Ari sighed.

I've dallied long enough.

Ari was silent until Pulse and his mate drew apart. They smiled faintly. That smile faded, though, as the pair turned their backs on Ari, and began to hop away. Hastily, Ari packed their supplies and stomped out their fire, taking off after the pair's retreating backs.

Pulse turned towards them, flashing his tail in a short, sharp signal. Although Ari was still new to their language of lights, they could read it easily.

Stay!

They slowed, and then stopped, heart breaking.

They held up a clenched fist. Circled it, opened their hand, hoping that the message was right.

Why?

We must go, Pulse flashed back, ears drooping slightly. He gestured out across the plain, blinking. *New home out there.*

Ari made no gestures but stared back at their friend in disbelief.

But...

Pulse glanced past Ari then, and to the distant sparkle of lights across the plain, where the pack was sleeping. He did not light up, but the message was clear.

You have them.

Ari's blood felt cold. They did not answer, even as Pulse left them standing alone on the plain, until the glow had faded from the heather around them.

I... suppose I do.

Ari folded their hands across their chest, and shivered slightly. *Pulse was miserable with the group.* They thought in frustration. *Why can't I just be happy for him? For... for anyone.*

At a slow walk, Ari returned to the edge of the campfire.

Bailey... Reina... and now Pulse. They're all where they're meant to be, and they don't need me. So where am I meant to be?

Slowly, Ari forced themself to eat and sleep. No one came to lead them away this time. By the time they opened their eyes, the group was already gone, indistinguishable from all the other lights.

Ari felt deflated. They wandered alone across the plain, keeping an eye on the horizon, but never again taking it upon themself to pursue the lights. Messages rippled across the distance, inane gossip mostly, with occasional useful tidbits.

Twins born today! Celebrate!

A friend has left us! Keep them safe!

Food scarce by this way!

Stay off our turf!

The twinkling glimmer burned itself into their eyes, until Ari finally lowered their gaze, keeping their eyes on the mosses at their feet. They walked for a time without looking up, fearful of the knot that was growing in their throat.

That was a mistake.

When they looked up, all the lights had gone out.

Ari's blood ran cold.

That can only mean one thing.

Ari looked up, but by the time they realised they were being hunted, it was already too late. The great, void-like shadow of enormous wings fell on them. Fear closed in from all sides, numbing them, even as the great talons locked around their chest. With a great flurry of wingbeats they were hauled bodily from the earth. The ground fell away as though in slow motion.

Instinct took over, then, and Ari whipped the knife from their thigh, and plunged it into the limb that held them. Before they knew what was happening, Ari was sent spinning back to earth, and hit the ground with a sickening crash. A half-closed claw thudded down beside them.

As Ari lay where they were, heaving deep breaths, a violent sickness came crashing in. The pain, the bruises from the fall, were suddenly an afterthought. Their head spun, throat closed up as they dry heaved violently. A sudden, terrible agony racked their abdomen, and sent them trembling. They curled up into a tight ball on the ground and waited for it to pass.

Ari gagged, groaning, and writhed in pain. Horrible familiarity flashed briefly through them as they thought back to the sickness of the Riftworld, ignored for so long. Could this be the same?

Tears welled in their eyes, and lights bled in their vision.

What's happening to me? they wondered, as the sickness faded into nausea. *Could it be food poisoning? I've taken all the necessary precautions.*

They heaved a shaky breath.

I've no way of checking for illness.

Finally, after what felt like a lifetime, they were able to

sit up, and with small, staggering steps, they found their way back to a water source. Luckily, the creature that had been hunting them did not return; they would have been an easy target had it not been wounded. They found shelter just beneath the edge of the ravine and slept the hours away.

At first, Ari woke only to eat and drink. They could barely keep food down. The soft tinkling of the stream taunted them. They ate, slept, woke briefly, and slept again. Even when they felt well enough to get up, Ari felt bloated and heavy. Their head spun even when they stood still. With supplies running low, though, they were forced to get up and forage regardless. On the way, they needed to sit and rest frequently.

Bit by bit, their appetite drained away. In its place lingered nausea, and fatigue.

They knew they should eat, but somehow, they couldn't stomach it. The feeling of meat on their tongue, or the sweetness of fruit, left them gagging. The scent of the spores in the air made their head spin, and the sick feeling in their belly intensified.

Ari huddled alone under the jagged skeleton of a dead tree, wrapping their cloak tightly about them as they struggled to warm themself by the fire.

Ari rested their chin on their knees and closed their eyes as they tried to quell the dizziness. They thought again back to the strange creature that they had scavenged in the swamp. *That was where it all started. But… it's been weeks since then.*

Slumber claimed them almost against their will.

Soon after the Riftmaster woke from a sleep choked by memories, and in a moment of feverish self-deception found themself running a hand across their belly. *Could I be…?*

They shook away the thought as quickly as it had come. *No. No, that's not possible. Oliver is…*

Ari choked softly, hugging their knees.

He's been dead for years now.

Even still, the thought brought a hollow feeling into their belly.

Perhaps they would never know what killed them.

Perhaps no one would ever know.

Ari opened their eyes as something brushed against their side. They raised their head, peeking out over their knees, and found a light-hopper with torn ears and slim sides standing beside them, a bold red fruit clasped in small paws. It held the fruit out to them, and they held out a hand to receive it.

But then a white light filled their vision.

Ari clung to their knees and braced themself for the pain, the sensation of falling, and the feeling of being thrown from one world, into the next.

…But it never came.

Another small flash broke through their closed lids and Ari looked down as Pulse dropped his offering and fled into the undergrowth.

Ari raised their head, looking around them in evident surprise. The campfire still crackled before them. The tree's dead branches whistled quietly above.

A low boom echoed out over the plain as a dark, streamlined shape soared overhead, glinting in the starlight. Ari knew that sound. They knew it all too well. Their chest sparked with dread, and then swelled with an unexpected glimmer of hope.

A Renohaiin scouting vessel. The empire is here.

With renewed strength flowing through their limbs, Ari struggled upright and slung the satchel over their shoulder.

The vessel was low; it wouldn't be far before it came in for a landing.

Stumbling, shivering, and with one hand tightly folded across their belly, Ari stumbled after the ship.

Chapter 5
The Vessel

It couldn't have taken long for the Riftmaster to reach the newly landed vessel, but it felt like an eternity. They staggered across the open plain, stumbling and occasionally sinking to their knees, heaving laboured breaths before hauling up onto leaden limbs and carrying on. By the time they reached it their vision spun, and eyes were wild. The plain seemed to tilt beneath them.

The vessel was not a large ship, but it was a familiar one. It sat on the open plain, sleek and black with plates of crystal making up the hull. Ari paused for just a moment, a mixture of familiarity and grief making them hesitate. The last time they had been on board such a ship had been centuries ago. Only years after they'd lost Oliver and their family to the Rift; the sight of it brought back the pain fresh and new.

Three of the Renohaiin's small crew had already formed a barricade against their approach, while a small number took readings and samples of plant life in the nearby vicinity.

The crew showed little diversity; a team of six tall, slim creatures with segmented bodies like mantises, and four, quick, nimble arms. Their top-heavy torsos were counterbalanced by short, thick, dragonfly-like tails.

The Renohaiin had small mouths with two tiny, tusked mandibles either side. Two large eyes faced forward, and two small, slitted eyes were protected by thorny brow-growths. Their scaly carapaces shone in the half-light.

Although the Empire was well-known for a penchant for taking in stragglers of the Rift, Ari only saw one other species among them. The seventh member of the crew was a stocky little creature with its body covered in wispy grey hair. This one received a tray of samples from a colleague without leaving the cargo hold. He didn't even look up to see what the fuss was about.

No matter.

The crew waited expectantly, with weapons cocked. Like the vessel before them, the guns Ari had once known as plasma florets had changed little in the centuries since they served. They vaguely resembled the bloom of a flower made from Renohaiin chitin, but Ari had no doubt they were even more powerful now. Ari would have no choice but to grovel.

Ari removed one of the necklaces wound around their neck and approached in full view, holding their arms out with palms outstretched, in a clear display of submission. The pendant of their necklace hung across one outstretched palm; a tiny carving of a Renohaiin exo-skull.

Several of the crew took defensive positions in front of the loading ramp.

"Comrades!" Ari called, slurring slightly as they switched to the Renohaiin tongue. "I am Riftmaster, Navigator of Sector Seventeen in fleet 1501. As a refugee of the Rift, I Humbly ask your aid."

They approached. Step by step, feeling their limbs beginning to quiver under their weight, and the strain of hope.

The plasma florets were trained on their chest.

"Navigator?" clicked one of the crew. Uncertainly, the weapon was lowered. Then he barked out a name.

"Captain Malgas! It speaks our tongue."

Another of the crew, who had been watching closely,

began to approach. Captain Malgas was a highly decorated creature, with an impressive crest upon the brow that spoke of lifelong access to the resources needed to produce tough exoskeletal chitin. The elevated status of captain was worn as both a badge, and a warning. Although the iridescent-dipped tips of her crests indicated that human society would have considered her female-presenting, she, like the Riftmaster themself, carried little that could be misconstrued as feminine grace or charm. Captain Malgas was a creature of sharp angles and chitinous points, with tightly drawn mandibles lending her a suitably severe expression.

She moved towards them cautiously, and as she neared the speaker took a respectful step back, dipping a half-formed crown, and quickly relaying what they had said.

Ari saw the captain squinting, four eyes twitching into lens-like focus as she examined the pendant in their palm. "That team is defunct," she said flatly. "Your sigil is years out of date. Which star cycle did you serve?"

Ari's brow creased with the effort of remembering. "1560 through to 1563." They said, hoping the mostly-random numbers were close enough.

Several membranes flicked over the captain's eyes. It was a subtle expression, but undoubtedly one of surprise.

"Atomic type?"

"Carbon-based."

The captain hesitated. "I'm sorry, Navigator. Our current systems cannot sustain you."

"But–…" Ari felt the strength leave their limbs. It was as though hope alone was keeping them on their feet, and now they felt the days of sustained effort and sickness dragging them down like lead weights. "I… I can't…"

They felt themself fall forward onto their knees, tremors racking their stocky frame. Their bones felt as though they had crumbled into sand. Somewhere, they heard themself gasping for air.

But their vision had already faded into black.

***

"Captain Malgas!"

Malgas' impressively crested head twitched towards her subordinate as a stunned exclamation reached her receptors. After a brief moment of appraisal cast over the steel-blue Renohaiin standing before her, the captain's mandibles clacked an invitation to continue. She took a step back from the crumpled form at her feet.

"Yes, Osai?"

"Captain! Are you well? What did it say?"

Malgas glanced back towards the Rift-walker at her feet, sigil still clasped in fleshy paw. "It's dying," Malgas said. "Illness eats it from inside. We'd be foolish to invite it on board."

"Why would we invite it on board?"

"It claims to be the navigator for a defunct scouting vessel."

"Do you believe it?"

"Not in the slightest."

Clearly, the sigil was stolen. Under ordinary circumstances, Rift-walkers had not been welcome on Renohaiin ships for cycles. If it spoke the truth, it had been out here for many more lifetimes than was plausible for a warm-blood. She wasn't about to start giving leeches the benefit of the doubt now.

That said... the sigil was very, very old. In the time that it was made, the Empire may have been new enough that Rift-walkers would have been an asset.

"So... what are your orders, Captain?"

"Scan some tissue samples and leave it here. Unless you have a better option, Osai...?"

The steel-blue Renohain signalled a negative, and bent hesitantly at the creature's side, a device with a delicate needle poised to take a sample from one of its limbs. Malgas took the time to look around, watching the rest of her crew as they collected samples of the surrounding area.

With the excitement of this curious encounter dying down, most of her crew had simply begun to hastily continue their work.

As Malgas' gaze landed on each of the crew in turn, their actions became quicker, more frantic, as though speed would guarantee a greater level of success.

A clack from Osai drew Malgas' attention again. She glanced down curiously, taking in the creature, now with blood running from a cut in its forelimb. Red blood. Iron.

"You'll need to see this, Captain."

"What's your analysis?"

"Iron blood. Primarily carbon based. But listen, Malgas… There are traces of iridium binding to the carbon in its cells."

Malgas froze. Her mandibles quivered lightly as she thought.

"You're certain?"

"Yes."

"So… this sickness…"

"It… Would appear so."

Malgas' gaze snapped from Osai to her crew. "Nuudren! Ganir!" Two Renohain turned sharply towards her. "Help Osai bring this creature on board. Make sure it is restrained, and be prepared for anything."

She turned towards the *Vestige*, to where a small, furry figure still hovered uncertainly in the entrance. "Hoss– Bring Omea at once!"

The target couldn't fight them in a state like this. Couldn't resist.

Malgas watched as, between eight arms, Nuudren and Ganir hoisted the unconscious Rift-walker between them. It struggled faintly, weakly, against their touch.

"Where to, Captain?" Nuudren asked.

"To the Medbay. Whatever happens, we cannot let this creature die."

***

Senses deserted the Riftmaster. Sights failed them.

All they knew in that time was pain.

Clacking voices exchanged incredulity when the world spun briefly back into existence. Ari kept coming back to find that shocked murmurs had heightened into furious, broken debates.

They felt everything. The needles in their skin. The sturdy, carapaced arms that held them throughout.

Why aren't they sedating me? Ari thought, desperately, as they felt something like ice flooding their veins. *Do they think me too much of an alien to feel pain?*

Luckily, when the tubes were settled and the pain was dull but constant, exhaustion and darkness finally crept in.

When reality faded, they heard children's laughter, familiar and warm in their ears. The voices of their two youngest, distantly but unintelligibly arguing.

And somewhere, somehow, someone called out a name that wasn't theirs. Their belly dropped; their heart filled with nostalgia.

"Aria... they're looking for you."

Who? Ari tried to ask. *Who's looking for me?*

Their eyes cracked open, searching for the source of the voices, but instead of a familiar face, they instead saw a blurred ceiling of bleeding UV lights and sleek black crystal. The sound of laughter and children's voices slowly faded from their ears.

When their eyes drifted closed, they saw reddish leaves rustling in a faint, warm breeze.

"Aria, I really don't think that–"

Time made that voice feel warped and unfamiliar. But even still the sound of it swelled in their heart.

Ari didn't dare open their eyes again, as they strained through their memories to catch even the faintest glimpse of his face.

"Who? I think you might have the wrong Rifter," they heard themself say, although they hadn't moved their lips.

"Aria, now's not–"

"I've told you, my name is Riftmaster. And if you want to keep your belly full, you'd do well to remember it," Ari's voice said.

"*Riftmaster,* then," the name was spoken with a sigh.

"Better," the Riftmaster said. "You should really think

about dropping the attitude too, but we can work on that later."

"Riftmaster… I just don't think this is a good idea."

"Why not?"

"We can't just… waltz into a camp of these… *aliens* and expect to come out alive. What if they eat us? What if they rob us?"

"We're the only *aliens* here, Oliver. Besides, they're peaceful to outsiders, so just follow my lead."

"How do you know?"

"I've traded with them before. Besides… we're doing this for your sake, not mine. Remember? You can only survive so long on luck."

Ari's eyelids flickered. Again they searched in vain for the source of the voice. But the figures standing over them were anything but human.

"Oli… ver…" they spoke out loud, briefly surfacing from a sea of dreams. Ari was appalled by how weak and thin their voice sounded. Ashamed by how much it hurt.

As their eyes closed, the image of the woods returned.

"Listen… If you're really that worried, you can stay here. Hold my satchel for me, if you will."

"What if the Rift takes you?"

"Then it takes me. It makes no difference."

"But… you'd have nothing. Nothing at all."

"It doesn't matter. I'd cope. At least you'd have supplies then."

"But…"

They felt their voice grow taut with frustration. "But what, Oliver? What do you want me to say? The Rift won't wait for us. I'll be quick."

"What will you do then? When I'm gone?"

"What do you mean? I'll carry on, the same as I always have."

Though the conversation continued, the voices grew hazy and distant. *Oliver…* Ari opened their eyes, flinging their head from side to side as they searched for him once more. And this time, they found him; as their gaze lit on the sleek, crystalline floor beyond their bedside, his image hazed into view. They saw him locked in the cold chill of death, blood oozing from the corner of his mouth and onto the shimmering tiles. *Oliver!*

Ari thrashed. Immediately, clawed hands that felt like hard, scaled leather came to hold them down. Their arms were lashed to the frame beneath them, and legs restrained.

Oliver's body faded from their vision. Ari's heart broke once more, just as it had the first time, and the last. But even as they fought to clear away the memory, the sleek, crystal structure of the room remained.

It took them more than a few minutes to realise that the sleek black crystal and sterile lights were real. Renohaiin tech, uncannily similar to those on the Riftworld they had visited with Bailey.

There was something on their face. Their lungs were being pumped with air that tasted of sulfur. Finally, they were awake. But they didn't feel lucid. Winding knots of external veins delivered the nutrients to their body that they could not find by any other means.

The Riftmaster tried raising their hands to feel for the shards of his knife but found their wrists bound by cold metal. And in any case, they felt their skin exposed to open air, devoid of any comforting weights or even the Renohaiin pendant. Armour, jewellery, and everything in between, all had been removed.

Only their scaled undergarment remained. It clung tight enough to their body, perhaps, that it had been taken for no more than a second skin.

Fear remained, too, pumping through their veins like cold ice. And then something else… Something strange, that didn't feel like their own. Ari felt cold relief unperturbed by the sight of death. Innocent concern, and the feeling of a warm, filled belly, clashed with the tears gushing down their cheeks and the horror of the images still stuck in their brain.

Ari squeezed their eyes shut, willing the peaceful visions to return, and clinging to the comfort.

Oliver… please, come back to me.

Ari's eyes jerked open as they heard a soft clinking sound. With a great effort, they shifted their head once more. It was like pushing through honey. The tubes running from the mask across their face strained to pull them back, but they resisted, and watched. A steel-blue Renohaiin in a form-fitting suit was moving beside their bedside. Tubes of suspiciously blood-red matter swirled in its grasp, whilst cabinets of other substances lay half-opened, or scattered across all available surfaces. Three silk-bound books lay open beneath a broad, translucent screen of symbols, and although Ari couldn't see it from here, they knew each one would read in Renohaiin script.

A long, nimble claw moved from the control panel to tap at the surface of a glass orb filled with fluid, creating the strange clinking sound once again.

As they watched, the Renohaiin adjusted the screen with one free arm, and with the final one, tapped out a series of notes.

Ari watched for a while before losing interest. Their vision was too hazy to read the notes.

Gradually, Ari felt the aches and pains return, and with it, the realisation of where they were. As lucidity returned, all traces of sleepiness faded, leaving them alone with their hollow heart and fear. With their mouth filled by oxygen tubes, and their eyes flitting wildly, they forced out a low grunt.

The medic turned towards them, curious. It blinked a few times, with all four eyes and a few extra membranes than were strictly necessary, as if checking to make sure that the Riftmaster was really still alive. And then the medic approached. Cautiously, and with long, spindly fingers that twitched like insect legs, he gently removed the oxygen mask from Ari's mouth.

First, they felt the cold chill of the air falling on their face. Then, a sharp pain as the breathing tubes slithered out after.

Ari took a harsh breath, then coughed. The air in here felt thin. But a few deep breaths later, their chest heaving and nostrils flaring, they had regained composure.

Beneath them they felt a smooth, plasticky bed frame. Glancing down, they saw their bodysuit shimmering with iridescence under the bright lights, their prone body running parallel to a tangle of tubes. Needles had been poked into their veins; they must have had some kind of technology that had been used to see beneath the skin. They could feel by the aches that their arms were covered in bruises.

"Welcome back, Navigator," the medic said.

From the way that the Renohaiin was decorated, with undipped tines and a plain suit woven with shimmering threads, Ari could see that the medic presented as male, or at least had not progressed past that point of his life cycle yet. And although Ari still found emotions difficult to distinguish in the insectoid race, they thought he sounded significantly relieved. "How are you feeling?"

"Horrible," Ari said truthfully. "Did you beat me up on the way into the ship?"

"Hardly," the medic said. "You put up quite a fight for one on the brink of death."

Ari huffed softly, half in amusement and half in exasperation. "That explains the bindings." Ari's gaze followed the tubes from their inner arms and towards the pumps that kept substance flowing through them, out of them, and away for further tests. "Looks like it took a lot to pull me through."

"Yes, you could say that. Your veins were full of toxins, and you were horribly malnourished. We didn't have a lot to feed carbon-based lifeforms, but we were able to find some sustenance pellets that you responded well to."

At Ari's glance, the medic crouched at their bedside, two of the creature's nimble arms holding them steady, and the others removing several tubes. Ari winced at the sudden, sharp pain, and watched blankly as their blood formed into small, round pearls between the scales. They knew that there might be side effects close to follow, and they didn't look forward to it. *My body will have something to say about alien lifeblood in my veins, for sure…*

"Sounds like it would have been easier just to let me die," they said softly.

"Oh, definitely."

Ari blinked, expecting some elaboration. Unfortunately, though, the Renohaiin medic was unwilling to continue. Ari considered for a second.

"…well… In that case, I think I might be okay to look after myself from now on. If you'd like to drop me on the nearest life-bearing planet, I'll keep going by myself."

"I'm afraid that won't be possible."

"Why not?"

"We will need to monitor your systems closely, to make sure you respond well to the transfusion."

"With the amount of resources that will take, it would be far more efficient to cut your losses and let me go, don't you think?"

"I'm sorry. We're not letting you go." The medic hesitated, tilting his horned head, mandibles quivering in hesitation.

There was a long pause, before Ari finally sighed. "I'm an ex-Renohaiin veteran myself," they said. "I understand that you have orders. That being said…This kind of vessel is used for searching and scouting, not conquering. What were you looking for?"

The medic clacked softly as he thought.

"We were sent to search for the element of iridium. It's rarely produced naturally, but in some ecosystems it is essential."

"What about me…?"

"Your body contains a high concentration of Iridium. It was what almost killed you. That armour you were wearing contained high concentrations, too."

"My armour…?" Ari thought back to the swamp, and the strange creatures they had found there. Harvested for materials… And then eaten. "…Oh, god damn it."

"What is it?"

"I found something. Large, pale. Dead. My armour is made from their hide and bones. I ate from it."

"You *ate* it?"

"Yes."

"Why?"

Ari blinked several times at the question. "Why do you think?"

One by one, membranes slipped into place over the medic's eyes, until the final lids closed. His mandibles trembled as he recomposed himself, before finally flicking open his eyes once again.

"Might that creature be what you were looking for?"

"…We'd need to take samples."

"You have my armour."

The medic hesitated. "I'll… let Captain Malgas know. Thank you. I'm afraid I… can't do much more than that."

Ari sighed. But, with their wrists bound and the majority of their organs still being fed nourishment via tubes, there was very little else they could do. "Thank you, Medic. I understand."

"Please, call me Omea. Since you are awake, I must go report to our Captain. You should rest in the meantime. You may be stable, but not enough to survive the Rift. It will take a while before we reach our centre of operations at cruising speed."

"Okay then. I'll keep that in mind."

"Thank you, Navigator."

"Alright. And… Call me Riftmaster. It's been a long time since I served."

"Noted, Riftmaster. I'll let them know."

The Renohaiin medic's claws clacked gently against the crystalline floor as he left Ari alone to their thoughts, and the gentle hum of their life support systems.

Chapter 6
Renewal

"Omea tells me that the host has been stabilised, Captain."

Malgas did not look up from where she ran fingers nimbly across the translucent screen before her. She was clearly absorbed in some administrative task or another. But in the bright lights flooding the captain's chamber, he saw the tension leave her shoulders immediately, a low whistle escaping between her mandibles.

"I'm happy to hear that. Thank you, Osai."

For a time, Malgas continued in her task, sweeping pathways from shape to interconnected shape, as she cast out a series of codes into the unknown. Finally, she stepped back from the communications board, four arms folding before and behind her chest.

She glanced back and found Osai patiently waiting for her to finish. Malgas swept past him, ushering with a silent flick of her segmented tail. With fluid, adamantine grace, she moved a little more than three strides before collapsing down into a high-backed chair, resting her crest back into a specifically designed hollow so that she could stare beseechingly up at the sterile lights shining above them.

With soft clacks of his claws against the floor panels, Osai followed, taking a place opposite.

"So, the host," Malgas said finally, after what felt like forever. Her mandibles twitched in something resembling a smile. "It's stable. How stable?"

"It's responding well to treatment. Omea removed the transfusion tubes shortly after it awakened."

"Did it speak any more?"

"From time to time. It wants to know why we're keeping it here."

"That's reasonable. Is it…" Malgas hesitated, lifting her head to look directly at Osai, who although sitting, was poised sharply upright. "…confirmed, then?"

"Yes, captain. This is the one we were looking for."

Malgas leaned forward slightly. She reached out, a single carapaced hand outstretched. Her mandibles trembled. "Do you realise what that means, Osai?"

Malgas shaded her eyes with a single membrane. Shrouded eyes met.

Osai did not answer but reached forward to clasp her hand in two of his own.

"…It's over… We did it. And… Of all the vessels out there searching, it was the *Vestige* that found what we were looking for."

"…And her crew."

Malgas' mandibles quirked. "That was implied."

"But we shouldn't get ahead of ourselves, Captain."

Malgas let out a whistling sigh. "Of course. We still have to get it back to the base of operations." She twisted back towards the communications board. "Did the Rift-walker give you any kind of identification?"

"It claimed that its name was Riftmaster. Why?"

Malgas clacked thoughtfully. "I reached out to the station. Requested any information they had about the defunct Fleet 1501. Information is sparse. Mostly paper records that were transcribed for completion's sake."

"And?"

"The Riftmaster was on them. Either this is a case of identity theft, or this Rift-walker is telling the truth."

Osai froze. "But… that was generations ago."

"It was. But we know that the Rift can extend lives

beyond any reasonable measure, and that the way time flows in the Rift can be... unpredictable. There were other, more..." Malgas' mandibles quivered. "...Concerning... things in the files, though."

"Such as?"

"Riftmaster belongs to a race called... human. A warm-blooded, carbon-based lifeform. Records would suggest that this species is typically... rather fragile. We do not know the system or planet of origin."

"That adds up. Is there anything else?"

"When it was a part of the Empire, the Riftmaster was... unreliable, to say the least. It was once a captain, but was demoted to navigator after a case of desertion. Then after another demotion, it was put to training new recruits in survival skills. Apparently, the Old Empire deemed it too much of an asset to banish completely. This Rift-walker had a knack for surviving even the most hostile planets virtually unscathed... however, it was also known for going to extreme lengths to avoid conflict."

"So it left?"

"It was on one last mission when the ship was wrecked. An early ship, with faulty fuel converters. The team was presumed dead, and the fleet declared defunct, but no bodies were ever found."

Osai was silent for a time. "So... What you're saying is..."

Malgas glanced back.

"Make this Rift-walker comfortable. We need to be sure it stays happy, safe, and on our side."

"Right."

Osai rose with a long, fluid movement. He paused only briefly when Malgas called after him.

"And Osai?"

"Captain?"

"Warn the crew to be cautious. It would seem that we have a bit of a troublemaker on our hands."

***

Although Ari soon lost track of time, they were relieved to find that their health was gradually improving. The nausea left first, and then their appetite returned with violent force. Ari spoke to Omea about the possibility of bringing them solid nourishment to fill their belly.

Omea was hesitant. There were few rations on board suited to their bodily needs, and as it was, they were unlikely to make it back to the Renohaiin homestead on what little they had. But if they were to keep healing, Ari needed the strength. They couldn't last on nutrients administered directly to the bloodstream forever.

It was a process, though. They had to be weaned from the medication gradually, removing the tubes for only a few hours at a time. When they looked down at themself, Ari felt their blood run cold as they saw the outlines of their bones beneath their scales. They had been strong, once; their endurance unmatched by any other human on Earth... or at least, they liked to think that was the case.

But now...

This sickness had really pushed them to the brink. It could take months to get their fitness back to where it had been before. Perhaps even years.

I was well overdue for a case of food poisoning. But this... this was too close.

Finally, when Omea returned to cautiously remove their tubes and loosen their wrist straps, they were able to sit up without their head spinning. They silently vowed that that would be the last time they slept tied down.

From then on, the Riftmaster ate what little food was available to them, and although the crew tried to ration it strictly, it was never enough. The sustenance pellets that fizzed and swelled into a tasteless grey gruel would never feed them longer than a few hours. The human body needed more energy to function than the crew had prepared for. Ari was used to searching for their food, but on a sterile spaceship such as this, they knew that finding anything more than what they'd already eaten would be unlikely. Even if the Renohaiin equivalent of a rat had found its way on board somehow, the crew were always vigilant about stowaways.

Every time the door to the medical wing fizzed open, Ari expected Omea to bring bad news instead of a meal. When the time came, he did not speak but instead held out a pale blue pellet. Ari's stomach dropped.

"That's it?" they asked. "We're all out?"

Omea nodded sadly. "I'm afraid this is the closest we've got. It's still based on plant matter, but it's from our hearth-world."

Ari gnawed nervously on their lower lip. In a pinch, they'd tried to last on other forms of Renohaiin sustenance before. But it had never gone well. Their body always rejected what little nourishment cold be gained. Either they'd vomit, purging even more vital nutrients from their system, or they'd be bedridden the rest of the trip with severe food poisoning.

"How far do we still have to go?" Ari asked. "How long?"

"We're several star systems away… Three lunes, at least."

Ari paused to translate. If they were remembering correctly… Three lunes, or lunar orbits, was something akin to two months.

"You said this ship can enter the Rift. Right?"

"Yes. The ship's casing is made from bioreactive rift-crystals. It was built to enter the Rift. But Riftmaster, I'm sorry, we can't."

"I've been in the Rift for thousands of years, even sick. I'm sure I could handle one more."

"I'm sorry, Riftmaster. We have orders."

"I'm feeling better. We could get there sooner–"

"I'm sorry, Riftmaster. You are too precious a cargo to waste like that."

"Feed me poison and you will be wasting it anyway, *Medic*," Ari finally snapped. *So stop lying to me!*

"I'm sorry, Navigator. This is all we have."

The medic dropped the pill into a small glass bowl. it fizzed and frothed into a rich blue-black colour, swelling up to fill the container. Ari watched it with fascination, and disgust. But their stomach let out a faint, and pitiful growl.

They'd have to pick their poison; in a few days they'd begin to atrophy, and eventually die of starvation. Or they could drink this… and die slower, and more painfully, of gradual poisoning. It would be a long, terrible few months, but they might just make it out on the other side.

Ari let out a breath, slowly raising their hands to receive the glass bowl. They raised the thick, foamy broth up towards their lips to drink. And then they swallowed. It tasted thick, salty and bitter. A shudder ran up and down their spine but they forced it down anyway. Perhaps a small amount would be easier to stomach. A few mouthfuls would be enough for an hour or two. Ari placed down the container by their bedside, and lay back against the plasticky surface beneath them.

As they settled into place, Omea nodded approvingly. "We will monitor you. If need be, we can stop at a colonised planet on the way… but the captain doesn't think it will be necessary."

Ari's brows furrowed. "We'll see. I know what my body needs better than anyone."

***

To Ari's surprise, the sickness did not arrive. They remained comfortably healthy, at least as much as they could given the circumstances. After a few cautious meals, they finally began to finish the slop with more gusto.

Ari was naturally suspicious, and kept an inner checklist of things to stay alert for. After every first sip they'd hold up their hands, flex fingertips, and scan their brain for any telltale signs of grogginess. They'd work out some simple mathematical puzzles, to ensure their mind was working at full capacity. But the gruel didn't appear to be drugged.

Perhaps they've changed the recipe.

The only thing, which was admittedly strange enough, happened fairly frequently. A small, emotional quirk had begun to make itself known within their mind as though they were feeling the emotions of someone else. A small spark of contentment, joy, and a quaint sort of curiosity tugged at their mind even as the rest of them was alert with suspicion and doubt. They had felt it before, on first opening their eyes aboard the vessel. They felt it each time they awoke, before their sense of self had truly settled in. And yet… even now, as they eyed the medic with suspicion, an isolated part of them felt strangely cheerful.

And they felt it the most in the moments before blinking off to sleep, the feeling of being wide awake, and curious. It was as though something, somewhere, was probing their mind.

Does the Renohaiin Empire have that sort of technology? they thought. *I would certainly hope not.*

But when their body spun with pain was when the intrusion felt the most out of place.

Omea often attended them and seemed oblivious to their inner turmoil. For the most part, they did not voice it, instead preferring to stay on the subject of their progress, and the things that had changed since Ari had served, which was something akin to seven hundred years ago.

As someone who entered the Rift only briefly, Omea was equally curious about how it affected Ari.

"You told the captain that you served once. But you disappeared, and your fleet is long gone. What happened?" Omea asked one day, as Ari tentatively sipped at their bitter breakfast. It had been slightly warmed today, but that didn't make it taste any better. If anything, the temperature change only made it worse.

They stuck their tongue out as they thought of a suitable reply. "I…" Ari tapped a foot against the ground uncertainly. "I've just been away for a long time, that's all. I'm a Rift-walker… that's just how it is sometimes."

Ari hastily drowned the rest of their gruel to avoid further questions. Finally looking up, they let out a breath with a sigh.

"Does the empire still value rift-walkers?"

"Rarely for off-planet work. Too unreliable."

"This ship can enter the Rift. You must be using rift-crystals for that. You do know they can also be used to prevent Rifting?"

"Yes. We have implants for those that desire it. But few will deal with the constant tingling, and fewer still the prejudice. But you'll sometimes find them working in complexes or city-domes."

"Hrm. You'll have little need to study them anymore, now that you can use the Rift?"

"That's correct. You are interested in joining us?"

Ari hesitated, but gave no indication of their thoughts. "Perhaps," they finally said. "Nowhere is safer than the Empire. Even daily rations feel like royal treatment compared to some of the planets I've lived on."

Omea's mandible quirked. Ari didn't think it was a smile.

"That would make sense."

Ari paused for a moment, waiting to see if the medic would say anything more. It seemed he was finished, though. Finally, Ari spoke again, lightly changing the subject.

"Scouting ships weren't anything like this when I served. Things have changed a lot."

"That's rather ironic. The *Vestige* is one of the Empire's most outdated ships. She's one of the last of her kind; just wait until you see some of the others."

"Even still... I never thought you'd ever be able to enter the Rift willingly."

"Well, the Empire has expanded. We have colonised more planets than ever in recent years. Our soldiers are more diverse than any other faction across the known universe. So naturally, our ships have changed to accommodate that."

"You mentioned it has some biomechanical components?"

"Yes! Riftworld crystals, mostly. The Rift will only really transport objects with some sort of biological components, so we need to design our ships accordingly."

"Fascinating. I'd love to be able to explore it, sometime," Ari coyly glanced over towards the locked door that led to the rest of the ship. "So long as it's okay with Captain Malgas, that is."

"Of course. I believe she'll be happy to see how far you've come; and especially pleased for the chance to show you that you are not a prisoner here."

Ari straightened up, surprised, their cheeks flushing slightly. "I never said–" Ari trailed off, then shook their head slightly. "Never mind. I would be very glad of the opportunity to see the rest of the ship, and express my gratitude to the crew. Some freedom will make the rest of the journey far more pleasant. Thank you, Omea."

The Renohaiin dipped his head slightly and turned to leave. The insectoid creature rested fingerlike digits in a slight indentation in the wall. After a slight pause, he drew back, and the door slid open.

"Wait–" Ari said quickly.

The medic turned slightly towards them, a few membranes flicking across his eyes. "What is it, Riftmaster?"

"Do you think you could bring me my clothes?"

* * *

As the door slid open once more, Ari sat upright. Omea approached, holding a bundle of familiar leathers and hides. Ari sighed with relief. They shimmied themself over to the side of the bed and swung their legs over the edge.

The crystal tiles were cold against their bare feet. Their legs trembled faintly under the weight of their body. Without their armour, they felt exposed and lumpy in all the wrong places; and their bones stuck out rather unappealingly.

"Here you are. I don't see how this will assist you against the vacuum beyond, but…"

"So long as your colleagues can't see my squishy parts, that's all that matters."

Ari readjusted their scaled bodysuit first of all, taking care to flatten down their chest. They tied it in place behind their neck with a messy knot, and freed their hair with an added sweep. It fell across their shoulders and chest and down their back in fiery cascades. It had grown – just how long had they been on board? They pulled on the breastplate made of blue-tinged carapace and secured their pauldrons, tugging their fashionable half-cape across their shoulders. Then came the leather boots and shinguards. Finally, they fastened a few belts in place before draping a loincloth across the belt at their middle.

"This seems exceedingly complicated, Riftmaster," Omea said with amusement.

"Yeah, well, they don't come off very often," Ari answered as they carefully wound their necklaces into place. Teeth, bones, crystal pendants... all of them souvenirs, and some thousands of years old. Ari noticed that some of the sharper beads had been removed.

They let out a long breath as they saw that the fragment of Riftworld crystal remained. The clusters stood out sharply against their chest. Ari held onto the hope that one day, they'd be able to put it to good use.

Tilting their head down, they held out their arms and examined themself. Chest flat, scales shining, and dignity safely restored, Ari relaxed.

After that, they looked around for anything more, but that was all.

Ari looked up at Omea accusingly.

"Where's my satchel?" Ari asked.

"It's in the cargo hold. You won't be needing it here. We can't risk you bringing potential weapons or poisons on board, especially if you are to be given free reign of the ship."

"Fair enough," Ari said with a shrug. *I wouldn't trust me either.*

"Anything else?"

"There was a length of hide, too," Omea said. "But I didn't think it wholly necessary..."

"Are you joking? That's the most important part!"

Omea's mandibles clacked. Ari wasn't sure whether it was mirth or irritation, but a few moments later, they were alone again.

Although Ari wondered at first if they had offended the medic, he soon reappeared. Ari grinned, opening their arms to receive the hide he held folded in his arms. After a moment's consideration, they swung it over their shoulders and tied it in place with a woven twine.

Then finally they stood feeling whole again, cloak and all.

"Now, how about a tour?"

"Indeed. So long as you're feeling well enough, that is."

Ari nodded. "Perfectly."

Omea rested his long, exoskeletal fingers into the hollow beside the door once more, and Ari nodded lightly as it slid open. "Back in my day, we used our ranking pendants," Ari mused, as they stepped on through.

Omea clacked softly in acknowledgement. "Those pendants are too easily forged, stolen, and used by unauthorised personnel. Nowadays, the digits of each crewmember are scanned and put into a database. Unless you are one of our crew or a commanding officer, you will not be able to move around the ship freely."

It sounded like a warning as much as an explanation.

Noted, Ari thought, eyes sparkling with interest.

As they wandered down the sterile, shimmering corridor towards the mess hall, Ari took a moment to remind themself of everything they knew about the Renohaiin race, and this crew in particular. Of eight crew members, seven were Renohaiin. And the last one, Ari wasn't sure.

Of those, Ari knew that three were male-presenting – or at least, were in that stage of their life. They knew this for how they decorated themselves, and in particular the jagged crown above their eyes. The Renohaiin life cycle was most similar to ants, and even then only tangentially. Nothing ever went unplanned among their kind, with sometimes decades passing between conception and birth.

There were four stages in the Renohaiin life cycle: larva, juvenile, male and then egg-carrier.

And it made a difference. As all three sexes could be experienced in one lifetime, there was little difference in the treatment of each. The dipping of an egg-carrier's horns was done entirely by choice, and some, those who preferred masculine presentation (or none), could choose not to dip their tines, or never to progress at all.

Such pronouns as 'he' and 'she' rarely entered Ari's vocabulary except for convenience's sake; but in addition to being a useful way of helping to telling the crew apart, the Renohaiin language was one of the few alien tongues that made the distinction.

Speaking of distinction…

Names! Names… What were their names?

Ari racked their brains but had heard only two. *Omea is the medic. Male-presenting. Malgas is the captain, the matriarch. Female-presenting, with dipped crests.* As for the rest, Ari did not know. The thought made their stomach drop a little bit. Names were a point of pride when it came to the Renohaiin. To know someone's name was to show them a great deal of respect. To ask someone's name showed ignorance, and no one wanted to be seen as forgettable.

As Omea stopped to open the door, Ari paused.

"Omea! I am terribly sorry to disrespect the kindness of captain Malgas and her crew, but… What are their names? I must ask, before I embarrass them."

Omea clacked his jaws once more, but this time Ari was certain it was mirth.

"Peace, Riftmaster. You were never told. They understand this."

The door slid open, and Omea ushered them inside.

Immediately, seven sets of eyes turned towards Ari. As soon as they stepped through the doorway they stopped, heart hammering, before offering a hasty double-palmed salute and dropping into a bow. "Greetings. I am Riftmaster, Ex-navigator of the now-defunct crew 1501. I would like to express my humblest gratitude for taking me on board in my time of need…"

Ari trailed off as they felt a hand rest against their

shoulder. They turned to see Omea gesturing them forward, closer to the rest of the crew. Obediently, Ari followed. Captain Malgas stepped out to meet them first, her iridescent carapace radiant in the sterile lights of the ship, towering over them by more than two feet.

"Riftmaster," Captain Malgas said, outstretching her arms in welcome. "So you're finally awake."

Malgas tilted her torso slightly forward in a bow, as low as she could without overbalancing. She held three palms outstretched, as she placed the final hand across her chest. "It is an honour to meet a Navigator of the Old Empire. Especially one with such a reputation."

Ari had never been particularly tall, even on their home planet. But among these slender creatures, they felt both dwarfed and stocky. Captain Malgas' bow brought her slightly lower than their eye level, as was custom. Ari's cheeks flushed red and anything they had been about to say escaped their tongue. "The honour is all mine, Captain. You know me?"

"We have the information on every fleet in history, at our fingertips. The files mention you by name."

Ari chuckled nervously. "All good things, I hope."

"Not necessarily. But always surprising," Malgas said pointedly.

I'm not sure if that was flattery or threat, Ari thought. *But whatever it is, it's working.*

"Please, if you'll allow me, I must introduce my crew."

Malgas gestured first to a blue-grey Renohaiin with an impressive crest of horns atop his head.

"This is Osai. Clutchmate to Omea, and one of the Empire's finest scientists."

Osai bowed slightly, but Ari couldn't help noticing that his gaze lingered on his brother.

"This is Nuudren. Ecological expert, with a specialty for uncharted planets. If we have not visited a world, she is the one who will help us prepare for its creatures and climate."

A lime-green Renohaiin looked up from her place, mandibles twitching in a slight smile. She didn't seem eager to be distracted from her pulpy meal for long, though.

"This is Ganir. She specialises in the study of the Rift."

Ari bowed, and Ganir bowed back. "It must have been quite a task to come this far."

"I could say the same," Ganir said. Her eyes were bright. "I've always wanted to meet a Rift-walker."

Here, the only non-Renohaiin crewmate glanced up. But Ganir seemed not to notice them.

"Are there none on your home planet?" Ari asked, glancing at the fluffy creature only briefly.

"There are some. But you... you serve the Empire for so many orbits that they started counting in star cycles. You disappear and are presumed dead, and then thousands later you appear, completely unscathed. There are very few manage to survive this long, with or without our help. I'd love to hear about your travels."

"You want to hear my stories?" Ari laughed softly, a weary smile tugging at their cheeks. "I'm afraid I'll have no choice but to indulge you on that. Prepare for a long journey home, my friend."

"I look forward to it. The things you must have seen. The things you must know! I'm certain you could expand our knowledge by a thousandfold."

Ari's smile became a faint wince. If it was accuracy and evidence Ganir was looking for, the process of storytelling was about to get a lot less exciting. "I'm sorry... In that, you may be disappointed."

"Many areas of science are disappointing. The Rift is not one of them."

As Ari gave a slight bow, Malgas moved on.

"Eidhoin, our engineer, is currently piloting the vessel. I'm sure you'll meet her soon. Our last crew member is Hoss. Our navigator."

Ari finally met the gaze of the small, pale, hairy creature they had glimpsed when first approaching the ship. The only non-Renohaiin member of the crew, and a bit of an outcast, it seemed. Unlike the others, Hoss was less than half Ari's height. He was small, chubby, with wiry hairs and huge, batlike ears; a poof of colourful fur tipped a long and whiplike tail. To Ari's surprise, Hoss seemed more hesitant to introduce himself. He was eating with small and nimble paws, using the tip of his tail to whisk patterns across a tablet screen, and did not raise his head to look at them even as the captain spoke.

As he finally turned, Ari saw that along with a glowing crystal placed perfectly on the centre of his forehead, a spiderweb of wires spread between his ears.

"It's a pleasure to meet you," Ari said, with a bow. "Navigator Hoss."

The small creature blinked up at them with beady eyes, and then spoke in heavily accented Renohaiin, that clattered his teeth and rasped in his throat. "Rift-walker. I feel we will get along," Hoss said softly. "It's been a long time since I met another."

A thrill of excitement ran through Ari's blood. They looked up, indicating Omea. "The medic said Rift-walkers are rarely used for off-planet work," they said, lowering their voice.

"Well, this is a rare sort of crew."

The side of Ari's mouth twitched. "Why is that?"

"Sometimes, we are needed for more than factory work. Navigation is one of the few instances where our usefulness outweighs our unreliability."

The edge of Ari's mouth twitched.

You didn't answer my question.

Glancing up, Ari noticed Malgas watching them. Ari offered Hoss a parting bow and withdrew.

"Well? Would you like to see the rest of the ship?"

Ari nodded eagerly, before adding, for clarity: "Of course!"

Ari left Omea behind in the mess hall as Malgas took the reins. The captain showed them between various tiny laboratories, storage units, and control rooms, all of them significantly smaller than what they were used to. Even the medbay seemed somehow more cramped when they passed it again. But the overall structure of the ship itself was quite familiar from their old days as a navigator.

The layout itself had not changed much, and the placement of the rooms was largely the same. The most notable difference was that multiple engine rooms, one on either wing, had been merged into only a single one at the centre of the ship. Ari was informed that the engines also doubled as generators to power the rest of the ship's mechanics in a pinch, but unsurprisingly they were not allowed to see. Malgas explained that she feared it unsafe for them, but Ari didn't think so. The crew probably didn't trust them enough to show them such volatile areas of the ship. They couldn't exactly blame her.

The cockpit was significantly sleeker than what they remembered. Beneath a massive window of translucent crystal, it had fewer buttons, sliders and levers than they remembered, the majority replaced by a large screen, with a few blinking lights. The sight of the stars for the first time in weeks made their heart pump slightly faster with excitement, despite the fact they had never learned to pilot a ship. A hologram projector shone various symbols onto the starscape beyond, including a greenish target that seemingly indicated the direction of the Renohaiin space station.

Ari looked at the target curiously, their heart leaping slightly.

Could this be? They dared to wonder with a flutter of hope. *My ticket back to Earth?*

They never could have imagined that the opportunity would arise so soon. The hard part would be finding a way to use it for themself.

"Riftmaster?" Malgas asked curiously, coming up beside them.

Ari shook themself back to the present. "Er… If the ship can show you where to go, why do you need a navigator?"

"There are a lot of reasons," captain Malgas said. "On exiting the Rift, the stars will have changed position and we may be outside of the mapped regions in our database. A navigator can point out familiar stars and galaxies that computers may not recognise, and help us reorient. They are an important part of surface expeditions, and if we are voyaging beyond the boundaries of the colonies, where the signals cannot reach us. In many situations, a navigator is the only thing that can lead us safely home to our host planet."

As she spoke, she wandered ahead of them down the corridor. Her strides were long, but slow. Her claws clacked softly against sleek surfaces. Ari's hurried footsteps echoed back in a pitter-pattering rhythm.

"This one should look familiar to you," Malgas said as she opened a door. "…Navigator."

The navigation room had changed significantly. Ari remembered a room full of books and documents, ancient starmaps drawn in red ink onto translucent silk, and compasses carefully crafted for a range of magnetic fields. Whilst a few old books and documents could be seen lined neatly on shelves beneath the countertop, Ari's gaze was drawn to the table itself.

Looking down into the sheet glass, they saw patterns of a thousand stars projected beneath the glass, shining back at them as if they were looking into a well of open space.

Some of the stars they recognised. A few constellations stuck out to them. A few systems they knew. Stepping back, they could see that the stars formed what looked to be a great whirlpool.

"I know this galaxy," Ari said.

Malgas' optic membranes flicked across her eyes. "You do?"

"Yes. My home planet orbits one of its stars. Back there, we called it the Milky Way."

Ari fell silent, gazing in awe at the patterns that seemed to shift before their very eyes, glistening, twinkling, and shining.

"Where is it that we're going?" they asked after a time.

Malgas peered into the starmap, all four eyes narrowing. "I'm not a navigator, but… I believe it to be somewhere around here."

She pointed to the empty space between three parallel stars.

Ari narrowed their eyes. As she removed her digit, they strained to see if there was something in the empty space that they'd missed. "The space station was built some distance away from any solar system, then."

"Indeed," she said. "It's the perfect distance from our local colonies, and our home planet."

Ari nodded. "That makes sense."

"You will see why soon enough. I expect you'll find our space station to be a place of great interest. But we have a long way to go yet."

Ari nodded. "I know," Ari said. "We still could enter the Rift. I've been doing it for star cycles, it's not about to kill me now."

"You are not ready, Riftmaster. This is too important of a chance to waste. You'll understand one day."

Ari's brows creased. "I'm sure I will," they said, hoping they sounded more certain than they felt. For some reason, they didn't like this. Their stomach knotted slightly as they thought. A shiver rode down their spine, and with it, came that feeling again; a delicate twinge of curiosity, and contentment.

All will be well, it said. *You are alive. You are healthy. You are among friends.*

All is perfect.

And for a moment, Ari felt inclined to believe it.

This is what I wanted, they reminded themself. *To not be alone. To be safe and happy. Among people who care.*

"Have you finished looking? There is yet more to see."

...And the crew seem to really want me here.

Ari stirred as though blinking away a dream, glancing up. They realised that they had unconsciously placed a hand upon their belly. The hairs along the back of their neck prickled slightly with unease, but they pushed it down, shaking their head.

No. I have somewhere to get to, somewhere to be. Is this sickness of mine really gone? Or is it just waiting for the right moment, festering in my mind?

"Yes, I'm finished."

Feeling their stomach silently knotting, Ari followed

Malgas out of the navigation room and into the labyrinth of corridors again. "I have to say, Malgas," Ari said carefully. "It has been wonderful seeing how far the Empire has come whilst I've been away. Technology has advanced in ways I never could have foreseen. Thank you, truly."

"It has been my pleasure, Riftmaster."

Ari kept an eye out for the cargo hold as they walked, but they caught no glimpses. As they followed her back towards the med bay, they glanced once again at each and every room they had entered, every dead end and corridor.

There was no sign of an escape pod, and their hope of using one to return to Earth gradually receded back into a dull ache at the very back of their brain.

Chapter 7
The Creature

Travelling on board the *Vestige* brought back memories Ari thought had been squashed thousands of years ago.

Sleep cycle after sleep cycle, it was always the same. The terrible laments of a grieving mind that ached to go back to where it had all begun.

It brought back the warped fragments of memories.

Whenever darkness closed in on Ari's vision, they felt the warmth of the fire around them, and saw the familiar reaches of another world. Purplish leaves rustled quietly in a faint breeze. The humid air bit with the faintest tang of sulfur, a cloak of translucent steam hanging in a low, low blanket above the ground. When they gazed out beyond the trees, the boundary of the clearing flickered and faded away into obscurity.

Ari walked towards the edge of the clearing, but there was nothing beyond the fog. The foliage trembled, tree branches hanging on empty air.

Even still, they knew this place.

Slowly, Ari returned to the fireside and knelt.

Under their palms, Ari felt the soft surface of the fabric they had been folding, deftly pulling knots tight so that the sleeping hides could be easily transported. Beside them, a humble campfire burned with bluish hues. The

Riftmaster looked up from the task at the telltale rustle of someone entering the clearing. Their eyes sparkled with curiosity; Oliver had not been gone long. Surely, he couldn't have a meal for them already?

They saw a shape emerging from the darkness, and their brows quirked with surprise as they lifted their gaze to see a familiar figure. "Oli... Oliver?"

There was something wrong. Oliver's face flickered in their vision. Too sharp. Too lanky. His hair, grey-streaked gold, had stolen the intricate formation of Reina's quills, the taut lankiness of her vaguely humanoid body.

Oliver... they thought, gazing out at his inhuman face. *What have I done to you?*

Feeling faintly sick, they glanced down to see what he was holding. A brightly coloured bouquet of alien flowers rested against his chest.

This isn't him, Ari thought, far too fleetingly. *So why do I want so badly to believe that it is?*

"Some of those flowers are toxic, Oliver. We can't eat those," they said.

"Uh," Oliver's cheeks flushed, and he glanced away. "They're not for eating."

"Then why...?"

"I just thought you'd like them."

Ari looked at the flowers, blinking a few times. They stared, confused. They supposed the flowers were actually quite lovely; jagged petals formed elegant, speckled cups of blue and lilac.

The closer they looked, though, the more sinister the flowers seemed to become. They rippled and throbbed, their stems segmented like insect legs. Ari took them anyway.

"Well, I suppose I do." Ari slowly settled a grip, taking careful effort to avoid the thorns as they lifted them from Oliver's bony fingers. "I never pictured you for a romantic, Oliver." They paused for a moment. "You made sure there were no bugs on this, right?"

Oliver's eyes widened. "Uh-?"

Ari smiled slightly, amused as they took a quick check beneath the leaves and petals. "I jest, Oliver, they seem clean enough. What should we do with them?"

"I… hadn't thought that far ahead."

Ari stifled a laugh but cast their gaze around regardless. It landed on a fallen trunk of gnarled, knotted foliage, twists of ivy forming numerous holes in the husk. Pools of water had formed at the bottom of some of the hollows.

Ari approached the log, and as they absentmindedly rearranged the stems, heard Oliver's voice.

"You know, in all my years, I've never met a woman like you."

They looked up, and found him standing exactly where he'd been left, arms knotted over his chest.

Ari scoffed softly. "It's been a long time since you've met anyone to compare me to… and even longer since I've considered myself as such," they said. "…but thank you, I suppose."

Oliver bowed his head slightly. His sharp jaw kept on shifting, the stubble along his cheeks quivering briefly into quills, and back again; but it was, for the moment, unmistakably him. As they looked down at his scruffy jawline and hazel – or were they blue? – eyes, Ari found themself drawn back into the familiarity. For just a second, they felt at home. The Riftmaster placed both hands upon the twisted trunk, and hoisted themself up to settle there. They patted the space beside them, and Oliver moved over, obediently settling himself beside.

"Now, what is this really about?" they asked, direct.

Oliver hesitated. "Aria… what would you consider us?"

Ari opened their mouth to reply, then thought better of it. They spent a moment thinking. "I'm not sure, anymore," they admitted. "It's been a long time since we felt like mentor and apprentice. You're a survivor now in your own right."

Oliver nodded. "I've felt the same."

The two of them sat in silence for a moment. Ari looked at the flowers, that seemed to wilt before their very eyes, and rearranged the stems again. "Are... you wanting to leave, Oliver?" they asked, leaning back on their palms. "You could probably make it out there, with some supplies and a bit of luck."

Oliver turned towards them in surprise.

"Aria... of course not. I can't see any kind of future out here without you." Oliver avoided their prying gaze. "That's... that's what I wanted to talk about."

Ari wasn't sure why, but they felt their stomach sink. "What do you mean...?"

"Aria... I... I've fallen in love with you."

***

When they awoke, they were another step closer to their destination and a step further away from the apathy that for so long had kept them safe and whole.

Each time they slept, the same Oliver greeted them with the same warmth, the same comfort, the same urgency. The same faintly inhuman attributes that seemed to fill the holes in their aging memory.

Things were changing. Each time they stood upright, received a health check from Omea, and ate, they felt more and more pressure. They had to keep moving, to return to the Rift and leave these happy memories to fester.

Uneasiness fluttered in their belly, and itched in the back of their mind.

Even when their mind ached from pure exhaustion, they tossed and turned before they inevitably slept. Things didn't seem to be adding up. They thought about seeing the ship from the ground and compared it to where they'd explored with Malgas. There had to be an escape route. And not just because they were unnerved; no, for the most part, they felt quite comfortable. But when it came to being outnumbered seven to one in an enclosed space, it was always good to have a way out.

Every time they woke from slumber brought them nearer to the Renohaiin base of operations, and the truth of what made them such valuable cargo.

The more they thought about it, the more ominous it seemed.

There must be a lower wing of the ship, there has to be. But how would I get to it?

In their free time, they took to exploring the ship, speaking to the other crew members, and learning just how much had changed. Captain Malgas allowed them free reign, except for several restricted areas which they were unable to see.

The mess hall allowed them a welcome break from the isolation of the med bay, and a momentary reprise from their role as important cargo. After the first meeting with the crew, they would rarely see more than two or three of them in the mess hall at a time. Malgas sat mostly alongside Osai, the scientist who seemed to double as a second-in-command. Nuudren tended to sit with Ganir and sometimes Osai. Hoss always ate his meals alone.

Oftentimes, they'd accompany Hoss into the navigation room, peering out of the broad windows and watching the stars go by. *They mentioned that they could stop at a colony for supplies if need be. I wonder if we'll be passing it soon?*

Hoss seemed to enjoy the presence of another Rifter, and although he spoke little, he never stopped them.

Looking out of the transparent window of the Navigation room, Ari saw the distant shapes of planets circling the warmth of their sun. Of those three, one was blue.

Water. Habitable, maybe. And if I'm not mistaken, it's in the proper region of orbit.

Ari turned towards Hoss, a question in their eyes that they were afraid to ask. He couldn't know their plans. None of them could.

Hoss watched them, looking into their eyes. And for just an instant, they thought he might have understood.

"You know, we Rift-walkers have a bad name because of people like you," he said after a lengthy pause.

Ari startled, eyes wide with surprise and momentary panic.

"Back when I served, we were respected among the Renohaiin," they said after a brief stutter.

"Maybe once. But not now. I had to fight hard in order to earn my place on this ship."

"Why would you want to?"

"Why wouldn't you? You can go anywhere at any time, and you have a crew to watch your tail. It's the best way to keep on Rifting, only with more freedom, and less fear." Hoss paused, little black eyes flickering. "I'd hoped it might help me find my way home, one day."

Ari blinked. "The perfect life for a Rifter, then."

"It would seem that way, wouldn't it? I serve under the condition that I may never leave except into domed cities, and always with the implant itching under my skin." With a small hand, Hoss gestured to the spiderweb of wires across his forehead, out of his reach. As Ari realised what it was, a terrifying shiver swept over them. They opened their mouth to speak, but Hoss continued. "The fact that I've survived longer than any of their generals means nothing. All it means to them is that I know how to be selfish, just like the rest."

Ari winced faintly. "When I served, the Rift was anomalous, and unknown. Rifters were rare, and revered."

Ari glanced away. They didn't respond for a while, so Hoss filled the silence for them. "How long have you survived out here, Rift-walker?"

Ari's lip quirked into a faint smile. "Thirty-seven star cycles," they said. "Many of them alone."

"Thirty-seven…" Hoss murmured, shaking his head. "I've lived three. Only a little longer than my kind's natural lifespan."

"My race lives less than a single star cycle."

"How? How have you made it that long?"

Ari shrugged. "Luck, mostly. Luck, and selfishness. I try not to burden myself with the problems of worlds when they don't concern me."

"Doesn't that bother you?"

"Hardly. I'm not harming anyone so long as they don't harm me. That's just the way it is."

"It doesn't have to be."

"What are you saying?"

Hoss' ears pricked for a moment. He opened his jaws for a second, reddish teeth flashing, then closed them again. "What do you think I'm saying?"

Ari turned away, back towards the well of stars and the milky way that bloomed as though alive beneath their fingertips. They didn't answer, but the question had stirred a creeping dread in their gut.

Perhaps this ship has escape pods that will even allow me to enter the Rift. It's a long shot, but if they do, then… Ari looked out beyond the planet and to the stars.

Perhaps I could even use it to get back to Earth.

Ari rose, and left Hoss to his work without saying another word.

Wandering at a slow meander back towards the Mess hall, the Riftmaster replayed in their minds everything they knew about the ship. They flicked through their memories of every room. Except, of course, for the generator room that they had yet to see. As they passed the generator room. Ari's hope suddenly rose.

In the old ships, they used two generators, one per engine. Now they only use one. But that's not including the lights, the controls, the power to the rest of the ship… and the coolants needed to keep it all there. The engine room is the most important room on the ship, and this seems like it would be far too small to contain so much equipment.

It has to lead to a lower wing, I'm sure of it.

They returned to an empty mess hall alone, and were deep in thought as they added the required amount of water to the blue tablet they had become accustomed to. As they drank yet more warm and bitter mulch, they thought again about everything they'd seen. The crew collecting samples from the plants and soil. Hoss receiving samples into the loading bay. A bay which they had *not* seen.

Ari swung their legs over the edge of the bench, downed the rest of their putrid meal, and looked towards the door.

They had to find a way down. There had to be *something*; a ladder, a hatch entrance, a hidden trapdoor. Anything. And it had to be hidden in the generator room.

Ari looked up abruptly as the whirring sound of a door opening reached their ears. Hastily relaxing, they turned to see Captain Malgas, stirring a cup of nutrients for herself.

She had noticed Ari's presence before they noticed her. Their eyes met. Ari hastily glanced away and lifted the broth to their lips. However, a soft clink told them that Malgas had placed herself next to them anyway.

Putting a safe distance between them, of course.

Although they tried not to show it, Ari found Malgas more than a little bit intimidating – though not for the reasons they would like anyone to think. Ari was not a jealous person. But she was tall, slender and her movements spoke of a lifetime of militaristic training. Her natural, chitinous armour shone; her species was perfectly adapted to a life among the stars, and Malgas was a prime example of that. Her expression was never anything less than severe, and she seemed absolutely unflappable.

They'd never spoken to her alone, before. They were almost afraid of what she'd say.

As Ari scrambled for a suitable greeting, the captain unexpectedly spoke first.

"It would seem you've made yourself at home," she said.

Ari breathed in a small amount of gruel and coughed it back up out of their nose. Regal as ever, they covered it up with the back of a hand. "Of course, of course. With no small thanks to you."

"No gratitude needed. It's been a pleasure having you on board, Navigator."

After wiping their nose, Ari smiled sheepishly. "Riftmaster, if you please. It's been a long time since I was a navigator."

"I know. The records say as much."

"They seem to say a lot, don't they?"

"More than you'd probably want to know."

Ari grunted nervously. "Do they say how I… left the position?"

"What, that you were fired?"

Ari's cheeks flushed bright red. "Not fired! Demoted!"

"That's just as dishonourable!" Malgas' mandibles wavered, but she clacked with mirth.

"Yeah, well… I became a trainer after that. I was too good to lose!"

"I know," Malgas said. "…And then you disappeared."

The smile left Ari's eyes. "Not intentionally." They glanced away. "Never intentionally."

When Malgas spoke again, her voice sounded gentle, but stern. "Riftmaster… What happened, truly?" She paused. "Omea tells me you were reluctant to answer him."

"It's… nothing really. Just… the Rift. You know how things are."

Malgas tapped her claws against the tabletop. Ari guessed that she was growing impatient. "It's been a long time, Riftmaster; I won't judge you. I won't tell the crew. And I won't update the records."

Ari realised then that they were being ordered.

"Oh, no. I didn't commit any crimes, if that's what you're implying. The ship went down on a training mission, that's all," Ari began tentatively. "We all escaped, but there was no way back to base. Communications were gone. I helped the rookies survive, and bound them to me in preparation for Rifting. Being a Rift-walker was in this case, both a blessing and a curse. We wouldn't stay on that planet long."

"So you took them with you." Malgas said in wonder. "How?"

"Rift-binding. My… I used to do it a lot. You tie around them a length of clothing or give them an item which has been with you through the Rift. I usually use my necklaces, because it has to be touching the skin."

"That seems… exceedingly simple. But it worked? For all of you?"

117

"For a time. I wasn't just… going to leave them out there. Nature would have had its way with them in a moment."

"…and then?"

Ari avoided Malgas' gaze for a moment before replying, voice even. "I left them on a Riftworld."

"You left them!?"

Ari paused briefly, between sips.

"Yes, I did. It's not as bad as it sounds. If you've ever visited a Riftworld, you'll know. There are towns, and traders, and taverns… Rifters tend to pick up the Renohaiin language, and you'll find nowhere safer than a Riftworld. It had everything they needed to lead a happy life… or to start trying to find their way home."

"And that was it, then?"

Ari lowered their gaze, and smiled grimly. "You ask that as if I had a choice. I'm a Rift-walker. I don't *have* that kind of luxury. If we kept going I would have had to keep driving them on, through countless hostile worlds… Keeping alive those shreds of hope that we might end up on a colonised planet, until they either died of old age or were picked off one by one by predatory lifeforms. And I know which outcome I prefer."

Wondering only briefly if Malgas found their curtness on the matter offensive, Ari hastily drowned the rest of their gruel to avoid further questions. Finally looking up to see Malgas' gaze still fixed on them, they let out a breath with a sigh.

"You've been through that before," Malgas said.

Ari froze, the hackles rising on the back of their neck. Their legs stiffened, but they forced themself to stay seated, and not react.

"Don't lie," Malgas said. "I can see you want to."

Something in Ari's stomach turned. Their insides quivered, vision blurred. "I was a parent." They finally said. "My children came with me through the Rift, but they got old. My… partner and I found them a safe world to live on. Star cycles later, I found what was left of them."

They fell silent.

118

Malgas did not reply for a time. "A parent," she echoed. "As a Rift-walker, I would have thought that impossible."

Ari sniffed, forcing a wan smile. "It wasn't always intentional."

"Ah. I would not know."

Ari nodded. They looked up at Malgas' face, their gaze trailing over the colourful tines of her crest. An egg-carrier… a parent, or someone who planned to be. "Are you a parent, Malgas?"

It was now her turn to hesitate. "Yes. I am," she said quietly. "I was a progenitor on one of our most advanced colonies. The last time I saw it, there were vast and sprawling cities among cultivated oases. Most stayed there, turning it into a new hearth world. But some became captains of their own ships. I watched all of their first flights."

Along with the unmistakable hint of pride, there was something else in Malgas' tone.

Even between two species with light years of separation, there were some things that never changed.

Ari noticed that without realising it, the two had drawn nearer to one another. Ari finished the rest of their gruel without pulling away.

Malgas began to eat as well, sucking up the fluid through a narrow tube. They waited until she paused before speaking again.

"How long will it be now, do you think, before we reach the base?"

"Only two rotations. Not long at all."

That's two sleep cycles, for me. Ari felt a shudder run from the tips of their fingers down to their toes. The journey felt as though it had passed in an instant. Recovery had blurred the days into weeks. And now it was almost over.

"Since we're almost there, Malgas… Could you at least tell me why you kept me here?"

"You have quite the rich history, Riftmaster," Malgas said tentatively. "We… thought that the Renohaiin empire could learn a lot –"

Ari smiled sweetly. "I don't believe you. I'm more trouble than I'm worth, and we both know it. Omea knows it. Even the records know it."

Malgas was taken aback. In her faltering silence, the Riftmaster knew that they'd snared her in her own lie.

"I'm sorry, Riftmaster. I don't…" With no one else to fall back on, Malgas turned back to her gruel, inching away from them. "I don't have the authority to share that information."

"All right," Ari relented. "It was worth one more try."

"You'll understand soon enough. If nothing else, I do promise that it will be worth it." Malgas blinked. "Can you trust me, Riftmaster?"

"I… I'm not sure. But I suppose I have no choice."

Doubt shadowed the corners of their eyes. As Malgas replaced her straw, Ari excused themself and rose. Malgas' mandibles quirked as she nodded a farewell – leaving Ari to feel a faint fizzle of aggravation.

As they wandered back down the corridor towards the med bay that had become their home, they knew without a doubt that they needed to find out the truth. More than that, they needed to find a way off the ship.

Ari slept, ate, and slept again, their thoughts frenzied with pent up energy and useless plans. One rotation to go. Not much time. They paced in their room, feverish with the need to go.

As welcome as the crew had fought to make them feel, there was something sinister in the way they coyly dodged around details. Ari was cargo. They were valuable. The fact that they had served only made it easier to pretend there was another reason to keep them aboard.

Ari examined the med bay with renewed scrutiny. Searching for all the things that had been used to pull them back from the brink. Anything sharp, anything they could use. They searched in vain for the glass transfusion orb that had pumped sterile alien lifeblood into their veins.

But they were nowhere to be found. Hidden smartly away, somewhere out of their reach.

Ari needed the crew to bring it out again. And soon.

It was only a day before their precious cargo would reach its destination. The crew couldn't risk losing it so close to their goal… could they?

Omea came to check on Ari as he always did when they awoke, bringing them nourishment. But this time, they dragged out their motions while insisting that they were fine. Drawing out the worry. Lying with the truth.

Omea had very little choice. He stuck around to prepare some instruments, performing some final checks.

Ari waited until Omea turned his back, and dropped the container to the floor. A splatter of blue liquid flew in all directions and Omea spun round in fright. Sadly, the bowl didn't break.

"I… I'm sorry, Omea. Maybe I'm not as well as I thought."

"How do you feel?"

"Dizzy… Nauseous… weak…" They shook their head. "I suppose I'm more nervous than I thought. Would you like me to help clean up?"

"No need. Should I prepare for another transfusion?"

"No… I… Maybe later. Perhaps a short walk will help. I'm terribly sorry."

Ari waited until Omea had opened the door for them, before stepping out for their walk. With an exasperated clacking sound, Omea began the long task of cleaning down the medbay whilst they were gone. Ari wandered. They looked once again down every corridor and dead end, but found nothing. The doors to most important rooms were locked; a stranger would not be allowed to access them unauthorised.

The mess hall was the only one they really had clearance for. The navigation room, maybe. And even then, they needed Hoss' help to get in.

Ari wandered, pacing for a time, and stopped in front of a locked door.

The engine room *had* to contain a way down to the lower deck. Unless the entire crew used hidden vents, there was nowhere else it could be.

And even if it didn't, well… what choice did they have now?

Ari slowly made their way back towards the med bay. The door was closed, presumably for a complete sterilisation. Perfect.

Backing away, Ari made their way towards the cantina. They entered the room, leaning heavily against the door frame for a brief moment, as though trying to hide it. They moved, and began to slowly prepare another meal as they took in the surroundings.

There were only a few around today. Ari glanced around. Hoss sat at a far-too-big chair, stuffing rounded cheeks with a greenish paste. The engineer was tending some wires nearby, and as though she sensed something wrong, Malgas stood.

"Captain Malgas," they said softly.

Their captain looked up, and then moved towards them cautiously. "Riftmaster– you look… unwell. Are you alright?"

"Actually, I… I was hoping to go for a walk, when my head began to spin. I very much need access to the medbay, but the door… it's locked."

They did not sound quite so pitiful as to indicate a clear farce. They spoke quietly, yet matter-of-factly. They paused for a long moment before continuing.

"I thought I was going to be fine. But it's getting worse."

Malgas approached them. As she placed a hand against their back, they grunted, and leaned their full weight into her, bringing the bowl of slop to their chest.

They looked up at her as if in a daze.

"You are worried about reaching the space station." Malgas said. "Try not to be afraid. That will only make it worse."

"The sickness… the one you found me with. You didn't cure me, did you?"

Malgas did not respond.

She held them upright, and supported thcm as they walked. A small groan escaped their lips. Soon they found themself laid down once more with two gentle arms supporting them. Another two gently removed the food from their grasp. Ari didn't open their eyes. Their breaths quickened to match their racing heart.

They heard the clinking sound of Malgas preparing equipment. Their heart raced and they fought to steady their breaths. *Come on, leave! How can I get you to leave?*

Their breaths faltered. Then they spoke.

"Am I dying, Malgas?" they asked faintly, just barely managing to hide a smile.

Too much? If she calls my bluff, this is all over.

But their plea seemed to scare the Renohaiin captain into action.

"Stay where you are," she said, putting down her tools. "I'll call Omea."

"W-wait! Malgas…"

The door fizzed open, and closed. Her clicking footsteps echoed away down the hall.

Ari sat up. They seized their abandoned bowl of nourishment, threw some at their face and the rest at their bed. Then they kicked the equipment down.

The equipment that the Captain had been using was only half readied. They seized it. The transfusion orb shattered into pieces, and they hid a shard of glass beneath their cloak. Then they hurtled themself down onto the bedframe, looking very much like someone in their death throes. They gasped for breath, eyes clamped shut, and sprawled as though mid-struggle.

They heard the door slide open, and then closed. Ari didn't move until they heard someone racing to their bedside. As they cracked their eyes open, they saw Omea enter the room, and to their relief, he was alone. "Malgas," they gasped fervently, opening eyes wide. "Where is she?"

"She needs to pilot the ship. She'll be a while – but don't worry, I'm here now–"

Ari waited until the medic knelt by their bedside, frantically preparing liquid and tubes that were already attuned to their systems. In that momentary lapse of caution, when he was seized with panic they lunged, grabbing Omea by the neck and whipping the glass shard from its hiding place.

Moments later, and Ari was upright, pressing Omea up against the wall. They pressed the shard into the joint between Omea's exoskeletal plates, where the tender throat flexed beneath. "If you dare scream, you'll never make another sound again. Understand?"

Omea's genuine fear as he looked into their face, splattered with blue, and twisted with anger, sent a wave of guilt crashing through their chest. But Ari needed to know the truth. They would not allow themself to be taken in before they even knew where they were going, and why.

Shaking mandibles clacked an affirmative.

They slowly released their grip on the medic's windpipe.

"Now tell me why you need me."

Omea hesitated, eyes wide with fright. A thin membrane flicked over his eyes, mandibles twitched, but he didn't speak. "Omea..." they said softly, warningly, twitching the shard of glass so that he briefly felt its bite.

Omea scrambled to answer. "It wasn't you we were looking for. It's a chemical in your bloodstream. Your cells contain traces of Iridium, which should have killed you. There are very few creatures that have managed to incorporate Iridium into their natural biology, and I'm assuming yours is not one of them."

"...That's correct," Ari said, at length.

"As I suspected."

"Then... what happened?"

"The change is caused by only one creature in the known universe... a parasite. It produces chemicals which alter the structure of your cells to–"

The medic's words faded from Ari's ears. Suddenly their stomach dropped, and they felt as though they knew where this was going. They remembered the body that they'd found in the swamp, which their armour had been taken from. The chunks taken out of local flora flashed into their mind, and the island cleaned of almost everything alive. The recently-dead creature which seemed to have been starving before being crushed by the tree it was feeding on.

There had been no way, then, to test the chemical compounds of the creature's blood… but there was a strong chance their tests would have warned them of the toxins in its blood.

Ari shook their head and forced themself to listen to Omea's terrified babbling.

"– the parasite's influence means you can absorb nutrients from things you wouldn't normally, and moreover–"

They felt their gut sink, but almost laughed out loud in terrified mania.

"I… I have a p… A parasite?"

"That's right."

They shook him by the shoulders. "Where?!"

Omea clattered frightfully, but gestured down towards their belly.

Ari froze for a moment. As if in a trance, they removed their cloak, and tied Omea's four arms to his sides before gagging him through the mandibles with a diagonal strip of fabric. The medic protested, stifled squeaks emerging from beneath the hide.

Ari turned their back on him, pacing erratically, breathing fast. *I have to get it out.*

They heard the medic struggling against his bindings. If they went through with this, would their body begin to return to normal? What about the Renohaiin food still in their body? Horror slid through every vein, their skin crawled at the thought of something living inside of them. *I don't care if it's useful. I'm not spending another second being a vessel for this thing.*

Their own emotions were joined by a feeling of confusion and a flash of fear, and this time they knew that it wasn't their own. Ari's head spun, stomach clamping hard with nausea. As though the parasite felt their intent, they also felt the soothing touch of comforting calm, like

125

a mother cat's gentle licks. The feeling made them hesitate, but only for a moment.

The damn thing is manipulating me.

Finally they stalked over to the corner of the medicine room, took a deep breath, and jammed their fingers into their throat.

The process was quick, and unpleasant.

Soon they found themself kneeling and gasping over a pool of blue liquid. Finally, they reached out and sifted through the mess with shaking fingertips. The Riftmaster could already see that there was a lump in the otherwise liquid pool. And it was *moving*. They pinched it between thumb and forefinger, and lifted out a slime-covered worm, roughly the size of a clenched fist. It had a squished, puglike face, and six huge eyes; Ari might have thought it cute in any other circumstances. Six stubby feet searched in vain for ground. With droopy little jowls, a mouth void of any sort of teeth and wrinkled, maggot-like skin, it was clear the creature was never meant to survive out here.

Ari spat a blue glob at the wall, wiped their mouth with the back of a hand and stalked over to Omea, ripping the gag from between his mandibles. "If you want it, have it," they snapped, shoving the dripping parasite in the medic's face. "Just let me go!"

"We can't!"

"Look! I didn't ask for this. I've been complacent, but I'm politely asking you to take back your damn worm. *Please*."

Omea shook his head.

"The Renohaiin system can only handle liquid nourishment, there's no way any of us could swallow *that*. And bar that, what do you think has been making our food edible? By removing it now, you'll *die*."

"You're not serious."

But the realisation was dawning. Ari lifted up the squirming creature to look into its eyes. It let out a pitiful squelch.

"Ick!"

Ari threw the creature onto the floor, their skin

crawling. The little creature bounced once, then curled into a terrified ball. They slowly looked up at the sound of Omea's voice.

"I am serious."

"So you need me to host it. What will you do then?"

"We'll do whatever it takes to keep it alive until we can safely extract its venom."

"Venom?" Ari felt a cold chill. "What about me?"

"You…" Omea trailed off. "You need be alive for the parasite to survive. We'll do everything we can to keep you that way."

"But… the venom… You're going to trigger its death struggle, when it can kill something like…" With a flash of horror, Ari remembered the creature crushed under the fallen tree. Its hide like steel, and its bones iron-like. Huge as a draft horse, with six stocky limbs. "…*that*?"

"The venom has not evolved to work on creatures like you. You've survived small doses before. I'm… sure you will again."

"What do you mean, I've survived it before?"

"The parasite reacts to strong emotions like fear or anger. If the host is in danger, the parasite will react by trying to eject itself… usually killing the host." Omea swallowed. "Like when we found you."

Ari paced. Back and forth, back and forth. This explained everything. The sickness, the nausea, and everything in between. Finally they looked up.

"I almost didn't survive, Omea… What if next time I'm not so lucky…?"

"You'll save thousands of lives, Riftmaster. Is that not enough?"

At that moment, they recalled Malgas' words. *It will all be worth it.*

For what? Were the Renohaiin really planning on using the venom to save lives, or were they just planning on using it to build weapons for conquest? For the Renohaiin empire, saving and killing people could be virtually indistinguishable. Ari realised that they didn't want to know.

Ari looked down at the creature, and then to Omea. Their expression hardened. "I don't care about saving lives if I'm not there to see it. Now… tell me how to leave the ship."

"There's no way–"

"The ship must have escape pods. No fleet captain would be stupid enough to go without. Tell me how to get to them."

"Riftmaster–"

"I don't want to needlessly harm you, Omea. But this can be a lot more painful than it needs to be." Ari yanked one of Omea's arms out of their bindings, and the Renohaiin's optic membranes fluttered fearfully. Ari extended the medic's hand and held it steady. They felt their fingers shaking but tried not to let it show. The medic's insectoid digits quivered, as though he knew what was coming.

"Okay! Okay… There's a ladder in the generator room down to the passages that the engineers use to tend the engines. The cargo hold is down there too, at the back of the ship. The pods are loaded into the exit chutes, accessible only by crew…" Omea trailed off, mandibles trembling. "Please…" he said again, softer this time. "You don't need to do this."

Ari felt the palms of Omea's hand, soft and slightly furred beneath the exoskeleton of his knuckles. Four segmented fingers tried desperately to curl away, shimmering steel blue in the sterile half-light. Ari ran their fingers over the joint between hand and wrist, where the exoskeleton split.

They felt sick to the stomach and struggled to keep their hands from shaking. "Thank you, Omea," Ari said, avoiding looking into his four terrified eyes. "And… I'm so, so sorry…"

Their grip tightened on the shard of glass.

"Wait–!"

"…But I'm dying on my terms, not yours."

Ari reached for the gag and steadied their breaths as they tied it back in place through Omea's mandibles.

128

Before they could think, they clamped their eyes shut, and then snapped the medic's wrist at the break between exoskeletal plates. A quick twist, and a surgical slice, and they held his severed hand in their palm.

Ari heard a scream force its way out from under the gag.

"Don't worry, it'll grow back," they said, although their voice betrayed the guilt. Heart pounding in their ears, they tore a strip of hide from their cape to carefully bind the wound, as best they could. It was rough, but they knew when the rest of the crew found him, he'd receive the proper care.

They took in the sight of him, tightly bound in their cape, and shivered slightly.

I told you this was the most important part.

Slowly, Ari stood, picking up the parasite in their palm. As they looked at it, a surprising swell of pity twinged their lips. The creature shuddered, curling in on itself against the cold, but as they lifted it, it huddled into the warmth of their hand, like a child huddling against its mother. Time would tell if they really would die without it, but… they supposed it would be best to take it with them, just in case.

This isn't your fault, anyway. Nasty little thing, but you are just doing what you were made to do. Ari let out a sigh of resignation. *Perhaps we can even find you a new host out there. Someone who doesn't know enough to care.*

They placed it against their chest, and then after a moment's consideration, slipped it into a fold in their underarmour. Their leather belts should keep it out of trouble, while their skin kept it warm and safe. They felt it squirm a little, then settled into a comfortable spot at the curve in the centre of their chest.

Finally, they raised Omea's hand, unfurled the fingers, and placed it in the indentations by the door. With a hiss, the way opened up, and Ari hesitated. "I really am sorry," they said, before stepping out. "But you have to understand, you are practically strangers to me."

The door slid closed behind them, and Ari let out a

breath. Hiding the severed hand and the shard of glass under their chestplate, they slunk away from the medbay, and hoped that they would be lucky as they made their escape.

Chapter 8
The Flight

Ari hurried through the corridors, their footsteps quick and silent as the grave. Every time they turned a corner, they expected someone to be waiting around the bend. Every moment of silence they expected a warning siren's wail.

As they rounded the final bend before the engine room, Ari passed someone coming the opposite way, and as they saw the blue-grey carapace and wide, blue eyes, their heart almost stopped. How had the medic escaped? Then they took a breath.

Instinctively, they bent forward as though in pain. Face still splattered with blue, they certainly looked the part.

"Osai," they called, over the deep hum of the ship's engine as they tried to still their hammering heart.

Omea's clutchmate dipped his head slightly. "Riftmaster. It's a surprise to see you. Malgas said you were sick."

Ari nodded. "Still am. But feeling a little bit better now."

"Is that so?"

"Mm-hm."

"Well, I can't imagine Omea would let you leave the medbay if you were still unwell."

Before them was the engine room; but they couldn't

possibly access it with Osai here. They thought quickly.

"Omea… has had an accident. The transfusion orb fell. He…" Ari paused to gather their thoughts, closing their eyes briefly. "He was injured, and some important instruments have been compromised. It was of the utmost importance that I get help while he stayed to salvage what he could. You should go to him."

Osai blinked. "Why didn't you inform me sooner?"

"I am… in pain… and not well versed in emergency etiquette. Quickly, now. I must go to the cockpit and inform the captain."

"You shouldn't be upright. I should get her."

"N-no… There might… Malgas could have emergency equipment that could help me."

"The labs…" Osai clacked, but trailed off.

Ari hunched over slightly. Their voice was only a little above a whisper. "I… don't have clearance."

Osai stared at them for a moment, and they briefly wondered if he knew.

"Go to your brother," they said finally, pleadingly. "He needs you. And I… I need him, too."

Osai looked into their eyes for a moment longer. Finally, though, he turned on his heel and hurried away.

They waited until his footsteps had receded, then spun around and hurried the rest of the way towards the engine room.

They had to be quick.

Ari pulled Omea's hand out from under their breastplate, unfurled its fingers, and placed them into the correct slots. The door hissed open before them, and they quickly shut it behind them. A wave of searing heat and sulfur-scent hit them squarely in the face.

They stepped into the generator room and closed the door behind them, plunging them into half-light.

Before them, generators roared. Coolant and bio-reactive fluid pulsed through tubes of clear silicone, and they felt the engine thrumming with tremors through the crystal plates beneath their feet. Ari ignored it all, hurrying forward.

When they finally found the stairs that Omea had mentioned, they could have cried out with relief. Already, they felt sweat beading on their forehead, feeling like they had been sitting in raw sunlight for hours.

The ladder wound disorientingly around the edge of the cylinder-shaped room beneath them. Ari hurried down, letting themself drop as soon as they knew they could land safely. At the bottom, they opened another door with Omea's severed hand.

They stepped past it into a wide corridor that was marginally less hot than the engine room. They bounded past branching pathways to restricted and storage rooms.

Cargo hold, cargo… Aha!

They almost cried out with relief as one final door opened up into a room that made up the belly of the ship. Before them were stored crates, emergency supplies, and of course the sustenance pills that kept the crew alive. But there were more important things to find. Ari wove through a labyrinth of boxes, panting and glancing wildly around. And finally, they found what they were looking for. They swung their satchel over their shoulder, and were relieved to find their dagger nestled in its depths. Finally they looked around for their spear. Unable to see it, Ari backed away, satchel swinging at their side. *I don't have time to keep searching. I can only hope it's been hidden further inside.*

They placed down the shard of glass in its place.

Of course, the only thing they truly needed to find was a way off the ship.

But perhaps while they were here, they could buy themself valuable time. In all likelihood, the cargo hold held more than enough nourishment for multiple journeys. But if they could cut down that supply, they could force the crew on an emergency supply run, buying Ari precious time to get lost in the Rift.

Perhaps the escape pod would even be able to take them home to Earth.

Ari didn't want to cause any significant damage to the crew or their livelihoods. Just a major inconvenience.

They looked around, carefully searching among the stored goods for something they could use. But any sort of engine fuel would be carefully stored away from anything flammable. Ari dug in their satchel for a moment, and pulled out a small bundle of tester herbs.

It pained them just to think about using it as kindling… but it would have to do.

Fumbling at their neck, Ari removed a shard of Mountain-dweller's horn and a fragment of Oliver's knife. Then, they stuffed their satchel full of as many sustenance pills they could carry, replaced them with leaves, and struck a spark. The pills burned with thick and acrid smoke. It would buy them time; but it would also lead the crew straight to them.

Ari had to move.

Even though the lower deck of the ship was notably smaller than the upper one, the cargo hold still felt massive. But if they could just find the pods…

They slunk once more through stacked boxes and supplies, weaving their way to the edge of the room, where they followed the folded ramp.

It wouldn't be here. Omea said they're at the back of the ship.

Ari's thoughts were cut off as a shrill siren tone began, ringing through their very bones and startling them into moving quicker. A few white lights flashed into life, casting stark shadows around the cargo hold from the boxes and crates, playing tricks on Ari's eyes. Omea had been found. They had to squash a momentary flood of relief; the poor medic really didn't deserve to be in pain, but, by extension, neither did they.

It wouldn't take long for the crew to work out where they'd gone. Omea had told them, and Osai had seen them; and it was only a matter of time before their movements would be tracked. That is, if they weren't already.

Ari hurried along the edge of the cargo hold, their grip tight on the disembodied wrist they held, almost as though it would help to keep them safe. They hadn't got much further when they heard the first shout from their pursuers

"What's burning!?"

"It's the pills! Hoss! Put it out!" barked someone. The faint echoing tap of claws reached their ears before another voice barked "Find the Rift-walker! Subdue it by any means necessary!"

Ari's blood ran cold. Dropping their head, they ran faster, slinking like a fox towards the end of the ship.

Movement.

Ari wasn't sure if it was a rogue shadow or a crew member, but they drew their knife anyway. With the siren wailing, its telltale hiss was inaudible.

They sprinted to duck behind a chute.

A crate beside them burst open, scattering pills all over the pristine floor. Ari ducked, and ran.

"Don't shoot! We need them both alive!" the voice seemed to come from nowhere, and everywhere.

"Flanking!"

They're trying to drive me, like sheepdogs herding sheep. But it's not going to work.

Finally, they reached a dead end, and the telltale curvature of a massive door.

"Move in! Get it away from there!"

Ari fumbled around the edges of the frame, feeling around with Omea's cold fingers until they found the slots.

There was a hiss, and a click. The door began to slide open, agonisingly slow. Ari squashed themself through before it had finished opening, and then shoved it closed once more.

A semicircular room lay beyond, and Ari cast their gaze about frantically, sides heaving. Amid the flashing lights and the crushing fear, they saw the outlines of chutes arranged in a semicircle, in appearance like enormous tubes half-buried in the vessel floor. The pods would be contained within, ready to go at any moment. Each individually sized for the crew member that was supposed to pilot them.

A docking bay… yes!

Ari moved between each of the doors, pressing Omea's hand into each slot until… yes!

Just as the doors began to open, Ari crammed themself into an escape pod and strapped themself down, lying lengthways and gazing up at a dark control panel. They frantically hammered at the buttons, but nothing stirred. They felt sweat beginning to bead on their forehead. Their sides heaved; until Ari noticed a darkened hollow in the centre of the control panel. Of course.

They shoved the hand, one last time, into the central hollow, and one by one, the buttons pulsed into life, light shining in waves over the control panel. Finally a pair of digital screens lit up. A radar. The control panel was like nothing they'd used before, but even still, they thought back to what they knew.

"Get it, get it!" Malgas shrieked, her clattering voice trembling through the walls of the chute. "Stop the pressure!"

Oh, give me strength. Eject, eject!

Ari struck at the buttons with all the force they had left, and they felt the walls of the escape pod closing in around them, securing them. The little creature in their clothing let out a little squelch of fear, and huddled into their chest, but they could provide no comfort.

Come on! Let's go!

They heard something scraping at the chute outside, but the process had already begun. There was the faint hiss of escaping gases, and then Ari felt their stomach lurch up into their chest.

Ari was pressed between crystal and sheet metal, a thin layer of uncomfortable fabric standing between them and the cold walls beyond. They closed their eyes as they were launched out into space. And then they were alone.

***

Malgas' limbs felt tight with rage. Her mandibles shook, gaze dark with the membranes shading her eyes. How could they have been so foolish? How could *she* have been so foolish?

She had thought that the Riftmaster had started to relax around them. Trust them, even. Rift-walkers were selfish; there had never been any doubt in her mind about that. To survive for that long, there had to be some degree of separation between yourself and others. But for an instant, Malgas had thought there was a reasonable creature hiding beneath its hot-blooded shell. Likeable, even.

And that was what enraged her the most.

It must have been toying with her. With all of them. It had used the knowledge that they needed it alive to trick and swindle the crew of the *Vestige*. Leaving them stranded miles from home, having decimated their supplies to ensure they wouldn't follow. But more than that, the Rift-walker had mutilated the very medic who had brought it back from the brink.

And yet… *Malgas* was the one who had believed its lie. She was the one who gave it that opportunity. It should have been her with an arm bound. Or it should have been her to stop it from happening.

Malgas let out a hiss, releasing the pressure that had built up in her chest. The crew surrounded her, looking towards her for their next orders. It seemed that each one was afraid to speak first, so after a lash of her tail, she spoke for them. "This isn't over yet. Help Hoss put out the fire."

"That won't be necessary, captain."

The short, stocky Rift-walker appeared in the entrance of the docking bay. His off-white fur was stained with soot, ears laid back. "The fires are out."

Malgas relaxed slightly. She nodded appreciatively, lower arms falling to her sides. She turned to the rest of the crew.

"Thank you, Hoss… In that case, salvage whatever you can and recalculate our supplies. We need to know how long we can last so we can hunt this creature down."

As Nuudren and Eidhoin scrambled to obey, Malgas beckoned Hoss with her tail. "Walk with me. I'm going to check on Omea."

Hoss lowered his ears, and hopped slowly alongside her, his jerking motions casting him a little ahead of her with every jump. "I'm sorry I couldn't be any more help, Captain." Hoss said, when they were out of earshot.

The ship rumbled beneath Malgas' insectoid digits as Ganir began to turn the ship towards the wayward escape pod. Malgas' mandibles quivered in frustration.

"It wasn't your responsibility, Hoss."

"You are angry, still."

"Not at you."

"Then, who?"

"I acted outside of my training, and endangered all of us."

"Such is the nature of this mission, Captain. It is… not often… we must go to such extreme lengths to avoid hurting something. We cannot neutralise this target, or it may die. We cannot scare it, or it might die. We must act with the utmost caution… but in this case, it seems we showed too much."

"That… is true." Malgas flexed her mandibles as she considered. "Hoss? You were a Rift-walker. What do you make of this one?"

Hoss considered. "I don't think it was feigning everything. I think it liked to look at the stars, and enjoyed being a navigator again. I think it liked the company, too. But… Perhaps it has just lived so long that it cannot imagine handing its future over to someone else."

Malgas grunted. "…Or perhaps it has something out there that it can't afford to lose."

***

Ari felt dizzy with relief, but they knew they weren't out of the woods yet. They settled their grip on what they took to be the joysticks, slowly turned the pod, and engaged the thrusters. Something spluttered into life, and the pod lurched forward, spinning out of control in empty space.

Nope, nope! Wrong button, wrong button!

Ari rapidly became dizzy. They struggled to stabilise, seeing the ship flash repeatedly by in their small window of vision. Finally, they managed to slow the spinning, and then stop, thrusters angling so that they burst briefly towards the *Vestige* before banking away.

Okay, okay. I'm back on track.

They frantically pushed more buttons.

Come on, how do we Rift? Can we Rift? I have to get away from the ship.

They saw the parasite float across their vision with a small squeak, tiny legs reaching hopelessly for empty air.

We have to get away from the ship.

They reached out, scooping the little creature out of the air, and brought it to rest atop their head. Tiny claws wound their way into the Riftmaster's auburn hair.

As they fumbled with the buttons, Ari felt themself squirming uncomfortably against the cold, hard space around them. It was not designed with comfort in mind. *Though I suppose comfort has a different meaning when you have an exoskeleton.*

A moment later, they heard a click, and a faint whirring sound.

Ah… Aha! I have it! Ari had to quell the urge to yell with triumph, wanting to preserve what little air they had. But their grip tightened, they reached upwards, and pulled a lever above their head.

Their field of view faded into whiteness. Ari felt the pain of the Rift, along with a feeling like being torn clean in two. They felt the pod lurch forward as though falling, gravity pulling them onwards. Finally, they hit the ground with a judder, the pod rolling to an unsteady halt in a crater of its own making.

The pain lingered under their skin; when they raised a trembling hand, the veins snaking down their wrist were aglow.

Well… they thought at length. *…That's new.*

With some difficulty, Ari opened the hatch, and found themself blinking in bright sunlight. They heaved in desperate breaths, gulping the cool, sharp air. A vast plain stretched out before them, rippling in the wind. Shining grasses and heathers shone in hues of steel blue, shimmering beneath the sky like an ocean. Distant rock formations were silhouetted against the setting sun. They looked up, into a lime-green sky that was ribboned with clouds, and felt their spirit swell. A fine sprinkling of rain washed the sweat from their skin.

They stood upright, but found their legs shaking too much to support their weight.

So finally, they settled down on the nose of the escape pod. They felt a little tug on their hair, and raised a hand to gently lift the parasite from their head. Now that it was dry, its skin was soft as velvet, and it looked towards the sun with all of its eyes narrowed against the brightness that it so rarely saw.

As the wind played softly with the curls of their hair and the rain swept a shimmering curtain of rainbow light across the plain, Ari finally let out their breath.

They'll never catch us now.

Chapter 9
Fugitives

Ari rested by the crashed escape pod, taking in the sight of the wind creeping over the grass and revelling in the feeling of solid ground beneath their feet. They waited until they had recovered as much strength as they could.

But the feeling of the Rift lingered in their skin, burning, itching, fizzing in the back of their neck. They reached up to scratch it and felt something cold and hard beneath their fingertips. *What is that!?*

Ari scratched and tugged, hooking their nails under the object and wrenching it off of their skin. Pain lanced through the back of their skull. Fluid poured down their shoulders, and Ari threw the object to the ground.

Fragments of broken rift crystal gleamed wickedly up at them, flickering faintly in the dark among a tangle of bloodied wires.

A rift crystal? their blood ran cold. *...They put the implant in me. The same one as Hoss had.*

They didn't want me to know about this. They were trying to prevent my escape.

Ari raised their hand and rubbed the back of their neck. A splinter remained half-buried under the flesh. They hooked their nails under it, trying to claw it from the wound, but only managed to drive it deeper.

It throbbed with itching, stinging pains. When they lowered their hand, it was covered with blood. Their breaths were heaving, their throat tight. Ari dug in their satchel and pulled out a scrap of fabric. They pressed it to the wound, and felt the sharpness of its point against their palm as they examined the knot of bloodied wires and alien tech.

In the meantime, they had other things to worry about.

As long as this stays stuck in me, I won't be able to enter the Rift.

Although their limbs screamed for a rest, their heart throbbed with adrenaline. They needed to put as much distance between the escape pod and themself as possible. *There might have been a tracker on board,* they forced their breaths to stay calm, thoughts reasonable. *But tracker signals take days to travel across systems, weeks to travel light years. They won't catch up to me for a long time yet.*

Before they left, they paced around the outside of the pod, desperate for a way into its shell to find anything useful – especially the Rift Crystals that undoubtedly powered it. With them, Ari might have been able to force the Rift to open, and perhaps even follow their traces back to their home planet once more. But the panels were tightly secured, its shell welded with meteorite metal and sealed tight against pressure loss and debris. They tried and failed for a few long minutes to open it up from both the inside and out. But with only a few sparse supplies on their person and nothing that could possibly pry open the panels on a spaceship, Ari finally gave up.

Their hope of using the pod to return to Earth gradually faltered and died.

I have to get away from this place. The sooner, the better.

The Riftmaster had plenty of food, and a filled waterskin. But they needed shelter. Then they could take the time to think. They had the crystal cluster against their chest and one still stuck in their neck. Somehow, they would need to find a way to power them. Then, and only then, could they begin to make their way offworld. Ari doubted that the vessel would be able to locate them then. They'd just have to be more cautious when it came to approaching ships in future. The Renohaiin empire would definitely remember that they had mutilated an innocent medic, and took something the Empire deemed important.

...Knowing the Empire, that's probably a good thing.

Ari set off towards a series of jagged rocks rising from the plain – small mountains ribbed with bands of colour. There, perhaps, they would find a cave.

Banks of clouds rolled overhead across the lime-green sky, occasionally showering them with a swirl of misty rain.

As Ari walked, they felt their body shift, though. At first, a dull fog began to settle in over their brain, and a lethargy crept into their muscles that made it harder and harder to keep going. Then Ari's stomach began to turn in knots. Sickness rose with wretched familiarity into their throat. *Not again,* they thought, as suddenly they began to fear that the medic was right. *Could it be true that the parasite was the only thing keeping me alive?*

The sun had long set by the time that Ari reached the foot of the barren formations. They explored, gathering some materials for a campfire, even though they knew that the smoke would give away their position. *Still... Helps to be prepared.*

Finally, they sank down in a hollow in the rock and curled up, crossing their hands across their belly, and letting out an audible groan. *Feeling like this, and I can't even warm myself by the fire.*

Feeling something brush against their skin, Ari glanced down, and the face of the parasite popped out from under the fabric resting against their collarbone.

They met its gaze, imagining those big eyes pleading them to do the unthinkable.

Ari shivered, feeling all the more sick, and turned away. They rifled in their satchel for a moment, emptying out the pouch of pills into the bottom of their bag. In the depths, they saw the cold gleam of the pommel of their knife. They smiled half-heartedly. *Ah yes,* they thought resignedly. *The one thing Malgas should have confiscated.*

After a moment's consideration, Ari lifted the dagger, sheath and belt from their satchel, and pulled their breastplate off over their head. They tugged the knot of their scaled bodysuit undone at the back of their neck. Letting their clothing fall to expose their bare torso to the cold, they gently removed the parasite and set it down beside them.

Shuddering slightly, Ari wound a belt around their ribcage and pulled it tight, sheathing the knife against the curve of their chest. When they tied their scaled suit back into place, Ari was confident that the weapon couldn't be seen. So long as the Renohaiin continued to assume that their scales were no more than a second skin, they would be safe.

The pommel felt cold against their skin, though, and the leather felt clammy, almost as though it was still coated in a layer of blood.

Ari shook their head. *Now is not the time; I have far bigger concerns than this.*

Finally, Ari reached to their side, picked up the worm by gently pinching the skin along its back, and dropped it into a leather pouch. A moment later, they tugged the pouch closed.

"There – dark, enclosed, and warm. Just like being in my belly, right?" they asked hopefully. A small squelch answered, and the bag wriggled briefly as the worm fought to escape. Ari gently set it down, and waited for it to grow still.

I'll give it until the morning, Ari decided, slowly stretching out in their refuge. *Maybe I'll feel better then.* They winced as another pain ran through them, but forced their eyes to close. Ari feared that they may never sleep, but as soon as the adrenaline had ceased pumping through their veins, their breaths evened and their body stilled.

They were asleep before they even had the chance to acknowledge their exhaustion, and this time they dreamed no dreams.

Ari awoke to the brightness of daylight, and squinted against the sunshine filtering into their little hollow. They raised a hand and brushed it over their belly, perking up as no pains answered them. *Aha! He was wrong!*

They sat upright, a grin stealing across their lips.

I'm fine on my own! I don't need–

Their gaze fell on the pouch that they had placed by the fireside. It had folded in on itself, the drawstring prised open from within.

Ari seized the pouch in both hands and looked inside.

It was empty.

Ari frantically looked around them. "Little thing? Creature?"

Where could it be? They asked themself, although they had a terrible feeling that they already knew. *How the f–*

A sharp sting of emotion cut them off, loud inside their head. It was happy! Joyous! Grateful!

Ari clamped their eyes shut, and heaved a sigh. "Okay, I suppose I can't argue," they muttered. "You can stay."

As though it understood, Ari winced as they felt another sharp jab of happiness. *I'm home!* they imagined it saying, *Yay!*

A moment later, Ari let out a faint chuckle, punctuated by disbelief. *I'm talking to a parasitic worm. This has got to be a new low.*

Ari tried to shut the little beast out, shuddering.

That being said, there were certainly worse things to be ailed with in the Rift. The little creature could even be helpful; the ability to eat almost anything was something they could have benefitted from a lot over the years.

Ari supposed that the pair of them could reach a state of peaceful symbiosis. It would be nice feeling as though they weren't quite so alone, too. They shuffled around in the hollow for a moment, pulling out a bowl and a sustenance pill from the depths of their satchel. They dropped the pill into the bowl with a gentle clatter, and then with a few drops from their waterskin, they soaked it through. Ari watched in fascination as it swelled, fizzed, and thickened. Soon, Ari was settled back with a bowl full of thin gruel, sipping it occasionally, and wincing at the bitter taste. The pills weren't exactly ideal, and wouldn't nourish them for long, but they would at least last until Ari managed to find a more nourishing and non-toxic food supply.

Finally, they stood up, brushing a thin layer of dust from their clothes, and stepping out onto the open plains. As they stood, blinking in the bright sunlight, they raised their waterskin to their lips and drank.

Alright, Ari thought. *Time to pave our way in this world.*

For starters, they knew the plains would not be a good place for them to stick around. Not only were they easily visible to potential predators and prey, but especially to any ships flying overhead. The rock formations that they had slept among were certainly a good start, but they were still far too open for Ari's liking.

Further on into the plain, though, the clusters became larger and closer together. In the distance an entire forest of formations spread out before them, as far as the eye could see. The perfect place to lose themself. And the worst place in the world to land a spaceship.

First thing's first; I need to find a water supply. Lowering their waterskin from their lips and raising their other hand, they shielded their eyes from the light, and gazed out over the steel-blue plain shining in the sunshine.

When it comes to broad, flat plains like this, water is spread thin. If there is any running water, there will be telltale signs. Large lifeforms will know where to go, and plants will flourish.

They set off, beginning to walk again, moving around the edge of the rock formations as they put yet more distance between themself and the escape pod.

Composed of layers upon layers of grey, blue and black stone, the rock made for a fascinating contrast against the green-hued sky, and Ari found themself feeling a lot safer as they hid in the shadows, though they couldn't help feeling that their off-white and iridescent garb would stick out somewhat. The cloak might have helped, but not by much.

No matter. If there are any creatures living here, I can make use of them.

They picked their way through large boulders and over ridged foothills, glancing around warily.

Although they searched, they didn't see any signs of a distant river or watering hole across the plain, nor did they see any large creatures. The most they saw was a bug flitting across their path, or scurrying out from under a rock. There was no sign of anything larger than their palm, and though they did at one point find a long, squirming crawler under a rock, it disappeared far too quickly to be caught.

That aside, its bright green exterior meant Ari was less than eager to try it.

Probably poisonous anyway.

As the hours passed, their stomach began to growl. Ari ignored it, until something else chimed in. An impatient feeling swept over them, and they froze despite knowing what was causing it.

Yes, yes, I know.

Ari sighed, and settled down in the shade. Once again, they produced their bowl and a sustenance pill. With the rest of the droplets they could squeeze from their waterskin, they prepared it. As they waited for the meal to form, a flash of light lit up the sky.

Already!?

From their little nook, Ari saw the vessel flying overhead, circling around to land. Although they knew they wouldn't be seen from here, Ari shuffled backwards and crouched among the stones, waiting tensely. Instead though, the vessel hung in the sky, hovering above the sprawling plain.

It's scanning, they thought with horror, as they peered out from a bed of grasses. *It has to be. Shoot!*

The parasite added in a little sprinkle of curiosity.

You wouldn't understand, little thing.

Looking down, they checked to make sure that their meal had properly formed into a liquid. As soon as they were certain it was ready, Ari raised it to their lips and drained it as quick as they could.

Raising their hand, they wiped a smear of blue from their lip with the back of their wrist, wincing as they felt a burp rise in their throat. *Maybe it wasn't ready, after all.*

Their passenger seemed more than satisfied, though.

At least one of us is happy.

Ari glanced up and saw the vessel's landing gear beginning to extend beneath it. It was creeping towards them over the plain, like a great black panther on the hunt. *That's my cue to leave, anyhow.*

Ari stood, gathered their belongings, and turned to run. They soon disappeared among the rocks, clambering up ledges and hurdling boulders as they lost themself deeper in the labyrinth. Once they were sure that they could not be seen, Ari made their way to the top of a formation and gazed around. In the distance, they saw a fragment of the plain. And far, far away into the centre of the labyrinth, they saw the bulbous shape of an alien plant.

In an instant, they were flitting from rock to rock until they reached solid ground again.

And then they began to press on into the centre of the formation, where they hoped an oasis awaited them.

***

The Rift-walker had not gone far. A leap of several solar systems had brought them to an uncolonised world, its air pristine and clean and its skies swirling with clouds. Somewhere across a rocky labyrinth, Malgas could see a wall of mist.

She dreaded the task of piloting through the bank of cloud; but it seemed their target had not reached it yet.

The blinking dot upon the window-screen told her that they were close.

When she wasn't needed piloting the ship, Malgas

made time to visit Omea, and found Osai crouched by his bedside. Osai did not look up as she approached, and settled beside the pair, kneeling on the cold floor. When Omea's eyes flickered open at the sound of her approach, his face brightened. The captain was relieved to see that he hadn't taken the injury too hard.

The cut was clean and precise, and he had suffered no other wounds from the Rift-walker. He insisted, completely seriously, that she ought to carry on with the mission – that he still had three working arms, and that they couldn't miss this chance.

Relieved, though slightly shamefaced, Malgas was inclined to agree.

As he relayed to her the events leading up to it, Malgas was appalled. It all seemed meticulously planned. From the glass, to the spilled food, to the sickness that had never existed in the first place.

"It was… odd, though. They really didn't seem to want to hurt me. There was always a choice, and I…" Omea winced. "I always took the easy option."

Malgas looked down at Omea and tried not to let the betrayal seep into her tone.

"So it knows, then?"

"Most of it," Omea said guiltily. "But not everything."

"And you… told the Rift-walker that it may die?"

"No. I told it we'd try to keep it alive. It… threatened to hurt me further if I didn't help it leave the ship." Omea paused, closing the membranes across its eyes. "I… am ashamed, Malgas. I asked it to be prepared for death to save lives but was unprepared to do the same."

Malgas did not answer. She couldn't.

Osai spoke up, then. "It was feeding you empty threats. I don't think that this creature has the killing drive we do. I have no doubt it already suspected how to get down into the cargo hold. It would still have escaped, Omea, and it would still have taken your hand."

"I disagree," Malgas said.

Osai finally met her gaze.

"I think it would easily kill to ensure its own survival."

"It acted in a state of blind panic after being told classified information. And it will continue to do so, continue to evade us, until it is caught, and restrained. Or… until we give the parasite another host."

"You know that isn't possible, Osai. Not anymore."

"Why not?"

"The parasite must leave willingly for it to properly adapt to a new host species. We could assure that… but that would mean endangering a member of our own crew, instead. And if there is another option, I will take it."

"Captain. With all due respect, that is why Hoss is here."

"Hoss is here because he is a fine navigator. Being expendable has nothing to do with it."

Malgas rose, a sudden and sharp movement like drawing a knife. "I'm sorry for drawing you into this, Omea. I'm glad to see that you're well."

"Thank you, Malgas… that means a lot." He blinked open his eyes. "Now, would you go and catch that Rifter for me?"

As Malgas wandered down the corridor back towards the cockpit, she found it bathed in the green light of another world. Taking the controls from Nuudren, she brought the *Vestige* in towards the plain.

***

At the centre of the maze, Ari found a safe haven. The green sky reflected on the still waters of a reservoir, sheltered from the rest of the world by a labyrinth of stone. Plants with thick trunks and great, swollen leaves grew from the deepest parts of its waters; and it was these that Ari had seen from the distant formations. A bright flower grew from each of their distant tops, like a beacon. Mosses and moulds clung to the surrounding rock faces whilst narrow tunnels wound their way through them, boring through layers of rock. Ari found plenty of places in which to shelter and hide, but they also wondered about their origin. Had they been formed by wildlife, perhaps? Or even an ancient civilisation, which had long gone?

Ari found immeasurable delight in exploring these caves, although there were no useful treasures. And in these times, the parasite often chipped in with small sparks of joy of its own. It seemed to answer them, even, two emotions twining together in a sort of unspoken conversation. Tentatively, Ari felt themself warming to it.

You're not so bad, are you? You're just doing what you do best.

The waters of their new home were often shrouded in fog, and smelled bitter as they knelt at the water's edge. Their testing revealed the waters to be a little too acidic for their liking; but that had never stopped them before. They needed fire to build a filtration system though, and so Ari was hesitant. Instead, they hefted rocks into the water to create stepping stones, and were eventually able to reach the bulbous leaves of the water-plants. When their knife sliced through the leaves, they found them not only edible, but full of fresh, and filtered water that tasted only mildly citrusy.

I wonder if I could grow these? They thought to themself, as they chewed through the skin, and sucked out the vaguely bitter juices.

They tied a fragment of Oliver's knife onto the remaining stem, and made a new, if slightly flimsy, spear.

The parasite, too, seemed quite happy with the change in diet; Ari felt its warm comfort in their mind, and imagined it curling up to sleep like a contented kitten. They smiled slightly despite themself.

After so long, it's almost nice to be eating for two again, Ari thought as they picked up another leaf.

Immediately after, though, Ari was hit by a wave of revulsion. They cringed.

...No, that's disgusting. I shouldn't be thinking like that.

They shook their head, redirecting their thoughts with a shudder.

Even still... reminds me of those days when I had a family to watch my back. Only, without the worry of anyone wandering off and getting into trouble, or Oliver breathing down my neck. The smile gradually faded from their face.

No matter what I did, nothing was right when it came to him. He really was a worrier.

They looked up, slowly placing down the half-eaten leaf. *Only because he cared, though.*

The thought left them feeling hollow, and the hand holding their leaf quivered slightly.

Ari raised their gaze towards the green-toned sky, and shook their head. *Well, I don't need to worry about pleasing anyone anymore.*

Except for you, little thing. And you seem quite content, so long as you're fed and happy.

Ari smiled slightly as they felt a wave of drowsiness in reply. It was too easy to imagine it taking the form of words:

I am, I am!

Although they knew that their pursuers would be close on their tail, Ari decided to stay for a time. Each night, they slept in a different cave, and in the morning they picked their way up onto the tallest formations to ensure they were still alone.

Ari was not the only one, though, to find this place; Ari jolted awake one day as a commotion reached their ears. They drew their knife and stumbled to their feet, darting away, and hid in the entrance of a small, sheltered cave. From there they saw an enormous, bug-like creature come bounding into the clearing over the rock formations. It moved with long, loping strides like a deer, claws scrabbling and scraping as it slid against the stone. Ari narrowed their eyes as they watched closely.

This isn't supposed to be here. Something must have scared it off the plain.

It didn't take long for the beast's pursuers to show themselves.

Moments later, a pack of six beasts leaped into the clearing, hurdling the gaps and racing across the stone as though they were nothing, clinging to surfaces with broad paws and six stocky limbs. Jaws made for crushing ended in a sharp and beaklike point, and ivory skin hugged tight to leathery carapace. Small, beady eyes flashed as they narrowly avoided their prey's desperate strikes.

Ari's eyes widened slightly in a moment of recognition.

Their memory flashed back to the carcase they'd found in the swamp. The armour that they'd stripped from its body suddenly didn't seem like enough.

But it can't be the same creatures… Can it?

Snapping, drooling, and hissing, Ari watched as the pack surrounded their unfortunate prey, and brought it down.

They tore into the massive carcase, gizzards swelling as they filled with fresh meat, and ripped it apart in minutes like the piranhas of Earth. Ari waited patiently, eyes wide, and breath bated. *Perhaps they'll leave me some scraps.*

However, as time passed and the creatures continued eating, hissing and squawking among themselves, it became increasingly apparent that there would be none left. They devoured all: carapace, hide, flesh, even exoskeleton. Some hours had passed by the time the creatures moved to the water's edge, drank their fill, and left.

Ari emerged what felt like a lifetime after that, visibly shaken. They approached the spot where the beast had fallen and ran a hand across the ground. But aside from the scuffs in the dirt, the beasts had left no trace that they were ever there.

The clearing didn't seem so safe after that.

Provided the Renohaiin crew did not find them, they might have been able to live comfortably here for quite some time. However, the longer they stayed, the more nervous they felt. In addition to the appearance of the predators, Ari knew they would soon be found, and although the ship would not be able to land nearby, it would only take so long for them to find their way through the labyrinth of stone.

The next sunrise, Ari awoke to find their clearing darkened by the shadow of the ship. Panic flared in their stomach as they crept through their tunnels like a rat, staying out of sight to the eye, but not to the sensors. The ship was hovering, perfectly still in its flight. And then a bright white beam shone down on the clearing, leaving a scorch mark on the stone beneath. With a flash of light, Eidhoin and Ganir appeared in the clearing that Ari had claimed for shelter.

They can't land... but they can Rift!?

Stuffing their satchel with as many stored leaves as they could carry, Ari squeezed into a narrow side-tunnel and wormed their way out of the clearing. They pressed deeper and deeper into the labyrinth, happening upon many more stagnating pools along the way. The ship did not activate the Rift again; perhaps the *Vestige* would have to land to pick up the foot scouts again.

Still, they were too close behind for comfort.

The sun set, and rose, and set again. The labyrinth of stone seemed to go on forever. At one point, the ground sloped upwards like a twisted mountain. And finally, Ari was able to hop onto a tall formation, and see that the labyrinth was coming to an end. Beyond, a vast and empty steppe, ranging from horizon to horizon, and nothingness as far as the eye could see. In the distance, a pack of ivory shapes moved across the flatlands, lurking around the edges of roaming herds.

Beyond, a wall of clouds crept slowly across the plain.

A cold wind washed over them, prickling at their skin. It was an unexpected gasp of winter, and it disappeared as quickly as it had come.

Ari gazed out over the steel blue grasses and felt their stomach sink. They glanced back the way they had come, and saw nothing but a sea of stone. Beyond that, the sleek, dark shape of the vessel hanging just below the clouds, creeping towards them.

Searching. Always searching. But Ari had no doubt the Captain knew exactly where they were.

Ari retreated back among the rocks and let the sun set as they considered what to do next.

The first day saw them eating through the majority of

their supplies as they lightened their carrying weight and found a new hideaway. Still they saw no signs of the Renohaiin crew, but at one point the scouting vessel veered past them. The scouts couldn't have been far behind.

The crystal still embedded in their flesh kept the Rift at bay, chasing away any hope of an easy getaway.

Across the plain, the cloud cover briefly shifted to reveal the peak of a mountain. A strong wind brought with it a wisp of snow. But the cloud cover over its sides never broke.

I have to go towards the mountain, Ari finally thought. *I can lose them in the blizzard. The Vestige can't be built for such a drastic change in climate.*

Ari shivered slightly.

But then again, neither am I.

The next day found the ship hanging above them. And no matter how far they ran, it was always there. They ate their way through the rest of their supplies and forced themself onto the most difficult tracks they could. Squeezing through gaps that scraped their fragile skin, knowing the Renohaiin's exoskeletons might be too broad. They ducked through narrow overhangs that could not be seen from the sky, and crumbled rocks over their path to render it impassable.

They knew for certain that there was no going back.

Finally they emerged out onto the open plain, and it was time to go. Breaking into a sprint, Ari took off across the grass, cutting a straight pathway away from the formation and across the miles towards the foot of the mountains.

It would bring them jarringly close to the herdbeasts and the pack of predators that guarded them, but the Riftmaster felt they had no other choice.

They had hoped that their roguish pathways would have at least delayed the ground scout teams from following. But it was only minutes before they heard the distant hum of an engine.

They cast a glance back towards the scouting vessel,

which was lowering itself towards the plain thirty feet behind them. There were figures emerging from the formations beyond that, tiny dots with terrifyingly long strides.

Ari's breath was already heaving, and the mountains felt no closer.

They wouldn't make it.

Ari swerved towards the roaming herdbeasts and the pack encircling them, shepherding the creatures together in a terrified cluster.

The *Vestige* withdrew its landing gear and rose from the plain, and the ship moved forward until it hovered directly above Ari.

Something was happening.

They thought they heard someone shout an order, but they couldn't be sure.

And fear caused their stomach to turn, the parasite's anxiety throbbing through their veins until it was all they knew. Ari's fingertips grew numb, and dizziness sent them stumbling. "Would you leave me be?!" they snapped out loud, holding themself steady on an upturned boulder and gasping for air. "Why now?! Why are you doing this?!"

The parasite jabbed back with a sharp stab of fear but didn't seem to understand. Frustrated, the Riftmaster wrenched themself on, disappearing among tall grasses and hiding in uneven terrain.

It's reacting to me, the Riftmaster reminded themself. *I need to breathe. If I just think, I can get through this.*

The herdbeasts noticed Ari's approach long before their captors did and cast terrified feelers into the air as they felt the throb of the ship's engine. They grew afraid, teetering on long limbs.

Ari considered themself lucky that they weren't the focus of these creatures; as large as draft horses and muscular like bulldogs, Ari felt certain of who would be the victor of an encounter.

Their heart pounded as they drew uncomfortably close.

Breathe… they don't need me.

The pack-beasts snapped, rumbling warningly and keeping their prey in place. With large herdbeasts present, and with such a number of them, they seemed to care little about Ari.

But as the shadow of the *Vestige* fell upon them, a hundred heads raised and the herd finally looked up.

Suddenly one broke formation, launching itself out beyond the herd and stumbling away across the plain. In the moment of distraction, others quickly followed.

Chaos erupted as herbivores sprang in all directions, the herd of thirty or so individuals scattering. Ari dropped to the ground as one launched over their head. The carnivores reacted quickly, recapturing one of them, and snapping its hind limbs with hardly a shake of the head.

At that first blood, a frenzy of killing erupted from the previously organised pack. Herdbeast after herdbeast fell, but more still took off and were scattered across the plain.

Ari poked their head out from behind a boulder and made a choice. As a herdbeast sprang past, they darted out to meet it, plunging their spear into its side and swinging themself up onto its back. It shrieked with fear and pain as Ari grabbed its feelers and wrenched its head in the direction of the blizzard.

Now go! Go! Go!

They fled across the plain, clouds and grasses blurring past.

The journey faded into a blur of adrenaline. Their mount bumped and juddered beneath them, hard carapace leaving painful bruises on their inner thighs. But, where once the Renohaiin vessel was always there, hanging over them, now it fell behind, lingering over the chaos.

If they're just scanning for living creatures… then I'll be just one point of many on their sensors. And yet, they found it hard to hang on to that tiny thread of hope. *But they can't be, can they? That would be far too easy.*

Clouds swelled ahead to meet them. A soft drizzle of snow soon began to fall, rapidly becoming enormous flakes. Whenever the herbivore began to sway from their path, Ari would wrench its feelers and drag it back on track. Finally, though, the creature's senses returned. It bucked, thrashed, threw them to the ground beside a steaming creek, and then disappeared into the fog.

The plain was nowhere to be seen, lost in the mist, and the ground sloped under their feet. Tilting their head upwards, they tried to see the mountains towering beyond them.

Grinning, Ari watched their breaths swell on the cold air, as they gazed up at the thick and heavy sky. Swinging their satchel across their shoulder, Ari finally ran for the nearest cover, reminding themself that celebration was not due yet; they needed to preserve their strength, and they were hardly protected from the cold.

Shivering violently, they stumbled across terrain that was knee-deep in snow, until the ground became rockier and began to slope. After a time, a threadbare tree loomed out of the mist. Soon they found themself weaving through a petrified forest, some branches clinging onto bulbous fruits that looked like pure ice.

There had been a time when Ari felt as though they could run forever. Now, though, exhaustion dragged at them; soaked through, their limbs felt like lead.

They followed the creek until it joined paths with a river, winding its slow way into a v-shaped valley. The snow evaporated into steam and mist flowed across its crystal-clear surface. To Ari's surprise, as they wiggled their fingers in its waters, it warmed them to their very core. They walked beside it, and from a bed of strange, hairy fungus growing from the riverbank they cut a thick cloak to lay across their shoulders.

It was damp, but carried the lingering warmth of the waters.

Soon, though, they were shivering again as they headed downstream.

I have to find shelter. I didn't plan well for this at all.

Among the petrified trunks, there was little. But on the other side of the river they caught sight of an uprooted tree, its roots catching the snowflakes as they fell to form a cave.

Ari kept walking, looking for a suitable place to cross

the water but finding solace in the fact that they wouldn't be journeying much longer.

As they hopped across a series of stepping stones, Ari saw the fog light up with a beam of white. Ari stared in dismay, freezing in place before realising they needed to move. They cleared the last few leaps in a terrified instant, slipping on the bank and splashing water up their leg. *That won't be drying anytime soon,* they thought in a brief panic, as they hurried up the bank.

Stumbling upstream, Ari soon found their chosen shelter, and huddled down into the small snow-cave.

They sniffled, nose and cheeks red with the cold, but pulled their new cloak tight about their shoulders. It was scratchy, damp, and probably full of creatures, but it kept the warmth in.

As Ari cast their gaze out of the hollow and out into the fog, they saw no sign of the ship. Far from being a relief, they were instead filled with worry.

The crew must have found a place to land.

Even as they tried to sleep, Ari's heart beat fast. They looked out over the snow, ears pricked to the whistling of the wind through the forest. But nothing appeared. Slowly, but surely, Ari's eyes began to close. But then a movement caught their eye. Ari's eyes snapped open, breaths quickening.

An unmistakable silhouette moved through the trees.

Ari stayed where they were at first. Still as the grave. Statuesque.

But as the figure drew nearer to the riverbank, they knew that they had been seen. Ari stumbled out of their shelter and fled over the riverbank and up the slope.

The terrain grew ever steeper until Ari moved at a zigzag. Finally, they were forced to scale bare, cold rocks, covered with a thin sheet of ice. Glancing back, Ari saw a figure weaving its way through the trees, alone. Shivering in the cold, they reached up for the next handhold. A rock split in half, cutting into their palm and clattering down into the valley below. Ari swung loose with a stifled cry, struggling to regain their footing.

Falling snowflakes mingled with a spray of red.

As they looked down, they saw how far they had climbed and their stomach dropped. Many metres below them, a Renohaiin soldier aimed their weapon.

They can't shoot! Ari reminded themself, forcing their breaths to remain steady as the vision blurred at the corner of their eyes. *I'd die from the fall, and they need me alive! They're trying to drive me, not kill me!*

Even so, Ari couldn't stay here. With no other choice, they regained their footing and continued climbing, leaving smears of crimson in the otherwise greyscale terrain.

Looking up, Ari picked up the pace, clambering faster up the mountainside and disappearing over the mountain ridge. *I made it!* They thought, as they slithered down the snowy slope on the other side.

For a brief, blissful moment, they ran with the certainty that they were going to escape. But then they saw their shadow cast starkly on the snow before them by a blinding beam of white light.

Ari glanced back, and immediately wished they hadn't. They ran, pushing for the petrified forest, yet knowing it wouldn't protect them. There was no escape now. Still, they fled.

The Riftmaster came slithering to a halt only when the silhouette of a Renohaiin loomed out of the dark ahead of them. Osai's neck and belly glowed white, carapace burning with brightness. The snow turned to steam as it touched him, sharp points taking shape from a silhouette of white.

Ari was surrounded. Trapped.

Ari heard the hiss of melting snow as someone appeared behind them, the Rift placing them exactly where they needed to be. Whipping around, the Riftmaster struck out in a desperate blow with their spear. The blow grazed Malgas' chest before the spear ground to a halt. They yanked the shaft, but it was dragged out of their grasp from behind.

Vision spinning, they lashed out instead with a clenched fist.

Captain Malgas caught one of their wrists in an armoured, insect-like hand, then the other. As if she was restraining a child.

Grinding their teeth in rage, Ari looked up to see her other two arms holding tranquiliser guns.

"Osai!" she barked.

Ari twisted their head to see her second-in-command holding a silken chain.

They struggled, but were quickly bound.

As the ship landed, Malgas lifted them by the arm and dragged them towards it. Ari fought with all the strength they had left, but they knew it was futile.

"How did you find me?" Ari spat, full of horror as they struggled against their bindings. But those, as well as the two crew members grasping their shoulders, were unmovable. "The tracker signal couldn't have reached you yet, and there are hundreds of thousands of life-bearing planets in the known universe. I should have been light-years out of reach. The Rift is unpredictable. Untraceable!"

The captain did not smile. There was no sense of triumph in her words. "That's for us to know, and for you to fear," Malgas looked into their eyes. "Nothing is unpredictable; we'll find you again and again, for as long as it takes. Either you come with us willingly, or we'll drag you in by the mandibles."

Ari stopped struggling and felt their stomach drop. The Rift *was* random. It had to be. Didn't it? There were times when a pattern had seemed clear to them as they looked at the sky and traced their path through the stars. And then they'd end up on a planet galaxies away, and they'd deem the pattern a coincidence. But orbits were ever changing, planets hid behind suns and turned on their axis. The longer they stayed still, the more the planets in every corner of the universe would shift.

Perhaps the Rift wasn't as random as it had always seemed.

"But the escape pod…"

Ari remembered the sight of hundreds of thousands of

stars sprawling out before them, in every direction. They could have Rifted anywhere. Even if she spoke the truth, hundreds of thousands of planets could have been aligned. They should have been long lost.

So that meant… *no.* It couldn't be true.

But none of it mattered. The Riftmaster could see no other way out. There was no escaping now.

Ari went limp as they were hauled back on board the ship, mind reeling.

Chapter 10
Ruins

This time, the medbay was deemed unsuitable for Ari's containment. With Omea incapacitated, Captain Malgas seemed to fear that they would take advantage of the medic's weakened state, and hurt him further. Of course, Ari planned to do no such thing. They didn't object, though.

They were placed in storage, with unstable tissue samples and crates, cuffed to the wall. Ari couldn't reach any kind of supplies even if they stretched, and they couldn't see any way out. Their wrists were bound together and fixed to the wall. Even though their knife remained sheathed against their chest, there was no way for them to reach it. The metal was cold against their skin. Ari doubted that the meagre weapon would be able to break their chains, in any case.

Their satchel, along with Omea's severed hand had been confiscated once more.

Nobody visited them at first. Ari didn't know how long they were sitting alone in hazard containment, silently stewing with rage. It might have been days, or weeks.

The only hint they had was the deteriorating state of their body. Their strength was not at its peak, and they found themself sleeping sitting upright, their back to the cold wall of the containment unit. They ached like they were eighty years old again. Always, the weight of the knife against their chest left them twisting with discomfort, and the only thing they could think in that dark, deep silence was what it symbolised.

To have it here with them was almost a crueller punishment than having it confiscated.

They awoke incredibly hungry, stomach growling. Usually food was brought and left just out of reach. They'd fight their way over to it and struggle to drink. Sometimes they reached it, sometimes they did not. Either way, they were left to fight against their chains alone.

Well... they supposed. *Not completely alone.*

Sometimes, they simply had to battle the hunger and try their hardest to blot out the pangs which weren't their own.

On one occasion, though, they were joined by an unexpected face.

When the door finally slid open, Hoss, the wispy-haired Rifter, trotted in. He held a small tray, piled high with the swollen leaves they had been feeding on. Ari blinked in surprise.

"Hoss," they said, with some trepidation.

"Rift-walker," Hoss answered, approaching without too much fear despite his small stature. "I'll be tending your needs until we touch down."

"Well, it's good to know they haven't forgotten about me."

Hoss let out a sharp huff that might have been a laugh.

"Forgotten? Malgas is terrified! Anything she leaves within reach could be used in your next escape. After a getaway like that, you're under constant surveillance."

"I suppose I shouldn't be surprised," Ari said with a slight groan.

They received the food with a measure of cautious gratitude into their lap.

"Indeed," Hoss said, as they began to eat with some difficulty. "It *was* quite the escape."

Ari swallowed their mouthful.

"I just did what I had to do. Is Omea recovering okay?"

"Just fine. The tissues are already beginning to reform."

Ari let out a sigh of relief. "Good. I almost feared that I had the wrong race."

"So you really didn't mean to cause any severe wounds?"

"Of course not. I bound it, didn't I?"

"You did. And not only that, you alerted Osai. Why?"

"I don't like to harm people if I don't have to. And on this occasion, well…"

"You felt it necessary."

"I did. I've been alive too long to just give myself up like that."

Hoss' beady eyes narrowed, his tail lashing once in frustration.

"You said something to Omea. You said '*I'm dying on my terms, not yours*'." Beneath the wiry fur of his muzzle, they could see the reddish shine of sharpened teeth. "What would your terms be? How do you want to die, Riftmaster?"

Ari opened their mouth, stunned, and then closed it again. They began to speak, but no sound came out.

"You are immortal. The Rift has failed to kill you. If you keep going as you are, your life will never end naturally." Hoss' voice had softened, but they didn't think it was to comfort them. "Do you intend to just keep going until you make the one mistake that costs you everything, and waste it all?"

Ari slowly closed their fingers into fists, their knuckles quickly turning white. Ari floundered for an answer before finally snorting out a sharp breath. "I… I intend to find my way back to my home planet. There's someone I care about there. One last one."

And then, Ari thought. *Maybe then the pain will finally end.*

"Which planet?" Hoss asked softly.

Ari bared their teeth in something resembling a smile. "As if I'd send the Empire straight to an unconquered planet," they said. *If nothing else, I think Bailey would end me.*

"So you won't barter? Not even for thousands of lives?" Hoss lowered his chin. "*Human* lives, not just Renohaiin."

Ari hesitated, a moment of doubt flickering in their eyes before they masked it with practiced ease. They lifted their chin. "Not even then."

Hoss was quiet for a moment.

"What about the one you want to get back to?"

Ari didn't reply, but filled the silence with gentle munching. Finally, they swallowed. But they carefully avoided his question.

As if the Empire would care about him.

"Is it true?" they asked instead. "What Malgas said?"

"What did she say?"

"That the Rift can be predicted."

Hoss' tail twitched. "I'm afraid I can't say," he said.

"Is that because of orders, or because you don't know?"

"My home planet has laws surrounding honesty," Hoss said, wrinkling his nose. "But withholding information is sometimes necessary. For both your safety, and mine."

Ari aggravatedly rattled their chains and didn't answer. Sometime later, Hoss broke the silence once more.

"Riftmaster... in the navigation room, you said you don't concern yourself with the problems of the worlds you visit. You don't even seem to care about your own."

"...I remember. Why?"

"I just wanted to remind you that now may be the time to reconsider that."

"So... You're suggesting I accept death as an option and give myself over to the Empire? For the sake of some grand purpose that you're not even going to tell me?"

"...Yes."

Ari paused, their lips tightening into a hard line.

"If I'd given myself up to the first one who wanted to use me for the good of their planet, I wouldn't be on this ship, and your kind would be just as screwed."

"I assure you, Riftmaster, there will never be a bigger

need than this. If I believed in the thing called 'fate', I'd believe unquestionably that it's the reason we found you."

"Hoss, I will not just give myself without even knowing what for. Your crew can try to use me all they like, but Hoss, I can assure you that I will never stop fighting them, escaping them, and fighting them again."

Hoss's small, beady eyes closed. He breathed deeply for a moment before blinking them open once more. Ari met his gaze. "Listen," he said. "It is highly classified information to those outside of the Renohaiin empire. But if you *do* manage to escape us, you will find out eventually." Hoss' ears twitched. "You were a navigator, once. That makes you at least a veteran. If I tell you now… Can you promise me you will consider helping us willingly?"

Ari looked into Hoss' eyes. They narrowed their own, and then slowly nodded. "For what it's worth, I will consider it."

Hoss hesitated before speaking. The Riftmaster could almost see him flicking through the translations and making a decision. Finally he spoke. "Firstly, Riftmaster, there is something you need to know. The *Vestige* is only one of thousands of vessels who were looking for you – or rather, the parasite inside of you. If it wasn't us, then someone would have found you eventually."

"Thousands? That can't be right. That would mean…" Ari trailed off.

"The Renohaiin Armada has been recalled."

Ari felt their blood run cold. After thousands of conquered planets and billions of inhabited worlds, the Renohaiin Armada had never, *ever* been recalled. "Recalled?"

"The word has already spread to the farthest corner of seven galaxies, and even further as we speak. Ships return to their host planets every cycle."

"That must have taken generations."

"It's an emergency frequency. Twenty-five parsecs every second."

"I didn't even know that was possible."

"Neither did we. This is the first time it's been used."

Ari met the navigator's gaze, and felt their stomach sink. "Why now?"

"Picture this," Hoss began tentatively. "A small predator. Low on the food chain, so it's fast, omnivorous. Capable of consuming and scavenging from almost any lifeform on any world. They need only one fertilised queen to be capable of rapid, uncontrolled reproduction for generations."

So… similar to rats, then, Ari thought. *Or ants, perhaps.*

"And?"

"Now picture the planet they came from; known to us as Vularis Prime. A hostile, predatory world. And it's huge; monstrously huge. A Vularian apex predator could swallow this shuttle in one gulp. And even the smaller ones…" Hoss trailed off.

"Go on?"

"They'd be many, many times larger than we are. On any other world, they'd become the dominant species, ravaging ecosystems and eating until there is nothing left."

Ari felt their heart rate begin to rise.

"So what you're saying is…"

"They've entered the Rift. And now they're spreading."

They remembered, in an instant, the large predators they'd seen. The bodies… those that they'd eaten, and taken hide from, and used. During their escape, the curiously familiar hunters that shepherded beasts on the plains. "Like an interplanetary virus," they murmured.

"Precisely."

Ari shuddered slightly. "And the Parasite…?"

"It's from their world. The Motherbeast was carrying it when she first entered the Rift. But she feeds her young via regurgitation, and it was lost."

"What makes it so important?"

A prickle of unease slid through their brain, and for an instant they weren't sure if it belonged to the parasite, or themself.

"If the host is in danger, the parasite is capable of producing a toxin that can forcibly eject it, killing the host in an instant. We need to try to replicate that toxin. It's the only thing we know capable of killing them easily."

Ari swallowed, feeling their gut clench with a sharp stab of fear. Shaking their head to force sense to return, Ari rose to their feet, scattering bulbous leaves.

"Where are they now?"

"Where are they not? Four of our colonies have already been compromised. They require heavy weaponry just to wound, which the empire can only produce so much of. But no matter how many we kill, it's all pointless if the Motherbeast continues to Rift." Hoss breathed out. "There are even a few small populations popping up in the galaxy you call the Milky way."

Ari's blood ran cold, their breaths coming fast. They looked down at their bound hands, away from Hoss, and away from their prison. There were only so many life-bearing planets in the milky way, and they knew for a fact that the Renohaiin empire would not care for the tiny, uncolonised planets that got caught in the crossfire.

"Why do you need me?" the Riftmaster asked. "Can't you just pass it on to another host?"

Hoss smiled wryly. "As a warm-blood, I was brought along as a suitable host. But thanks to you, it has adapted to carbon-based biology. It would be unable to survive inside of me now."

Hoss shook his head as though to clear his thoughts, ears flapping.

"So, Riftmaster… is that reason enough?"

Ari looked up, and tried to calm their racing heart, but they did not answer for a moment. "How long until we get to the space station?" They asked. "I need some time to think."

"Not long," Hoss said. "We should touch down soon. It's time to make a decision."

"Great," Ari muttered, mind reeling. They needed a way out, and soon. More than that, they had to find a way back to Earth.

So deep in thought, Ari had barely noticed that Hoss had picked up his tray and turned to leave.

The thick-furred navigator didn't look at them as he left the room, at least until Ari spoke.

"Wait," they said.

Hoss glanced up, eyeing them distrustfully.

"No matter the outcome of this... I thank you for telling me."

Hoss, however, turned away. "Coming from you, that doesn't mean a lot."

Ari's heart sank. "That's fair."

They watched as he locked the door of the containment unit behind him, and listened until his pattering footsteps had long faded to echoes.

***

"...I am not about to start assigning values to my crew now. That's not how I became captain."

Malgas' back was stiff, and her tail tightly wound. She sat facing Osai, the air between them crackling with tension.

"Then we have already lost, Captain. You need to know who you are prepared to lose. The Rift-walker is too dangerous to be left alive, and it has proven it, time and time again."

"When you brought Hoss to me, you did so as a fine navigator. Not as a host. When he came on board, you relinquished any authority you had over him to me. At that moment he became one of my crew, under my protection. I am Hoss' captain, and he takes orders from me. That is my final say, Osai. We are not beginning to sacrifice our crew today. Understood?"

"Understood."

"You are dismissed."

Malgas watched, mandibles taut, as the scientist left the cockpit. He did not look back, did not acknowledge the edge of her tone. And he certainly did not show any kind of remorse.

She was certain that this would not be the end of her troubles with Osai. As she watched him leave, the door slid open to reveal a small, white figure.

Hoss stood to attention, his ears lowered and face expressionless. He looked up briefly as Osai stormed past him, but then quickly looked back to Malgas.

"Hoss," the Captain said, slowly rising, and approaching the small creature. She checked ahead of her, to make sure that Osai was not entering the cantina. Instead he turned left, entering the med bay. "Come. I'm in dire need of sustenance."

Hoss dipped his head and sprang after her as she moved. "How did it go?" she asked.

Hoss didn't answer at first, as he took the time to gather the words. "Well, I think."

"Will the Rift-walker submit?"

"It will… consider it."

Malgas wasn't reassured. "That… is good, I suppose. Was there anything else?"

"It's trying to get back to someone. Just like I thought."

Malgas' membranes flitted over her eyes in momentary surprise despite herself.

As she gathered herself to reply, Hoss spoke again.

"Are you sure I won't be reprimanded for this?" he asked tentatively.

"Of course not. As your captain, all responsibility for the actions of my crew fall to me. Besides…" she paused. "It was my idea."

"Captain…" Hoss looked up at her uncertainly. "I don't deserve this. We both know where I should be."

Malgas looked down at the small, furry creature. They paused just outside the cantina. "You deserve my protection just as much as Osai or Omea."

"The rest of the crew doesn't seem to think so. I don't think so. I worry, Malgas; this creature does not want to help us. It doesn't care about saving lives. Doesn't even care about its own kind." Hoss looked up at her. "At least I know that I can trust me."

"Hoss… You have proven yourself as one of the finest

navigators in the Empire. I cannot risk losing that if there is another option."

Hoss did not respond.

In the silence, Malgas felt the ground beneath her feet began to throb with a low hum, the casing of the ship beginning to judder alarmingly. "We are entering the atmosphere," she mused. "It won't be long now."

Hoss grunted an acknowledgement.

"I suppose I should go make sure our prisoner is still secure. Who is on surveillance duty?"

"Nuudren, at the moment."

Malgas nodded, and then turned away towards the engine room.

"Captain," Hoss broke in, before she began to walk. He still stood expectantly beside the cantina door. "You should feed. You haven't taken nourishment since it escaped."

"I can take nourishment when it is secured. You go on ahead. I'll be joining you shortly."

An odd expression crossed Hoss' face. Without further protest, he disappeared into the mess hall.

Malgas began the journey down into the bowels of the ship, taking her time, as it fought against gravity and turbulence. When she reached the cargo hold, she was surprised to hear the pitter-pattering of footsteps behind her.

Hoss appeared, in tiny paws clutching a beaker of blue nourishing fluid.

She had only to take it, and then he was gone. Gratitude swelled within her cold chest as she slowly made her way to the hazard containment unit. Behind a sheet of crystal, the prisoner lay defeated. Chin resting upon its chest. For a moment, Malgas thought that it must have been sleeping, but then it raised its head, and the two locked eyes.

The human staggered to its feet, back still pressed against the wall, bindings safely secured to its fittings. It was still safely contained.

Malgas relaxed, searching its expression.

Within those small sheer eyes, Malgas was certain she saw the fires of rage burning, and she steeled herself. *This is not over yet. We're so close, but this creature is going to be fighting us every step of the way. We must prepare.*

How could so much anger be contained in its small, stocky body? For a creature so fleshy and inelegant, it had somehow managed to make everything so much harder. The Renohaiin typically considered warm-blooded creatures to be inefficient and primitive. It had no claws, no fangs, no mandibles. No tail, and only two limbs that weren't used for locomotion. Its moods were unpredictable and its natural armour was nonexistent.

But Malgas was sure that the emotions she'd seen it show were genuine.

As it spoke of its long-dead children, she felt something horribly familiar in its voice. And now, she saw in its eyes the same inextinguishable light.

For such a clumsy, fleshy, and awkward-looking creature, with its aggressive mane of hair and mysterious biology, she'd grown to feel a begrudging respect.

Now that it was back, the sheer panic she'd felt at its loss had given way to cool resignation and mild curiosity. There was nothing it could do now. They had won.

If I wasn't your captor, what could we have been? We could have learned so much from you.

Malgas stepped back from the crystal barrier as the ship tilted beneath her feet. A deep rumble grew from the bowels of the vessel, debris clattered against the hull. Malgas stretched out a hand, and steadied herself against a nearby crate.

We're here.

***

Ari raised their head as they felt a tremor running up through their feet, A low rumbling sounded from the outside as though the vessel were struggling to hold its shape. Soon, the gravity changed. They sank to their knees, disoriented, as they were pulled to the ground.

Soon after, they felt their head spinning as their weight lightened when the ship changed speeds. Finally, the world around them shuddered.

A few samples of materials rattled on the highest shelves, but none fell. The Renohaiin crew would not be so careless as to place anything sharp in their reach again.

The door hissed open, and captain Malgas stepped into their tiny world. She held a strip of hide that had been taken from their own supply cache. Holding them still, even though they were still bound, she gagged them. Behind her, Osai and Nuudren emerged, holding plasma florets at the ready. Ari narrowed their eyes, acknowledging the silent threat. Malgas said nothing as she unclipped Ari's chains from the wall and hauled them to their feet, shoving them roughly ahead of her.

Ari felt an arm upon each shoulder, and had no choice but to walk. They stepped into the loading bay, and light streamed in from the outside world.

Like it or not, they had arrived.

Chapter 11
Renohaiin

As the loading bay hissed open and the ramp unfurled, Ari kept their eyes trained on that sliver of the outside. First, they saw the maroon-toned sky, speckled with stars and ribboned with rich lilac smog, rocky debris and meteorites floating slowly by. Then, they saw radio towers built of sleek black crystal, interconnected tunnels and walkways linking them almost like a futuristic castle. Built over the generations by thousands of Renohaiin war generals, surely this was the central hub that had allowed for the study of the Rift. Vessels followed shimmering lights along carefully-mapped airways, and rarely detoured.

Meticulously constructed scaffolding frames braced a half-finished city dome and incomplete buildings stretched beyond the horizon. But there were no telltale sounds of building, crashes, clanks, the sight of workpeople clambering over their surfaces.

Deserted.

Even still, the *Vestige's* landing pad was one of many, a sleek and empty expanse of smooth meteorite plates held up from the ground by a set of supporting pillars. Ari craned their neck for a better look as the view widened, inch by inch.

A broken landscape hissed slowly into view, the planet's crust crisscrossed by vast cracks in the earth. Sheer cliffs of black crystal fell away into the crust of the world.

Ari drew in a sharp breath.

A Riftworld.

Aside from a maze of walkways and landing bays, the shattered earth beneath the city of ships was covered in a thin layer of lilac soil. Very little life seemed to thrive beyond the boundaries of the Renohaiin city. Ari saw the twisted remnants of discarded ship parts lying where no one ventured among the petrified remains of rotted mushrooms and twisted shrubbery. For the most part, though, the outskirts had been cleared.

Other than that, the stripped surface of the world was flat and smooth, largely devoid of places to hide.

Malgas pushed them forward, and they stumbled onto the loading ramp. The tip of the knife still sheathed against their chest jabbed roughly into them, almost as a reminder that there was no escaping this.

Finally, they looked up. The officers here must have been forewarned; there were four guards present, waiting to receive them. Of those four, two held plasma florets. The guards held them readied, in a silent threat.

Ari narrowed their eyes.

"Shouldn't we be using tranquilisers?" one of the guards clicked. "If we can't harm it, florets seem redundant."

Malgas didn't answer at first, instead risking a long glance at Ari. Finally, though, she clacked her mandibles, and spoke.

"The host understands our tongue, so you would do well to keep your clackers shut." She said first. And then... "Best not to risk it. If the parasite thinks the host's body is dying, it may try to eject, and end up killing it. But a light burn or two could help encourage it. Let this Riftmaster know that we are merciful."

Beneath their gag, Ari couldn't resist a disbelieving smirk. They rolled their eyes back towards Malgas to see if she was still holding her own gun. *Malgas, you sly son of a...*

The Captain returned their gaze evenly as she continued to speak. "But just in case, prepare another Rift-walker to host it. Atomic preference: carbon-based."

"It is gagged and bound. I'm sure we'll manage. Does it know what is at stake?"

Malgas' mandibles clacked. "The overseer requested the purpose of our mission be kept secret to prevent panic. I have ensured that his word is kept."

Ari heard the pat-pat-patting sound of Hoss' paws against the ramp falter slightly.

As Malgas finally let go, and handed them over to the armed guards, she spoke one more time. "Don't underestimate this one. The parasite couldn't have chosen a more problematic host."

"Noted."

"Be careful what you do."

"Don't worry, Malgas. We will ensure it reaches processing safely."

A guard grabbed their forearm, bound at their front. The other three surrounded them; one in front, two either side, and one behind. Ari struggled slightly, but even then, knew there was no getting away. Head reeling, they glanced back towards the only people they had known for so long.

They saw Omea being escorted from the ship, missing hand bound. Malgas had her back to them, glad to see them go. After all the trouble they'd caused, Ari guessed that they all were.

Only Hoss gazed after them, beady eyes unblinking. Ari met his gaze momentarily, then glanced back to the path ahead.

They were on the very edge of the crystal city, towers stretching high above them, and a smooth walkway stretching out ahead. *This looks like it wasn't made for walking. If they have transporters, I'll need to be fast. I can't let them get me any further into the complex. It will only be harder to escape then.*

They turned their attention onto the guards escorting them. Neither of them held anything sharp that they could use to sever their cuffs, but their gaze fixed on the plasma floret carried by the one in front.

They felt the guard behind them press the muzzle of his own into the back of their neck. It brushed briefly against the wound from the implant, and the shard of crystal still embedded within them.

Pain thrilled through Ari's body.

But they felt their brain ticking, heart pounded, and hope flared. Their hair began to stand on end. They didn't think, couldn't. In that moment they knew what they had to do. Ari clamped their eyes shut, leaned their head forward slightly, and then slammed it back into the barrel of the gun.

It struck squarely on the point of the crystal; pain flooded through the back of their skull as it shattered, burning heat sweeping up and down their spine.

A bright flash of light bathed the world around them.

There was a clatter as a floret dropped to the ground in the empty space behind them. The two guards that had stood there were gone in an instant, condemned in a moment to an existence away from everything they had known and loved. Ari yanked themself back, straining to get away from the two that remained.

They heard a commotion of shouts from around them and one of the guards let go of their arm, but they could spare only a single thought.

N-no… Why wasn't it me!?

As the guards regained their senses and started urging them forward, Ari pulled back as though to try to escape back to the *Vestige*. They kept resisting even as the guards jerked them forward.

They pulled and pulled until their limbs ached.

Another guard grabbed their arm, yanking them off their feet. They stumbled but kept pulling back towards the vessel. They waited, pulling, playing a furious tug-o-war with every ounce of strength they had. And then they sucked in a sharp breath and lunged forward, taking the guards by surprise.

Ari thrust their head forward. They felt the guard's

leathery optic bend concave beneath their skull.

The guard folded and fell hard to the ground, writhing in something that a human would describe as unfiltered agony.

Ari stood over him, chest heaving with uneven breaths.

They were dizzy with the impact, vision swimming, but they lunged for the plasma floret that had fallen from the hands of the Rifted guard. Dropping to their knees, Ari picked up the weapon in their hands before they could be stopped. They twisted around to face the remaining guard, knowing he wouldn't be alone for much longer. Malgas' crew lurched out of the *Vestige* to try to contain them.

Ari felt a warning twist in the pit of their stomach. The parasite felt their pain, felt the adrenaline pulsing in their bloodstream.

Breathe… breathe… I'm in no danger, here. But I'm sorry about this, little thing.

But they made sure it felt no fear.

Skittering backwards, they crouched and pressed the barrel of the weapon into their belly, looking from guard to guard with a promise in their eyes.

The safety is on. The full power of this thing can only be accessed with at least two free arms. What if it's not enough? Whatever I do, it needs to look real. They need the two of us alive.

A single trigger could only kill at point blank range; but in this case, it was enough.

A shock of emotion hit them. *What's happening?!*

They tried to reassure the uncertain consciousness that brushed against theirs. *Nothing. We're safe. I have this all under control,* Ari soothed silently.

Your heart is very loud! You're in pain.

They heard it too, throbbing in their ears. *Yes, I know. It was my fault. No need to fear.*

I'm afraid.

I know. But I'm not. Can you feel it?

"Fool! Get that thing off it! It won't kill itself! It can't!" Malgas' voice broke through their thoughts. They felt a thrill of triumph at the sharpness in her tone.

Is that panic I hear, Captain?

Another short, sharp breath whistled in through their teeth and they tightened their thumb on the trigger, making sure that all of them could see.

For all you know, I can survive this shot. Can it?

"Call for backup!" Malgas snapped to Osai. "Now!"

"What can backup do?!"

"What else can *we* do?! We can't shoot! We can't tranq! We can't risk it pulling that trigger."

The floret let out a faint but warning hum in Ari's arms. They tried not to show the panic that awakened in their chest and struggled to keep it steady as it vibrated in their grasp. But the guards had no choice but to step back. Ari cast their gaze around wildly, looking for an escape route. All around them, the walkway fell away into empty space. The drop below must have been ten feet or more; but they had no other choice. Still holding the gun to their belly, Ari backed away, step by step. Finally, they reached the edge and let themself drop, managing to catch themself into a tumbling roll that juddered their teeth and left their head spinning.

But regardless, they struggled to their feet and fled, cramming themself under a fragment of hull beneath the crystalline city. They heard guards clacking and clattering to one another as their disappearance was made known, and soldiers all across the planet were ordered into overdrive. They were gagged and bound; surely it wouldn't be a challenge to find them?

Ari squashed the thoughts down and sucked in another deep breath through their nose.

Focus on the now. No fear. I'm free.

Ari held the plasma gun in their palms and struggled to manoeuvre it to the back of their head. They pulled the trigger. A hollow thud echoed in their ears, sending their eardrums ringing. A wave of burning heat hit the back of their head. A moment later, the gag loosened from their face and they smelled burned hair. Ari patted out the burning patch, then pressed their palms forward into the dirt. With their lips free, they struggled to press the barrel of the gun to the silk that bound their hands.

A guard hollered somewhere nearby.

They pressed the handguard into their neck, feeling the upper trigger against their lips. They tightened their jaw, and curled out their tongue, wincing as they felt a low hum thrumming up through their teeth.

Ah!

Ari stumbled back. A small blue flame erupted from the ground. Their hands were burned, silk searing their wrists, but they were free.

Quashing the urge to bark triumphant laughter, Ari took off beneath the walkway, picking their way across the waste-strewn landscape beneath the city. By the time that backup had arrived, and soldiers began to descend from above, Ari had accustomed themself to the labyrinth of metal supports below. They crouched on the support beams between the ground and the landing bay, watching for any opportunity.

Wherever the soldiers walked, Ari heard a faint chiming tone, and realised with a thrill of terror that the Renohaiin were scanning for the iridium in their blood. They had to get away from here. They had to find a safe space to hide until the Rift came for them.

Or... perhaps there was another way. The Renohaiin space station was built upon a broken Riftworld; all around them lay the crystals with the capability to prevent or open the Rift.

Just like the one that pricked their neck with its jagged clusters.

Ari glanced down towards the weapon they held in their palm. The technology that powered it was far more complex than anything they'd worked with before, but the cells wouldn't last forever. Every battery needed changing eventually. Surely the same went for this plasma cell.

Deep in thought, Ari felt their neck prickle with excitement. But there was no time to think about it. For now, they needed a way out.

A shout erupted from below, and the Riftmaster knew

that they had been found. Ari's entire body tensed. A searing wave of heat hit the support beam they were sitting on, but they had dropped to the ground before it could so much as quiver. Shoving the floret into their belt for safekeeping, Ari stooped to pick up a length of metal piping from the ground. Keeping low, Ari fled, weaving through the wreckage and keeping to the shadows.

***

As they left the city behind, Ari felt as though they were stepping into a new world.

There was very little plant life here. Long-dead mushrooms had melted into soggy mulch or stood as petrified husks. Ari poked them tentatively with the pipe as they passed. No creatures had run beneath the city except for those brought by the Renohaiin. And out here, there were even less. Any Rifters that had once lived here were gone, either to the planet's hatching or the Rift.

As they travelled, a small moon slowly rose overhead.

I've never been to a Riftworld with a moon before, Ari thought curiously.

At first, Ari was filled with the uncontrollable thrill of having survived. But the more they wandered, the more the gravity of the situation began to weigh them down. Without their satchel, Ari was lost, and soon growing hungry for more than this planet had to offer.

Now, they had only the clothes on their back, the floret at their belt, and the pipe they still carried in their palm.

Oh, and of course the worm inside them.

Not exactly a winning combination.

Ari sniffed.

But I suppose I've been dealt worse cards.

Great fissures cut jagged vents across the surface of the planet, and Ari was forced to redirect their course often to find their way around. When the fissures widened, Ari would avert their course. They didn't want to risk ending up at a quarry, where the Renohaiin army was likely still mining.

They felt the chill of the crystal from Reina's riftworld home bumping against their chest. Its sharp edges and points prickled their skin, and a flare of hope rose in their chest.

Perhaps it would come in useful after all.

Ari searched in vain for one of the Riftworld's small, evenly-spaced ponds. But they found only the hole where one had been, and a gaping maw of black crystal piercing to the planet's core. No water in sight.

They weren't sure if it had been the Riftworld's hatching that had left this planet dead, or the Renohaiin army's ravaging for resources. So long as they lived, such things rarely mattered to Ari… But in this case, Ari decided that it did. Their satchel had contained thousands of years' worth of supplies; it made survival possible, if not a little too easy. Without it, they may as well eat dirt.

…But, they supposed that their passenger could make up for that. The little creature had been rather unhelpful as of late, but they remembered why they let it stay. In this case, it could be more than useful to them.

Ari had grown so used to feeling its emotions alongside their own that they barely noticed it anymore. But they found themself growing strangely worried at the lack of presence. Turning their thoughts inward, they reached out, feeling for its emotions.

You okay in there, little one?

Almost immediately, they felt a note of disgruntlement fizzing through them, almost as though it had been waiting for the opportunity to chide them.

Yes, yes… I know I threatened you. But I didn't mean it, okay?

It gave no indication of an answer, and Ari took that as an accepted apology. There was something else, though, something that Ari both noticed and shared.

Hungry!

Ari winced slightly. Not much they could do about that right now. Even if the parasite could help them digest most toxic substances, Ari didn't want to chance anything rotten or potentially deadly. They didn't yet know what its limits were… Although at this rate, Ari was going to have to find out rather soon.

As they moved across the barren wasteland, Ari heard a distant rumble, and they felt a jolt rush through them.

The armada had finally taken to their ships.

It's about time, Ari thought. The fleet was acting with a certain degree of caution, they imagined. Ari was armed with a plasma floret now, making it significantly more difficult to capture them unharmed. To surround and capture them on foot was the ideal scenario, but since they had passed the city's outskirts and pressed further into the unknown, that had obviously failed.

What they didn't know, was that Ari had other plans for the weapon. They'd have to use it soon before the fleet grew desperate. With an armada of ships scanning the planet from the air, Ari only had so long before they were found.

There was little shelter here, but they had to try to stay out of view of the ships as long as possible. They scurried like a rat between fallen caps and the husks of long-grounded ships as the search parties began to appear. Their presence would easily be picked up on scanners, it was true, but with any luck there would be false alarms. If a ship landed even a hundred metres away, Ari would have the chance to escape.

Uneven terrain would give them the best chance at survival.

With so few places to hide, Ari began to follow the fissures to the edge of the broken world.

Perhaps the immense slabs of crystal would offer them a measure of protection there. Perhaps the shards would even be too fragile to hold the weight of a ship. Ari felt their breaths coming quickly as they forced themself to move quicker through waste and sludge, winding through broken pieces of foliage from other worlds. In the distance they could see shards of the planet hanging just above the gravity field; and knew that they were going the right way.

A scouting vessel boomed as it soared overhead; there

was no way in hell that Ari hadn't been seen. They broke into a sprint once again, following along the jagged edge of the fissure. To their left was lilac soil, and the distant silhouette of the crystalline city.

To the right, jagged crystals fell away into a cliff that pierced right into the very centre of the world. Just looking into it made them feel dizzy; they could not see the bottom, and knew it went right to the planet's core.

They kept on peering over the edge and into the fissure, looking for caves just beneath the lip of the cliff.

They would not find me there. Or if they did, it would at least give me long enough to get off this planet.

As they moved, they kept their gaze on the ground; fragments of half-buried crystals poked up from the earth around them, sharp and dangerous.

Another crack joined them on their other side. The fissures would soon converge and Ari would reach a dead end; they slowed, hesitating.

No; I have to keep going. No vessel would land this close to the edge.

Ari finally came to the precipice. Standing upon the very edge, they looked out over the gash torn in the side of this once lively planet. They took in a breath in a sharp gasp.

I thought the Rift had run out of surprises.

The world fell away beneath them, a thousand fragments of the planet's crust floating beyond the stratosphere as though they'd broken away just yesterday. They glistened bleakly in the light of a thousand stars, the shadowy husks of trees still clinging to their surfaces.

And there, at the bottom of a terrifying drop, lay the long-dead carapace of the creature that had curled up inside, a hundred miles below. Over thousands of years, its flesh had rotted away, leaving only the exoskeleton of the vast newborn floating at the planet's core, now bearing a coat of dying trees and plant life. As a deep rumble reached their ears, Ari looked up sharply, and saw a ship silhouetted against the moon overhead.

Not a moon, they reminded themself. *…A meteorite.*

They couldn't stay here; if they hadn't been already, they would be seen. Ari backed away from the precipice and looked around.

In the distance they saw the familiar shape of a vessel landing upon the distant plain like a great black mosquito. Their heart sank. Ari felt slightly sick. They risked one last glance at the dead rift-whale before turning to peer out across a smaller crevasse.

The other side was many metres away from them; though there were no caves it was jagged, ridged, and covered in overhanging slabs and ledges. The Renohaiin armada would never be able to land a ship over there, and moreover, they'd have more than enough trouble sending soldiers in after them. If Ari reached it, they could perhaps use it to climb even lower into Riftworld's core. But the other side was too far to leap.

I need to be quick; if worst comes to worst, they can still Rift to the planet's surface.

Ari cast their gaze around, at jagged crystal spikes and then to the drop beneath them, where there was ample space to land on the crumbling skeleton, held together only by its own gravity.

But… would they risk it? This planet has a surface beneath the surface.

They would have to draw nearer to the vessel, and hope that the jagged cliff face presented an opportunity.

Ari set off, scanning the sheer cliff face across from them and holding their breath as it drew nearer. More and more, they closed the distance between themself and the vessel, until they could see individual figures clustered around the *Vestige*.

Their route back to the city was cut off.

Ari hurried along the very edge of the cliff, gazing out to the other side, only metres away. Just a little closer, and…

Looking up, Ari saw that the crew had fanned out across the plain, and were heading towards them. They could tell from the colours of their hides that it was Captain Malgas and her crew, with the exception of

Omea, and Hoss. Ari wasn't sure why, but they felt their heart sink.

This will have to do. I'm out of time.

They looked out across the fissure, at the jagged mess of crystals on the other side. One of them was flat enough to make for an adequate landing point, but they'd need to make sure they hit it just right. Aside from that, they'd need to climb, shimmy, and leap their way across the cliff face to get to a larger ledge.

It would be a drastic action; one wrong move could send them plummeting to their death, but it would buy them enough time to work with what they had and find a way off the planet.

They had little choice.

Ari took a few steps back, measuring the distance and trying not to let their fear get the better of them. They breathed deeply, but their heart kept on pounding. They felt the parasite responding acutely to their fear, even as they tried to squash it. It churned in the depths of their belly.

Don't do it! Scary! Unsafe!

It will be worse for the both of us if I don't, they thought, trying their best to calm it down. *Experimented on, tested, used for their own gain... They'll probably melt you down for your toxins.*

Fear!

Ari's thoughts didn't seem to be helping, so they tried their best to shut it out. They risked a final glance towards the crew. Florets readied, they were breaking into a coordinated sprint, shouting orders to each other across the plain.

Ari had only seconds.

The Riftmaster took a deep breath and set their gaze on the other side. It suddenly seemed so far away. Shoving the pipe into the belt against their back, they broke into a sprint. They hurled themself out into open space, and heard Captain Malgas scream. They seemed to hang there for an eternity over the abyss, before tumbling to a painful halt and smacking against the cliffside.

They sat there for a few moments, breathing heavily, feeling the adrenaline pounding through their skull. They wiped a hand against their forehead. Ari thought at first that the slick feeling was sweat, but as they glanced down at their palm, they found it covered in blood. Ari glanced up towards the edge of the cliff, and saw a figure standing there.

Malgas' face was full of thunder, her shoulders stiff. While two of her hands held a floret against her chest, the others writhed like insect legs. Ari saw Osai appear at her side, similarly armed. Ari stared at them for what felt like forever, before the Renohaiin finally exchanged a glance. Turning their backs, they disappeared from Ari's view.

Ari didn't know where they were going, and in this particular moment, they decided that they didn't care.

Breaths short and sharp, and forehead beginning to sting, Ari regained their breath, suddenly wheezing. They rested their back against the cliff face and panted, pressing a palm against their forehead to try to stop the bloodflow. Even still, they felt euphoric.

We made it! We're alive!

Heedless of a reply, Ari gave themself a few moments more to recover before slowly rising to their feet, shaking slightly, and leaned an arm against the cliff face. The brittle crystal creaked slightly beneath their weight, but they were certain it would hold.

Grasping onto a few overhanging clusters, Ari swung themself over empty space.

One hand after the other, they climbed further down the cliffside until they managed to wedge their feet into an overhanging ridge. They pressed themself into the cold stone, breathing sharply, trembling with the strain, and inched along its surface. Finally, after a few more minutes of climbing, a short upwards scramble, and a close near-miss, Ari sat on a wide, mostly-flat ledge, overlooking the exoskeleton hanging below in perfect stillness.

Here, they finally allowed themself to breathe, heaving the air into their burning lungs. After such physical exertion, their throat was parched. It felt like grit, and stuck together when they swallowed. They wouldn't have long. They badly needed food, water, and rest.

But more importantly, they needed a plan.

Ari removed the pipe from their back, the crystal from their necklace, and the floret from their belt, and set them in a corner between the ledge and the cliff face. It took Ari a moment to decide which object to examine first. But finally, they decided the gun would be the best starting point. It would be central to finding their way off this planet.

It took a long while before Ari was able to disconnect the power cell, but eventually they managed. Using the tip of their knife to ease the chitinous plates from the metal framework, they set the body of the gun aside whilst they examined it.

No wires… just the cell. Perhaps there will be more inside.

After a moment of consideration, they began to take it apart. Removing all the wiring they could find, they kept the circuit largely intact, but rearranged the plasma cell, replacing it with the crystal.

Without much in the way of supplies and nothing to start a fire, Ari drew their knife. With a sharp feeling of discomfort, they forced themself not to look as they raised it above their head and swept torso-length hair into a single fistful. In what proved to be a long, uncomfortable, and somewhat painful endeavour, they cut it short.

I knew that there was a reason I kept it long… Ari thought as they arranged it into a pile on the ground. With a shot from the floret, they set it alight. The stench of burning hair made them feel ill, and they covered it with their cape, hoping that the material was flammable. The flame took a moment to hold, but eventually lit up in a searing blaze, white-hot with the iridium hide. Finally, by its light they were able to begin.

Ari held the piping into the open flame. It was not made from the strongest metal, but it couldn't exactly be called flimsy. But, with most Renohaiin valuing chitin over metal, their alloys tended to have a low melting point. When it glowed red amid the white-hot campfire, Ari pierced a hole in its length with a fragment of metal.

When it had cooled, they used the flame once more to solder the wires to the crystal, threaded them through the pipe, and finally melded pipe to crystal in a makeshift setting. At the centre of the pipe, they re-attached the trigger, and completed the circuit.

What remained of the floret's metal framework, they sharpened with a stone from a necklace and turned into a crude, backwards-curving blade. They finally used it to seal up the hollow end of the pipe.

As Ari worked, the meteorite moon rose and fell overhead, shining an eerie life into the sleek black canyon. Spaceships soared, flying low overhead. Figures appeared up at the clifftop. Ari knew they would be seen, but they had some degree of confidence that they could not be reached.

As the fire died, they fed it with more and more scraps of their clothing, forcing the sputtering flare back into life. By the end of it all, their boots had been ripped down to their ankles, and their loincloth was completely gone. All that remained was their shining undersuit.

As the day wore on, exhaustion began to hinder their movements, and their hands became covered in burns. They had not slept in many days. The wound on their forehead was small, but it itched viciously.

Finally, Ari rested with their back to the wall, and lifted up the staff into their palm. The power cell inside rattled faintly, and twin blades gleamed dully in the light of the dying fire. A spiral of copper wires ran down its length, from the crystal at its base to hooked, asymmetrical blades – between which a small fragment had been placed. The floret's trigger stuck out from its side.

It was a crude object; haphazardly produced and probably inconvenient and unwieldy to use. Still, Ari stared at it in wonder until, finally spent, their eyes flickered closed.

But, through the darkness, the back of their neck kept on burning with a shivering pain. Ari opened their eyes, raising a hand towards it. Even the faintest touch was enough to sting. Ari steeled themself, then piece by painful piece, they dug out the shards of crystal that had burrowed into flesh, until the pain had dulled. Even then, they were certain some remained.

What if I'm never able to Rift again? they wondered. *What will I do then?*

Their gaze trailed down to the staff that now lay across their lap. *If this works,* they thought. *Then I'll have my answer.*

Finally they closed their eyes once more. *I'll test it when I wake,* they thought, as they drifted off into slumber. *Hopefully, the Rift will arrive, and I'll never need to use it.*

***

Nervousness made for uneasy sleep, but Ari managed to separate themself from consciousness eventually. They awakened twice each hour, casting their gaze up and out of the ravine. They couldn't tell just how long they drifted in and out of sleep, but Ari jolted awake as fragments of crystal rained down on them. Their eyes flickered open, and they blinked awake before shooting bolt upright and onto their feet. Fractured memories spinning into nonexistence, Ari turned their staff perpendicular to their body, craning their neck back and saw that they were not alone.

Above them, several Renohaiin soldiers were abseiling down the sheer crystal surface, towards their tiny hideaway. Ari's breath caught. They spun their staff and tightened their grip on the trigger.

There's a chance this might kill me. But what other choice do I have?

The choice seemed easy; would they rather die in agony with their blood full of venom, or die to their own hand?

Die in sacrifice for the empire and end my life meaningfully, or be lost to the abyss, forever.

It was unlikely to work, they knew. But…

I have to try.

Sucking in a deep breath and trying to calm their wildly beating heart, Ari raised the crystal in their staff towards the heavens. They looked towards the stars, the ever-changing map that they had followed for thousands of years. Then they pulled the trigger.

The power cell hummed; they felt the vibrations beneath their fingertips. The crystal pulsed with a faint white light that slowly spread to its sharpened points. Brighter and brighter, until it was nearly blinding. The hum deepened as Ari clamped their palm around the trigger again.

But nothing happened.

Fear lit Ari's gaze with a sparkle of wild fire. They had hinged all their bets on this; there was no other way out.

Their pursuers descended upon them, close enough that Ari could see the hope in their compound eyes…

Ari pressed themself against the cliffside, sucked in their breath and pulled the trigger one more time.

They heard the faintest *chink* as the pressure released.

The pain hit them immediately, more intense than anything they'd ever felt before. The light that filled their vision bored deep into their brain and lingered until they knew nothing else, their eyes rolling back in their head. They keeled over, feeling the power rushing through them as they let out a barely-human screech. And then they were falling, minutes passing as they spun through empty space.

It felt like they fell for an eternity. Falling, or floating; they couldn't be sure which. Perhaps their body was burning into nothingness; or perhaps it was already gone.

But then they hit the ground, cold water leaping up around them as they splashed to a tumbling halt. Where the water touched their bare skin, it hissed and boiled. The cold burned them to the core. They lay, partially submerged in a muddied mire.

Slowly, they pushed themself upright and onto their knees. The formerly dark crystal on the end of their staff glowed like a trapped star, a snaking crack bleeding white light into the shaded world beyond their vision. But somehow, it remained whole.

Bad! No! Fear!

It's alright! We're safe! We're alive!

They felt the fear sharp on their tongue. Poison tugged at their limbs like lead. Nausea raged in their belly. But, without stopping to consider, Ari cupped their hands in the water pooled around them.

It bubbled in their grasp. And they saw that their veins were marked by ribbons of bright, glowing light, alive with a fire that still itched and burned.

They began to drink.

It felt like so long since they'd wet their throat. And the cold seemed to soothe the worm inside of them. It stopped protesting. The nausea didn't worsen any more. Ari slowly clambered to their feet, using the staff as an aid. They raised a fist, though it felt heavy as lead, to the sky. Ari filled their lungs, yelled in triumph and punched the empty air. Every vein in their body pumped with adrenaline and pulsed with the light of the Rift as they called out, shaking their staff in challenge.

"Eat it, empire! You'll never catch this!"

Finally, they stumbled out of the mire and onto dry land. Crashing down under the welcoming boughs of a tree, they passed out.

Minutes turned into an hour as they gradually regained their strength, their heart rate slowed. They opened their eyes to see the mire lapping at a silty shore, shrouded in mist. *Tide's coming in,* they thought vaguely. They lifted a shaking hand, and found that the glow had faded from their skin, but the wound on the back of their neck was still on fire, throbbing.

They looked up, craning their neck back. It flared painfully, but they gazed up at the sky. Through the tree canopy and past a layer of smog, the twinkle of a few stray stars was visible. Somewhere beyond them, the world they had left behind. *I have to go. I have to get off this planet.*

They climbed into the branches of the sturdiest flora, and gazed up past the leaves and the mountains, into the deep nothingness of the sky.

Ari trained their staff and pulled the trigger just as a flash of light lit up the sky with brightness.

This time, the crystal didn't need any further encouragement.

A moment later, they felt their world spinning. Skin burning. Falling through nothingness. But this time, at least they knew they were alone.

Mostly.

As much as they tried to cling to consciousness, Ari was out cold before they hit the ground.

Chapter 12
Rift Rendezvous

By the time they came to, the pain had faded, and the world around them was stark with contrasting shadows. A sheer white sun blazed in an ash-grey sky, and the air was thick with the heady smell of decaying fruit.

Ari sat up. Wincing faintly, they rubbed their forehead and glanced around. The world around them looked washed in ash, almost as if their eyes were beginning to fail, or was being seen through a black-and-white television set from back home.

The distant, jagged mountain peaks stood out bleakly against the grey sky.

Ancient, gnarled trees loomed around them, scattered across the valley in sickly grey hues.

Glancing down at their hands, Ari saw that they stood out as the only flash of colour in a world of otherwise grey; but their scaled armour showed its hues only faintly.

Looking around, Ari saw jagged, unattractive foliage, and the ground was covered in faintly brown-tinted mush. They sniffed the air; the sweet smell of decay had reawakened the hunger in their belly, and they suddenly realised just how desperate they were.

How long has it been since my last meal? they wondered. *Five days, perhaps? A week?*

No matter what, they needed to find something. Ari wove through the jagged undergrowth, peering around at the world. With so little colour and no way of knowing what was good for them, Ari didn't know if they trusted anything, but the sparse woodland seemed, regardless, full of fruit. Plucking a black, leathery-skinned fruit from a bulbous trunk, Ari stumbled through the sparsely scattered trees, looking in vain for somewhere to settle down as they considered alternate ways to check for toxicity.

They supposed that the old-fashioned way would have to do.

Finally, they picked a handful of silver berries that dangled in a tantalising spray above their path, a few furry, nut-like seeds, and an odd pulsating object of questionable origins. Whether it was animal or plant, Ari couldn't be sure. Finally, they cautiously tested the backwards-curving blades of their staff on a tree branch, then used it to haul themself up into the crotch of a gnarled tree trunk. They set their prizes aside as they checked the weapon for any signs of warping. Finding none, they looked up.

The broad trunk was massive; wide, flat branches formed an interlocking knot in the centre that made for a good place to make camp. It was rather open; the tree canopy here was almost like another forest floor, open to the sky and bearing plants and fruits of its own. This second ground was threaded with interlocking tendrils that added stability and sturdiness, and presumably gathered nutrients. Some broad leaves even bore a layer of soil and moss of its own.

Roots above as well as below... how curious, Ari mused, as they sprawled out in the centre of the tree and from its comforting solidity began to gather rocks, stones, and twigs to build a platform for a campfire.

Whilst they weren't sure what they wanted to try first, Ari knew for a fact what they intended to save for last.

First, they took the large, leathery fruit, and cut it open with deft motions of their staff. Opening it up startled them; it was blue, true blue, and a brighter shade than they'd seen anywhere else on this world. Holding it beneath their nose, they sniffed. It smelled sour, but not wholly unpleasant.

Picking up the berries, Ari squashed one between their fingertips. The juices oozed a rich purple colour. They sniffed, and immediately felt a sneeze brewing in the back of their throat. Turning their gaze away, Ari violently let it loose, and heard the echoes bouncing back at them from all over the wood. Unnerved, they placed the berries aside.

Finally, they prepared to cut into the pulsating orb. Almost immediately, it unfurled. Startled, Ari dropped it, and a shocked terrestrial creature dropped between the tree branches and took off across the ground. Ari wiped their fingers on their clothing and shuddered.

I suppose I'll try the leather-melon.

Ari lit a fire that burned in sickly tones of white and yellow, and placed the fruit on a spit over the flickering fire. Almost immediately it began to bubble, and they were greeted with a warm, savoury smell. Their stomach growled.

"Almost there, little thing. You'll be fed soon," they murmured.

But the parasite didn't respond.

As the fruit cooked, Ari took to scraping some bark from the branches of the trees. Unlike on Earth, it was soft and malleable, almost like fabric. They cut off long strips and began to weave them together into a makeshift sling. *All I really need is a way to carry things. After that, I'll be good to go.*

Soon after that, the fruit on the fire began to liquify; Ari hastily lifted it off, using the skin as a bowl. It was not quite as solid as they'd hoped, but it would at least hold its shape. Ari blew away the steam, and listened to the crackling of the campfire, letting the silence warm them to the core. Finally, they took a sip. It wasn't bad; certainly better than anything the Renohaiin empire produced. Then again, Ari couldn't exactly blame them.

197

The Renohaiin couldn't taste foods the same way that humans could, so nourishment alone took priority.

Still, after so long eating nothing but sustenance pills and water-rich leaves, the fruit's bitter sweetness tasted almost gourmet. Ari slurped up half with vigour, before reluctantly setting the rest aside. *I'd best not eat too much at once. My stomach isn't used to it… and if I do end up poisoned, well… I'll need to be ready.*

Still, they licked the remaining juice from their lips, closed their eyes, and felt for a response. Deep in the crevices of their mind, they felt a small thrill of relief and joy. *That's right,* they answered silently. *We're safe now.*

Night fell, quickly and abruptly, and they wrapped themselves in broad leaves to keep warm, shivering. They had lost almost all of their possessions to Malgas' crew, including the things they used to keep warm; but it still felt like pure, unbridled relief to get back to their usual routines. It felt like they were finally home; back out in the wild, back in their natural habitat.

With their urgent needs satisfied, Ari finally looked up as the stars began to poke through a blanket of grey. And there, they saw traces of familiarity. Curiosity piqued, the Riftmaster examined them closely, and was able to trace their pathway back to the empty space where the Riftworld lay.

At first, it was an unnerving thought. *Maybe they will be able to follow me after all.*

But then…

Bailey… the Riftmaster was hit with a surge of euphoria that caught them off guard. They didn't realise how long it had been since they'd even thought about him. *With this staff, I'll be able to get back to him. If I just wait for the planets to turn… I might be able to find my way.*

The sparkle in their eyes slowly dulled, though, as they remembered something else.

The Vularian creatures… they're out here, too. If I get back to him, I need to warn him.

***

Over the next few days, Ari did little more than eating and sleeping. Contrary to their fears, they didn't come down with food poisoning, and supposed that the parasite was helping them more than they knew. Gradually, they became less hesitant to eat, and lost their wariness as they regained their strength. They found, soon, that they could cook the leather-melons whole, drink the fluid from inside and then reuse the empty skin as a water flask.

Gradually, they rebuilt their repertoire. And, when many sleep cycles later the night finally returned, Ari began to plan their route, gazing up at the sky. They saw the stars, familiar constellations that they had known for thousands of years from a whole new perspective. And finally they were ready to explore them again.

I'm quite a way out from the Milky Way. But if I begin to make my way to the outskirts of this galaxy, then I should soon be able to see it. I saw it from the Vestige; that means I should soon be back among familiar stars.

For the first time in all their years, Ari felt their heart swell with hope. Here, today, they were about to navigate the Rift. Control it.

They were going back.

But what will I find when I get there? They shook their head to chase away a faint niggle of doubt. *All I can do is get back to Earth, and warn Bailey.*

They tried not to think about what would happen after.

Maybe I can convince him to run with me.

Ari turned their attention back towards the most important thing. For a few more hours, Ari filled their belly and made sure to pack supplies. Their water pouch was filled, their sling tied across their shoulder, and their belly full. Their staff was freshly sharpened and its jewels glowed bright as the moon back on Earth.

Ari raised their staff, setting their sights on the brightest star. They pointed the cracked crystal towards it.

I'll see you soon, Bailey.

And then, they pulled the trigger.

Ari landed on the other side of the Rift and waited for the fire to die from their fingertips. It took a while longer for the glow to fade from their skin, and they shed light on their new world with a beaming grin.

As Ari closed the gaps between worlds, travelling with the staff became easier to bear. Powerful blasts of Rift-energy that had left them stunned and incapacitated became tolerable. Soon, it felt like any other Rift, and they no longer hesitated before using it.

More than that, their mind kept track of the planets they passed, both now and in previous years, reminiscing on planets that were in their reach. Whether the Rift was truly random or not, Ari found themself wondering at the grain of truth in Malgas' words. For, whenever they pointed their staff at the sky, they'd always... or... well, usually, find the planet they'd left behind, or the distant fleck of its system, sitting somewhere in the sky above them. Provided the view was clear, of course. More often than not, it would be too bright, too shrouded in clouds or fog, or simply out of view.

Sometimes they'd cast out for a star and end up solar systems away, having travelled a hundred lightyears further or in a different direction entirely. Not far off, they supposed, in the grand scale of the universe; but still almost unimaginable in its distance for a creature like Ari.

Perhaps some of the planets were not aligned.

They had always known that the universe was ever-changing; planets forever turned, always in orbit, hiding in the shadow of their suns. The stars themselves were shifting, some improperly positioned, even when they had been accessible before. Even now, the path Ari took between planets felt jagged and confusing.

In amongst wonder, Ari felt a creeping sense of dread. *Small populations have even been turning up in the galaxy you call the Milky Way;* Hoss's words lingered in their mind, repeated.

Rifters always use the same pathways, Ari kept on thinking. *And there are only so many life-bearing planets in the Milky Way. That means there's a higher chance than not that I'll run into them… or maybe even the Motherbeast itself eventually.*

Whatever the case, on reaching a new planet Ari would climb to the highest point they could find and wait for the sky to clear. With the staff at their disposal, they did not like to Rift blindly. When they had the luxury of choice, they liked to make the most of it. Often, they would need to wait until the planet's natural rotation allowed them a view of a new part of the sky, although it wasn't always facing the right direction.

On days like these, when time felt limitless, Ari would fill their time constructing elaborate starmaps from sticks, stones, and any natural materials they could find. Drawing lines in the dirt, they marked out their path through the cosmos. Although their efforts often drew the intrigue of the local wildlife, Ari found themself inching steadily closer to the planet they knew as Earth.

No matter the shape of the horizon or the colour of the sky, Ari never lost sight of that goal.

Finally they looked over the edge of a clifftop. Dense jungle fell away behind them, and ahead, the mirror-like stillness of a rich red sea. But they had eyes only for what lay above; in a sky of deep maroon flecked with scattered points of light, Ari could see an island of swirling, twisting clouds that lit the entire stratosphere. But they knew that those clouds weren't clouds at all; but a vast number of lights, each one a sun with its own system, and planets with their own story, each creature inhabiting their own tiny corner of an impossibly huge universe. Infinite possibilities awaited them across a river of dark red sky.

But raising their staff, the Riftmaster set their sights on only one. Ari held their breath before making the final crossing; with no more than a tiny click, Ari made the leap from the Andromeda galaxy onto the outermost stars of the Milky Way.

It had been weeks, and still they felt no closer.

Soon, though, Ari walked a path paved with memories. The scents on the air became gradually more familiar.

They recognised the colours and shapes of the foliage.

This might have been the very first planet I set foot on.
This might have been the first one I made my first kill.
This might have been the last I named.

Ari knew from their and Bailey's time together that Rifting between worlds left invisible traces. When a Rifter arrived or left, they created an imprint on a planet's surface with a high concentration of Rift Energy. On Earth, those places tended to breed superstition; whispers of gateways to hell, wormholes, and theories of a more conspiratorial air. Perhaps, now that they had control, Ari found themself re-using those same pathways.

It was wishful thinking, though; the oldest memories were foggy at best, and at worst, barely decipherable. There was no telling whether a world was the same or whether this strange species of tree just bore similar seed pods to somewhere else. These spiky orange berries vividly triggered a memory of utter delicacy; and yet tasted like rotten fish soaked in honey.

Familiarity alone wasn't enough to keep them alive.

Even still, their travels had brought them so painfully close to Earth. Once when they first left, and again when they met Oliver. Then, years later, when they met Bailey too.

If Bailey could just see me now, they thought. *How much has changed.*

Ari's heart ached as they thought back. Their mind wandered back to the Riftworld where they'd both learned so much. Ari remembered returning to the cabin to find Bailey studying as though he was home again, greeting them with a warm smile. Though they had always known in their heart of hearts that for him, the Rift would never feel like home, for a moment Ari imagined what would have happened if they'd never left him behind.

Would he be here with me now? Would the Empire have come after us both?

Ari smiled wanly.

Bailey would have given himself up in a heartbeat to

save lives, they thought. *He's better kept out of this. All I need to do is make sure he gets away.*

More and more frequently they found themself wondering about the worlds they passed through, straining back through the nostalgia to find the truth.

Did they visit this planet with Oliver, or Bailey? As a family, or as a duo? *Were there three of us here, or five, or perhaps nine? Or was it just me?*

The more they searched for the answers, the more Ari found themself facing memories of happier times. Their mind echoed with the familiar sounds of creatures leaping above homes long crumbled; the smells of cooking.

We were here with Adeline when she was only tiny, I'm sure of it. And we came back when Toby and Polly were only toddling.

Ari kept looking down towards their empty arms and expecting to see the face of a newborn gazing back at them, their eyes so bright and new.

How close we must have come to reaching Earth. How different things might have been if we had.

Perhaps if they had, their children might still have been alive, and Oliver too.

Ari's heart grew heavy, their fingers cold, as they opened the way to the Rift and forced themself to go on, to keep on leaving the memories behind. They could think forever about the what-ifs. But it wouldn't raise the dead, or clean the blood from their hands.

The stars crowded close as they travelled, spinning, swirling, rearranging themselves into recognisable shapes.

Ari's breath grew thick with anticipation.

It won't be long now.

As the glow faded from their skin and the fire from their veins, Ari raised their chin, gently sniffing the air. As the whiteness faded from their vision, red leaves gradually faded into focus, gently rustling all around them.

This place… They thought. *Could this be?*

Gentle winds whispered like an omen among the crimson foliage. As they took their first step forward and began to walk, they felt memories replaying before their very eyes. Memories of those first few weeks, as Oliver struggled and Ari toyed.

As they walked forward, Ari's boots crunched among the remains of long-dead ferns, choked and strangled by the tendrils of familiar flowers from other worlds. What had once been planted in their garden alone had spread; and now they formed a colourful blanket across the forest floor where ferns had once fed on the coils of dappled light.

Ari wrestled with relief and revulsion, and ignored the damage that they had hand-sown, along with the herbs that had guided them through so many worlds. And this time they knew for certain.

The planet where we first met.

Even in the peaceful, blissful quiet, Ari's breaths came quickly, their heart pounding in their throat.

I can't stay here, they realised.

Everywhere they looked, they saw fragments of a time long gone, the ghosts of memories played. In the cries of the creatures of the woods, they heard Oliver's enraged shouts, while Aria's impish giggle hid in the sound of the wind.

Even the leaves are the colour of his blood.

Ari spun around, mind reeling, as something rustled in the undergrowth beyond their sight.

No...

Every fibre and muscle prepared to see the impossible visage of a familiar face, Ari took an anxious step back as they stared, hypnotised. Their legs tensed. *Go,* they told themself. *What are you waiting for? There's nothing here! He's gone!*

Their own laughter hung on the air in their bated breath. The bushes rustled again in warning.

Why are you doing this to yourself? You're only going to be disappointed.

Ari didn't wait to see what emerged. Forcing the life back into their limbs, they finally fled, heart pounding in their chest, running until lungs ached. Finally, they skidded to a halt and pressed their back to the trunk of a tree, clutching their face as they let out choked sobs. Their head was spinning, stomach turning. As though for the first time, Ari remembered just what they were carrying inside of them.

Why this? Why now?

Danger, danger!

Ari felt acid rising in their throat. *I'm not in danger!*

Then why are you afraid?

I'm not afraid! Just give me a moment... Please, little thing, just make it stop.

You're lying! I feel your despair. It tightens in the walls around me and pulses in your blood!

I'm not! Please, just leave me be.

I will! Just let me out!

Something writhed.

No! Ari's stomach dropped. *No, I won't! Stop trying to escape!*

Ari swallowed it down despite the discomfort of both passenger and host.

It tried again, sending lancing pains through their entire body. Sweat beaded on the Riftmaster's forehead as they hacked and choked, tears streaming down their face and vision blurred.

"No!" They spluttered out between retches. "There is no danger here, can't you see? Stop! Please, stop!"

Ari struggled to control their breaths, swallowing one more time and closing their eyes. "Stop trying to leave…"

Ari kept their head down and focused on their breathing, trying to blot out the pain. *I can't let you leave. I can't be on my own again.*

"Little thing, you're all I have now."

And as long as you're inside me, no harm will ever come to you. I promise.

It took time, but they were finally able to raise their head without losing their last meal. They rested their head back against the trunk of the tree, gazing up into its branches as tears rolled down their salt-encrusted cheeks.

Ari shook their head slightly, scrubbing the tears from their face. *It's over… why does it hurt so much?*

Slowly but surely, they staggered to their feet, leaning heavily on the staff with the blades planted in the ground by their feet. They felt for the trigger… but then stopped themself, steadying their breaths.

I need to calm down. This is a safe planet, a respite. If I Rift like this, I'll be doomed.

Finally, they turned their gaze to the forest floor, trying to avoid seeing anything else.

I can't believe I'm back… after so long. There can't be many jumps left before I reach Earth. Of that I'm nearly certain. I just need to find somewhere to see the stars.

So, with agonising slowness, Ari made their way to what felt like the top of the world – clambering up onto a lonely plateau spread out beneath the stars. With only stray stands of trees, it was almost easy to pretend that they were standing on a different planet altogether. There they gazed up past the clouds and beyond the reaches of their memories, and there they saw a single star.

As much as I'd like to get away from this place… If I'm to leave this planet, I'll need to prepare.

It took Ari several days to gather the courage just to leave the plateau and step once more into the forest's familiar eaves. They gathered flowering tendrils of the plants that had escaped their garden, restoring the supplies that had taken them so far.

They resisted sleep as long as they could, knowing that the dreams would come.

But eventually, they curled up in a hollow they had once known as home, closed their eyes and dreamed.

They heard rain pitter-pattering softly on unseen leaves around them.

They heard Oliver's voice, first. His low, hesitant tone and quick, nervous breaths made their heart skip a beat.

"So you're certain, then?" he asked cautiously.

Ari finally opened their eyes.

In this dream, Oliver had become even less human. A mane of quills framed his face, and a couple spiked his chin.

His body was long and lanky, curved like a frightened cat. His face was porcelain white; though they couldn't tell if that was the warping of their memory, or the fear.

As Ari looked into Oliver's frightened blue eyes, they felt their expression sour slightly.

"There's no need to look so shocked; it was bound to happen at some point."

"Well, yes, but… so soon?"

"Soon?" Ari laughed, a high-pitched, startling sound, instinctively emerging to cover any indication of how they truly felt. "It's taken almost a thousand years."

"Well, yes, but…" Oliver's cheeks flushed bright red. "You know what I mean."

"Anyway," Ari turned their back. "That's all I wanted to say. I just thought you should know."

"Aria, wait."

A large, warm, strong hand grasped their shoulder. Sharp talons drove into their skin, biting and alluring. Slowly Oliver ran his palm down their arm, winding his fingers into theirs. His palms felt rough against their own, and yet the gentle touch felt soft, and homely. Even still, they felt the cold burn of the golden ring on his finger.

"What will we do?"

"We hunt for our dinner."

"Aria… That's not what I meant." Oliver glanced down towards something they refused to acknowledge.

The Riftmaster didn't follow his gaze.

"Stop looking," they said sourly. "There's nothing we *can* do. We made our cake. Now we must eat it."

"But Aria, *listen*. You could get hurt. You could even die."

Ari didn't look at him. When they spoke, their voice was small. "I know."

"But you're still planning on going through with it? Out here? Alone?"

"What else can we do? Ollie, this is the Rift. All we can do is prepare. For the best outcome, and…" they turned their gaze away, raising a hand towards their belly. "And for the worst."

For what felt like the first time in their long, long life, Ari felt fear. Real fear. There was something inside of them that could one day tear them apart, and all they could do was wait for it to come. It was already affecting their mind, their body, their appetite, and everything in between. And even if they survived, the consequences of this could affect them forever.

They almost didn't feel like *them* anymore.

The Riftmaster had been expecting this for some time. Dreading it but expecting it. Even still, that didn't help to alleviate just how *wrong* it felt.

They could see no way out of this. No way to make it easier.

They were thousands of lightyears from the nearest hospital, and it was entirely up to chance whether they would end up there or not. If that wasn't enough, it was even more unlikely that the doctors there would be able to help them at all.

There weren't a lot of races in the infinite cosmos skilled in preparing for live birth. And Oliver was unlikely to trust any of them, anyway.

There was no hope.

For the first time, the Riftmaster was not in control.

Slowly, they let out a breath and sank down onto a mossy stone that rose to meet them out of the mist. Their legs quivered slightly as they buried their head in their hands. They felt Oliver's taloned hand rest on the small of their back and start rubbing.

"Aren't you scared?" Ari asked softly. "I might not make it out of this."

"A little bit," Oliver admitted, after a moment's hesitation. "Not as nervous as the first time."

Ari had to bite their tongue to keep a sharp retort. *It's almost as if your first time is the only important one.*

Finally they took a deep breath, and spoke. "In case you haven't noticed, we're on a completely different world." Though their eyes were dark with helpless anger, their voice was low. "…And your first child was born over a thousand years ago."

Oliver's jaw tightened. "I know, I know... but Aria... Take this from me," Oliver gently ran a hand across one of their cheeks and raised their chin so he could look into their eyes.

Reluctantly, they met his eyes – they were hazel, now. But Oliver's face was beginning to blur; Ari wasn't sure if it was with the tears in their eyes, or the memory fading away. "I think you'll make it through this. If anything in this universe *could* kill you, it certainly wouldn't be your own body."

"Oliver... That is probably the only thing that *can* kill me."

Ari fought to keep his image at the forefront of their mind as the dreams fizzled out of existence, and into consciousness. They awoke clutching the necklace of shards around their neck, their palms scratched red and raw.

It took them several more days to underprepare, gathering familiar fruits and stripping a hairy creature of its thick coat to make a new one of their own.

They resisted sleep until their eyes sank deep into the hollows of their skull.

Slipping one of Reina's quills from a leather band around their neck, Ari wove plant fibres into thread and stitched a new set of warm clothing. Even though Ari had the option to Rift to escape unfavourable conditions, there was one planet they hoped to stop by, however unlikely it was that its orbit and their path would align. If they did make it, though, then they would need to be *warm*.

As they threaded the needle back onto their necklace and let it fall against their chest, though, Ari caught sight of a familiar pendant that left them feeling hollow inside. Fragments of Oliver's knife gleamed in the starlight.

Ari squeezed their eyes shut and looked away.

The more they lingered, though, the more they felt as though there was something they had to do. Something important. Even when they were ready to go, Ari stood, hesitating on the edge of the precipice. For tonight alone, the sky was clear; and in the patterns above them, they saw the scattered array of familiar constellations.

Finally, they raised their hands to the back of their neck and untied the leather-wound shards. Just looking at the pieces was enough to bring tears to their eyes.

If I'd been given the chance, I'd have buried him with our family. But the place where we met… It's good enough, right?

Falling to their knees, Ari dug a hollow into the earth. They lifted the loop of leather from their lap, and held it above the small, makeshift grave. They watched the broken shards for a moment, entranced as they slowly swung, before lowering the necklace towards the ground.

With it hovering an inch above the bottom of the hole, they stopped.

No… It's not good enough, they thought. *I should wait until I reach Earth.* Ari looped the leather necklace back over their head and turned their back on this world that they had once known. After pressing down the disturbed soil with the heel of their boot, Ari tilted their staff towards the sky.

Another instant, and they were long, long gone.

Chapter 13
The Return

As their feet crunched down in a thick layer of pink snow, Ari was shocked by just how unprepared they were for the cold punching solidly into their lungs. Even after weeks of preparation, they hadn't expected the freezing air to hit them quite so hard, locking their limbs in place and sending a wave of shudders down their spine.

A few great flakes of snow circled them, settling in pink-tinged drifts, with one coming to rest on Ari's shoulder. A smile cracked their chattering teeth, just a little bit.

I'm here... they thought, excitement mingling with disbelief.

After Ari had left the red forest, the travel and the tedium of survival almost made it easy to forget that they had ever been there. They lived in a blitz of rift-pain and gathering warmth, lingering just long enough on each world to know that they would leap in a new direction.

Tucking their glowing fingertips under their armpits was just enough to stave off the numbness. A snowflake landing on the tip of their nose hissed and evaporated in the white-hot heat of the Rift. Ari's resolve wavered, just a little bit. Now that they had the opportunity to leave immediately, what was really the point in staying?

It would be so easy to just move on, to find somewhere more suited for human life.

Their breaths pooled in the air around them, and the slope was shrouded in fog, but they could just barely see the vast slope of a proud mountain range, stretching off into a deep red, nighttime mist.

It had been some time, but the mountains stood the same as they always had.

The stars hid behind a blanket of clouds faintly tinged with the colours of dusk. There was no telling which planets lay in formation between them and their final destination. They shook off the urge to Rift; now would be the perfect time for a final rest stop, on a familiar planet, before making the last few leaps towards Earth.

Ari's heart swelled to a flash of warmth.

I wonder how the Tribe is coping. I'm sure that Bailey would like to know.

Snow crunching beneath their boots, Ari trudged up the mountain. They remembered the way like it was yesterday, despite the pristine, unbroken whiteness of the mountain's slope. On the way, they passed a lonely, sunken hollow. Completely snowed in, only a few protruding supports remained where Seven-horn's home had once stood.

Further and further up the mountain Ari climbed, until the cold worked its way into their lungs. They walked until the clouds closed around them, thick and cold and shimmering with frost, before emerging out of the snowfall and into a clear, cloud-swirled night, with a blanket of fog swirling slowly under the apex of a deep crimson sky.

Finally they stood upon the very peak of the mountain ridge, looking down into the caldera of the ancient volcano. There they paused, eyes wide.

...How long have I been gone?

Ari remembered that, once, the crater sprawled below them had been filled with a smooth, unbroken blanket of snow, with only the slightest hollows to show where hidden entrances to the village lay. Now, though, Ari saw numerous ridges and hollows where the icy halls of the village had collapsed somewhere beneath.

Whether the Mountain's Heart had been abandoned, and simply fallen into disrepair, or some disaster had befallen the race of Mountain-dwellers, Ari couldn't tell from up here. An uneasy feeling crept into the pit of their gut, though.

Ari's grip tightened on their staff. They glanced up, breaths pooling in the air around them and drifting off into the sky. Just above the horizon, beyond the clouds and the mist that clung to the mountain slopes, the sky was clear and rich. And there, thousands of lightyears away, just beyond the enormous moon hanging above the mountain peaks, they saw the three shining stars of Orion's belt. *Won't be long now,* Ari thought. *I'll be quick.*

After a few moments of hesitation, Ari scrambled from the ridge and hurried down the slope, slithering through unseen drifts.

This world has never brought out the most elegant side of me, they thought with a grimace, as they sank waist-deep into the snow at the edge of the caldera. Shivering, they fished around in the snow. For a moment, they worried that they were looking in the wrong place, until their hand struck a pocket of air and the thin covering of snow caved to reveal the entrance of a tunnel, sleek and icy walls still intact.

Where the tunnels had once been well lit, smelling rich and warm with fur and brewing herbs, now they were just as cold and dark as outside.

Uneasily, Ari stepped from the snowdrift and batted down their clothes, shaking clots of snow from hide and hair.

I should leave, they thought. *This certainly doesn't strike me as safe.*

Ari let out a breath.

But perhaps there are things that can be salvaged from the depths. Bowls. Tools. Horns. The ice will have preserved any herbs left behind. Perhaps my garden still stands.

Ari stepped forward into the tunnel, and cautiously walked forward.

Although it had been… Four years…? Since they had lived among the Mountain-dwellers, the cave looked like it had been abandoned for far longer. In the time they'd been gone, entire tunnels had collapsed and become impassable due to heavy drifts. Ari found areas that had once been homes. The plinths that had held the Dwellers' cooking fires were all covered in a layer of ice. The hollows in the walls that were once used for storage had been long frozen over, various items still perfectly preserved within. Ari used some tools to chip their way through, and dig out some healing herbs which they stuffed into their makeshift bag. They searched among broken shards for small clay bowls that might have remained intact, but found none. For the most part, though, the walls had been picked clean.

As they wandered along a lonely corridor, they caught a glimpse of their reflection in the ice. Ari startled briefly, raising a hand to brush a hollow freckled cheek. They looked back into a pair of sunken eyes. *I'd tried to put on weight…* they thought. *But I look so… so…*

Ari turned away, unable to finish the thought, and continued their search.

Through a lot of luck, and after numerous dead ends, Ari somehow managed to find their way through to the other side of the mountain. As they emerged, the snow had settled to a light sprinkling of peach. The sun was beginning to rise above the distant caps of the tallest peaks, casting a pale pink light upon the swirling mists in the valley deep below.

And as they squinted off into the brightness of the slope sprawling beneath them, Ari's eyes widened in surprise.

Because, aside from a pristine, unbroken blanket of snow, there was nothing. No deep furrows left by free-roaming herds of mountain-crawlers. No keepers, wandering to brush their creatures' wiry fur or direct their attentions towards the most nourishing drifts of snow.

Not even hornless lambs, clambering, rolling and

tumbling across the mountain slopes in blatant disobedience of their parents' lessons.

The mountainside had never felt so empty.

Ari's stomach sank.

The healers… It was our job to bring them home. Did they ever make it back?

They swallowed, looking out across the deceptively serene beauty of the slopes.

Is this our fault?

They shook the thought aside. *No. Mountain-Dwellers are hardy. This is something else. It has to be.* Even so, the sinking feeling lingered.

Ari stepped into the open, weaving their way down across an exposed rocky path, down to the edge of the wide plain. Though the surface of the snow was unbroken, now that they were closer, Ari could see the marks of a well-worn path. Their hopes rose.

Of course. The Mountain-dwellers walk upon the snow, without breaking through. Perhaps the village is not completely abandoned after all.

They followed the track as best they could, before it could be covered by a sprinkling of snow. It must have been hours, perhaps days, since any Mountain-dwellers had walked this path; there was no telling where they were now. Along the slope of the mountain Ari followed, until finally they reached what appeared to be a few unceremonious lumps in the snow. Ari brushed a thin layer of snow from the surface of the smaller lump. Ari felt chills run down their spine as they uncovered a layer of pale pink fur, and the body of a fallen Mountain-dweller. The next covered mound was the same, a peach-coloured mountain dweller still clinging to a spear even in death.

Finally, from a mound that Ari had hoped was a home, Ari uncovered a misty-eyed head, preserved in all its ugliness by the sheer cold. Ari uncovered enormous, terrifying jaws, and an overhanging beak. They prodded it with the tip of their staff, but the exposed flesh had been frozen solid.

One of these things? Here?

Ari froze, stepping away from the frozen corpse, their breaths suddenly coming quickly.

They must be living in the valley, where it's warmer. I have to get back to the village, gather what I can, and get out.

Ari felt their stomach flutter with unease. Or... perhaps it was the parasite. It was growing harder and harder to tell.

What if they're taking refuge in the village? I'd be trapped there along with them.

Fear! Go, soon! Its emotions rang out sharply like an alarm bell.

Ari shut out the emotions of the parasite and tried to think logically.

The tools and materials of the Mountain-dwellers are unmatched. If I can find any to bring with me, it will be well worth the risk. Besides... Ari tightened their grip on their staff. *I have a way out now.*

Out, out! Get out!

Ari trudged back through their own prints towards the rocky tunnel, turning their back on the formerly pristine world, and leaving the Mountain-dwellers where they had fallen. They threaded their way through the great mountain crevasse and wound their way back into the village centre.

From this angle, the village centre could finally be reached. Only a small fragment of the room was still traversable, though. The rest had collapsed in on itself and was blanketed in snow. The great, towering walls of slick ice were threaded with cracks. Ari could hear them creaking ominously in the piercing silence, barely held upright by the support of ancient bones.

Legend said that the Mountain's Heart had not been built; the Mountain-dwellers' oldest stories said that it had been created when a herd of great mountain-crawlers took shelter from a storm in the belly of this ancient volcano. Over the course of many days, they were buried, succumbing to the deathly cold. Their bodies had long since rotted away, leaving great halls of ice beneath the snow.

Now, their bones stood as both support for the village, and a reminder to always bow your horns to the Mountain's will; for the Mountain-dweller race survives not of their own volition, but because of Her mercy.

Ari could not speak for the truth of the legends. But what they could speak for was the wonder they felt even now as they wandered among the crumbled ruins, picking their way through the village's remains.

If the Mountain's Heart had been made by the padded hands of ancient Mountain-dwellers, it was a marvel of ingenuity, and a wonder of their ancient world. If it had, as the legends said, been naturally formed, then it was a wonder of nature.

Ari listened to the echoes of their footsteps and looked around as they grasped for their memories of the ancient paths. Many of the entrances to the market hall had been blocked up by walls of snow. It didn't look like they had collapsed, though. This simple security measure was something unique among the Mountain-dwellers; it was not meant to hide them, but to enclose heat.

Seeing this made Ari's chest well up with a small flare of hope. Perhaps they were not alone after all. Perhaps some of the tribespeople yet lived.

The entranceways within the village had never been sealed before, but glancing back towards the collapsed ceiling, Ari could see why it was necessary now.

Ari approached the sealed entrance that they knew concealed a curving pathway into the village's depths. They placed a hand across the seal, and pushed. It was as fragile as ever, and the snow was soft, and relatively fresh. Ari created a big enough gap to step through, and then took their time rebuilding the seal.

Ari had never been good at sealing entranceways; no matter how often Seven-horn had tried to teach them, they had always somehow managed to fail. Even lessons geared towards teaching bleating little lambs had failed. All Ari had been left with was numbed fingertips and a greater respect for the generations of Mountain-dwellers who had perfected the technique.

After a few collapses, they finally gave up and left a tiny hole.

Even though much of the northern village had collapsed or fallen into disrepair, the southern side of the village was, wondrously, mostly intact. The pale red light of the sun rising above the mountain cast an eerie purple glow around them as Ari wove their way down into the depths of the village.

The Riftmaster's hollow was never in a prime location; their alliance with the Mountain-dwellers had been at times shaky, and generally rather prejudiced. Nobody else had wanted to sleep against the rough, stone wall of the mountain herself. As well as being a place riddled with superstition, Ari's hollow was also one of the coldest rooms in the village, although it still didn't hold a candle to the piercing chill outside.

Before they had claimed the hollow, it was generally used as a storeroom for tools, herbs, pelts and food. Ari hoped that after their departure, it had been reused for that purpose again.

Its location meant that it was probably the sturdiest room in the village, as well as being in the very belly of the mountain. If any supplies had been kept there, Ari knew that they would remain intact.

Ari moved, slowly, and cautiously, around the steady spiral into the lowest part of the village. Always, they kept an ear out for any sign of the Mountain-dwellers, or anything else that moved in the dark. The deeper into the village Ari pressed, the more the shadows pressed in on them. Where, once, the village would be lit by cooking fires and torches, the darkness within the belly of the mountain was choking. Ari held out the glowing crystal on the end of their staff to light their way and felt their heart rate mounting as they rounded every corner.

Other than the darkness, though, the village was largely the same. Beneath the top floor of the village, very few tunnels had collapsed or fallen into disrepair. The pathways had not changed. Finally, Ari stood holding their staff before the sealed entranceway of what had been their home for so long. Ari wasn't sure why, but they felt a flutter of nerves in their belly.

The entrance is sealed. Someone must be inside… Or perhaps the supplies I'm looking for.

Resting the blade of their staff against the icy ground with a clink, Ari breathed out a small puff of steam, hesitating with their palm hovering above the seal.

Can I remember the intricacies of the mountain tongue? The correct etiquette for apologies?

They spent a moment thinking it over, before shaking their head slightly. *In and out. I'm not staying long.*

Ari felt a faint twinge of curiosity react to their nervousness but didn't feel the need to clarify.

They pressed their hand against the seal and pushed inward. As they lifted their hand away, they saw blue light streaming from cracks in the barrier. It took a moment longer for the snow to fall away, but when it finally did, Ari felt a wave of warmth hit them. A stream of bright firelight blinded them. Ari blinked, squinting as their vision came into focus. Their eyes widened in surprise, as they took a step forward.

The first thing Ari saw was a ring of spears pointed at them. They raised their hands and staff in submission, letting out a guttural rumble from deep in their chest as they prepared to speak in the Mountain tongue.

"P-peace! I… come in peace, friends!"

Ari saw terrified eyes widen in surprise, and formerly drooping ears prick.

"What… is this?!"

"The stranger speaks our tongue!"

"How? Why?!"

And then, above all the rest, came a sharp, familiar bleat.

"Riftmaster?!"

Ari's eyes widened. They lowered their hands to their sides, and stepped through the broken seal. And there, before them, they saw the face of an old friend.

"Four-horn Keeper," they breathed. "Or have the seasons changed your name?"

The peach-toned Dweller's head dipped, and spear lowered. As though by some unseen signal, the other Mountain-dwellers did the same. Now that they were no longer under threat, Ari could see that the group before them was small.

Nineteen Mountain-dwellers were crammed into the rocky hollow, most huddled around the cooking fire.

Was this all that remained of the proud Tribe of the Mountain Heart?

"They have. I am known as Chief Eleven-horn, now. My days of tending the crawlers are long behind me," the Chief said, moving towards them. Although Ari was by no means tall, they still towered over the diminutive goat-creature.

Ari reached forward, and the Mountain Chief's pad was placed in their palm.

"It's been so long, old friend."

Chapter 14
The Motherbeast

In the Mountain's Heart, it was rare for a Mountain-dweller to go by a first name. Here, experience was vastly more important than role. So the prefix telling their number of horns became, for all intents and purposes, a Mountain-dweller's name.

In only a few circumstances did the importance of a Mountain-dweller's achievements exceed their number of horns.

To become Chief was one of those.

Thus, how Four-horn Keeper had become Chief Eleven-horn.

As soon as the Mountain-dwellers realised that the stranger knew their Chief, Ari was ushered into the small hollow and made at home. In return for such hospitality, Ari offered the Mountain-dwellers what little food they had managed to scavenge from the village's stores.

The Mountain-dwellers gratefully accepted the gift with more than a little surprise.

Despite limited supplies, a diminutive Mountain-dweller with pale pink fur and white speckles set to work cooking a thin, slimy soup, and another two draped a familiarly heavy pink cloak across Ari's shoulders. By the time Ari sat down, the majority of the group had settled down to eat, and Ari heard the soft buzz of warbling voices echoing through the icy halls.

They looked around at the circle of Mountain-dwellers.

"I'm sorry, Riftmaster, we have only so many bowls," Chief Eleven-horn said, noticing their hungry glances at the group despite meagre rations. The creature pronounced its words carefully and spoke slowly, to make sure Ari understood.

They caught more than a few glances cast their way, but the Mountain-dwellers spoke too quickly for Ari to catch any words.

As the Chief sat beside them, Ari told, in their rumbling tongue, of how they had left the Mountain Domain behind.

Through it all, Chief Eleven-horn listened with ears pricked and expression dull. "...So tell me again. You were taken by the Rift down in the valley?"

"There was nothing we could do. There is no way of preventing the Rift. But we did all we could to ensure the healers made it back up the mountain."

"As they said."

"So... they made it back?"

"Only two. New-horn Forager, and Seven-horn Speaker were lost. Of the two who returned, one was wounded beyond our repair. He could never walk again."

Ari watched as another of the group returned his empty bowl to the cook.

"I'm sorry."

"Sorry? It was thanks to you that they made it home at all. Mountain's mercy, they gave everything they had to ensure that chance was not wasted." Chief Eleven-horn looked up towards the cook. "Three-horn!" The Mountain-dweller gestured with a flip of an ear.

The speckled Mountain-dweller filled the empty bowl and hurried over. They offered Ari a small nod and held out a steaming bowl of translucent black slop.

Ari brought the warm bowl to their chest and blew the steam from its surface.

"Riftmaster, this is Three-horn Forager. You and your

kin helped save this one's life-giver from the valley. It was born shortly after their safe return."

Three-horn Forager dipped its head slightly, ears lowering respectfully.

Feeling the bowl warming their chest, Ari nodded in silent greeting to the Mountain-dweller.

As the creature retreated, Ari swilled the watery broth, before taking a long draught. They had not tasted Mountain-dweller cooking in quite some time, but they knew for a fact it had been better than this. Ari supposed that the few luxuries they had when it came to cooking had long been abandoned.

"My apprentice was devastated that he couldn't save Seven-horn," the Riftmaster said softly.

"Your apprentice. The other creature of your kind, yes? I remember Seven-horn was quite fond. Whatever happened to him?"

Ari felt the lump grow sharply in their throat. They blinked back a few tears.

"He found his way home," Ari said. "And we parted ways."

"You are from the same place. Why didn't you stay?"

"I had to go. The Rift wouldn't wait," Ari swallowed, but the lump remained. "And besides, even if the Rift let me, I... I don't know if I belong there, anymore."

Eleven-horn looked at Ari closely. "Well, you don't seem too worried about being here, and a lot has changed since you left. Six seasons has never felt so long."

"Well, I... Suppose it's not just that. To be back among my own kind... I'd feel more out of place among them than I do among you. There are so many things to consider; etiquette, technology, how things have changed with the passage of time... I hardly remember anything. Even when I lived there, I felt out of place." Ari paused. "Did you say it had been six seasons?" they asked. They narrowed their eyes slightly, trying to work out how long it had been. If they remembered correctly, a single season on the Mountain was almost three human years. The mountain only had two, though; two phases of the year that Ari liked to call Winter and Worse Winter. "For your kind, that's not long at all."

Chief-eleven horn slightly inclined its head.

"The Ruiners came shortly after you left."

Something clicked in Ari's mind, and they abruptly remembered the bodies in the snow. Their stomach sank. "Ruiners?"

"Yes. Creatures far larger than we. It started with mountain-crawlers disappearing from the edge of the herd. Then someone saw them hunting our beasts. There was only one at first, wounded. Dragging one leg in the snow. We ignored it; thought the Mountain's Mercy would take care of it. Then as the seasons passed, more came. We tried to defend our beasts and our home, but they followed us back into the village. Killed many. They have been living in the central chambers, where it is warmest."

Ari's blood ran cold, and they almost dropped their broth. "They are living in the village?!"

"Yes. We collapsed the tunnels to seal them off, but they still wander sometimes."

Ari fell silent, in disbelief and awe that the Mountain-dwellers would destroy their ancestral home. But, if the Mountain Dwellers were anything, they were survivors.

"So… you're all that's left?"

Chief Eleven-horn glanced back at the small group clustered around the fire. "All that decided to stay. Can't speak for other Tribes, or the ones that left." Eleven-horn lowered its gaze. "As far as we know, they were all slaughtered."

"Why didn't you leave, too?"

"These ones were too small, or too proud, to make the journey. Now there are too few," Chief said sadly.

"So… You're just going to stay here?"

"We have nowhere else. They will kill us if we try to go."

"Well… then…" Ari hesitated, glancing down at their staff. "How about you come with me, between worlds?"

"How?"

Ari raised their staff, showing it to Eleven-horn. The

glow of the jewel on its end reflected in the Chief's wide black eyes. "This staff can create pathways between worlds. We can leave those creatures behind."

"Where will we go?"

"I don't know exactly. I've visited hundreds of worlds, though, so I'm sure we'll find somewhere cold."

Chief glanced around. "All of us? The entire Tribe?"

Ari looked around.

Secretly, Ari wondered if the solemn little group could really be called a tribe anymore. "Of course. You sheltered me when I needed it, all those seasons ago. I should like to do the same for you."

"Why?"

"Those creatures are ruthless. They are from another world, so they do not follow the laws of your mountain. Now that they're here, they're not going anywhere."

"How do you know?"

"They are the reason I'm here. I seek to warn my apprentice."

Chief's eyes were wide, and the Mountain-dweller blew out a small huff of cold air. "Our... our mountain may be dying, but it is all we have ever known. We are already so few, but... I am afraid of what lies beyond. We all are. I... I *may* be willing to leave our home behind, but I cannot speak for the others."

Ari nodded, slowly. "I understand. It's a lot to consider. But if we leave, you will at least have a chance to live free again."

"I'm not certain. If we are to die, it should be on Her slopes."

Ari slowly inclined their head. "Then I must ask you to simply consider it. It would break my heart to leave you to your fate, but if you insist, then I won't force you."

"When will you be leaving?"

"Soon. I was hoping to search the village for supplies, if you'd allow me."

"If there is anything left to be found, you are welcome to it. Provided that you bring us any herbs, you are welcome to return to us for shelter."

"Thank you, Chief."

Chief Eleven-horn turned away, and Ari did the same. As they glanced around, they suddenly found that Chief wasn't the only one watching them.

Suddenly self-conscious, Ari muttered to Eleven-horn "Are they listening?"

Eleven-horn's ears tilted slightly. "Not as much as they wish they were. Your speaking needs much work, Riftmaster."

Ari blushed, but smiled. "Noted."

***

Before their venture out into the dark depths of the village, Ari accepted the Mountain-dwellers' gracious offer of shelter. They slept as they had slept all those years in the Mountain-Dwellers' domain, huddled under a heavyweight blanket of mountain-crawler skin.

Completely still, the weight helped to soothe them into slumber. But the cold stone felt sharp under their fingertips and the earth was rough under their back. As sleep crept in, they were buried under a blanket of memories. The discomfort of rock and bare earth took them back to a time of aches and pains.

The needs of their growing body had been getting harder to ignore. They had had to rest more frequently. They remembered waking up with aching bones. In dreams, time stretched. Had it been months or years? Did the Rift make this process slower, or was everything happening as it should?

Ari had no way to tell.

Even unconscious, they were exhausting themself. They stood upon a small plateau of rock within a void of nothingness. They did not remember this world, not the smells or the stars or the shape of the horizon. All they remembered was the anger, and the formations of stone that appeared beneath their feet as they moved. This tiny island of land in the void felt like a stage, and they felt like a dancer, to be watched, to be admired, to be ridiculed.

They felt round as a snail shell, off-balance and strange, and yet they were far too angry to stop. Oliver raised his weapon to block a jarring blow that sent his pristine teeth rattling. He pushed back, but for now his arms were no match for the sinewy muscles that locked in their broad shoulders.

Ari thought they saw a flash of fear steal across Oliver's half-human face, and their eyes glittered with satisfaction. They drew back, aiming another perfect strike. The blow jarred his arms, the impact rippling through his skin and wavering in his image. Finally his spear was wrenched from his talons and clattered to a halt, sticking vertically out from a bed of moss.

Oliver flinched, chest heaving, as he found the opposing spearhead pointed directly at his face. His shoulders sagged, breaths ragged, as it was raised away from him. His quills were dishevelled. His blue eyes were slitted, snakelike.

They met his gaze and just for an instant noticed the familiar fear in his eyes. Even at the end of the sparring session, Oliver's spear was clean. Theirs, though, shone with a faint red sheen.

Ari growled, spinning the weapon in their grasp, as they stepped back.

Red droplets showered the world around them, scattering the void with a cascade of crimson. But by Oliver's lack of wounds, they finally realised that this wasn't a part of the memory. Or, at least, they hoped not.

"Again," they said finally, nodding towards the fallen weapon, chest heaving. "I'm not finished yet."

"Aria, when–"

"Riftmaster," Ari corrected bitterly. "We stop when you finish letting me win! Now pick up your spear and fight me!"

"I… Ari…"

The Riftmaster picked up Oliver's spear and stalked back towards him, offering him the shaft. Oliver took a step back.

"*Riftmaster*," he said placatingly. "I… I don't want to spar. And I don't think you do either."

Ari gritted their teeth. They tried again to offer him the weapon. "I want to spar," they said. "I've got to keep fit somehow."

"Do you want to spar, or do you just want to be angry?" As he spoke, they glimpsed a pristine white fang flashing beneath his lip.

Ari said nothing, letting a breath hiss out between their teeth. "I want to spar," they said again.

"Well… I'm not sparring with you again until this is over. We can't do this forever, Aria."

Ari's eyes sparked with rage, but they didn't reply.

Oliver glanced down. "Especially not now."

Anger still pulsing through their veins, Ari drove the spearhead into the soil at their feet and stalked away. They settled themself down on a boulder that emerged from the darkness, bringing their knees up towards their belly. They were too big to curl up completely.

They hid their grey eyes behind their forearms as they quietly seethed.

A moment later, they heard the soft shuffle of footsteps on a carpet of moss. Oliver's shadow fell upon them, towered over them. They still didn't lift their head.

"You're afraid," Oliver said gently. "That's where this is coming from."

Ari didn't answer at first. *What an inane observation,* they thought. *Of course I'm afraid.*

"I thought you felt better about this," Oliver added, hesitating.

He knelt down in front of them, hunched like a cat, and gently unfurled their arms. They let him look into their teary eyes.

"I've been through this before," he said. "I'll be here for you… for both of you. No matter what happens, I'll be here. You'll make it through, I promise."

Ari looked away. For just a moment, they wanted to believe that this was really him. They opened their mouth. Closed it again.

Then they spoke as though the thought had never crossed their mind.

"Oliver… It's… not… I've been thinking."

"…about what?"

Ari opened their mouth to reply, but the words faltered in their throat. They found themself briefly falling back through a childhood leeched of its wonder and joy by fear of what lay after death. Teen years that were throttled by the expectations of their ancestors.

They wanted to speak, but found they couldn't say the words.

A long time ago, Ari had promised themself that they would never become their parents. That they would live their life happy, alone if they had to. What was the point in becoming a parent if all you could do was hold someone back?

But now, after all this… Even after fear of the pain, of the risk had dulled, something new arose; fear for what their child could become. There was no choice out here. No matter how constricted Ari had ever felt in their lifetime on Earth, out here you could grow up to be only one thing: a Rifter.

Their only options in the Rift were to keep going or lie down and die.

Ari returned themself to the memory at hand.

"Do… do you think they'll ever be happy?" Ari asked.

Oliver's expression fell. "I think that our son or daughter will be happier than we ever could be."

"How can you think that?"

"They won't know anything else. They won't have to leave Earth and struggle to survive. From the very beginning, our little one'll have you guiding them every second of the way. I can't think of anyone better to teach them out here."

Ari looked down as he held their hand, gaze blurry with tears. A hooked claw gently stroked their palm. They sniffed.

"The wonder, the beauty, and the absurdity of the Rift will be all they know," they murmured. "They'll never feel forced into a job or a home or a marriage, or shackled by human laws. They'll be free. Of death, of judgement, of all the trappings and complications of our world." They raised their head. "And... They'll never have to lose us."

"Exactly," Oliver squeezed their hand. "There's nothing we can do but try."

Ari's lips cracked into a faint smile, they lifted a hand to stroke his scruffy, sharp stubble. "They just need to get here first."

Oliver smiled back. He extended a wicked talon and pointed towards their belly. As he leaned near, they saw a deceptively tender light in his eyes.

"...And finish tormenting their poor mommy."

He jabbed his finger sharply forwards, prodding them in the belly, that wicked claw piercing through. They saw a spray of ruby droplets erupt from the wound and for just an instant the world was bathed in red.

They were awakened from slumber by their own piercing scream.

The real world came crashing in in a haze of nausea and agony.

When their blurred vision finally spun into focus, they were beneath the mountain, surrounded by the warm shapes of the Mountain-dwellers. Numerous small black eyes were fixed on them, dazed and confused, before slowly settling back to sleep.

The comforting scent of warm fur swelled around them.

They caught their breaths, heartbeat steadying as they blinked away the tears and slowly eased themselves upright. Whenever they blinked, their head spun, and they tried to focus the dark shape of a rock somewhere in the corner, while they breathed deeply and pressed their consciousness down on the creature hiding within them.

Panic! Fear!

Little thing... we're safe. It was only a dream...

Gradually, their vision began to settle, and the knife edge of sickness gradually dulled. They swallowed, looking around.

A couple of Mountain-dwellers who guarded the door turned towards them. Ari rubbed bleary eyes with the back of a clenched fist.

They yawned softly, but their stomach told them that returning to sleep would not be a good idea.

They expected it to be a long time before the other Mountain-dwellers awoke; the small, sturdy creatures spent much of their lives in torpor against the cold, sleeping far longer hours than any human. Generally, they slept and woke on alternating days.

So, Ari began to carefully ready themself to leave, gathering their supplies under the watchful eyes of the two Mountain-dwellers who had been tasked with staying alert.

Ari used the blanket that Chief had given them as a cloak, tying it in place on their chest with a loop of leather. The mountain-crawlers' hide was one of the warmest materials they had ever found in the Rift; its presence would be invaluable.

I've missed this, they thought, with a flash of warm nostalgia as its weight closed around their shoulders.

As Ari readied themself to leave, however, it seemed that hunger had become a far more powerful force than torpor. The Mountain-dwellers were beginning to stir, sending tired-looking glances their way as they moved between the groggily sprawled out forms.

Ari paused just before the snowy seal, glancing back. They found Chief Eleven-horn finally awake, wiry fur sticking out in all directions.

"Going already?"

"Yes. Not far, though; I want to see what I can find. I'll return soon."

Chief nodded slightly. The guards stepped back as they pressed lightly on the snowy seal, leading to a large section falling away. Ari stepped out of the hole a few moments later, allowing the guards to begin rebuilding it with nimble pawpads. By the time Ari glanced back, the hole had shrunk significantly, and before Ari's very eyes, it disappeared with a final pawful of snow. The silence gave way to a quiet hiss as a last trickle of snow poured onto the ground.

Okay. Alone time.

I'm here! the parasite chimed in, with a thrill of excitement. Clearly, it didn't much understand the situation at hand.

Okay. Not-entirely-alone time.

Ari's footsteps echoed around the icy tunnel as they pressed further and further into the depths of the village. It was dark; the only light shimmering faintly from above, where the unbroken ice let light shine through vaguely translucent cracks. It was far colder away from the cooking fire, too; icicles hung from doorways that had once been well-maintained, and frost shimmered, growing thick upon anything left behind.

No cooking fires remained; Ari found only the deserted remains of the village that had once been bustling with activity and life.

Six seasons, Ari thought with wonder, and a pang of grief. *That means it's been almost eighteen years since Bailey and I left. It feels like only moments ago we fled the valley.*

Any ruins near the Mountain-dwellers' hideaway had been emptied, the nooks and crannies used to store herbs and foodstuffs picked completely clean. Ari found a few shed horns and stored them safely away in their makeshift knapsack.

The ridges of a Mountain-dwellers' horns were perfect for starting fires and crafting tools of their own; whilst they were here, they wanted to find as many as they could.

Mildly disrespectful, Ari thought with a cautious glance across their shoulder. *But what the Chief doesn't know won't hurt it.*

They found a few scattered tools as they wandered; mostly ice picks carved from long, curved bones, and fire-starters. Spears were left stuck in walls or gently resting where the owner had left them. Although the staff bumping against their back was serving them well, Ari picked one up anyway. Any kindling that remained was too wet or frozen to be any use. As they moved higher up into the heart of the village, though, Ari found a little more that could be useful to them. Mostly, they found forms of nourishment, and although they had promised to bring them back to the group, Ari hid a few mouthfuls' worth in the depths of their pack.

The world around them grew steadily brighter as they neared the surface, and as they moved along a slowly spiralling corridor, they became aware of a quiet creaking sound. It was low at first, repeating along with a low click. And then the sound grew louder. Closer.

Ari's breath caught. They ducked into a side tunnel, peering out into the hallway, expecting something to appear any moment now.

And although the sound kept on repeating, kept on growing louder until it felt like it came from all around them, the source never appeared.

Ari's heart hammered in their ears, the pounding of their blood filling their mind.

And then a shadow fell upon them.

Ari glanced up. Through the faintly translucent walls of the tunnel, they saw a great shadow above them, walking along a tunnel that paralleled their own. Each time its paws came down, they saw the outline of six great claws. One end tapered to a long, pointed snout; while the other ended rather abruptly.

Though they couldn't see more than its paws, they could imagine it clearly; a great creature, with six stocky limbs and jaws made for crushing, with small eyes and bare skin, and sides rippling with boorish muscle.

Ari slowly stepped out of their alcove and stood directly below the beast.

As it passed above them, Ari heard deep, huffing, gasping breaths. It walked lopsidedly, one limb dragging beneath it with a high-pitched scrape. Not that that seemed to stop it. Ari waited until it had moved on along the tunnel.

Do I follow it? They thought for a moment, curiosity outweighing logic. But then they shook their head. *No, that really would be tempting fate. These pathways likely converge at some point.*

So, Ari backed away. They felt their heart pounding still in their chest, and took a deep breath, trying to steady themself.

Something is happening, the parasite's fear reached them, a fear that could have originated only in one place. *Why are you afraid?*

Don't worry, Ari soothed again. *We're safe.*

They looked up, peering along the tunnel above them as they tried to see more. But the beast had long gone. In a way, they were lucky; there was no way that it could have seen them beneath it.

But also, Ari's curiosity had been piqued.

Could that have been the Motherbeast? They wondered. *Eleven-horn said the first Ruiner they saw was wounded.*

Ari's excitement mounted.

I know they can be killed. I've seen them dead. Perhaps the Mountain-dwellers would even help.

Ari shook their head, their eagerness faltering.

Even if the Mountain-dwellers helped take down the Motherbeast, their world is already compromised. There are others here, too. And... That may not even be **her.** *She may be bigger, stronger, hidden away. I may have just heard a wounded soldier, like the one lying dead outside.*

Ari turned back, and slowly began to walk, soon breaking into a sprint. They moved the way they had come, leaving the beasts to their own devices, and the tunnel empty.

But if I can, then... there may be no need to warn Bailey at all. We could stop this plague in its tracks, once and for all.

Chapter 15
Forming Plans

"I know that these creatures can be killed. I have seen it; in poison, starvation, as well as by your kind's spears. If we band together, we may be able to come up with a solution that can stop this scourge from spreading.

"…So, if you'll stand by me, I think we could take down the Motherbeast, and save your world," Ari finished their proposal grandly, fanning out their hands in a silent plea.

The assembled Mountain-dwellers exchanged glances. One of them timidly raised a pad, just as Ari had suggested.

"Yes?"

"…Can you repeat that?"

Ari's heart sank. They looked around and found all but Chief Eleven-horn staring at them blankly.

Oh no… again?

Ari sighed, rubbing their head and struggling to remember how it had begun. Finally they obliged. This time, they slowed their speech, hoping that their pronunciation was, if not correct, at least adequate.

As they finished again, they found the young Mountain-dweller's pad waving at them.

Ari braced themself for another round.

"…Yes?"

"How do we know which one is the Motherbeast?"

Ari's shoulders relaxed.

"I… I'm not certain. We'll need to get closer to find out for sure. She is the one that gave birth to all the others. She will bear signs. She may be bigger, rounder, and I'm hoping that she is wounded."

Glances were exchanged. Low burbling mutters passed between the small gathering of Mountain-dwellers.

Finally, Chief-Eleven-horn stood up. "I will propose a compromise."

The Mountain-dwellers fell silent, ears pricked and listening. "We can scout. Two of us will be inconspicuous. If we can find out which of these creatures is the Motherbeast, then we will stand by you."

Ari's eyes shone. "Thank you for that, Chief Eleven-horn," they said softly.

"No thanks. We will bring down the walls of our home if it means we will be safe again."

"I have a feeling we might need to."

Eleven-horn bowed slightly. "And if it cannot be done… I will go with you to another world."

The other Mountain-dwellers exchanged astonished glances as the Chief looked back at them. "We are survivors. The last gasp of the Mountain's Heart. Sometimes drastic action needs to be taken to make it through. I know not what happened to the others, but I intend to survive."

To Ari's dismay, the other Mountain-dwellers said nothing.

"…I just hope it does not come to that."

The Chief looked back at the Riftmaster once more. "In any case, we should start preparing."

Ari nodded. "You know these tunnels best. Walk me through the plan."

***

Ari's muffled footsteps felt painfully loud against the

silence. Distantly, they heard the dull hum of the wind trapped in the caldera outside. Chief's footsteps, on the other hand, were silent; Ari found themself glancing frequently to their side to ensure that the peach-furred creature was still walking with them.

After what felt like a lifetime, Chief Eleven-horn spoke out loud.

"You are too silent. Are you afraid?"

"No. Just thinking," the Riftmaster said absently. "Back to the time I lived here."

"It was long ago. I'm shocked you remember our tongue at all."

"Well… it doesn't feel like so long, in the Rift. I can't believe it's been six seasons since we left."

"Indeed. You have been missed," Chief said.

"Really?" Ari asked in disbelief. "I thought I was here out of mercy alone."

"No. Well… among the Keepers at least. We missed your nimble fingers to tend the crawlers. And your… notable stature, too. The herd missed you, as well."

Ari's brows rose. They tried to imagine the gigantic, worm-like creatures showing emotion, and couldn't help but smile.

"How can you tell?"

"They kept trying to wind their tendrils around us during grooming. They did like your warmth, but it was quite the problem for a while."

Ari's smile broadened as they imagined the Keepers trying to fend off the unwanted affections of a bus-sized pink worm.

It had been so long; Ari had almost forgotten just how grateful they were to the little creature beside them. Since leaving the world of the Mountain-dwellers, Ari had not thought much about this world and those they had left behind.

It was a strategy they had adopted more out of necessity than a lack of care.

Now, though, they found themself thinking back.

In the beginning, the Riftmaster had had only a single

friend in this world; the diplomat and advisor known as Seven-horn Speaker, who possessed something that the other Mountain-dwellers rarely saw the value in. Seven-horn was curious, believing that learning would reveal new facets to survival. Seven-horn saw a stranger where many other Mountain-dwellers saw a monster.

In return, Ari taught Seven-horn their birth tongue, and told stories of the worlds they'd seen.

The kindness of that singular Mountain-dweller had made it possible for Ari to thrive in their world.

Despite Seven-horn teaching them the Mountain Tongue, they were mostly ignored when they tried to speak it. No matter how fluent they thought they were becoming, it was never enough to earn more than a passing glance.

Ari had no horns, and by extension, no power here. They were treated as an infant, even among the newly-grown.

The only exceptions were the Keepers, who lived outside of the village's walls. With their help, Ari was able to earn their place on the Mountain's slopes, and slowly work their way into the society of the Mountain-dwellers.

Four-horn was the Riftmaster's mentor among the keepers; the Mountain-dweller who now walked beside them as chief had taught Ari all they knew. From how best to groom the fur of the mountain-crawlers, to how to remove the ice from between their toes.

Being taller gave the Riftmaster a significant advantage among the keepers, but also meant they were subjected to some of the worst tasks. Ari didn't think they'd ever forget the horrors of cleaning out a blocked excretion tube.

For creatures that fed exclusively on the microbial life flourishing in snowdrifts, they managed to accumulate a terrifying amount of debris.

But through it all, Ari moved up in the world.

In time, the Riftmaster was finally able to move out of Seven-horn's hollow and into the village; even if their home there was cold, small, and uncomfortable. And a season after that, they were finally given a Mountain-dweller's horn by the chief, a symbol of their acceptance into the tribe.

Shortly after that, Bailey arrived; and with Ari's hard-won status among diplomat and keeper, they were able to ensure his survival.

It was a steep and jagged road, full of hurdles. At times it felt like they were sliding down rather than climbing up. But without Seven Horn, and then Four-horn, to help them up, they would never have lasted long on the cruel slopes of the Mountain.

Ari jerked back to attention as the Chief Mountain-dweller spoke once more.

"This was where you saw it, yes?" Chief asked, looking up towards the dimly-lit ceiling above them. Since the sun had passed its zenith, the tunnels were flooded in darkness once more.

"That's right. The sun was above. Its shadow falling through the ice. It didn't see me."

"This is alarming. The Ruiners rarely venture this deep."

"Well, it's not here now."

"Yes. But stay alert."

Ari fell silent as they pressed deeper into enemy territory. But the tunnels remained quiet, and the duo alone. Ari kept their staff gripped against their palm, holding it horizontally against their side. Chief Eleven-horn, meanwhile, adjusted both pads around the shaft of its spear.

The Mountain-dweller's ears pricked.

"Anything?" Ari whispered, knowing that the Mountain-dweller's hearing would be infinitely more effective at keeping them safe.

"Yes," Chief Eleven-horn rumbled under its breath. "They're ahead of us. In the collapsed sector."

Ari nodded slightly, falling in behind Chief and letting the Mountain-dweller take the lead. "If anything comes," Ari whispered, "signal me."

Chief Eleven-horn's ears flicked in acknowledgement. The pair pressed forward, moving beyond the frozen tunnels and through collapsed drifts of ice and snow. Eleven-horn showed them a way through a labyrinth of caverns that had once been interlinked tunnels, and Ari soon heard what the Chief had long acknowledged; the scraping of claws, and slow huffing, and hooting breaths. At one point, Ari heard the high-pitched squeak of escaping air, and a low, rumbling vibration passed through the ice under their feet. Ari's heart almost stopped for a second until they heard the sound of a scuffle filling the tunnels.

A moment later, a small, wounded creature scurried out of an archway, squeezed into a narrow side tunnel and disappeared, the echoes of its footsteps drifting into silence as it fled. Ari froze, glancing sideways at Chief Eleven-horn.

The Mountain-dweller wasn't looking at them, though. Ears pricked forward, they lifted a paw pad and signalled. Together they dived after the wounded Ruiner, following its retreating footsteps and cramming themselves into the narrow tunnel where it had disappeared.

A scrape, a huff. Time passed; seconds felt like days.

Then Ari saw a shadow fall against the ruined hide that had once been a thick and insulating carpet. They saw a flash of light in small and beady eyes, and then she appeared.

A beast, with six stocky legs and enormous claws, and great jaws that tapered into a beaked end.

She had no ears; no visible way to pick up the vibrations of the surrounding world, but her beak was gnarled with ridges. Velvet skin hugged tight to the rippling muscles beneath a sturdy carapace, and the body ended in a tailless nub.

And she was *enormous*.

One great, clawed midlimb dragged against the ground as she walked, and Ari saw that her shoulder bore an unmistakable relic; the cauterised wound from a Renohaiin floret.

This world is free of the Empire, Ari thought, as they caught their breaths tight with horror. *This one must have come from somewhere else.*

They listened until she tramped and scraped her way past their hiding spot and along the tunnel, until her breaths had faded even to Chief.

Then Ari placed a hand on Chief's shoulder, and swung their arm in a wide gesture back towards the way they had come. Wasting no time, the two squeezed out of their hiding spot and scurried back towards the deeper tunnels. When they were out of the collapsed ruins and back into the narrower, more maintained tunnels, Ari slowed, panting.

The creature didn't have any ways that Ari could see of tracing vibrations in the air – certainly no large, cupped ears or obvious holes to draw them in. But that didn't mean hearing was out of its power.

After checking around to be certain they weren't being followed, Ari spoke, voice only a little bit above a hushed whisper.

"That's her," they said. "The Motherbeast."

"How can you tell?" the Chief asked in surprise.

"The wound she carries is a plasma burn. It's from another world."

"I thought it might be frostbite. This creature does not appear to tolerate cold as well as we."

"If it was, then she'd be missing that limb. No, that's a burn wound." Ari shuddered slightly. What kind of creature was this, that it could survive a fully-powered plasma blast, and keep on living? Not only that, but keep on breeding, and infesting worlds like a disease?

"Well, it doesn't appear to affect her much."

"No. The empire says they are virtually immune to heavy weaponry. I wonder if they can feel pain at all."

"Then how do we kill her?"

Ari's lips tightened in a hard line. They thought back to the creature sprawled under the remains of a fallen tree. Smaller, yes… but the same creature. "I've seen it done before. I know she can be killed."

"If you are convinced, then I believe you."

"We need to get back to the others. I think I know what we need to do."

Chief Eleven-horn looked up at them expectantly.

Ari closed their eyes and took a deep breath before they spoke once more. "It may be time to bring down the village."

Unsurprisingly, the Mountain-dwellers were not so eager to destroy what remained of their ancestral home. As Ari sat surrounded by the pitiful group, their ears were filled by a barrage of panicked bleats and shocked rumbles that were not easily quelled by Chief's reassurance. In the end, it may have been a combination of the gravity and the knowledge that they would be doing what remained of their world some good. Eventually, they all fell silent.

Ari felt the doom on the air as realisation hit. These Mountain-dwellers were all that was left in the once-proud village. And now they had to let go of the very last thing that remained of their old lives.

Ari said nothing, out of respect for the Tribe's loss. Ari pressed down the thought that they had felt the same thing a thousand times before, feeling that now was not the time to speak. Did it come from empathy or apathy? As much as they knew that the first time always hurt the most, Ari also knew that they had never had to make this terrible, terrible choice.

"…but there will be a life for us, beyond these walls, and beyond these slopes. With the Riftmaster, we can find a new mountaintop to call our own, and another world where we can be safe."

"And there, we can build our Tribe anew?"

"Yes. We will be legends one day, in new halls, on new slopes."

"What about Her? What about Her mercy? She has protected us for so long, since the beginning of our time."

"Our Mountain must protect Herself first; that mercy has run out for us. If we stay here, we will die. Though we are leaving, we will never forget Her."

"And this creature… it has the key?"

Ari slowly bowed their head, tilting their staff to show them the crystal gleaming on the tip. "I do. The key is here, in this staff. And I promise I will guide you to a safe place in the universe. No matter how long it takes."

There were no more questions, after that. Gloomy glances were exchanged, and mutual unhappiness filled the cave like miasma. Eleven-horn was given a thousand questions, only some of which the Mountain-dweller could answer.

Ari finally managed to get the Chief's attention after the hubbub died down.

"So, tell me… how did you bring down the missing sector of the village?"

"With disrepair, cracks appeared in the foundations. With heat and spear, and careful placement of some spittleberries, we exploited those cracks."

"Spittleberries?"

"They were medicinal, but they burn ferociously, cracking and spitting. We sometimes burned them on the cooking fire during celebrations. They will widen the cracks."

"Got it. Do we have any in the village?"

"Yes. The healers had many, for numbing wounds. When the caves were abandoned, we stored some away."

"Will pulping the berries increase their effectiveness?"

"Yes. Try it and you'll see."

"Got it. How will we get out?"

"If all goes to plan, the cracks should spread from within. We will weaken the central supports first, and then the outside edges of the village so that we can escape. We need to push the tunnels to the brink of their durability, and then get out before the structural integrity fails. Before we begin, we should have an evacuation plan, and we should trigger the final cracks as close to the edges of the village as we can to make our escape inevitable, and theirs impossible."

Ari's blood ran cold as the realisation struck that the Chief must have been preparing for this moment far longer than they could have known.

They continued speaking to the Mountain-dwellers about the task at hand, as though it was no more than a casual conversation on a sunny day. Although the other Mountain-dwellers were largely silent, Ari always felt eyes on them.

After the details were laid out, Ari asked that Three-horn bring some spittleberries for them to experiment with. Ari was amazed that the innocuous, tough, brittle plant matter could be useful at all. It looked to them like no more than a frozen vine, with a few faintly translucent, ice-coloured berries and no leaves. But they had a long time ago learned not to underestimate the plants under their feet.

Ari ushered the Mountain-dwellers from a rocky corner of their humble abode, and placed the berries on a ledge.

Ari reached down into their tunic, and withdrew the knife from their chest. They heard it hiss gently, the sinister sound sizzling into their brain.

But they paid it no heed.

With the tip of their knife, they cut off a small segment of the stem, and then removed a single berry.

Unwinding a necklace from around their neck, they held the fragment of Mountain-dweller's horn at arm's length. Using the blade of their knife, they struck a spark onto the length of stem. It caught alight almost immediately, popping, cracking, and sparking in a reaction that lingered.

The Mountain-dwellers watched, unsurprised.

As Ari set the berry alight, however, it whistled softly, before bursting in a small spray of flame. The seeds on the inside fizzed, and kept burning for a while longer before being vaporised.

"May I borrow a bowl?" Ari asked Three-horn.

The young Mountain-dweller obediently brought them a clay bowl, and watched as Ari began to pluck each of the berries in turn from its length. After a couple, they used the pommel of their knife to grind the berries down into a fine, translucent paste.

They removed their knife only when the paste ran

smooth, and scraped a small amount onto the charred rock-face where they had tested the individual components. With the tip of the knife, they scored along the edge of the vine, removing a length of bark. They placed one end of narrow strip into the ground-up mess of berries, then Ari lit the other end and stepped back.

It curled, spitting and sparking, as a tiny flame ran along the fuse and finally reached the ice-coloured pulp. The pulp caught alight quickly, flame flaring quickly and wildly. It spat, it flared, and then just before it disappeared, burst into a shower of sparks, with an audible pop.

As Ari looked around, he noticed the Mountain-dwellers removing their pads from their ears.

"What do you think?"

Eleven-horn nodded approvingly, but the other Mountain-dwellers exchanged worried glances.

"Will they hear us?" Three-horn asked worriedly.

"No," Ari reassured. "They have no way of picking up vibrations. Even if they do, their ears are not sensitive like yours."

"Have you any longer lengths of spittleberry vine? We can use them to carry the flame from a distance."

"We do, but not much. Spittleberries were rarely used for this purpose, and it's been a long time since anyone has been out to gather them."

"So this is it, then?" Three-horn asked, bleating voice small.

Ari hesitated, then nodded. "I suppose it is. Are you ready?"

The Mountain-dwellers stared back at them without answering. Finally, Chief Eleven-horn spoke. "I don't think we'll ever be ready for this. But we must press on, regardless."

Ari glanced away, towards the sealed door. "I suppose that'll have to do, then."

***

Over the next few hours, whilst the Mountain-dwellers prepared and slept, Ari scored the spittleberry vines in order to create lengthy strips. By tying these together, they made fuses of a metre or two long. In the cold, their fingers fumbled, and finally laid open their palm with the tip of their blade.

Dropping their knife, they pressed their palm into the icy walls. Their gaze strayed to the knife, its blade splattered with red.

As they did so, they caught the way it shone in the icy light of the cooking fire, as though it was hungry for more. Ari shivered.

Awful familiarity rose in their brain.

Things haven't changed since then, they found themself thinking. *You're still going out of your way to kill.*

Ari shook their head, trying to fight off the ice that crawled in their mind. *No. This isn't just for me. This time it's for the good of the many. Just one creature has to die, and then we'll be free.*

Besides, it's not going to be me scoring the final blow. Not this time.

A questioning thrill coursed through them, but they paid it no heed. The process was fiddly, but when they weren't causing themself bodily harm they found it rather relaxing, if a little boring. By the time they were ready to go, their chilly fingers were covered in cuts. The Mountain-dwellers clustered together by the snowy seal to leave their hollow one final time, as Chief Eleven-horn looked over its tiny kingdom forlornly.

"Today we Mountain-dwellers climb to new heights," Eleven-horn said quietly. "We leave our eternal Mistress and take to the stars."

The Mountain-dwellers watched in silence as Chief Eleven-horn turned towards Ari.

"In this creature's hands I place my trust, our history, and the future of our tiny Tribe. If I am wrong on this today, then our fate is sealed. So… I shed the mantle of Chief."

Ari glanced down in shock, and met Eleven-horn's gaze.

"Until we find new slopes, the Tribe of the Mountain-heart exists no longer."

Ari swallowed a growing lump in their throat.

"So, Riftmaster… Do not let us down."

Ari slightly inclined their head.

"I promise, I will do everything in my power to ensure that the Tribe lives on."

Seemingly satisfied, Eleven-horn turned away.

The former chief broke the seal and let the covering of snow fall away. Then it stepped out into the empty tunnels that had once been their home.

Ari took a step forward, and moved to stand by their old friend's side. After only a moment's hesitation, the Mountain-dwellers followed, moving together in a sombre silence to follow Ari and Eleven-horn's lead, leaving their refuge open to the cold stillness of the air.

Chapter 16
The Mountain's End

Ari followed the spiralling corridor into the belly of the mountain. They stopped just as brightness began to filter in from above, and then in whispered murmurs and hushed exchanges, they identified their escape route. The village's hidden entrances, sealed by snow, were numerous; but if the village caved, they would need a pathway guaranteed still to stand. So, the Mountain-dwellers suggested that they use one of the rocky tunnels that had been formed by the flow of ancient lava.

Ari had been aware of only a few, but as they suspected, there were plenty more, sealed by snow and known only by the Mountain-dwellers.

The plan was deceptively simple; gradually weaken the village from the depths upwards, until the icy walls could no longer support the weight of tunnels and snow. Then, as the ice began to crack, get out.

After discussing their roles, they split up. Three-horn and a small party fanned out across one wing, each carrying bowls of spittleberry paste.

Eleven-horn, meanwhile, went to scout in the very belly of the beast, to make sure that the Motherbeast was here at all. If she was by some cruel chance out hunting, or scouting the lower sector of the village, this would fail.

Ari used a scrap of leather to begin spreading the spittleberry paste across one of the cracks that had been pointed out to them by Eleven-horn. When the crack had been sufficiently packed with paste, they stepped away, and admired their work.

Only one more thing.

Ari took a strip of the plant stem that was to be used as a fuse, and began to work it into the crack, making sure that the flame would take. Finally finished, Ari looked around for more cracks. They only had to move a short distance along the corridor before finding another, this one almost cutting through to the snow beyond.

Ari knelt, and began to smear the spittleberry paste along its edges.

After so long, the village really has fallen into disrepair. I never thought such an ancient structure could possibly be this fragile.

As they did so, Eleven-horn returned.

"She's here," the Mountain-dweller said gravely.

"Did you see any others?"

"Yes. Many wander the tunnels. Hungry. We will need to be careful."

Ari nodded. "We're deep, so it shouldn't be an issue."

"They search deeper by the day. And our smell is strong. We must go quickly. Are you done?"

Ari glanced back at the crack. Their work here seemed so small. So insignificant. "Are there any more cracks to fill?" they asked.

Eleven-horn shook its head. "The others should take care of that."

"Where are they?"

"Arranged all the way around the village. Each has an escape to return to. When all is over, we meet outside on the slopes."

Ari nodded slowly and stood. "I'm done, then. Would you go check on them? Make sure their fuses are long enough. As soon as we light them, we need to get out."

"I'll do so."

The Mountain-dweller disappeared in an instant,

leaving Ari alone in the dark. They looked around, watching the faint gleam of the ice surrounding them. Listening to the haunting sound of the winds howling outside, as well as occasional creaks and rumbles from deep in the belly of the village.

So long as the fuses are lit, we'll make it out.

Ari tried to reassure themself, shivering in the dark and the lonesomeness. It was hard to feel confident when everything was so cold, and when they knew that the Ruiners were so close.

Their stomach wavered, as though their passenger felt the uncertainty.

No fear… you know there's no fear. Don't you?

Ari glanced up as they heard the distant scraping of claws passing above them, through a sealed-up tunnel. A deep, snorting breath followed it. And then a quiet snuffling.

Ari remained still, listening out for the Mountain-dwellers. *They never come this deep, so why would they have any reason to now?*

But the Ruiners were hungrier than ever; it seemed that their uneasy truce was close to ending.

We have to go. Now.

Ari removed a necklace from over their head. It had been made here, in the cradle of the village, from the two halves of a Mountain-dweller's horn.

"Light them! Light the fires!" they bleated out into the dark. A moment later, they heard a faint hiss.

Soon after, the sound of pattering paws. A small group of Mountain-dwellers soon thundered into view, and Ari struck a spark with the two beads of their necklace. It didn't light.

Ari's heart pounded. They tried again.

Still nothing.

Mountain-dwellers were swarming around them now, panicking, burbling deep in bleating voices.

Ari's stomach dropped. They hesitated for a moment. Then they struck one more time and the fuse at last ignited.

"Yes!" they gasped with relief. "Let's get out of here!"

As one, the group fled for the rocky tunnels.

Though the voices swirled around and over them as though a thousand conversations were happening at once, Ari caught onto a single important detail. They were not alone down here.

"What?!" Ari skidded to a halt. "What did you say?"

"Something is licking up our work," Eleven-horn answered. "We could only light a few. Come! No going back!"

Ari's blood ran cold, their heart hammered, and they almost forgot the way. *I just hope it's enough.*

In their wake they left great heaving puffs of steam as they ran. As they neared the cusp, Ari heard the great creak, the pop, the crack of the great cracks widening. The village under the ice gave a great moan, and the ground shifted under Ari's feet.

A Mountain-dweller tripped ahead of them, but Ari wasn't about to stop. They sprang over it like a startled doe.

"Let's go! We've almost made it."

Even in the dark, Ari saw a great void ahead of them, and hurled themself forwards. A great maw of stone loomed up around them. They clattered to a halt against solid ground, and the other Mountain-dwellers tumbled into the tunnel after them. The icy path behind lingered open for just an instant, and Ari thought they saw the gleaming light of eyes somewhere at its end… only for the tunnel to suddenly fill with snow, sealing behind them as the village collapsed under its own weight.

"Keep going, friends! We will be buried if we stay here!"

Ari stumbled on in the dark, holding onto a patch of wiry fur and hoping that it was Eleven-horn's.

Through the rocky tunnel, Ari saw a light.

They struck out towards it and lurched into daylight under a clear sky the colour of rose quartz. The mountain slope spread out ahead of them, a pristine sight of clear whiteness above the cold grey fog of the valley. They ran, slithering down the slope away from the tunnel mouth, and heard a deep rumble from somewhere below. The snow hissed as it shifted around them, and then there was silence.

Breathing heavily, Ari watched and listened.

A chorus of bleats, both excited and mourning, reached their ears.

Along the slopes, Ari could see other groups beginning to emerge, huddling together in fear and grief.

An array of tiny groups of four and five, Ari was struck by just how empty the mountainside looked. But, with only them and the Mountain-dwellers, this world looked bright and beautiful, dramatic under the great red sun.

The Mountain's Heart had stopped beating; but they were alive.

Ari spread out their arms and squinted their eyes against the brightness, stepping out onto the snow and then twirling with relief, treading glorious patterns in the snow. The Mountain-dwellers surged down the slope to meet them.

But they weren't alone for very long. Back in the tunnel's entrance, Ari thought they caught the darkness shift. A moment later, a small cascade of snow spilled out of the gaping maw. Ari's grip tightened on their staff, and they held it at the ready. Their heart skipped.

A moment later, a shape materialised from the wreckage; a great beast hauled itself out into the open. Wounds poured blue blood out onto the glittering snow. It raised its muzzle to sniff at the air, then limped up the mountain slope. It wasn't as big as they remembered. Perhaps the tunnels had made it seem far larger.

They checked its wounds, dripping blue blood onto the snow.

It's not the right foreleg. This isn't her.

Perhaps she had died within?

Ari could only hope so.

But it was moving. It would not do to stay here. They had to go before it could lick its wounds.

The great beast stamped and rumbled; Ari felt the vibrations running up through their feet.

What is it doing? Ari wondered. Then their blood ran cold. *Could they possibly be… communicating?*

It paid them no heed, pausing, and then limping on. After a while it stopped to begin digging frantically through drifts of snow. On the slope high above them, Ari saw a hunched shape emerge… then another, and another.

"The village. They are emerging from the village."

"How can they still be alive?" Ari breathed. "Their carapaces must be crushed. They paint the snow blue with their blood."

Ari watched them emerge like ants from an anthill, working together as they dragged something, struggling and bleeding, into the open. The smaller creatures clustered around the bedraggled shape, whose ragged breaths could be heard all the way down the mountain slope.

"The Motherbeast…" Ari slowly fell to their knees in the snow. "Even now, she's alive."

Before Ari's eyes, the Ruiners clustered around their wounded mother, tongues scraping over broken carapace and bloodied wounds.

The Ruiners were weakened. Many lay dead within those walls. But there were some who had survived, and as long as *she* lived on, their efforts would be for nothing.

Ari's vision blurred. Bitter tears formed in their eyes and streamed down their cheeks. Their hands shook, their grip on the shaft of their staff tightened. It had all come down to this; their only hope had been to bring down the village.

Rage lit a fire in their belly that spread throughout them like the venom in their veins.

What else could they do?

Mountain-dwellers across the mountainside drew their spears and, eyes burning with a shared purpose, stalked up the mountainside. Another of Eleven-horn's tiny group followed suit.

"What are they doing!?" Ari asked, bewildered. "We're outnumbered. They might be weak, but there's still no hope of winning."

"My people have lost everything," Eleven-horn said, sadly. "We did not bring our village down for nothing. This may be the only chance we have to see this ended."

Ari stared in horror, in sadness, as a Ruiner raised its head, little eyes finding them, and opened its jaws in a deep rumbling snarl. As though it knew, it hauled itself away from the Motherbeast and was stumbling towards them. Others began to follow, leaving bluish smears in the snow. Some went to meet the groups of Mountain-dwellers on the slopes. The Motherbeast stayed where she was, sides heaving where she lay.

Ari stared, hypnotised, until Eleven-horn raised its own spear. The Mountain-dweller stood tall with stance bravely set, ready to fight for the only family it had left. With a jolt, Ari raised a hand and grabbed Eleven-horn's shoulder, stopping the Chief in his tracks.

"We can't take them like this," Ari pleaded. "We must go. You still have a Tribe to lead."

They looked into Eleven-horn's eyes. Their vision blurred as tears formed unbidden.

"Please," they said. "Call them back."

Eleven-horn looked back at the tiny group of five who stood loyally by its side, spears held fast, and heads bowed. Then the Chief looked out across the mountainside, to where the Mountain-dwellers and the Ruiners were beginning to meet. Spears flashed, and bellowing warcries reverberated across the mountain slopes. The Mountain-dwellers attacked in the biggest groups they could muster; but they were scattered like flies from a corpse as the first Ruiner lashed out. A dying shriek rang out across the slope, echoing back up through the valley as the first Mountain-dweller fell.

And then the next. And the next.

Finally, a single Ruiner came crashing down.

Re-energised, the Mountain-dwellers' frantic assault continued.

They're dying, Ari thought numbly. *They're going to wipe themselves out, and there's nothing I can do.*

Ari shook their head, splattering frozen tears onto the

snow. The grip on their staff tightened. They glanced down, looking at the glowing crystal on its end. *Maybe there is one last thing.* They swallowed, lower jaw trembling as another tear wound its way down their cheek.

Or… just maybe… there are two things.

As if in a trance, Ari began to climb up the mountain's slopes, wading through knee-deep snow.

So there isn't just one thing left that I care about, after all.

They stalked past the scrum of fighting, writhing Ruiners and terrified Mountain-dwellers, their cries like ice in Ari's brain.

No living creature moved to stop them.

The Motherbeast had gathered her legs beneath her and was slowly hauling herself onto her feet. Blood pouring from a myriad of cuts, one limb twisted out of shape, she supported herself on four of her six stocky limbs and raised her head to the sky.

She swung her head to look around. She gazed past them along the steep slopes, down into the fog below.

There was nowhere to go but down.

Ari tightened their grip on the trigger of their staff. They could see the muscles rippling under her thick carapace. The snow that reached their knees barely made it past her enormous paws.

They tried to block out the blinding fear. The nausea. The pain that was pumping through leaden muscles.

"You can see me, can't you?" they yelled out to the Motherbeast, challenging in their own native tongue. It sounded hoarse. Otherworldly. "You want to escape? Then escape!"

She began to limp towards them, sniffing at the air with great, snorting breaths.

"But you'll have to get past *me* first!"

They held their staff beside their body, tilting it in challenge. It might as well have been a toothpick to her. Their voice was high with mania, the skin around their eyes pulled taut.

Their heart was pounding, the blood roaring through

their veins. They felt the brush of fright against their consciousness but blocked it out.

The Motherbeast closed the distance, step by painful step, pouring pools of blue blood onto the snow.

She lunged, with jaws splayed wide.

Ari leaped forward, sinking their staff into a crack in her carapace and swinging themselves up towards her shoulder. There, they plunged their blades into an open wound and hung there. The Motherbeast screamed and reeled back, spraying blue blood onto the snow and swinging them violently, but she did not die. They yanked the staff back and tumbled onto the snow as she swept out a huge forepaw, claws like knives.

With every movement, lethargy tugged at their limbs. Every motion, their stomach turned. They just barely managed to dodge another strike, diving back onto the snow and tumbling winded to a halt.

Fear! No! Their stomach lurched as the parasite fought to eject. Sweat beaded on their forehead as they refused to let it. They fought to steady their breaths.

The entire world seemed to tilt beneath their feet.

They were met with a sick realisation that dropped right into the pit of their stomach.

If she doesn't kill me, Little Thing will.

But there was no going back now.

Keeping their distance, Ari lurched to the side and rammed their blade into her carapace. The attack drew no blood. They remembered abruptly how hard it had been to cut that hide with a hunting knife alone.

The Motherbeast stalked forward, step after terrible step. Across the battlefield, Ruiners were beginning to make their way towards their queen; abandoning the struggle with the few Mountain-dwellers that remained.

Even now, even wounded, they'd come to the aid of their mother.

The terrible familiarity that rose within them dragged their limbs to a halt. Breathing heavily, they retreated step by step.

In that moment of hesitation, the Motherbeast turned

and smacked them with an enormous paw. The Riftmaster was cast, flailing, into the air, and spun helplessly as they hit the ground. Their staff clattered to the ground somewhere close by.

Ari's chest heaved and they lay where they had fallen, their ragged breaths billowing up into the air.

This wasn't going to work.

The Motherbeast limped after them, sensing victory, and a meal that would go a long way towards tending her wounds, along with those of her young. *No...*

Ari struggled up onto their knees and groped for their weapon. They leaned their weight on its length and slowly stood.

Strings of translucent drool hissed in the snow around them. The Motherbeast towered over them, great, hot breaths pouring a blanket of mist.

And then she went in to swallow them whole.

There was no time to dodge. All they could do was grip their staff and clamp their eyes shut.

Superheated darkness closed in around them, wet blue walls crushing from every side. Something moved in the dark, winding around them. Before they had time to comprehend, fleshy tendrils gripped tight, and dragged them into darkness. The air was thick; unbreathable. They could do nothing.

Blood roared in their ears. In the darkness, they could feel the parasite's acute fear, searing in their blood like needles.

Their stomach convulsed in a violent wrench of agony, but Ari knew that of all the places, to lose it here would be to give the universe to her hold.

No! I'm not dying today, not here, and not like this!

In a last fit of desperation, Ari forced their staff out ahead of them, turned it perpendicular to their descent, and jammed it into the fleshy walls. The blades anchored, burying deep into the bare, vulnerable flesh either side of the Motherbeast's gizzard.

...And then light burst through.

The world rocked, forcing the breath from Ari's lungs.

The gurgling scream that reverberated around them was cut short.

The tendrils that gripped them loosened, slowly letting go, and then they were ejected violently onto snow that melted and steamed in their wake. She collapsed onto the mountainside, rivulets of blue blood pouring from her wounds. The Motherbeast thrashed briefly and was still.

With their parent gone, the Ruiners that had stumbled to her side cried out, lost. Three lay dead. One lay dying.

Ari staggered to the Motherbeast's side, tears forcing their way out of their eyes. Their vision blurred. Emotions spun, helpless and confusing. The Motherbeast was dead; the worlds she could have claimed were now safe. But in the process, the Riftmaster Ari had taken another life. And the life of a parent, no less.

…And it was not enough.

Her life ended here; but her orphans were still scattered across the universe. Even now, the remnants of her brood were clawing their way out from the belly of the mountain, tearing up and eating their way through every planet she had left to them.

Ari choked, the snow freezing the tears to their cheeks, the blood steaming from their armour and the tip of their weapon. A bead of blue slowly wound its way down the wires. As they watched, it slowly began to turn red.

Ari hastily looked away.

But it pooled in the snow from her open maw, coils of steam rising in the cold. Ari stumbled towards the Motherbeast's side. Their fingertips brushed her massive paws, stretched out in the snow.

I'll leave you here. If your kin don't bury you, the snow will. But… a part of you should come with me. These claws will taste blood again; truly a funeral fit for a Rifter.

Eleven-horn came trudging up the mountainside to meet them, Three-horn hurrying in its wake. Ari staggered to their feet, pitching forward. Their vision tilted, belly spun, but they hastily righted themself and went to meet it.

A small group followed after. Some were wounded, one left a trail of blood in the snow.

The young Mountain-dwellers' eyes were immeasurably sad.

"It's gone," Ari said. "The Motherbeast is gone."

"You killed her…" Eleven-horn breathed.

"Even then, these slopes are not ours anymore," Three-horn said softly. "We are scared."

Finally, Eleven-horn looked down to the mountainside, to a single wounded Ruiner still striking out towards them. Three legs dragging along the snow, it made its slow way up the slope. Its progress grew slower and slower, but it was still coming.

Ari readied their weapon, hiding the fact that they hadn't the strength to fight.

But the wounded Ruiner dragged itself slowly past them, before slumping to the side of its mother's cooling body. It draped its great head across her paws and did not move, even as the battle raged on.

Eleven-horn came to the Riftmaster's side. Lowering its horns, the Mountain-dweller glanced back at the mountainside, where its kin still struggled and died.

"Is anyone else coming?" Ari asked. Their voice felt rough, their chest tight.

"This is their home – they would rather die on Her slopes than leave the Mountain."

Ari hesitated. Slowly, the Riftmaster opened their arms, and beckoned the tiny tribe into their sides. They swept the diminutive creatures up beneath their cloak and gestured with their staff up towards the sky. There, they searched for a star.

Just above the horizon, Orion's belt shone true and bright.

Ari paused for a single moment; casting one last glance out towards the still form of the mother and the Ruiners tearing into the last remaining shreds of the Mountain's Heart. Then, before they could change their mind, they squeezed their eyes shut, Ari tightened their grip on the trigger. They felt fire flare through their skin, and grunted in pain, eyes clamped shut against the brightness. The ground dropped away beneath them. A mere five Mountain-Dwellers let out shrill bleats of fear and pain as they fell into nothingness.

For a precious moment, Ari realised that they had failed to warn them of the Rift's burning. And then the ground appeared beneath their feet. Ari sank to their knees in a pile of leaf-mulch amidst a circle of fallen Mountain-dwellers, and looked up towards the rainforest canopy.

There, they saw knots of titanic branches, fruits long-rotted, or eaten into nothingness. The scent of decay leeched into Ari's brain like a poison.

The gnarled trunks of struggling plants drooped slightly under their own weight, stripped of lichen and gnawed beyond recognition. Fallen trees could be seen criss-crossing beyond the distant treeline, and Ari saw the shapes of a few branches that still held the rotted ghosts of lantern fruits.

Every leaf on every tree had either fallen or been eaten, every fruit ripped from its branch. The forest once aglow with lantern-lights and beauty had succumbed to wreckage, and now all that remained were bleached skulls of the creatures that had caused this, lying on flowerbeds of Ari's tester herbs that still grew, wild and untamed. Their tendrils bored into the trunks of titanic trees, having escaped their garden and grown wildly out of control. Their beauty contrasted with the ugliness of decay.

A few flying creatures winked and glimmered among the branches, but other than that, Ari saw nothing that was as it should have been.

Against their will, Ari's eyes welled up, tears gushing down their face.

This world, too? They thought to themself. *Amazonia was beautiful. It was hospitable. It kept us so safe. And now…*

Ari swallowed.

Earth… What if Earth has already succumbed?

They forced themself to their feet and looked around to

where the Mountain-dwellers were helping each other up, fur stained in various tones of brown and green. They stuck out from the earthy tones, and already they were starting to loll out tongues and pant in the heat.

Pain shivered through Ari's abdomen and rolled like lead weights through their muscles. Their vision wavered at the corners of their eyes. They needed to rest.

"We need to find shelter," they declared. "I need a moment to think."

Chapter 17
The Final Choice

The Renohaiin empire was crumbling.

When the news reached the colonies that the Empire had failed to catch a single warm-blood, fear and strife had spread like wildfire. With the overseers involved in trying to find weapons powerful enough to stop the Vularian menace, troublemakers found themself suddenly free to begin uprisings and organise rebellions.

As the wheel turned, the Renohaiin empire had begun to lose their grip.

Colonies that had stood for generations began to crumble as the rumour spread that a single person had been enough to throw the Empire out of balance. *So what,* the ringleaders asked, *could a whole planet accomplish?*

Was one life worth all of this?

Malgas sat alone in a laboratory that was almost empty of people, looking out to a sky that was almost empty of ships. The few figures that wandered the streets below looked dark and lonely from up here. A beaker of blue-black liquid sat, cold and half-finished, upon a surface before her. Her undercarriage had grown tight; her abdomen thin with malnourishment.

Tiny figures loaded up the *Vestige* for one last try. An attempt that she wouldn't get to see.

The Riftmaster had nearly ruined her.

But, then… Captain Malgas had nearly ruined herself.

In a sense, Osai was right; Hoss had been a natural choice for a navigator because he could, in a pinch, become a host. But that wasn't the only reason. As his captain, Malgas was duty-bound to keep her small crew safe. But the ship that could have saved countless worlds had become the one that doomed them.

Her own pride had been her downfall.

Hoss would have given himself up in a moment. He wanted to see the Vularian Rift-walkers defeated as much as she did. He had just as much to avenge. He was here for that reason. Because he was one of the few who was more than willing to die.

But that didn't matter anymore. What did matter was that because of her, they were doomed.

Captain Malgas looked out of the window and through compound eyes watched as her old vessel began to lift off. It, along with the last vestiges of hope, took off and disappeared over the horizon, on one last search.

But Malgas knew there was nothing more they could do. Gently pushing the beaker of nourishment away with the tips of her claws, former Captain Malgas slumped down and hid everything away behind her hands.

It was over.

* * *

Ari managed to find shelter large enough for all of them under the buttress roots of a titanic tree.

As soon as they were out of sight, they sank down into a heap, groaning, and slept in brief and fitful intervals.

Fever raged under their skin, and nausea curled like a snake inside of them. They crawled to the edge of their shelter and expected at any moment to lose it all. Finally, they collapsed at the entrance of their abode and lost consciousness.

Breaths heaved. Dreams did not come.

The parasite was killing them; but it was a hindrance they could not live without.

For most of the night, Ari said nothing to their companions. Looking at the world around them wrought a strange sense of grief. Although they'd heard just what the Ruiners were capable of from Hoss, it was as though they hadn't fully believed it.

Perhaps the acid rain had been their downfall. Or, perhaps they'd met their match in the form of this world's predators. Or, perhaps they had simply moved on to greener pastures, sweeping in a wave of destruction across the surface of this world.

Perhaps the rainforests of Amazonia could recover; some creatures seemed to have stayed out of their reach, at least. But the devastation they had left in their wake could not be denied.

Life here would never be the same again.

It was as though the hope had evaporated before their very eyes. The Earth was almost within their grasp, but what if the Ruiners had got there first? All they'd wanted to do was warn Bailey. To get him to leave the Earth before it inevitably succumbed. But even if he did leave – and Ari knew that Bailey would never leave the people that he loved – the Ruiners would still be out there. Still spreading. Still devouring. Still reducing planets to ruins.

It would only be so long before another entered the Rift.

Ari could see it now; over tens of thousands of years, the light of life across the universe winking slowly out until nothing remained. Even the great whales from beyond the universe suffering. Would the newborns, freshly hatched from their Riftworlds, be able to Rift through a lifeless universe?

As time passed, there would be no future out here. Not for Bailey, not for Earth, or for the refugees of the Mountain's Heart.

And Ari... well.

They probably wouldn't live to see it at all.

They were dying. And there was only one thing in the universe that could possibly save them, and destroy the Ruiners for good.

Ari raised their head for the first time in many hours as something rustled. A pale shape came into focus before them. Eleven-horn's fur was muddied and matted, and his nostrils flared with the heat. But the creature spoke with dignity despite evident despair.

"Riftmaster… We can't stay here. The air is thick, too warm, and the scents are overwhelming. We must find new slopes."

Ari glanced across at the little huddle of Mountain-dwellers, clustered together in the dark as if hoping they could keep each other cold.

"Do you know where our new home may be found?"

Ari swallowed.

In all their years, they had never considered themself a hero. In their time in the Rift, they had lied and betrayed, gambled and tarried, hurt and even killed. Anything that was necessary to survive. And yet… As Ari looked into Eleven-horn's hopeful eyes, they truly felt as though they had made a mistake.

No longer will you die in the halls of your home, surrounded by the memories of your kin. I've doomed you to die all the way out here, a thousand light-years away from the nearest snowfall.

And all alone.

"I don't know, Eleven-horn," they choked out around the lump in their throat.

Ari looked to the stars.

Thousands of constellations twinkled above them through a web of bare branches. But the Earth was nowhere in sight. Instead they saw the Mountain-dwellers' star, and the zigzagging pathway of twinkling flecks that marked the way they had come.

Ari swallowed, slowly rising into a sitting position.

I can stop this. Even if I don't live to see it through, perhaps Bailey will.

But I need to make it back to the Empire.

"Mountain-dwellers," Ari said softly. "I know where we must go next."

Eleven-horn looked at them expectantly.

"As you can see, this planet, too, has suffered to the wrath of the Ruiners," Ari took a deep breath. "If you look around, see that it has been eaten bare. No matter where you go, they will one day follow. No slopes will be truly safe for you until these creatures are extinct."

They paused, looking around at the grave faces of the Tribe who hung on their every word.

"But I know someone who can help."

Ari let those words linger for a moment before continuing.

"It may mean that I am unable to find you a new mountain home. But I promise you, I will find you somewhere safe... One day. And until then, you'll be cared for."

Ari's throat closed up slightly as they saw the dismay, the betrayal, cross the faces of each Mountain-dweller in turn. Finally, they looked towards Eleven-horn, but its expression was unreadable. Head lowered, peach-toned mane fell over its four eyes. Ears were back. The chief was perfectly still, as though frozen in place.

"But... you promised," Three-horn said. "You'd find us a new home."

"Safe is not home," Eleven-horn finally said, in a tiny bleat.

Ari swallowed. "I know... But as long as the Ruiners are out there, no mountain... no planet will ever be safe. Not for you, not for me, not for my apprentice."

They glanced up towards the starlight that leaked through the branches above. "But... Perhaps I can change that."

Ari heaved a deep sigh.

"I just... need you to trust me, one more time."

Ari met Eleven-horn's eyes. The Mountain-dweller slowly nodded, as Ari held up their staff.

With no other choice, the Mountain-dwellers clustered into them, huddling near.

Well, then... Ari thought. *I suppose this is it.*

***

Ari and the Mountain-dwellers travelled in relative silence. At first, the Tribe was afraid of the staff and the pain that it brought, the fiery heat that spread beneath their skin a terrible discomfort. But, as each planet brought new sensations, they soon accepted that the pain was just a part of this new life, and they tolerated it without much complaint.

Often, they would linger on a planet for days at a time while they awaited the planet to turn and the stars to align. It was a struggle; it had been many centuries since Ari had had to worry about keeping so many others alive, and even more than that, the Mountain-dwellers' bodies needed dramatically different conditions to their own.

While they required the same compositions of sustenance, the Mountain-dwellers required low temperatures in order to digest it. Without the correct conditions to keep their bellies cold, the food stagnated, rotting in their gut.

Soon Ari wasn't the only one suffering with sickness. But the tiny group bore the pain without anger.

This was the price they'd paid for leaving their home.

Bit by bit, Ari's health was declining as the venom seeped through their veins. Though the source of their fear was long gone, the aftereffects lingered. Sleep became harder and harder to shrug off, and they struggled to keep food safely inside of them. They began to fear that they would not make it back to the Renohaiin empire on time.

Ari had hoped that they would encounter a suitable planet to acclimate the Mountain-dwellers on the way to the Renohaiin space station. At least then they would feel at peace when they gave everything up.

Until the very last planet they would bear this flimsy hope.

But none were cold enough. Some were too rocky. Even those that bore a sprinkling of snow simply did not have *enough* snow. Or sometimes, it was not the right kind.

"This snow is powder-snow. Ours was great flakes. It will never be so deep, here."

Ari almost argued more than once.

But then, in their mind's eye, they pictured the long-bleached bones of their children. Remembered the fate that came with not knowing a planet's cycles and seasons. If they did not choose carefully, the same fate could befall this humble tribe.

So, Ari knew that they had to let the Mountain-dwellers choose; only then, would the guilt of leaving them be easier to bear.

But the day drew ever nearer that they would need to part ways regardless. Planet by planet, star by star, Ari and the Mountain-dwellers inched nearer to the shattered Riftworld. Finally, Ari knew that there was no hiding it any longer. This planet's nights were cold, and their breaths steamed on the foggy air as they gathered the husks of leathery fruit. The Mountain-dwellers gathered around a meagre campfire, and the buzz of conversation was low and sparse.

Ari slowly settled down in the small ring of Mountain-dwellers, cheeks and nose flushed pink in the cold, and gently placed the fruits to heat at the foot of the fires.

The Mountain-dwellers glanced up as they did so.

At first, Ari had not cared to learn all their names; Eleven-horn and Three-horn being the notable exceptions, of course. But in their journey, each of the Mountain-dwellers had settled into some semblance of a role among the group. As the son of a healer, Three-horn Forager took it upon itself to comb the local flora for edibles.

Another pale Mountain-dweller with impressive, curving horns decided that its role was to be crafting. Ari was informed that its name was Seven-horn Tinkerer, and as much as Ari had tried to keep old doors closed, the revelation brought a faint ache to their chest.

The final two were the youngest, and quietest. Former apprentices among the tribe before it met its bitter end. As tradition decreed, their names were New-horn and

First-horn. Although Ari had thought them siblings at first, only one of them was Eleven-horn's child.

The two generally kept to themselves, and rarely talked to Ari.

Ari didn't dare find out more than that. They didn't want to make parting ways any more bitter than it had to be.

I'm doing this for Bailey, they told themself. *Besides… I'm giving them another chance.*

Ari was surprised to find that the Mountain-dwellers had a far easier time detecting toxins than they did. Sharp, twitching little noses picked up all but the faintest traces of poison, so they were easily able to distinguish what was edible and what was not.

Ari noted the way their tails wiggled with relief at the chill of this world, and eyes seemed brighter than they had in many days.

This was not home; but it seemed the Mountain-dwellers were finally settling into their new life. They had finally found their footing, just as the rug was about to be swept from under them once more.

Ari stared into the fire, chin against their chest, and said nothing for a time as the Mountain-dwellers delicately fed on their fruits, cringing only slightly at what they could only assume was an appalling taste for them.

Ari smiled lightly.

If one was to survive in the Rift, disgust was one of the very first things they needed to lay aside.

Ari cleared their throat, and the burbling voices subsided. Goatlike faces turned their way one by one. Kneeling, Ari rested a head above the other settled Mountain-dwellers, and their stature must have borne some authority. When they spoke, they were listened to, and they prayed that everyone understood.

"We have come far. But… this is the last planet we will see together."

Eleven-horn looked up in dismay. "We have not yet found our home."

"I know," Ari said. "And for that, I can only apologise."

"What will happen?"

"As I've said before, you will be safe. There are other beings on our next world who are well versed in other tongues and cultures. They will take good care of you."

"Will it be cold?"

"They… they have plenty of colonies in cold places. There will be plenty of places you can go. It just… Might be more crowded than what you're used to, but I'll make sure you're provided for. All of you."

"Where will *you* go?"

Ari didn't answer for a moment, seeming to wilt into themself somewhat. They hadn't wanted to consider that, even with their final destination so close at hand.

"I… Won't be going far. They need me. They're going to use me to wipe this scourge from the universe." They lowered their gaze. "Forever."

"When will we leave?" Eleven-horn rumbled, purring tones only a little louder than the faintest breath.

"Two days," Ari said. "That's when we'll see the star."

"And after that?"

Ari closed their eyes.

"Then we Rift."

"And then?"

"Then you'll be on your own."

The former chief didn't answer. Ari did not sleep that night, lying awake and scouring the skies. They saw no more traces of the Renohaiin empire.

They were probably out scouring distant systems in the futile hope of finding Ari again.

They certainly wouldn't expect the fugitive to leap directly into their open arms.

Two days came and passed in what felt like an instant. But to Ari's utmost surprise, the Mountain-dwellers never left their side.

On the dusk of the third day, Ari clustered their companions close and finally raised their staff towards the sky. They tightened their grasp on the trigger, and clamped their eyes tight shut.

This is it, little thing. You're finally going home.

Chapter 18
End of the Line

The feeling of falling seemed to last an eternity. The ground felt hard and flat beneath their feet. Ari's eyes cracked open as the pain faded from their skin. The space-station was almost empty of ships; The sky above was dark and filled with stars. The metal of their staff tingled against their skin.

The moon glowed bright over the horizon, silhouetting dark spires of radio towers and the occasional ship flashing by.

They had arrived back at the landing bay, empty aside from a few roaming guards on patrol, who shot them second glances and then scrambled to summon backup. Ari soon heard shouts erupt from nearby watchtowers.

Swallowing the nausea in their throat, Ari rose. The Mountain-dwellers clustered around them, ears flattened back in fear.

They removed their makeshift satchel and offered it to Eleven-horn. They raised their staff above their chest and faced the circle of guards, who paced, uncertain whether to pull their triggers. But Ari was tightly encircled, the Mountain-dwellers standing frozen in terror at their backs.

"Don't shoot," Ari said. "If I die, all hope will be lost."

At Ari's words, a guard flinched. As though they

expected something to happen. But then a steel-grey figure pushed their way through the crowd.

At the sight of Omea, hand bound against his chest, Ari almost let out a bark of relieved laughter, but stopped themself.

"Hoss," Ari snapped immediately. "I need to speak to Hoss."

Omea stared at them coldly, optic membranes twitching slightly. "Hoss is gone, Riftmaster. They went out to try to find another way."

Ari's blood ran cold. Their knuckles turned white as they tightened their grip around the staff.

"What about Captain Malgas?"

"Malgas has been demoted. You cost her reputation dearly."

"But she's here, on this planet?"

"…Yes. She's here."

"Then… I will answer to no one but her. Bring Malgas to me, or I re-enter the Rift." Warningly, Ari raised their staff to the heavens. Instinctively, desperately, the Mountain-dwellers huddled close, even though Ari had no intention of pulling the trigger.

"Why her?" Omea asked.

"She treated me with kindness, and without pity, considering she knew where I was going. I should hope she'll do the same for these creatures as well."

Ari cast a glance down towards the Mountain-dwellers, and met Eleven-horn's fearful gaze. Finally, they looked back up at Omea.

"…And if my final words are heard by anyone, I want it to be her."

"I… I'll see what can be done."

Omea turned, and melted into the crowd. Ari heard clattering whispers begin from the assembled guards, and their grips on plasma florets tightened.

It could have been minutes or hours. The moon slowly crept across the sky overhead. Ari busied themself picking out their pathway through the stars, casting their gaze back towards the celestial pathway leading back to

Earth for what they knew could be the last time.

"What is going on?" A familiar voice rose above the hubbub, and Ari let out a breath as Malgas swept into view. Although the Renohaiin race was notoriously hard to read, the sudden stillness of her body hinted at pure bewilderment.

Ari slowly uncurled their fingers from the metal and let their staff clatter to the ground.

Malgas' eyes widened.

"…You returned. Why?"

"I offer my aid. You have to stop these things."

"Aid? You think anyone will believe you, after all you've done? It would be a fool's errand to take you in conscious."

"Then bind me. Break me. Sedate me. But take me in now. I'm unarmed. No more tricks! All I ask is that you help these creatures, as best you can."

Ari held out their wrists, palms turned outward.

"Rift-walkers?"

"No. Refugees. I brought them with me from a planet ravaged by the Vularian Rift-walker."

Malgas' mandibles twitched slightly at the mention of the creatures' home planet; knowledge that Ari realised they should not have shared.

Malgas gestured with an arm, and a guard cautiously stepped forward, producing cuffs made from Renohaiin chitin. Clearly, they hadn't expected the appearance of such a high-value prisoner.

Ari waited as they were cuffed and bound. They met the eyes of the guard who was tending them, before turning back towards Malgas.

"All I will say is… I had to see the devastation for myself before I could truly believe what the Motherbeast was capable of."

"You saw her?"

In a fleeting moment of distraction, Ari wrenched the Motherbeast's claw from their belt and dropped it at Malgas' feet.

"I killed her."

Malgas fell silent. In stunned amazement, her mandibles flexed.

"I… don't believe you," she said tautly.

Ari cursed not having the foresight to take a sample from the titan's wound. "She bore the wounds of a Renohaiin plasma gun. Left mid-shoulder. One paralysed limb. There was not a single doubt in my mind that it was her. Not even as she lay writhing on the snow."

Malgas' mandibles quivered. Slowly, she knelt, to pick up the enormous claw from her feet. Slowly, tentatively, she turned it over in her grasp.

"Iridium veins…" she said at length. "You did see her." Malgas looked up sharply. "How did you do it?!" she demanded.

"We collapsed a village on her."

"And you survived."

Ari bowed their head. "We all did," They glanced around at the Mountain-dwellers, still clustering around them, letting out frightened yet dignified bleats in their native tongue. "Captain Malgas… these creatures, the Mountain-dwellers… They may not look like much, but they are some of the most hardy, loyal, and hard-working little creatures I've ever met. I hope the Empire keeps them safe."

"I'll be the judge of that, Riftmaster. Omea!"

Malgas switched seamlessly back into the role of being a captain.

The steel-blue medic materialised through the crowd once more, holding what appeared to be a plasma gun.

"Take readings."

Omea pressed the machine against Ari's forehead, and they felt a momentary flash of fear. A moment later, though, Omea spoke.

"The parasite lives."

"Come."

Ari felt the strength leave their limbs. Their legs buckled beneath them. A Renohaiin soldier on each arm kept them standing.

The air filled with noise and chaos. Soldiers scrambled

to find containment for them. Their arms were bound, their legs chained. But as someone brought a gag to bind their face, Malgas stopped them.

With Malgas grasping one of their arms with two strong limbs, and Osai on the other, Ari was led towards a small transport vessel, its structure not dissimilar to the hazard containment in the ship, and left the Mountain-dwellers behind.

"I'm sorry," Ari rumbled softly. But nobody answered them.

They strained for a glance back, and for an instant caught a last flash of a Mountain-dweller's helpless gaze. But there was nothing else Ari could do as they were loaded into a small transport vessel alongside their captors.

The Tribe they knew is dead. And I'm the one who pulled the trigger.

When the door closed, they were plunged into pitch-darkness and there was no way that they could see beyond. Without a rumble or a purr, or even a hum, the vehicle began to move. It slid smoothly across function-built walkways, and Ari felt like they were in the belly of something huge and terrifying.

There was no going back now.

As they were driven, Ari felt the air change. They struggled to peer out through the translucent crystal. They saw, vaguely, that they moved along a long and sterile corridor in a narrow street between towering, irregular structures. For an empire built on order, the architecture here was crooked and chaotic, with jagged points and overhanging ledges, as though it were built from the very foundations of the ruined planet.

The city-dome was half-crumbled, supported by scaffolding and unfinished.

"I have to say, Riftmaster. I wasn't expecting you to return. I thought the Empire had fallen. Thousands deserted, after your last escape."

Ari swallowed. "Why? Surely you have other colonies."

"We do. But in the current climate, it is difficult keeping them. Even on clean planets, revolutions and uprisings have taken us by surprise. Fear runs rife on new colonies. The hope of a poison – a 'cure', if you will, was one of the only things keeping us in their good graces. And when the wrong generals caught wind of the fact that we'd failed to capture even a single warrior…"

"I've lived thirty-seven star cycles, captain Malgas. I always said that if I was to die, I'd do it on my own terms."

"This is more than a simple saying, Riftmaster. You escaped an empire, thrice. You created a staff to control the Rift… and leaped between worlds of your own accord." Malgas paused, letting her words linger, her disbelief thick upon the air. "…And then you returned. So what makes now different?"

"I have control. And… clarity. Even if I don't get to see the results, I'll be glad knowing that at least someone can."

"Who?"

Ari opened their mouth, then closed it again.

"Why do you ask?"

"Curiosity. And to make sure you don't change your mind."

"I…" Ari hesitated again. "I'm doing this for my child." Ari glanced away. "Or… well… a… apprentice. I took him in when I found him in the Rift, but when he found his way home I… I let him go. I didn't know him for very long, but…" the lines deepened around Ari's eyes. "He is all I have left."

Ari let out their breath in a long sigh.

"In the beginning, he was why I escaped. I wished to warn him, back then, but…" they paused. "His planet may already be gone."

There was a brief moment of silence.

"I see." Malgas' mandibles twitched. She hesitated for a moment. "If I could have, I would have done anything to warn mine, as well. Anything."

Ari lowered their gaze.

"I… I'm sorry. I didn't know," they stammered. They had almost forgotten that Malgas was a parent. But the way she had talked about them lived on in their mind.

"I don't talk about it often," Malgas said simply.

"What… happened to them?" Even as they said it, Ari had the horrible feeling that they already knew.

"Their colony was one of the first to be consumed. I have yet to receive word if any still live."

Ari's blood ran cold. "…How many?"

"Seven were on missions away from the colony. They live, at least… but seventeen are still unaccounted for. If there's a chance I could save even one… I'd take it."

"And that's why you needed to capture me."

"Yes." Malgas paused. "I never imagined that a warm-blood could understand."

Ari smiled slightly. The irony was not lost on them. "There have been many times that I've thought the same of a cold-blood."

Malgas didn't look at Ari in the dark, seeming deep in thought. But her grip on their arm did not grow any stronger. Finally, the vehicle drew to a halt. They were lifted out and tugged into walking without gentleness.

Numbed by anticipation, Ari thought back to their days spent aimlessly wandering as they searched fruitlessly for a way home. And the first sign they had found there of something amiss in the Renohaiin Empire.

"Which colony was it?" they asked.

Malgas' optic membranes flicked in surprise. "Why would you want to know?" she asked.

"I met someone out there, on a Riftworld. A refugee from a recent colony. She thought they were sent into the Rift as punishment, but… thinking back, perhaps it was an evacuation. I don't want to create unnecessary hope, Malgas. But perhaps, if what you said about the Rift was true…" Ari met Malgas' four small eyes, and, for just a small moment, her expression was readable. "…If it can be traced… Then perhaps some of your kin still live."

"It was the ninth colony of system forty-four."

Ari simply smiled.

"Where can I find this refugee?" Malgas asked. Her tone was cautious, but her grip on the Riftmaster's arm tightened as they walked.

Ari thought then, of Reina. Of her wish to live, long and happy, on a world which was free of Renohaiin rule, though her new home was perhaps destined to one day break. Their smile faded slightly.

"That, I can't tell you."

They left their intent clear. As a navigator, they were expected to know, and Malgas knew that. *If I can do one more thing before I sleep… let it just be the right thing, one more time.*

"In that case, I'll find them myself." Malgas glanced away. "Thank you for bringing this to my attention," she said stiffly, and then was silent for a time.

Ari could tell that she was trying hard to break the silence.

"Which planet are you from?" she finally asked.

"Hm?"

"Your homeworld. If we are to eradicate this scourge from the universe, it could be good to start there. We owe you that much, at least."

A flash of nervousness grew in Ari's belly. *I can't… can I?* But they forced it down and shook their head. *But the Ruiners came so close… What if Earth succumbs?*

"Maybe," they said quietly.

"Tell me about your home planet," Malgas said again.

Walking was becoming harder, and their limbs felt like lead; they put more weight on Omea and Malgas with each passing moment.

Omea gripped Ari's arm tightly, claws digging into their flesh as the Renohaiin squeezed them through a narrow doorway. Ari tipped their head back to look around, and could see the walls lined with familiar instruments, books intricately carved with covers of Renohaiin chitin. The room was small; barely more than a cubicle, and nothing like the Renohaiin laboratories they were used to. It was barely large enough for the small party who now entered it.

Perhaps it was to ensure secrecy; or perhaps the inherent cosiness of it hoped to be less threatening, and offer them a greater chance at survival. Perhaps it was never intended to be a laboratory at all.

Tubes of fluid were knotted across the floor, all of them leading to a wide central plinth.

Upon it, there sat a half-sphere, its surface fragmented and jagged with crystalline plates, opaque. It was taller than Ari was by far, and long enough to settle a small Ruiner. The remaining space around it was narrow, with each corner purposed for a specific station. Wires and tubes knotted the rim like an eldritch birds' nest. The water within was crisscrossed by a spiderweb of silken and chitinous plates. It must have been built long before the Empire had known just what kind of creature the parasite would choose for a host.

For a moment, Ari's resolve faltered.

They swallowed the nausea that rose within. Struggled to support their weight for a moment.

Shivering slightly, they dragged their thoughts back to the matter at hand. Malgas had asked about their home planet.

To give this information now could condemn Earth to a long and painful process of alien colonisation. It could mean that Bailey, and everyone he loved, would be forced to assimilate and work for the Empire, submitting to cold-blooded overlords who wanted to help, without taking the time to learn what humanity really needed.

It could save the Earth, and kill it, all in a single blow.

Ari was giving themself up, but even now they were resisting, right down to their core. Their legs shook, their eyes bleary. They had to force their limbs to take every step. Even as the venom dragged the life from their limbs.

Even now, their body resisted. Their mind still screamed that it wasn't their time.

"Riftmaster…?" Malgas' voice broke through. They realised that they had been silent for a minute or more. Thinking. Considering.

Finally Ari spoke.

"It's nearest to the second starbase, twenty degrees between it and your host planet. It is currently in the… er… probably the highest of the Galaxy's arms. The sun is small, orbited by a system of nine celestial bodies. Our planet is the third in its system from the sun… with a single even smaller moon. The system is seventy degrees out-of-orbit from Betelgeuse, by four hundred lightyears, and known by our kind as Earth. I marked it on some old starmaps back when I was a navigator…" Ari hesitated briefly. "…Only then, I marked it as a dead planet, stripped of all useful resources by hostile natives."

Ari glanced down at the ground through lowered lashes. "I was lying, though. Mostly."

Malgas' expression did not change.

"Earth…" she repeated softly. She slowly drew to a halt beside the crystalline device that would soon become their coffin. They could see through the translucent crystal that it was filled with a clear fluid. "I'll remember that."

"The Ruiners… they came so close. You'll really make sure it's safe?" Ari hated how thin their voice, how powerless they felt. "And then you'll leave it alone…?"

Malgas' optic membranes flicked noncommittally. "When we reach Earth, that will be for the Overseers to decide," she said. "I'm sorry, Riftmaster."

"Well, will you tell them this?" Ari added quickly. "Settlement may not be wise. You'd be stupid to set foot on its surface or even enter the atmosphere with a large number of ships. The *Vestige* could be fine, but… Our kind is militaristic. Our world, polluted beyond belief and filled with weapons far too powerful for the needs of its people…" They trailed off. "…Even I feel like an alien among them."

Ari couldn't tell if Malgas believed those words. But no matter what happened, the Earth was in the Empire's claws, now.

"If you try to colonise, Earth will fight," they finally said.

"They all fight," Malgas said, as she hooked her claws

into some unseen lever beneath the rim of the pod. "It makes no difference."

There was a soft click, and the topmost plates began to slowly lift apart like the petals of a wicked mechanical flower. Plates slid aside, revealing a ladderlike structure. It wouldn't be easy, but Ari would be able to use them to climb inside.

As they watched, though, Omea activated something else; and the cradle of fluid began to slowly lower into its plinth, giving them a better view of the shimmering pool within.

They didn't much like the idea.

"Riftmaster… Would you please ready yourself. We will need access to every vein."

Ari nodded. Slowly, mechanically, they removed the clothes from their body, peeling back armour that clung to their skin like layers of grime and filth.

Malgas watched, shocked, as they removed their scales and exposed their real skin. There was no point in preserving modesty, here; their human body was the same to the Renohaiin as an animal was to humans.

"You're telling me that you were clothed the entire time!?" Malgas asked, appalled, as she looked them up and down.

Ari didn't reply, flushing only slightly. That was one tiny triumph, at least, as they offered her one last sly smile and a wink.

"Enjoy it while it lasts," Ari said. Their tone wavered slightly despite themself.

Malgas' mandibles quirked. Perhaps she saw the funny side as well.

But it didn't last.

"Now… Enter the capsule, for me."

Omea took their clothes with open arms. Three hands spread towards them, unafraid, while the other was tightly bound in silk bandages. Omea's mandibles quivered as they noticed Ari's gaze.

"It is healing well," Omea said, mildly.

"I'm…" Ari hesitated, a lump rising in their throat. *All that pain I caused, and in the end, it was all for nothing.*

Their voice croaked as they spoke aloud. "…I'm glad to hear that." A lump rose in their throat. "…Thank you. And I… I am sorry."

Omea said nothing, but offered them a nod. Not quite an acceptance, but an acknowledgement, and for them, it was enough.

Ari turned away. They tried, and failed, to lift their weight up, to begin climbing into the pool. Their vision spun with every movement. *I'm dying,* they realised. *Even if I'd escaped, I'd have no antidote to my own fear.*

A moment later, a comforting hand rested on their shoulder. They looked up and met the gaze of Captain Malgas, offering a nod. They allowed her to haul them, gently yet firmly, up and over the spires of crystal. Her hands rested under their arms and upon each of their hips with a firm, sturdy grip and settled them in the enclosed pool of airy fluid. Their lithe form barely made a ripple. And then Malgas straightened, peering down from above, as she might have watched a larva in its silken cradle.

The liquid felt chilly against their skin, and their hair stood on end from head to toe. Ari shivered as the slime lapped against their ribcage.

The crystalline petals felt like the bars of a cage stretching above them as they gazed up and out at the faces of their captors.

Leaning down, Omea gently inserted the tips of needles into their inner elbows. Ari felt a sharp, indignant pain in their abdomen, and then the nausea faded slowly away.

Malgas lowered them further into the liquid, enough to cover their chest.

Thankfully, the bottom and sides were enclosed in a thin, cushioning layer of leather.

Not that my comfort will matter for very long.

Ari didn't struggle.

"We're about to start life-support processes. It won't hurt, but the parasite may not like this. Ready?"

Ari tried to suppress the shudders of fear. Before they lay back against the padded inside of the crystalline capsule, Ari spoke.

"Captain Malgas... I have one last request." They paused. "When you reach Earth, would you find someone for me? His name is Bailey. If he's still there, he'll be wearing a Rift Crystal. Probably the only one on Earth. I... I want him to know what happened to me."

Ari lowered their gaze, hoping that the ulterior motive didn't shine in their eyes. For they hoped – no, knew – that Bailey could save their life. He was the only one they knew who would at least try.

But...

"And... If, by any chance, I die... Please, give him everything that was mine. He'll need it one day."

They looked into the Captain's eyes. And although she was far from human, Ari could have sworn they saw gratitude there. Gratitude, and some sadness, too.

"You might not die, Riftmaster."

"But... if I do...?"

Malgas gave no indication that she had ever heard.

Their eyelids began to droop. Ari forced them open again, horror flooding through their veins. But already they were beginning to sink beneath the surface. They sat up. "If... If you can ensure the Ruiners are dead, then Earth will already be safer," they murmured. "Thank you, Malgas."

"Don't thank me. And don't try to fight the sleep... It's already in your blood. Just breathe deeply, and let go."

Ari's eyes slowly slipped closed. The chill gradually closed around their cheeks, then their nose, and tugged on their hair. Fluid found its way into their nose, and they coughed. "Captain Malgas...?" Ari raised their head, slightly above the surface. Their voice was slurred.

"I'm here."

Ari hesitated, trembling. "...I'm scared."

There was a pause. When she finally spoke, her voice was faint. "I know."

But there was nothing she could do. They both knew that. After a time, though, she said their name. "...Riftmaster?"

Their eyes cracked open. Ari hadn't realised they had closed.

"Can I provide some sort of comfort?"

Ari couldn't say. Their throat closed up. When they spoke again… their voice emerged as a little more than a squeak. "Could you… hold my hand?"

Now that it was said out loud, the admission sounded foolish. They felt foolish. Foolish and alone.

But moments later, they felt fingers close over their hand. They gripped it, feeling hard carapace and soft, velvety palm.

They moved their lips, but no sound emerged.

And then sensation faded away altogether.

Let go…

Ari struggled to cling to wakefulness. They opened their mouth, and their lungs began to slowly fill with fluid.

The darkness behind their closed lids gradually faded into white.

I've let go a thousand times. What makes this time any different?

Something turned in the pit of their belly, and they felt a spark of fear.

The emotional thrill felt distant, separated somehow. Somewhere, they felt that the fear wasn't their own.

Their own mind felt largely empty. For the first time in a long while, they felt content. It could all be over soon, and they were okay with that.

I've done everything I can.

Faces flashed before their eyes, the faces of their parents full of rage on the night they ran away from home. More than five thousand years had made them blurry. Ari hardly recognised them anymore; they ached for one last look at the faded, grubby, muddied photograph buried at the bottom of the satchel that Malgas had most likely burned.

Stay awake. One more moment.

They saw the face of a long-dead love in his death throes, felt the prickle of his stubble as their lips pressed together one final time.

They wondered, briefly, if anyone remembered Oliver Patterson back in his hometown in Michigan. His children back on Earth would have grown up, grown old even. They might still wonder what happened to the father who had left them so long ago. Perhaps they might even still search sometimes, through old records and vintage newspaper articles, to see if anyone had seen him since.

His wife would be long gone, now.

Ari saw their own children flashing before their eyes, one by one by one. A thousand years, it had been. And still their faces shone as clearly as the day they had been lost. In the known universe, not a single image of them remained; and soon the only remaining memory of them would be lost to oblivion.

That scared Ari more than the enclosing dark.

Their names. Remember their names.

The visions grew hazy and blurred. Their memories fragmented, Ari put the names to the faces and held them close.

Adeline, Toby and Polly… Peggy, Pip, Martin, Katrina… Lily, Evan, Karen and Lucy…

Ari's eyes squeezed shut. Tears mingled with the liquid closing in around them. The light that had been falling on their closed eyelids winked out. They were shut in, and alone.

Adeline, Toby, Polly, Peggy… Martin… Polly… Adeline… Toby…

As thoughts became harder and harder to maintain, Ari's mind finally settled upon a clearer image. Fresher. One that arrived unbidden. Ari looked into those brown eyes that were bright with tears and traced over lips that mouthed the words 'goodbye'. Their gaze trailed over hair that was slicked with a fine rain and shimmering under a deep grey sky.

Bailey…

The memory of him came clearer, and easier, but the knowledge that he was gone felt no easier to bear. Even if, with luck, his light would keep on shining for a long, long time to come.

You have a home and a family to return to, and all because of me.

As it all faded away, Ari was left with a single final thought.

So why aren't I happy…?

The question lingered only a moment longer. Consciousness finally slipped through their fingers, and the Riftmaster drifted away.

Chapter 19
The New Line

The moon had set. The Renohaiin base of operations stood silent and lonely. But across the ruins and the shattered crystals, a sputtering engine began to purr. This was an ancient ship; older even than the *Vestige*. Its Rift-drivers seemed barely functioning.

Malgas had spent days repairing it, bringing its dusty interior back to the brink of collapse. When the *Vestige* was recalled from its final voyage, Malgas sought out her crew, silently appealing for Hoss, Eidhoin and Omea to join her at the landing pad. As silent as the grave, they followed her out into the crumbling wasteland.

Malgas introduced them to her new project as she would to a new crewmate. Hoss and Eidhoin glanced at one another, afraid of this new fire in her eyes. Afraid more of faulty equipment than her being caught, Hoss brought navigation tools, and fished what he could from the wreckage. Eidhoin repaired the engine, and had the generators humming, growling, and coughing.

"Captain," Hoss said urgently. "Are you sure we will be able to get clearance for this?"

"We're not getting clearance," Malgas said, as she jammed a tool under the control panel. Lights blinked and sputtered into life. "This is just something I have to do."

"But, Captain. You could be reprimanded, or worse."

Malgas sat back in the pilot's chair. She looked towards him. "I know."

"Then, why?"

Malgas hesitated, as though afraid to acknowledge the possibility out loud. "They might be still out there, Hoss."

Hoss' small eyes widened. He exchanged a glance with Eidhoin, and they offered one another a small nod.

After that, their repairs carried on with increased fervour. The moon cycled on, rising and setting.

Finally, they stood outside, looking upon the once-decrepit ship, repaired with crystal and sheets of plate metal. Malgas' eyes were bright. She blinked with a few membranes, as though she didn't believe it was truly finished.

"Thank you," she said, looking at each of her crew in turn. "Thank you so much."

Hoss nodded, ears tall with pride.

"I won't forget this," she added.

"Of course not," said Eidhoin. "We'll be reminding you every step of the way."

"You're not thinking…"

Omea drew a rolled-up parchment from a pouch in his uniform. "I got clearance."

For a moment, Malgas was dumbstruck. "How?"

"We have an idea of where to go, and a lead on a lost colony. We gathered our limited resources and put together a ship from nothing. The Overseer has nothing to lose. They would be foolish to miss that chance."

Malgas' mandibles flexed. She struggled to put the words to the feeling. Finally, she simply said "Thank you."

And then she led her tiny crew on board, taking them into their positions behind the cockpit. It was more cramped than what they were used to; but this was a vessel once intended for a crew of eight, just like hers. Malgas flicked switches and tapped buttons, seeing the panel light up with ancient runes.

The engine coughed, sputtered, and finally rumbled into life.

"We'll need to make a supply run at the nearest colony," she said. "It'll allow us to upgrade the ship, at least."

She activated the thrusters and the ship lifted unsteadily from the surface of the ravaged Riftworld. The landing gear creaked as they curled into the belly of the ship.

"And then, after that… the Riftmaster's home planet."

"What?! Why would you want to go there?! We've had enough trouble with *one* human!"

Malgas' mandibles quirked.

"If the Riftmaster dies, we'll need an alternate host," she said. "And if this… apprentice cares just as much about the Riftmaster as it cared about him… then he may come willingly."

Malgas flicked a few levers, and something groaned in the belly of the ship.

"Besides," she said. "It's on the way to system forty-four."

The city pulled away below them, smaller and smaller. Tiny shapes – the scientists who had inherited the world – watched them go.

The next time she returned, perhaps things would be different. Perhaps then the fight would have truly begun.

"How *is* the host?" Malgas asked.

"It's alive," Omea said, scratching newly-forming knuckles. "Seems to have built up some resistance to the toxin. There's still a very low chance of its survival, but…"

"Good," Malgas said, unable to hide a smile. "Hopefully the synthesis is going well."

"You hope it lives?"

"I do. After all the trouble it gave us, it almost seems a shame for its life to end this way," she said, a little bit wistfully.

"I suspect it will be with us a while yet. Not even the Motherbeast could kill that thing," Eidhoin said. "Though I'm not sure whether to be happy about that, or dread the day it awakes."

"Hopefully it will be on our side when it does," Malgas said.

Hoss scoffed faintly. They looked at him. "I doubt that."

Malgas glanced back at Omea. "It was stable, then?"

Omea clacked an affirmation. "There wasn't really a way to tell. But the last time I checked, its lips kept moving in its sleep. I expect it's dreaming."

"Do aliens dream, I wonder?" the Captain said.

"Some do, some don't. I've studied it, a little bit. I wonder what it's dreaming about."

Captain Malgas smiled sadly. "About a happier time, no doubt."

Epilogue
A New Beginning

There was no discomfort here. No exhaustion. No pain or aches from the climb. There was no wind, no scent. Only the cool pressure against every inch of their skin. An embrace they could never escape. They melted into it. This was comforting; this was home.

"I didn't think I'd ever see you smile again," Ari heard Oliver's voice rise from somewhere below them.

Something was wrong, but Ari just couldn't quite put their finger on why. With him, they'd take any moment they could get.

"Well… When you're leading a life like this, you need to learn to make the best of things."

Ari peered over the lip of a mossy precipice, and saw the smile spreading across his bristly cheeks. They extended a hand to help him up.

Oliver eyed that hand and shook his head. His quills softly rattled with the motion.

Ari raised an eyebrow, and tipped their head, eyes sparkling with humour. "What? A man's fragile ego can't handle a helping hand?"

"It's not that. I just think you shouldn't be pushing yourself," Oliver said. "It's bad enough that you insisted on coming up here in the first place."

Ari scoffed, withdrawing back over the edge.

"I'm pregnant, Oliver, not broken," they said a moment later.

"I always thought it was the same thing."

They answered him with a snort.

"You would."

Oliver spent another moment catching his breath, before finally hauling himself up after them. His claws scraped against stone, a hiss of effort emerging through clenched teeth. Rocks clattered down a hundred metres of rocky cliff face beneath him as ancient layers of stone dislodged. By the time he appeared, bedraggled and hunched like a cat, he was gasping for air.

Ari glanced at him only briefly, before turning away. They were settled down on the edge of a wide, flat plateau, sitting with their legs swinging over the edge, grey eyes watching the gilded clouds slowly roll by. The sunlight danced on a rose-gold sea. With hair shining red like molten copper, and swollen sides heaving, it didn't take long before they noticed Oliver's lingering gaze.

"What?" they asked, grinning.

Oliver hesitated, stammering, before choking out the words. "I just… Don't think you've ever looked more beautiful than you do right now."

Ari scoffed but didn't reply. "Beautiful is a… strong word for someone like me. I don't think I remember the last time you called me that."

"Probably because I knew you'd hate it."

"Yeah, probably."

Oliver slowly approached to stand beside them, with all the familiarity of partners of more than a thousand years, before sinking down to seat himself at their side. As they lightly grasped his arm, they felt the goosebumps forming on his skin. When he turned to look at them, he was smiling slightly.

"What did I tell you?" Ari said quietly, eyes shining.

"Hm?"

"This view… It's worth it. Right?"

Oliver raised his head, about to protest. But then he must have seen the way that their eyes were shining. The way that those cheeks dimpled with their broad grin, and the ageless joy in their expression.

"Yes," he said finally. "It was worth the climb."

Ari turned back to admire the view, but Oliver's eyes remained on them, combing over every wayward strand of hair and taking in every freckle.

They both knew then that the feelings of that morning would stick with them forever.

Silently Oliver inched closer and pressed his side into theirs. One arm slowly snuck around their waist, talons resting softly against their rounded side. Slowly, his eyes trailed down towards their belly.

Ari's body had never been particularly feminine; from the moment the pair had met, the Riftmaster had been short, squat, and lithe with muscle. They were fiery, disobedient, at times arrogant. And yet, this new rounded curve added a touch of femininity that they knew he would miss.

Although he never would have said it out loud, Ari knew Oliver liked this look on them.

So naturally, they couldn't wait to get rid of it.

The edge of Ari's mouth quirked with mischief.

"My eyes are up here, *dearest*."

Oliver startled out of his reverie, and fumbled for a reply, flushing red. He sputtered momentarily for something to say before finally falling silent.

"My darling, I still wish you wouldn't push yourself like that," he said. "You should take things easy. It won't be long now."

Ari laughed. *Of course.*

"And allow myself to grow out of shape?" they asked, in mock disbelief. "No way. We'll need all the strength we can muster if we want to protect the little one."

"I have enough strength for the both of us," Oliver insisted, looking slightly hurt.

Ari rolled their eyes.

"Tch. Speak for yourself. But, when the time comes, at

least we won't be wishing we'd made the most of the quiet while it lasted."

Oliver shook his head, sighing. "Perhaps motherhood will be just the thing to temper your fire," he said, only half joking.

"You know," Ari replied, smiling sweetly. "Sometimes I hate you with every fibre of my being."

"Every time you tell me that, I only love you more."

Ari's lip twitched upwards in a faint smile, before they offered him a small wink.

There was a momentary pause. "So you're excited, then?" Oliver ventured, after a while.

Ari sniffed, shrugging slightly. "Excited is a strong word." They hesitated. "But… I'm not wholly dreading it, at the very least."

Oliver slightly inclined his head before turning his gaze out towards the distant horizon. They followed it out to where the curving silhouettes of skyfaring beasts could be seen arcing in and out of the clouds like dolphins, playing and twisting in the sunrise.

Silence reigned between the two for a time as they basked in the warm sunshine of another Earth.

"Are you nervous yet?" Ari asked, after a little while.

"Maybe a little," Oliver replied. "I'm still not as nervous as the first time."

Ari let out a quiet huff and didn't answer.

"Well… My first time, at least."

"Nice catch," Ari said, voice dripping with sarcasm. "You know, this time will be different."

"I know," Oliver said. "My wife actually listened to me, for a start."

"Oh, hush up," Ari scoffed, though their smile never faltered. A moment later, they turned back to the open sea. "But… there is also the matter of the Rift. We will have no doctor out here, Oliver. I'm expecting you to cover for me while I'm–…" Their gaze flickered. For a second they couldn't find the words. Finally, they folded their arms across their chest, resting them lightly on their belly. "…less than able."

They glanced away for a moment.

"I'll always be there to provide for my family," Oliver said. "You know that."

Ari glanced towards him, as though trying to work out if he was joking. Finally, though, they shook their head. "It's not just about providing. We can both do that. But… I might not make it out of this, Oliver." Ari fell silent for a moment. "And even if I do, I might never be the same."

"Don't worry about anything, Aria. Just rest. As the man of the house, it's my duty to make sure you have everything you need."

Ari grunted, watching in vague disbelief as he puffed himself up, but said nothing.

Seeming to notice their doubt, Oliver's expression softened. He slowly reached down and took their hand, intertwining his fingers with theirs. "We'll make it through, Aria. We always make it through. You'll see."

Ari looked up at him, grey eyes gazing into blue. They hesitated another few moments before leaning their weight into his. Oliver rested his lips against their forehead, planting a series of kisses beneath their hair.

"I hope you're right," they murmured.

Oliver took them into his arms; they leaned their full weight into him and felt his hands stroking along their back.

They gazed deeply into his eyes and glimpsed their reflection staring back at them.

Despite youthful appearances, the memories of two thousand years lived within those eyes. And yet, this was new territory for both of them. It was hard to believe that after so many years, there were things that the esteemed Riftmaster had yet to do.

"Do you have any advice?" Ari asked, from where they had buried their face in his neck.

"Advice?" Oliver asked. He thought for a moment. "On parenthood?"

Ari nodded into his shoulder.

Oliver thought for a moment. "Parenthood is all about sacrifice."

"Sacrifice?" Ari chuckled slightly. "You're really selling it to me, Oliver."

Oliver smiled.

"It's true, though. When the time comes, it won't be about us anymore. Our kids will need to come first, no matter what. Times like this… all those days we spend climbing mountains and exploring forests, taking risks… Even just the days we spend together, indulging in each other's company."

Ari gazed out towards the copper-hued horizon, a faraway look in their eye. "Those days won't exist anymore."

"Exactly. From here on out, we'll need to think of them first. Sometimes the right decision to make won't be the easy one. But so long as we are together, I don't think it'll ever be the wrong one."

"What about us?"

"Well, I for one, think that so long as our kid is happy, I will be too."

Ari slightly inclined their head. They didn't respond for a while. Sometime later, though, they swung their feet onto solid ground, and stood up, brushing traces of moss from the front of their clothes. Oliver watched curiously as the Riftmaster cast one last, longing look across the rose-gold sea.

Slowly, Oliver stood too.

"Are you finished here?" he asked.

"I'll never be done with this view," Ari said, with a smile. "But I'm starting to get hungry, and…"

They winced slightly, placing a hand upon their swollen belly. After a moment's hesitation, Oliver did the same. Ari looked into those ageless eyes they loved so much, and took in the faintest scent of Earth that lingered on his breaths even now.

"It won't be long," he finished for them.

Ari nodded. They tilted their face up towards him, and he pressed his lips against theirs. Ari's heart swelled. He kissed them again, regardless of their calloused skin, and the chapped lips that were a little scratchy to the touch.

As Ari leaned into him, Oliver wrapped his arms around them, lifting them onto tiptoes.

They lifted their feet from the ground as they were twirled against the cool dawn wind. They felt his arms about them and felt a happiness burning inside them they had briefly thought they might never feel again.

Again and again, Oliver kissed their lips until the Riftmaster giggled and squirmed.

Finally, he raised his face from theirs, just far enough that they could look into one another's eyes once more.

They looked into those blue eyes, and just for a moment saw him as he always had been. Just Oliver. Human, and flawed, and wonderful in all the wrong ways.

"Ollie," the Riftmaster murmured, and planted one last kiss on his stubbly lips. "I love you."

"And I love you." Oliver nuzzled nose and mouth into their forehead, closing his eyes. "My beauty, my love. My Riftmaster."

They snorted with laughter before replying. "Now, now. That's far too much."

Oliver laughed, gave them one last hug, and then placed them unsteadily onto their own two feet.

"We should go. We need to prepare."

Ari nodded, smile fading into a look of serenity. The fear had left their eyes, leaving only a cool void of acceptance.

"For the worst outcome, as well as the best."

The End

Acknowledgements

So, we've reached the end of this long, long road.

In the time since I started writing *Renegade* three years ago, there has been a global pandemic, three lockdowns, and three years of married life. We got a new hamster (who is now a little old man), renovated our home, got into plant care (and killed a few). Finally, we opened up our very own book shop, BookWyrm. *Renegade* has, in that time, been one of the most teeth-clenchingly frustrating and rewarding books I've ever worked on.

Before we go, I'd like to say a few words to those who have helped me along this journey.

First of all, thank you so much to the lovely folks over at my publisher Elsewhen Press. They were the first ones to give *Riftmaster*, and me, a chance in the labyrinthine, and incredibly difficult world of traditional publishing!

Secondly, I'd like to thank the folks over at Elvet & Bailey, especially Gemma and Dan. This little independent shop was one of the first to give *Riftmaster* a place on their shelves when it first released, and Gemma and Dan were the very first to read *Renegade*'s first draft! The feedback they provided helped to grow my confidence in this bizarre little book, and to realise that maybe, just maybe, it was ready for the next step.

I'd also like to thank Andrew Joseph White, the author of *Hell Followed With Us*. It's always incredible to meet an author who you look up to, and I was absolutely honoured when Andrew agreed to help me with a later draft. His in-depth feedback was absolutely invaluable to making *Renegade* the book it is today. And the lovely, shiny quote he wrote for the blurb was an absolutely incredible bonus!

I'd also like to thank my husband and fellow BookWyrm, Chris. As always, he hasn't read *Renegade* yet. Chris always likes to wait until my books are released before reading them, as he worries that any feedback he gives will change it too much. Even still, he's always happy to listen to my plans and plots, and bounce back with ideas and thoughts. His additions were an essential part of the planning process and maybe by the time *Renegade* is in print, he'll have forgotten just enough to read it spoiler-free. Except, perhaps, for the beginning. And the ending. And the themes. And the tone. And the... oh. If you're reading this, I'm so sorry, Chris!

And finally, thank you, the reader; whether you're one of our wonderful customers in BookWyrm or you stumbled on this book by pure chance, I appreciate every single one of you.

I'm sure that the Rift will come again, but until then—thank you so much for joining me in this journey!

Elsewhen Press
delivering outstanding new talents in speculative fiction

Visit the Elsewhen Press website at elsewhen.press for the latest information on all of our titles, authors and events; to read our blog; find out where to buy our books and ebooks; or to place an order.

Sign up for the Elsewhen Press InFlight Newsletter at elsewhen.press/newsletter

Riftmaster

TALES OF A COSMIC TRAVELLER

Miles Nelson

How do you hold on to hope when you're being repeatedly wrenched between worlds?

College student Bailey Jones is plucked from his world by a mysterious and unpredictable force known as the Rift, which appears to move people at random from one world to another. Stranded on an alien planet, he is relieved when he meets a fellow human, the self-styled Riftmaster, who is prepared to assist him. Although curious about his new companion's real identity, Bailey hopes that, with years of experience of the Rift, this cosmic traveller can help him find a way to return to Earth. But first, as the two of them are ripped without warning from one hostile planet to another, Bailey must rely on the Riftmaster to show him how to survive.

Riftmaster, an adventure, an exploration, is concerned with loss, and letting go, while still holding onto your humanity and identity, even when life seems hopeless.

ISBN: 9781911409915 (epub, kindle) / 9781911409816 (264pp paperback)

Visit bit.ly/Riftmaster

The Forge
& The Flood

Miles Nelson

When history itself seems written to keep them apart, can two radically different peoples really find it in their hearts to get along?

Sienna is an Ailura. His kind live on the lonely island of Veramilia, bound under traditions forged by countless generations.
Indigo is a Lutra. His kind goes with the flow, having lived as free as the ocean waves since the beginning of time.

When a great calamity strikes and the Ailura are forced to flee their island home, the Ailura and the Lutra come face to face for the first time in known history. In these turbulent times, it is Indigo and Sienna who are chosen to find a suitable habitat for the displaced tribe. One a princess destined to rule his kind, the other the only son of a would-be chief, the pair seem like a natural choice.
 But as friendship blossoms into something more, and their journey takes them further and further from known lands, the wanderers begin to uncover secrets hidden among the ruins. Secrets which suggest the two species may not be as alien to one another as previously thought.

ISBN: 9781915304100 (epub, kindle) / 9781915304001 (184pp paperback)

Visit bit.ly/Forge&Flood

Life on Mars
The Vikings are coming

Hugh Duncan

Racing against time, Jade and her friends must hide evidence of Life on Mars to stop the probes from Earth finding them

Jade is on her way to meet up with her dad, Elvis, for her sixteen-millionth birthday (tortles live a long time in spite of the harsh conditions on Mars), when she gets side-tracked by a strange object that appears to have fallen from the sky. Elvis' travelling companion Starkwood, an electrostatic plant, is hearing voices, claiming that "The Vikings Are Coming", while their football-pitch-sized flying friend Fionix confirms the rumour: the Earth has sent two craft to look for life on Mars.

It then becomes a race against time to hide any evidence of such life before Earth destroys it for good. Can Jade and her friends succeed, with help from a Lung Whale, a liquid horse, some flying cats, the Hellas Angels, the Pyrites and a couple of House Martins from the South of France? Oh, and a quantum tunnelling worm – all while avoiding Zombie Vegetables and trouble with a Gravity Artist and the Physics Police?! A gentle and lightly humorous science fantasy adventure.

Cover artwork and illustrations: Natascha Booth

ISBN: 9781915304124 (epub, kindle) / 9781915304025 (400pp paperback)

Visit https://bit.ly/LifeOnMars-Vikings

The Magic Fix series by Mark Montanaro

The Magic Fix

**The Known World needs a fix or things could get very ugly
(even uglier than an Ogre!)**

"Did we win the battle?" asked King Wyndham.

"Well it depends how you define winning," answered Longfield, one of the King's royal commanders.

In fact, the Humans are fighting a losing battle with the Trolls. Meanwhile the Ogres are up to something, which probably isn't good. Could one flying unicorn bring about peace in the Known World? No, obviously not.

But maybe a group of rebels have the answer. Or perhaps the answer lies with a young Pixie with one remarkable gift. Does the Elvish Oracle have the answer? Who knows? And, even if she did, would anyone understand her cryptic answers (we all know what Oracles are like!)

The Known World is in danger of being rent in twain, and twain-rending is never good!

Did I mention the dragon? No? Ah… well… there's also a dragon.

ISBN: 9781911409731 (epub, kindle) / 9781911409632 (240pp paperback)
Visit bit.ly/TheMagicFix

The Enchanting Tricks

The Known World is still not fixed… and things <u>have</u> got ugly

In the Goblin realm, Queen Afflech was doing remarkably well considering the circumstances. She had seen her husband die, and both her sons killed within the space of a couple of weeks. That kind of thing does tend to bring you down a bit.

Losing three kings in a few days looked rather careless. But of more concern to the Goblin warlords was whether it looked weak to their enemies. They suspected the Humans were behind one death and the Ogres behind another. The Pixies were no threat, the Trolls would probably soon be killing one another again, and the Elves were irrelevant (or, to be precise, just annoying).

Meanwhile, King Wyndham wanted to show the Goblins that Humans were not to blame (apart from the two that might be to blame). Petra, the most famous Pixie in the Known World, knew exactly who was to blame and wanted to rescue them. Lord Protector Higarth was determined to help the Goblins with their predicament, whether they wanted Ogre-help or not.

But on the plus side, the dragon's gone; and there are still plenty of unicorns… maybe they can somehow solve everything?

ISBN: 9781915304193 (epub, kindle) / 9781915304094 (270pp paperback)
Visit bit.ly/TheEnchantingTricks

The Avatars of Ruin series by Tej Turner

Book 1: Bloodsworn

"Classic epic fantasy. I enjoyed it enormously"
– Anna Smith Spark
"a stunning introduction to a new fantasy world"
– Christopher G Nuttall

It has been twelve years since the war between the nations of Sharma and Gavendara. The villagers of Jalard live a bucolic existence, nestled within the hills of western Sharma, far from the warzone. They have little contact with the outside world, apart from once a year when Academy representatives choose two of them to be taken away to the institute in the capital. To be Chosen is considered a great honour… of which most of Jalard's children dream. But this year, their announcement is so shocking it causes friction between villagers, and some begin to suspect that all is not what it seems. Where are they taking the Chosen, and why? Some intend to find out, but what they discover will change their lives forever and set them on a long and bloody path to seek vengeance…

ISBN: 9781911409779 (epub, kindle) / 9781911409670 (432pp paperback)
Visit bit.ly/Bloodsworn

Book 2: Blood Legacy

The ragtag group from Jalard have finally reached Shemet, Sharma's capital city. Scarred and bereft, they bring a grim tale of what happened to their village, and a warning about the threat to all humanity. Some expect sanctuary within the Synod to mean an end to their hardships, but their hopes are soon dashed. Sharma's ruling class are caught within their own inner turmoil. Jaedin senses moles within their ranks, but his call to crisis falls mostly on deaf ears, and some seek to thwart him when he tries to hunt the infiltrators down.

Meanwhile, Gavendara is mustering its forces. With ritualistically augmented soldiers, their mutant army is like nothing the world has ever seen.

The Zakaras are coming. And Sharma's only hope of stopping them is if it can unite its people in time.

ISBN: 9781911409991 (epub, kindle) / 9781911409892 (474pp paperback)
Visit bit.ly/Blood-Legacy

Book 3: Blood War

Coming soon

BY DAVID M ALLAN

QUAESTOR

When you're searching, you don't always find what you expect

In Carrhen some people have a magic power – they may be telekinetic, clairvoyant, stealthy, or able to manipulate the elements. Anarya is a Sponger, she can absorb and use anyone else's magic without them even being aware, but she has to keep it a secret as it provokes jealousy and hostility especially among those with no magic powers at all.

When Anarya sees Yisyena, a Sitrelker refugee, being assaulted by three drunken men, she helps her to escape. Anarya is trying to establish herself as an investigator, a quaestor, in the city of Carregis. Yisyena is a clairvoyant, a skill that would be a useful asset for a quaestor, so Anarya offers her a place to stay and suggests they become business partners. Before long they are also lovers.

But business is still hard to find, so when an opportunity arises to work for Count Graumedel who rules over the city, they can't afford to turn it down, even though the outcome may not be to their liking.

Soon they are embroiled in state secrets and the personal vendettas of a murdered champion, a cabal, a puppet king, and a false god looking for one who has defied him.

ISBN: 9781911409571 (epub, kindle) / 9781911409472 (304pp paperback)
Visit bit.ly/Quaestor-Allan

THIEVER

Change is not always as good as a rest

After the events in Jotuk at the end of *Quaestor*, Anarya is no longer a Sponger but is now a Thiever – when she takes someone's magic talent they lose it until she can no longer hold on to it. Worryingly, the power also brings a desperate hunger to take others' talents, just as the false god did. As Anarya struggles to control the compulsion, Yisul is fraught with worry and seeks help for her lover. But Jotuk is in upheaval; the Twenty-Three families are in disarray, divided over how the city should be governed.

In Carregis, the king seeks to establish himself as an effective ruler. First, though, he must work out whom he can trust.

Meanwhile, the priestesses of Quarenna and the priests of Huler are having disturbing dreams…

Thiever is the much anticipated sequel to David M Allan's *Quaestor*.

ISBN: 9781911409977 (epub, kindle) / 9781911409878 (386pp paperback)
Visit bit.ly/Thiever

About Miles Nelson

Miles was born and raised in the distant north, in a quaint little city called Durham.

He studied video game design at Teesside University, graduating in 2018. Since then, he has taken a step back from coding to work on his writing career, and has since led several masterclasses with New Writing North.

He has been writing all his life, and although Riftmaster was technically his fourth novel, he likes to pretend the first three don't exist. Whilst he is primarily a sci-fi writer who loves long journeys, strange worlds and all things space and stars, he has also had brief flings with the genres of fantasy and horror.

He often writes stories highlighting the struggles faced by the LGBTQ+ community, and tries to include themes of empathy and inclusivity in all he does. Even then, though, Miles stands firm in the belief that this is not the defining element of his stories. And although he tries to represent his community as best he can, these themes are never the main focus; because he believes that (in most cases) a person shouldn't be defined by their deviation from standard norms.

Outside of scifi and fantasy, he has a deep-rooted fascination with natural history, and collects books told from unique perspectives (be they animal, alien, or mammoths from Mars). The older, the better; his oldest book is just about to turn 100!

He currently lives in Durham City with his husband, Chris, who so far seems unworried by Miles' rapidly growing collections.

Printed in Great Britain
by Amazon